His voice caught her off guard.

He hesitated slightly, and when he spoke, it came between heavy breaths.

"I don't think I've ever wanted a woman . . . the way I want you. Since that first night . . . in the red room." He pulled back just enough to look in her eyes. "Tell me you want me, *chère.*" His voice came so low it was barely audible.

"You know I do," she whispered.

They went totally still in the moment, no movement—just the connection of their gazes and the insistent beat of her heart against her rib cage.

She said it again, even softer this time. "You know I do."

His next kiss came shockingly gentle . . . She thought for a few moments that maybe she'd be content to just stand here and kiss him all night long.

Her breath grew more labored until she realized she was kissing him harder, pulling him closer, thinking, *Touch me, please touch me*, sure that if he didn't, she would die.

"Toni Blake writes powerfully erotic stories."

—STELLA CAMERON,
New York Times

:licious praise
of Toni Blake.

Praise for *The Red Diary*

"Heart-stopping sensuality! A sexy, compelling romance you'll want to savor!"

—LORI FOSTER, *New York Times*
bestselling author

"Sexual tension that is hot, hot, hot! Toni Blake writes the kind of book I want to read!"

—ELIZABETH BEVARLY, *New York Times*
bestselling author

"This beautiful story . . . will bring tears to your eyes . . . writing [that] comes from the heart."

—*Rendezvous*

"*The Red Diary* is one hot story . . . very sweet and quite lovely."

—*Romantic Times BOOKclub Magazine*

In Your Wildest
Dreams

ALSO BY TONI BLAKE

The Red Diary

In Your Wildest Dreams

TONI BLAKE

WARNER
FOREVER

NEW YORK   BOSTON

Warner Forever is a registered trademark of Warner Books.

Cover design by Diane Luger
Book design by Giorgetta Bell McRee

Warner Books

Time Warner Book Group
1271 Avenue of the Americas
New York, NY 10020
Visit our Web site at www.twbookmark.com

Printed in the United States of America

First Paperback Printing: July 2005

10 9 8 7 6 5 4 3 2 1

To my mom and dad,
who always encouraged me to follow my dreams.

Acknowledgments

They say you should write what you know. When you decide to ignore that advice, you must find nice people who are willing to share their knowledge with you. For help with research, my thanks go to:

Barbara Robichaux, tour guide extraordinaire, for answering many various and sundry questions about New Orleans, and also to Gloria Alvarez, Winnie Griggs, and the other ladies of Ninklink who provided helpful pieces of info on the city;

Captain Bill Shewmake, for answering my questions about the bayou;

Carrie Loque, for help with the fictional drive to bayou country, as well as being my Cajun French connection;

Author Maggie Price, her brother Major Richard Neaves, and Brian Hoehler, for answering a wide array of "cop questions";

Daphne Wedig, for tidbits about life in the advertising world;

Sarah Patrick, for her expertise in fine bed linens; and

John Abbott, manager of Muriel's, for a wonderful

personal tour of the restaurant's party rooms, which were the original inspiration for this story.

I hope I got everything right, and any errors come with my apologies.

Additional gratitude goes to:

Renee Norris, for her brilliant and insightful critique of the manuscript—I'm indebted!

Robin Zentmeyer, for lots of brainstorming, and also for traveling with me to New Orleans for research. I know eating beignets and drinking hurricanes was very hard work, and I appreciate the sacrifice!

My agent, Deidre Knight, for early feedback when this book was just an idea in my head;

Jackie Floyd, for early brainstorming, not to mention constant moral support;

Bobbi Casey, for teaching me to crochet, which inspired that part of the story;

Michelle Combs and Martha Poston, for letting me borrow the part about the angels;

Heather Lester, for hanging out with me in the red room at Muriel's at a party back in 2001—and listening as I chattered endlessly about how I *had* to use it in a book someday!

And to Michele Bidelspach, Karen Kosztolnyik, and Beth de Guzman of Warner Books, for being so supportive and wonderful to work with!

In Your Wildest Dreams

You see her in shadow. Curves and lace. Her presence draws you closer, deeper into a dark room.

Her face is hidden behind a Mardi Gras mask, red feathers fanning outward. Black sequins outline her eyes, eyes so powerful they leave you helpless as you move slowly but surely toward them. She lounges on a chaise beside floor-to-ceiling windows, waiting, watching.

Outside the window rests a balcony of twisting iron, and moonlight—shining through the square grates to highlight her body. The room takes on the color of deep ruby red, but that and the windows and the balcony are all peripheral because you see only her.

You want her with a force that turns you inside out; you fear she can see all your secrets, that they're written on your face, in the clench of your fists, in the heat you know burns in your eyes. This is more than sex. More than you want to feel. But it's pouring out of you like a liquid thing. You can't stop it.

Your eyes drop to her breasts, hugged by low-cut black lace with a rose embellished in red on each cup. You kneel before her and let your hands close over them, your fingers curling into their softness. Through the lace, firm nipples jut into your palms. Your stomach contracts. You're trembling now.

You squeeze, caress, bend your head to kiss through the bra. Her gentle moan shoots straight to your groin. More, you need more of her.

Reaching up, you slip your fingers beneath one black strap and slide it from her porcelain shoulder. You grip the edge of the scalloped cup, pulling down. You lower your mouth to one pink nipple, hard as a pearl as you lick, suckle her, want somehow to take her inside you.

As you inhale her scent—sweet roses—your hand glides down over her smooth stomach into the lace panties below. She sighs with pleasure, and touching her that way nearly buries you. There are things you want to say to her, desperately, but you can't find the words. Maybe there are no words, nothing to describe what you're feeling. You're not a man gifted with a silver tongue—and besides, if you want to use your tongue to make her feel good, there are better ways.

Releasing the hard peak of her breast, you tug gently on the black panties, where you find that same red rose inlaid on the front, until she lifts and lets you draw them down her thighs, over her stockings and sexy black heels. When she parts her legs for you, you think your chest might explode. You've never been this hungry for a woman. Never. You can't wait another second before dragging a long, slow lick up her center.

She sighs at each stroke of your tongue, rising to meet you. You're making love to her with your mouth, praying she knows it's lovemaking, also scared she knows. You've never let a woman's need become the biggest part of sex for you, but in this moment, your desire is secondary—this is all about her. Her. Her.

She slows her rhythm, but accentuates it at the same time, lifting higher, harder. You know she's getting close. Your only reason for existing is to make her come. You wonder if it's possible you could come, too, just from this.

A low, keening cry from above.

Fingernails grazing your scalp, hands coiling into tight fists in your hair.

A glance up to the black sequins finds her eyes shut; she bites her bottom lip as she leans her head back against red pillows.

Come. Come for me. Now.

As if on your silent demand, her cries deepen, stretch, fill the room as her sex fills your mouth with even more intense strokes. Your hands curve around her ass to help her, lift her, and it goes on and on, this orgasm from this woman whose face you can't see but whom you still need so much.

Finally, she relaxes, her pelvis easing back to the chaise, leaving you with the taste of her on your tongue, the sight of her closed legs below you. You lower one last, delicate kiss at the juncture of her thighs. Perfect fulfillment.

Chapter 1

It was only by chance that she sat before a mirror as she rolled the silk stocking up her leg. She saw herself in the glass, wearing only the stocking and a pair of satin cream-colored panties.

"Get a thong," Melody had instructed her. "It'll make you feel sexier."

Stephanie had ignored that part. She hadn't particularly *wanted* to feel sexy.

But as the second stocking whispered up the smooth skin of her calf, thigh, the lace top resting only a couple of inches from her crotch, a hint of titillation rose there, unbidden.

"It takes more than a pretty dress," Melody had said. "You have to *feel* it. *Sell* it. You have to *be* it, or you'll never fool anybody."

Sell it. Those were the two words she'd plucked from Melody's advice. If Stephanie was adept at anything, it was selling. Products. Pitches. This was a little different, of course. No, a lot different. But that didn't mean she couldn't pull it off.

She glanced back at the cheval mirror in the corner of her room. She'd never seen herself look so purely sexual.

Getting to her feet, she stepped into the ivory cocktail dress, sliding her arms through spaghetti-thin shoulder straps, reaching behind to the zipper. The fabric pulled close, again sending an unexpected tendril of awareness through her body. Awareness of self, of her own sensuality.

Strange, the journeys life led a person on—strange what someone could make themselves do for love. If anyone who knew her could see her now—sexy dress, strappy shoes, about to plunge into a decadent city's underworld—they wouldn't believe it. She could hardly believe it herself.

Fastening a bracelet, she glanced to the bedside clock. Ten-thirty. "Plan to arrive just before eleven," Melody had said. "That's prime time at the hunt."

A fresh shot of trepidation whirred through her. *Wait a few minutes and maybe you can convince yourself it's too late, past prime time. You can take off this silly dress, put on pajamas, and watch TV or read a book.*

Only problem was, if she didn't go tonight, she'd have to go tomorrow night, or the next night. And every night she talked herself out of it was another night Tina was missing.

Letting out a sigh, she took one last look in the mirror. She didn't even recognize herself.

Maybe that was a good thing.

Half an hour later, a cab pulled to a stop on an ancient, narrow street, delivering her to her destination. She felt sinfully beautiful. She felt naked. She wished she were anywhere else.

"Chez Sophia," the driver said.

She handed the polite middle-aged man a ten over the seat. "Keep the change."

Stepping out into the sultry night, she watched the taxi dart away and battled a brief second of feeling too alone. Put her in front of a roomful of hard-nosed CEOs in a sharply cut suit and she was a confident, eloquent woman in perfect control of everything around her. The stark contrast of where she was—*who* she was—tonight, struck once more.

Yet she'd come too far to turn back. So she took a deep breath and turned toward Chez Sophia, staring up at elegant fern-hung balconies, all curving wrought iron and grace. That quickly, the aura of the place began to surround her, the sensation nearly as cloying as the sticky air.

Moving toward the front entrance in heels that clicked on the sidewalk with each stride, she subtly tugged upward on the bodice of her low-cut dress in some last-minute stab at self-preservation.

But no. She wasn't here to be herself. All her suits were at home. She'd come to be someone else—someone she could never really be. Biting her lip, she gently pulled the clingy fabric back down, maximizing her cleavage. *Feel beautiful. Not naked.*

"Good evening, miss. Welcome to Chez Sophia." The twenty-something doorman wore a white shirt, red vest, black tie.

She manufactured a smile. *Sell it.* "Thank you."

He motioned toward the interior of the grand saloon, abuzz with people drinking, smoking, laughing. A Dixieland trio played in one corner, the large bass briefly drawing her eye. "Our high-tech dance club is straight down the hallway, the Zydeco Lounge is to the right, and—"

"I'm here for the private party." That's what Melody had told her to say.

The doorman's eyes changed. To disappointment? Lust? Surely she was thinking too much. Either way, his gaze dropped boldly to her cleavage before he brought it back to her face. That's all she was tonight—cleavage, curves.

"Through the doorway past the stairwell," he said.

"Thank you." But she could no longer meet his eyes. *Damn it, you're supposed to be selling it.*

As she walked farther into the club, she decided now would be a good time to start doing just that. *If all you are is cleavage and curves, sell* that. *Feel it. Be it. Like Melody said. Just for tonight.* Everything depended on it.

Men watched as she passed, clearly thinking her a different sort of woman than she was, even without the knowledge of the "private party" she'd come for, and again the juncture of her thighs suffered a slight tingle. Strange, maybe even shameful, to feel that *now,* yet as she was drawn more deeply into the place, she understood Melody's advice. She couldn't do this halfway. If she were to pull it off, she *had* to let herself feel every forbidden bit of it. So as she exited the door past the stairwell, she attempted to relish the fresh sensitivity in her breasts, to embrace the soft, slight throb between her thighs.

A large, dark-skinned man wearing a familiar red vest and black tie waited outside the door. "Private party?"

"Yes." She'd turned the one simple word silky, sexy. Practice.

"All the way to the top." He pointed up a wooden stairway painted white. Old brick walls surrounded the steps on all sides, and as she ascended, she realized she was outside again, in an enclosed courtyard. It seemed as if she were traveling a maze to reach the soiree tucked deeply within Chez Sophia—but she supposed that made sense. A thin line of perspiration trickled between her breasts.

Four half-flights of stairs later, she found another doorman, this one young, blond. "Welcome to Sophia's private party." He held the door open with a ready smile.

A wild sense of nervousness barreled down through her chest as the reality of what she was about to do struck her full force. But as she entered the room through red velvet curtains drawn back by gold cord, she struggled again to condense her feelings to the sensual, the sexual— nothing more.

The scene before her was awash in elegance, from the crystal chandeliers to the gentle clink of wineglasses to the soft jazz permeating the air. Men in well-tailored suits stood chatting with beautiful women in cocktail dresses, some shimmering with sequins and beads. Others sat on the plush couches and graceful divans that sprinkled the space in bold splashes of scarlet, amethyst, cobalt.

That's when it hit her. *I can do this.* Outwardly, the crowd didn't appear unlike those in *her* world. This was just another cocktail party. The only difference was that instead of selling an ad campaign, tonight she was selling *herself.*

She scanned the crowd for Tina. Her heart sank when she didn't find her, but she hadn't expected it to be that simple anyway, and now she had to mingle, pretend, convince. She had to flirt. But she was horrible at flirting, so even if this was all about selling, something she *could* do, she needed a drink to bolster her courage.

Clutching her small sateen purse tightly, she made a beeline for the long mahogany bar to one side of the luxurious room. A dark-haired guy stood behind the expanse of polished wood operating a blender, his back to her, as she climbed up onto a bar stool. A moment later, he stopped the blender and turned. "What would you like?"

Her heart nearly stopped just from looking into his eyes. He was everything she'd never been attracted to. Rugged. Unshaven. Unabashedly sexual without even trying. Midnight black hair framed his strong face, along with several days' stubble curving across his upper lip and chin. One wayward lock of hair dipped onto his forehead, drawing attention to deep, sensual brown eyes. Warm and chocolaty, a place to drown. A black T-shirt stretched across a muscular chest and broad shoulders, a hint of a tattoo peeking from beneath one sleeve. The forbidden sense of arousal already coursing through her veins deepened.

He cocked his head slightly. "Did you want a drink, *beb*?"

She finally caught her breath. "Um, yes. A Chardonnay, please."

As he reached for a stemmed glass, she dug in her purse, placing a twenty on the bar, all the while fighting her reaction to him. This wasn't her. She didn't get excited by a guy on mere sight. Especially not one who looked so . . . dangerous.

When he lowered her wine to a square napkin, his eyes fell on the cash. "What's that for?"

She blinked. "The wine."

His narrowed gaze only added to the sensations between her thighs. "Ladies don't pay."

She softly pulled in her breath. "Oh. Right." His tone said she should have known that. She shoved the bill back into her purse, then reached for the glass, taking a large swallow.

"First time here?"

What sort of accent was that? Something slightly Cajun? "Um, yes." She nodded, softly, trying to quit feeling like a schoolgirl. Here she'd finally begun to think she could control this situation as efficiently as she controlled the rest of her life, and this darkly sexy man was already turning her soft and vulnerable, emotions equally as foreign as the sensuality currently pummeling her.

Time to take back control, to start doing what she'd come here for. And the bartender seemed like a good place to start.

Sell it, she reminded herself, reassuming her silky voice. "I was hoping to run into a friend of mine here. Maybe you know her. Tina Grant?"

His brows knit slightly, making her wonder what he found perplexing about the question. "Your friend in the escort business, too?"

She nodded.

He shook his head lightly. "No, *chère,* afraid the name doesn't ring a bell."

Strike one. Fortunately for her, she had more than three tries, but just like when she'd first entered the room, she'd simply hoped against hope that maybe she wouldn't have to look any further.

As she took another sip of wine, his slow smile blazed all through her, heating her skin with the same force as the sun breaking through the clouds on a hot summer day.

"What are you smiling at?" She forgot the silky voice, too curious to find out what prompted that wicked grin.

"Just thinkin' you probably been sittin' on that stool longer than anyone ever has."

She lowered her chin, confused. "Oh?"

"Girls don't come here to sit and have a quiet glass of

wine, *chère*. They come to work. They don't usually waste time." He shifted his eyes to the crowded room behind her and her chest tightened. "Not that it's any of my business," he went on, "but it's after eleven. Place'll start clearin' out soon."

She opened her eyes wider. "So early?" Melody hadn't mentioned that.

He gave a soft laugh. "This isn't exactly the main event of the evenin', you know." Then he tilted his head, his warm eyes penetrating her defenses. "Your first time here, or your first time *period*?"

For some reason, she refused to let him think she was brand-new at this. He already seemed to have the upper hand, and she didn't intend to let him keep it. "Just my first time here. And I'm not in a hurry."

He shrugged. "Suit yourself. But I'd hate to see that pretty dress and hairdo go to waste."

The sentiment reminded her once more: she was cleavage and curves tonight.

In her world, how you looked was only one part of your identity; here, *everything* was about the business of flesh. "Maybe you're right." She slipped down from the stool and lifted her glass. "I should . . . get to work."

His expression softened, but his eyes still had the power to burn into her soul—or at least the spot between her legs. "Good luck, *chère*."

That escalating sensation—no longer just awareness or sensuality, now pure desire—persisted as she immersed herself into the crowd. She took another sip of wine and repeated her new mantra in her mind: *Sell it. Sell it.*

Although, admittedly, part of her remained back on the stool peering up at the bartender. What had come over her? *It's just the dress,* she told herself. *And the evening's quest.* That was the only reason her body had reacted so strongly to the guy.

Just as she wandered aimlessly through a sea of suits and slinky dresses, wondering what her next move should be, a man's hand fell on her shoulder. She hated his touch instantly, the clammy feel of his palm on her bare skin, but forced a smile.

"Hi there, honey. You new in town? Don't think I've seen you before." The pushing-fifty guy sported a deep Southern accent and a beer belly beneath his expensive black suit. His graying hair looked unkempt, the style too long for a man his age.

Sell it. Unfortunately, it was much harder with him than with the bartender. "Um, yes, this is my first night here."

"That so? Why, I'd be more than happy to break ya in . . . so to speak." He winked. "I'm stayin' at the Fairmont. Real fancy place—we can get it on in style." He concluded with a laugh that made her stomach churn.

"I'm . . . sorry," she said, "but I'm already . . . spoken for. I'm meeting someone here. A prearranged date."

He looked crestfallen. "Well, I'm mighty sorry to hear that. But what say we get together another time real soon?"

She sighed. "Um . . . perhaps. I'm sure I'll bump into you again."

He flashed a leering grin. "That sounds damn good. I'll be lookin' forward to it."

As he was about to move off in search of greener pastures, she remembered her mission—and reached up to touch his sleeve. His lusty gaze beamed down on her. "Maybe you can help me with something. I was hoping to find a friend of mine here—she's fairly new in town, too. Her name is Tina—"

"I ain't much good with names, honey."

"She's blond, twenty-five, has a light complexion, and . . ." She trailed off, realizing she'd just described around a third of the women in the room.

Above her, the beer belly shook his head absently. "Sorry," he said, taking off into the crowd, clearly uninterested in helping her if she wasn't going to be in his bed tonight.

Jake Broussard popped a mint in his mouth and kept an eye on the blonde moving through the crowd. She was trying her damnedest to look poised and relaxed, but something about her didn't ring true. Maybe she acted a little too sophisticated, or maybe her updo was a little too severe, precise—not one pretty golden hair out of place. Not that he hadn't met plenty of working girls who pulled it off with class, but for some reason, he didn't quite buy Miss Chardonnay's claim of being a pro.

"Pour me another, Jake. And a second glass of wine for the lady."

He drew his gaze to Charles Winthrop, a married forty-something scotch-on-the-rocks who came in every Thursday night for a little adultery. The lady on his arm this evening was Tawney, a brunette Chablis who couldn't be a day over eighteen.

"Sure," Jake replied, scooping ice into a glass and reaching for Winthrop's favorite brand of scotch.

As he poured the drinks, Winthrop slid one hand from Tawney's hip up to the side of her breast. "Drink up, honey, and we'll head to a hotel."

Winthrop handed Jake a twenty and said, "Keep the rest." A common statement from the men who climbed the steps to Sophia's secret third floor. They figured big tips bought Jake's discretion.

What they didn't know was that he didn't care. He didn't care that Winthrop was screwing around on his wife, and he didn't care that, at the moment, he was doing it with an obscenely young girl, likely younger than Winthrop's own daughters. Once upon a time, he *did* care—about people, about righting wrongs, about trying to fix things in his own little corner of the world. But those days were gone.

"Have a good evenin'," he murmured as the couple strolled away. He didn't mean it. But he didn't *not* mean it, either. He really didn't give a damn either way, so long as he earned his paycheck. That's what life was about for Jake the last two years—earning a paycheck, and sleeping.

The paycheck was easy—he worked at Chez Sophia a few nights a week, setting his own schedule. It didn't take too many hours behind this particular bar to make a decent living when you picked up hundred percent tips all night long. And as for the sleeping, it was getting better lately. He hadn't had a nightmare in a couple of months.

But the thought brought to mind the dream he'd had the other night. He couldn't ever recall a dream being so detailed, intense. So erotically raw. What the hell had that been about?

It's your dick complaining.

Probably. Couldn't blame it. The last time he'd had sex had been . . . too long ago. But every time a girl came on to him these days, he found himself bored, apathetic. He just wanted to look the other way. Wanted to go home and go to bed. Alone.

Of course, other than the girls at Sophia's, he didn't run into many. Because other than work, he stayed in. Lifted weights. Slept.

"This is no way to live," Tony had told him a few weeks ago when he'd shown up at Jake's place unexpected.

"You live your life, I'll live mine," he'd said. "I'm doin' fine."

Tony had nosed around, peeking in the near-empty fridge, spying the piles of dirty clothes in Jake's bedroom. "Yeah, right. Fine."

Jake knew he wasn't fine just as much as Tony knew it, but he only wanted to be left to himself, left free not to feel—*anything*.

Now he remembered that waking up from the dream had left him with a vague, nagging sense of guilt that had stuck around for hours. Damn, couldn't even outrun feelings in his sleep. Couldn't even dream about something as simple as sex without it getting complicated.

Wiping down the bar, he scanned the crowd for Miss Chardonnay again. She wove slowly through the well-dressed men and scantily clad women, but seemed to be doing a lot more moving than stopping or talking. "Not gonna get picked up like that, *chère*," he mumbled.

Maybe she was a cop. He made a mental note to ask Tony if he knew anything about an undercover vice operation. But he didn't think things were quiet enough at the NOPD that they'd started actively pursuing misdemeanors. Not unless somebody knew for sure that other crimes were tied in. He knew Tony *suspected* they were, but since Tony didn't have enough to move forward, Jake doubted anyone else in the department did, either.

Or maybe she was a reporter, looking for a story. Prostitution was practically a tradition in the Big Easy, but the men who "shopped" here in the "high-priced hooker zone," as Tony called it, were often public figures, guys who expected discretion because they had a lot to lose. List their names in the newspaper and, well . . . he was sure that kind of exposé could garner any journalist some major attention. So that idea actually held a little water.

Either way, though, she was playing with fire. You didn't play games with men as rich and powerful as the ones who came to Sophia's third floor. If anyone else developed the same suspicions he had, things would get ugly real fast.

Not that he cared. He didn't.

She was a big girl—she surely knew what she was getting herself into.

He didn't care, but then . . . why did he keep watching her? Why did he give a damn why she was here? Since when did he even pay attention to the people who came to his bar? They were all drinks to him. Bloody Marys, whiskey sours, rum and Cokes. Merlots, Cabernets . . . and Chardonnays.

Over the next half hour, the lush interior of the room became more pronounced as the crowd thinned, pairing off for the evening and moving on to hotels or apartments. Once or twice, he saw the blonde talking—with other girls, a few men—and found himself wishing he could hear their conversations, since they would probably reveal to his practiced ear whether she was here looking to make money like a good little escort or whether she'd come for something else.

"Just don't say anything to get yourself in trouble," he murmured as he studied her across the room conversing with Malcolm Unger, a prominent local attorney and a whiskey neat—and just one example of a guy who wouldn't like finding out he was flirting with someone who might be a reporter.

By eleven-fifteen, only a handful of customers dotted the velvet-and-brocade room: a drunk parish judge with an expensive hooker perched on each knee, and a group of young corporate types laughing and drinking with three girls. And Miss Chardonnay, who strolled swiftly past the bar, high color in her cheeks, breasts bouncing gently with each step.

"*Chère,*" he said.

She looked up and, when their eyes met, stopped.

He held out one arm, motioning her closer.

Although she complied, wariness filled her gaze.

"Get yourself a date for the night?" He'd had to ask, couldn't help himself.

She pulled in her breath, looking affronted by the question. Nope, no way was she a working girl—they weren't that sensitive. "Dates" were their job. "Um . . . no, if it's any of your business."

Another dead giveaway. A woman who looked like that, in a room full of men seeking sex, and she hadn't found any takers? He tilted his head, let her see just a hint of suspicion. "I find it hard to believe a lovely lady like you didn't get an offer tonight."

She released a soft breath, looking nervous, but also determined. "I . . . made a few dates for *other* nights, if you must know."

Possible, but he still wasn't buying. The third floor was all about instant gratification. And damn if he knew why he gave a shit, but something just beneath her surface seemed so innocent that he had to press on.

Just this one last time, he promised himself. *Just this*

one last time, you can try to save somebody. After that, it was back to working and sleeping and not caring.

"Listen, *chère,* you got anyplace to be right now?"

She blinked, looking uncertain, and gave her head a light shake.

"Good. Hang around a little while."

Her eyes widened. They were a soft, inviting shade of blue. "Why?"

He let the corners of his mouth turn up slightly. "Nothin' too terrible, *beb.* Just want to talk to you a minute. What do you say? Stick around while I close up the bar?" He motioned to the right. "There's a little room just around the corner. You can wait there."

Her gaze sparkled with hesitation, a hint of fear.

Did she think he was going to proposition her? If his suspicions were right, he'd probably just scared her shitless. Good, that was the point. "How about it?" he asked again. "Stay?"

Miss Chardonnay bit her lip, then slowly nodded.

To his surprise, he felt that nod tightening his groin. "Good, *chère.* See you soon."

Chapter 2

Sex had never been her thing.

It wasn't that she hadn't had it—she'd slept with a few guys.

But she'd just never understood the overwhelming power sex had over people, the all-consuming force it seemed to be. And although she'd tried to "get it," she'd spent the last ten years, since losing her virginity in college, wondering what all the fuss was about.

Now Stephanie looked around the small room he'd sent her to, in awe. The outer room was opulent, but *this* space? Downright decadent. Red silk and velvet abounded. Even the antique ceiling tiles were painted red. Mounds of red pillows and bolsters, some with gold embroidery, others sporting large tassels, cushioned the lush red sofa she sat upon. Red brocade wallpaper provided the backdrop for sensual paintings with a Renaissance-period feel, featuring naked women draped with swaths of fabric. Warm, dark objects filled the room—a globe on a thick cherry pedestal, a grandfather clock—and countless red velvet stools and ottomans sprinkled the small space. A room that belonged in the most extravagant bordello, she thought. A room *made* for sex. A room that almost made *her* want to have sex. Everything in it made her want to touch.

She took a deep breath, emotionally tired.

When she hadn't been dodging men with a sexual gleam in their eyes, she had managed to ease into a few conversations with other escorts, but it seemed no one knew Tina. No one. It made no sense and Stephanie's heart dropped even further recalling each fruitless discussion.

By the time the sexy bartender had asked her to stay, she'd been so spent that she'd gone blank on how to respond. Instinct had said *run,* but her body had hummed with that same unaccountable desire she'd felt upon meeting him.

Not that she planned to *do* anything with him. It was surely just the wine and the necessary sensuality of the evening making her feel these things. Things she hardly ever felt. Earlier, she'd told herself she *had* to feel them tonight, and it had led to this: sitting here waiting for a stranger and having no idea why.

Her only productive thought at the moment was that maybe he could help her find Tina. Maybe he could give her other places to look, people to ask. Melody had promised this was *the* premier spot for high-priced escorts, but maybe there were other locations she didn't know about.

Stephanie looked up when he walked into the room— he seemed to fill the small space, and the mere sight of him set her senses on fire all over again. What was it about this guy? His eyes seemed to touch her physically.

He took a seat on the sofa across from her. Above his head, a naked woman lounged on a chaise.

When he didn't say anything right away, just sat there looking at her, the silence pushed her to speak. "What did you want to talk to me about?"

"What's your name, *chère*?"

"Stephanie Grant."

Like before, he gave his head a slight, questioning tilt. "You know what I find odd, Stephanie Grant?"

Her skin prickled. "What's that?"

"I've met a lot of escorts here, but you're the first one who ever used her last name. Any good escort knows usin' only first names keeps the fantasy real and the money flowin'."

Heat rose to her cheeks. It made sense, and only then struck her that there were probably privacy concerns, too. Why hadn't she thought of that? "Well," she fudged, "I didn't realize I was still on the clock."

She couldn't interpret his slight smile—she only knew his very presence made her hotter and more nervous by the second. His voice came low. "What I wanted to tell you, *chère,* is that I don't believe you."

She blinked and her heartbeat sped up. "About what?"

His sexy grin faded, but his eyes still bore through her. She wasn't used to having a man look at her with such intensity—not in business, and certainly not in pleasure. "I don't believe you're a hooker. And I don't know why you're pretendin' you are, but I got news for you, *beb*. The men who come here wouldn't like findin' out you're lookin' to do anything but take their money and make 'em smile. You don't wanna mess around here. You'll get yourself in real trouble, Stephanie Grant."

It was all she could do to keep breathing. "Why on earth would I *pretend* to be an escort?"

His serious gaze never wavered. "*You* tell *me*."

"I can't, because you have no idea what you're talking about."

He let out a sigh of irritation. "Look, I'm tryin' to do you a favor. You're gonna get hurt if you mess with this crowd."

"No, *you* look, I didn't come here to be harassed by a bartender. So I think I'll just be leaving now." She pushed to her feet, intent on marching from the room, but he stood just as quickly, blocking her way.

She drew in her breath and lifted her eyes to find their faces only a few inches apart. Their bodies too. His musky scent permeated her senses.

"How much?" he whispered.

She drew back only slightly. "How much what?"

"How much do you charge?" His warm breath seemed to infuse heat into her veins as the loaded question ran all through her.

"Why do you care?"

"Consider it a test." His eyes glimmered in the dim lighting.

Melody had told her how much, she was sure of it— but she'd never expected to get this far into a conversation about it, and the bartender had her rattled. "A hundred and fifty," she guessed, thinking it sounded like an appropriate amount for an upper-tier lady of the evening. Hadn't she seen movies, TV shows, where regular street hookers charged only twenty, thirty, fifty dollars?

"For what exactly?" he asked.

Still more heat consumed her. "For one . . . go-round."

He didn't smile, but his eyes filled with satisfaction. "Wrong answer, *chère*."

"What?" She hadn't known there *was* a wrong answer. He still stood so close that she'd have sworn she could feel how fast her heart beat.

"The goin' price for a lady of your caliber is four hundred an hour, two thousand if I want you to spend the night."

Her eyes flew wide as her chest tightened. "If *you*. . . ?"

Only then did his wicked little grin reappear. "What's wrong, Stephanie Grant? Do I make you nervous?"

"Of course not." *Sell it.* Somehow. "One guy's the same as any other. I just . . ."

He tilted his head. "Don't think a lowly bartender's got that kinda cash? Surprise, *beb,* I do. And if you're really in the business you say you are, this would be easy money. Not sure why you didn't leave with any of the other men, but maybe it's just my good fortune, no?"

"No," she said. Unequivocally.

His fingertips grazed the length of her arm, rising onto her bare shoulder to stop at the thin strap there. Heat filled his touch and it was all she could do not to shiver. "Why not?" he asked.

She had no idea how to answer without blowing her cover.

He saved her the trouble by sweeping a tantalizingly soft kiss across her lips, tasting of cool mint. Her body blazed with wild desire and she gasped, trying desperately not to feel—but at the moment, she felt more than any man had ever made her feel before. A stranger. In a modern-day house of ill repute. It didn't make sense.

But then, what did? Did it make sense that she was masquerading as a lady of the night? Did it make sense that Tina was missing—could be somewhere dead or dying for all she knew? Put in that context, her current circumstances seemed a lot less bizarre.

"What do you say, *chère*?" he purred in her ear, the soft

Cajun accent melting over her, warm and encasing. With that, he brushed another sinfully short kiss over her mouth, leaving the same hint of mint, the same liquid lust pouring through her as he smoothly swept her into a loose embrace, lowering her lengthwise onto the velvet sofa. She lounged among the plush pillows as he grazed his palm over her cheek, jaw, neck, in a slow caress.

She could have left a minute ago—she could have walked away. But she hadn't, too caught up in his dark allure, and now she lay beside him, reaching for an answer. "No," she finally whispered.

"No?" To her surprise, his sexy expression revealed a hint of amusement. "You came here tonight to make money, didn't you?" His heated voice whisked down through her, somehow making even *those* words sensual, tempting. "You came here to sell your body, *chère*. Why shouldn't I take you up on it? Unless . . ." His voice stretched out the *s* sound.

She bit her lip. "Unless what?"

He leaned near her ear, his voice quiet, deep. "Unless there's a reason you're resistin'."

Was she? Resisting? His palm closed full around her waist, his thumb brushing dangerously near the underside of her breast, and still she didn't make a move to leave.

"Unless," he went on, "you aren't what you claim. Unless you aren't really here to sell all these pretty curves." His hand glided down over her waist, hip, thigh, as if outlining her.

She heard her own breath, broken and labored, and wished the room were darker, wished it were okay to pull him to her and do everything she suddenly wanted to do. Press his body against hers, let him touch her—every-where. Take him inside her.

He lowered more soft kisses to her neck, then reached behind her ankle to slide his hand slowly up her stocking to the spot behind her knee. Her heavy breath mingled with his now, the only sounds in the red room.

"Last chance, *chère*," he whispered, his palm edging higher.

Even as a shot of hungry pleasure blasted upward, she said, "No. Stop."

He never flinched, only lifted his mouth to breathe warm in her ear. "Tell me why."

"What?" She could barely think.

"If you were really an escort, you wouldn't make me stop, no?" His voice was a low growl. "You'd let me have you."

His palm skimmed around to the front of her thigh, fingertips slipping across the lace top of the stocking, making her body scream with conflicting yes's and no's that all blurred in her mind for a fraction of a second, until finally she knew she *couldn't* let this go any further. *"No, I can't. Stop!"*

His hand stilled in place and he drew back to look at her.

She knew he was waiting for more, and it suddenly seemed stupid to have kept up the pretense this long . . . unless she'd really wanted . . .

No—that wasn't it! She just didn't like having her cover, however thin, completely blown.

"I'm not really an escort," she admitted softly into the still air.

She thought he looked at once disappointed but pleased. He withdrew his hand from beneath her dress and pulled it back into place, then sat up beside her.

She felt like an idiot, but slowly raised herself upright

as well. They stayed silent and the moment reminded her strangely of high school—nights of kissing and touching and wanting more, but finding the strength to say no. This was the part where everything turned awkward.

She drew in her breath lightly at the shocking memory—she'd nearly forgotten a time when she *had* known these feelings. She shook her head to clear it.

"Why'd you lie?" he asked, slowly raising his gaze.

Her lips trembled when she tried to answer. "I . . . need to find someone."

"Tina Grant," he confirmed. "How are you related?"

She looked up in surprise, but then remembered—escorts didn't use their last names, and she'd stated it both when asking about Tina and introducing herself. She sighed. "She's my sister."

Their eyes met. "How old?"

"Twenty-five."

He seemed to understand much more than she'd told him. "Twenty-five is all grown up, no? Old enough to do what she wants."

Stephanie let out a small sound of disgust. The last thing she needed was a lecture. She already knew part of Tina's decision might be *her* fault, and that alone was hard enough to bear without his superior attitude. "But she's missing."

She'd thought that would catch his attention, yet it seemed not to shock him at all. "Define missin', *chère*."

She took a deep breath. No reason now, she supposed, not to lay everything on the table. "She came down here from Chicago a few months ago, chasing a guy. When I finally heard from her, she told me the relationship hadn't worked out, but that she'd decided to stay anyway and become . . . an escort." When referring to her little sister, the simple word became much harder to say. "I was upset, of course, and tried to talk her out of it, but the next time she called, she'd already started . . . working." She stopped a minute, her chest aching from the picture the words created in her head.

"And?"

"And she didn't call the next time she was supposed to. And she hasn't called since. She refused to give me a number where I could reach her—and she hasn't been in touch with her old boyfriend, either, because I checked—so after weeks with no contact, I had to do *something*."

"Probably just didn't want to talk to you, knowin' how you feel about what she's doin'."

She released a perturbed breath. This guy just thought he knew everything, didn't he? He might even be right, but his matter-of-fact tone made her worries sound practically unfounded. "You sound just like the cop I talked to. I *did* try that route before coming to look for her, just so you don't think I'm totally crazy. But I couldn't get any help from them."

" 'Cause they know she's probably fine."

She pursed her lips. "I took it a different way. I figured they didn't care because, to them, she's just another prostitute."

He shrugged—annoyingly. "Either way, I'm probably right."

She blinked, growing more irritated by the moment. "So I'm supposed to let her drop out of my life, forget she exists? Even if she *is* fine, I still have to find her."

"Some reason you didn't hire a PI, *beb*? Most people who can't get answers from the cops would try that route."

"For your information, I did. But within a few days he

said the trail was cold. That left me no other choice than to track her down myself."

His gaze remained steady on her. "And when you do?"

"I'll talk her into coming home and putting this chapter of her life behind her. I'll help her find a job. Help her get over the guy. I'll be there for her, for as long as she needs me."

Jake thought about how to reply. Sounded to him like Miss Chardonnay was pretty controlling when it came to her poor sister. But since she already seemed pissed off, he wasn't about to tell her that. "So you thought it'd be a good idea to come trottin' yourself down to New Orleans and dress yourself up like a high-priced hooker?" he said instead.

She looked as sheepish as he thought she should. "It wasn't exactly my idea."

"You got a partner in crime?"

She dropped her glance slightly before raising it again. "A woman I met doing research on the Internet—at a site where prostitutes trying to get out of the business can go for advice. Her name's Melody and she's an ex-escort— high-priced—who used to work the French Quarter. She thought the best way to find Tina was to ask the people who might work with her, or who might be her customers. And she doubted anyone would talk to me if I didn't appear to be . . . one of them."

"Which is how you knew about this place."

She nodded.

He lowered his chin, wondering the obvious. "Any reason Melody couldn't ask around *for* you?"

"She doesn't move in these circles anymore. She's married now, with a baby, and a husband who doesn't know her past."

Jake shrugged—it was a good reason. Girls who chose this life didn't usually end up where Miss Chardonnay's hooker friend had. "Still a pretty stupid move," he couldn't stop himself from murmuring.

She cast him a sideways glance. "What was I supposed to do? And why do you care so much anyway? You've got an awfully vested interest in this for a bartender."

She was right—like it or not, his old instincts were showing. Still, if the woman had any sense, she'd be grateful. "The way I see it, I might've saved your life tonight."

She let out a wry laugh. "That's an exaggeration, don't you think?"

He gave his head a solemn shake. "It's like I told you earlier—you fool around with these people, you'll get hurt. It's dangerous to say you're sellin' somethin' you aren't."

Her ire seemed to calm a little, her next question sounding more inquisitive. "What makes you so smart about these things?"

"I see a lot. Hear a lot."

She looked at him long and hard with those soft blue eyes, clearly trying to see behind his. "Don't take this the wrong way, but you seem too smart to be a bartender."

He sighed. She sounded just like Tony, just like his mother. It made him feel tired, much older than his thirty-three years. "I used to be a cop, okay?"

"Used to be?" She bit her lower lip, looking puzzled. "You're not . . . working here undercover or something, are you?"

He shook his head. "No way, *chère*. Just servin' up drinks, that's all."

"Why? Why would you go from being a cop to being a bartender?"

If you'd been anywhere near this city two years ago, you'd know. But since she'd clearly missed all the newspaper articles and TV news spots, he wasn't about to dredge up his past. "Nosy little girl, aren't you?"

"I came down here to ask questions," she said with a shrug.

He looked away, planting his gaze on the painting above the couch a few feet away. "But I'm not lost, *chère.* Not the person you came to find."

Silence blanketed the small, lush room and he regretted bringing her in here. It was too intimate a space and he found himself wanting to kiss her again. He hadn't planned that part of it and he remained surprised that it had felt so good, that stopping had been so hard. His game of coercing the truth from her had been a mistake. He didn't want to want her—or anyone. He just wanted to go home.

"Maybe you could help me."

Her hopeful words drew his eyes back to hers. "Help you how?"

"Help me find Tina." She suddenly sounded full of fresh optimism—*misplaced* optimism.

"How the hell you think I'd do that?"

"Well, you used to be a cop. And you seem to know your way around the escort industry pretty well. Surely there are people you could ask, places we could search."

"Whoa there, *chère.* What's this 'we' you're talkin' about all the sudden? I don't even know you."

She sighed. "But I need help and I'm desperate. And . . . I could pay you." Her eyes lit with the idea and she reached immediately for her purse. "How much do you want? I can give you what I have now, and more later. However much you want to charge."

Ironic. Now *she* was trying to pay *him* for something *he* didn't intend to sell, either. "No thanks, *beb*. I don't want your money, and frankly, I don't wanna get involved in your problems."

She looked crushed. He felt it in his heart, like a little dart sticking there.

Damn it. Why wouldn't people leave him alone? Of course, he'd started this—but he'd made his point with her and was ready to call it a night. "Look," he said, "I'm sorry, but I got enough troubles of my own, okay?"

She didn't respond, only kept sitting there looking like the world had just come to an end, making the dart in his chest dig a little deeper.

"Take my advice and go home to Chicago, Stephanie Grant. This is no place for a woman like you." Jake got to his feet and walked out of the room, through the outer bar area, and exited onto the steps descending into the enclosed courtyard. The night air hit him like a brick—for a September evening, it felt more like early August.

But he didn't really mind the heat—he'd grown up with it. At the moment, it was just something to feel, something to fight, something to wallow in, something to think about as he walked home—something other than Miss Chardonnay and those blue, blue eyes.

Chapter 3

Somewhere in the distance, a siren split the night. As usual on his walk home, he hadn't seen a soul since passing some partyers near Bourbon. As he moved up the sidewalk deep into dark, quiet streets, it was just him and the ghosts. That's what Becky used to say, the reason she never felt comfortable in the Quarter late at night. "Too many ghosts." Jake didn't believe in ghosts, but he could almost believe he felt them tonight, too, peeking over balconies and lurking in hidden doorways. Once he even looked over his shoulder.

Because he was losing his mind, apparently. *Knock it off already,* he scolded himself. What a night. Must be screwing with his brain.

Despite the ghosts and the heat, he was still thinking about Stephanie Grant.

He could have helped her. If he'd cared—about her search for her sister, about the worry haunting her gaze. But he didn't. He might have cared about Miss Chardonnay's fate enough to let her know she was playing a dangerous game, and he hoped she'd heed the warning. But like he'd said, her sister was all grown up. It was none of his business if one more sad girl spread her legs for money. He'd gone way overboard with Stephanie Grant tonight—and he couldn't even account for why—but that couch, the red room, was where it ended.

Still, a warm tremor ran the length of his body. Clearly, Stephanie Grant was all grown up, too—with ripe curves, lush lips, and soft breath that had grown heated when he'd kissed her.

Not real kisses, though. Teasing ones; their mouths had barely met.

Then why did he still feel them? And what about her had made him care *at all* what sort of trouble she might get herself into?

Turning a corner onto Burgundy, he let out a sigh. What the hell had happened to him tonight? He saw breasts and curves and sexy dresses in Sophia's every shift he worked and it didn't affect him. But somehow Stephanie Grant had dug deeper inside him. From the start, she'd drawn a few smiles from him—a rarity in itself, even if they were the devilish sort. And when he'd ended up alone with her in the red room, something inside him had switched on. Something needful. Something he'd nearly forgotten about, yet suddenly there it was, rearing its head just like that old habit of taking care of people and fixing things.

But hell, hadn't that dream of the masked woman made it clear? His body was hungry for sex, that's all this was. *Quit overthinking it. Go home. Go to sleep.*

"Got a quarter?"

The voice drew Jake's eyes to a skinny young girl with a creamed-coffee complexion, long hair falling straggly around her face. She huddled in a narrow doorway, her knees pulled up to her chest like she was cold. Even in the dark, he could see her white T-shirt was dingy.

Stopping, he reached in his pocket and found a five-dollar bill—he'd shoved it in there instead of his wallet, a late tip just before closing. He leaned down and let it drop to the cracked sidewalk beside her as he fought a nagging sense of worry. Against his better judgment, he spoke. "It's dangerous out here on the street."

"Tell me somethin' I don't know, Einstein."

He flinched at her sass—it didn't match the rest of her. She tried to talk "urban black girl" tough, but he wasn't buying it. "Where'd you run away from? You should go home."

He sensed more than saw her roll her eyes. "Mind your own damn business."

When he'd been a French Quarter beat cop, he'd talked to street kids all the time, and had gotten a hell of a lot worse from them than this, but her attitude still irritated him. "You'll get killed, or worse, out here," he informed her.

"Thanks for fillin' my day with sunshine, dude."

Much to his surprise, he let out a small laugh.

"You think somethin's funny about this?" she snapped.

He shook his head. "No, I just think *you're* a pretty funny kid is all."

Another eye roll. "Yeah, I just did *Leno* last week."

He sobered. "You really don't have a way to get off the street, someplace better to sleep?"

"If I did, would I be *here*, fool?"

"Speakin' of sleep, kinda late for panhandlin', isn't it?"

She cast a quick glance up before lowering her gaze. "Easier to sleep in the day. At night—got to keep my eyes open, you know?"

Jake sighed. *Keep walking, man. Just like you told Miss Chardonnay, you don't need anybody else's problems.* He couldn't quite make his feet move, though. Just like he hadn't quite been able to let Miss Chardonnay walk away tonight, either.

"There's a place in the courtyard where I live—you could sack out there if you want. It's nothin' great, but safer than this."

For the first time, she deigned to actually tilt her head back and meet his eyes. "You for real?"

He gave a short nod.

Suddenly, her back went rigid. "What you want for lettin' me sleep there? 'Cause if you playin' me, mister, tryin' to get in my pants—"

He held up his hands and took a step back. "Whoa, whoa, whoa, *'tite fille.* I'm just tryin' to be nice, no? You wanna come, follow me. You don't, don't." With that, he turned and walked on.

"Hold up."

He stopped, looked back. "What?"

She hesitated slightly. "Got to get my stuff."

Fishing out half a roll of mints, he put one in his mouth, then shoved his hands in his pockets and leaned back against an old brick wall, watching the girl reach through a hole in the building's foundation. As she got to her feet, a ragged backpack hoisted to one shoulder, he noticed rips in the knees of her blue jeans, dark skin peeking through.

"Sure you ain't after nothin'?" Her eyes narrowed even as she moved toward him.

"Hell yeah, I'm sure!" Peter, Paul, and Mary—what the hell had he done to deserve this? He had things to be guilty for, but damn. He spoke firmly. "You're a little girl. And I'm not that kinda guy. Got it?"

She pursed her lips, nodding shortly.

Without another look in her direction, Jake started toward his place again. He heard her padding along behind him, but didn't slow his stride. He regretted this already. Damn it, he'd done it again, without even realizing. First the blonde, now this. When would he get it through his head that he couldn't change anything, couldn't save anybody?

A block later, he led the girl through a wrought-iron gate that had seen better days and into a neglected courtyard. A broken fountain jutted up amid chipped, jagged bricks and dilapidated concrete. Four sagging wooden staircases flanked each side of the yard, leading to second-floor apartments. Jake strode to one where he knew somebody had discarded an old mattress. "Here ya go," he said, pointing.

She nodded, spoke gently. "Thanks."

He tried not to hear the softness in her voice. "Don't think this is the start of anything, though. You're still on your own."

Her next quiet nod made him feel like an ogre. "Your neighbors gonna go callin' the cops on me?"

Was the girl blind? He shook his head. "Don't have those kinda neighbors."

He didn't look back as he crossed the worn brickwork to the stairs that led to his place. He was ready to call it a night. No more mister nice guy, he scolded himself. It never paid. Never.

As he slid his key in the old lock, something raked up against his ankle, drawing his gaze downward. He found the scruffy little dog that had been hanging around the building for days, bugging whoever happened to be coming or going. "You again?" The mutt was an aggravation.

As he opened the door, he used one shoe to shove the dog away before stepping inside. Turning the lock brought a sense of relief, the isolation he cherished.

Heading to his bedroom, he stripped down to underwear, walked to the bathroom, and splashed cool water on his face. He looked at himself in the mirror, studied his eyes, thought about the empty feeling low in his belly. He was used to putting on a show, being polite at Sophia's, but it wasn't real and it tired him. Miss Chardonnay had tired him tonight, too—even if something about that *had* been disturbingly real.

It would suit him fine, he thought, if he never had to leave the run-down apartment again. But then, if he didn't have to work at all, if he truly didn't have to go anywhere to make money, he'd head out to the old house on the bayou and just stay *there*. The idea made him look forward to his days off, when he could go home for a couple of nights of solace.

Out there, there was no Miss Chardonnay worrying him with her pretense or tempting him with her innocent blue eyes. There was no homeless girl who thought he wanted to get in her pants. Out there was the one place he could truly forget, truly withdraw, even more than he already had.

Returning to the bedroom, he turned back the covers and lay down. He closed his eyes and tried not to think or feel, tried to shut back down into that place of least pain.

But it wasn't working. The events of the night kept flashing through his mind unbidden, leading right up to the most recent. *"Mon Dieu,"* he muttered as he flapped the sheet back.

Getting to his feet, he walked to the kitchen, where he pulled a shallow plastic dish of microwave mac-and-cheese from the fridge. He padded to the door and set the bowl outside, glancing up the breezeway to see that annoying dog come running.

Re-turning the lock, he shook his head at his insanity. Jesus, when would he ever learn?

A dorm room, a candle's glow turning pale yellow walls golden. Her top is off, blue jeans too. Jason is kissing her breasts, turning her inside out—his hands are in her underwear. He's trying to pull them down, but she's saying, "You know we can't."

"Yes, we can, Stephie."

"We can't. We don't have a . . . you know."

He's kissing her neck, then whispering. "Yes, we do. I bought some, just in case."

"Really?" Why hadn't it occurred to her that it was that simple, a walk into a drugstore?

He nods against her neck, molds her breasts in his hands. She feels it between her legs. And it hits her that they really can do it, if she decides it's okay. And the big sex mystery will be over, at last.

She's afraid—but she wants to. Her heartbeat echoes through her whole body.

This time when he tries to lower her panties, she doesn't stop him. Biting her lip, she runs her hands down his chest and reaches for the snap on his jeans. She is saying yes. Yes.

It should have been a good memory, but it wasn't. Stephanie pushed it away.

Still, the power of the recollection remained jolting as

she lay in bed, covers pulled to her waist. The quiet room in the quaint bed-and-breakfast just beyond the French Quarter felt like her safe hideaway from the decadence taking place on the streets nearby. She absently listened to the laughter of a romantic couple, watched their shadows move past her window, but her mind was back at DePaul on the night she'd given up her virginity. Maybe the last time she'd felt such overwhelming passion that she'd lost herself in it—until tonight.

It was strange to suddenly realize she *had* once understood the power of sex, yet had somehow *stopped* understanding somewhere along the way. The encounter with the bartender had apparently brought back a lot of little slices of her past she hadn't thought about in a very long time. Slices she'd actually forgotten—experiences she'd somehow tricked herself into believing she'd never had.

Upon returning to the room, she'd traded in her sexy clothes for the silly cotton pajamas Tina had given her last Christmas—a blue background dotted with black and white sheep. A desperate bid to get back to her simple life, the simple *self* she knew. Unfortunately, though, that hadn't stopped the uncontrollable sensations assaulting her. Same as if she were still in that sinfully red room with that sinfully sexy man, her breasts ached and the juncture of her thighs felt heavy.

She wanted to keep telling herself it was just about the situation, the strangeness of pretending she was there to sell her body. And maybe that was what had started it back in the red room, but what she felt now was nothing manufactured, nothing made up to get her through the night. If anything, it had almost *not* gotten her through the night.

The man was downright intriguing with that smooth, steady voice and the way he managed to seem distant and aloof even as he nearly seduced her. She couldn't help thinking he was something of a bastard, but she also couldn't deny the desire she'd suffered for him—that deep, deeper, deepest desire she'd not quite believed she was capable of feeling. She closed her eyes in an effort to blot out the moment when she'd realized it was only a game.

It was the first time in her life she'd ever gotten that intimate with a total stranger, the first time she'd ever wanted to have sex with someone she'd just met. Desire had taken over, becoming the biggest part of her, that quickly. God, she didn't even know his name.

Thank goodness she'd found the strength to spill the truth and stop the insanity of his hands, creeping up her body. It was the first time, and the *last* time, too, she promised herself. She needed to get back on track and think about Tina. Her sweet, impulsive, go-with-the-flow sister.

Tina, Tina, Tina.

Sometimes Tina seemed far younger than her twenty-five years, but sometimes Stephanie felt older than her thirty—widening the gap between them even more. Once upon a time, they'd been close—when Tina was little, the baby sister whom Stephanie had coddled and cooed over, passed clothes down to, helped with homework. But somewhere along the way Tina had begun to suffer from the belief that Stephanie was the family's golden child, the achiever who garnered all the praise, and that Tina was the neglected daughter, always coming in second place.

The truth was, Tina had never worked as hard as Stephanie. She lacked ambition and made poor choices, and following her last boyfriend down here was just one example. Tina had refused to see that part of Russ's decision to accept a job in a new city was because he wanted to break up—even Stephanie had detected that, yet Tina hadn't.

Now, though, Stephanie couldn't help wondering if things would be different if she'd been more supportive, and less judgmental. If she'd been more constructive rather than just criticizing. She'd thought the bartender had acted superior tonight, but had *she* unknowingly acted superior to Tina for all these years?

Despite the fact that they'd not been close for a while now, Stephanie could scarcely imagine her sister out there somewhere selling her body. What must it be like? What had driven Tina to such a place? Her phone calls had been so cryptic, simultaneously cheerful and sad. Where was she right now? Having sex with a stranger? One of the rich, smarmy men Stephanie had met tonight? Or . . . she closed her eyes, unable to even give words to her worst fears, that something had happened to Tina, something awful. She couldn't possibly give up her search simply because she hadn't gotten any leads tonight—no matter what the unhelpful, know-it-all bartender said.

And as for what had occurred with him, it was an aberration, that was all. An aberration best forgotten, put away somewhere in the back of her brain where she filed anything that threatened her sense of control. Where she'd apparently buried *all* her encounters with passion.

It was vital she have full control over herself if she were to find Tina. And if the bartender wouldn't help her, she had no other choice but keep looking for her sister in the same circles she had tonight. It seemed the only way to bring Tina home.

You float on dark bayou water, your skin moist with the humidity hanging heavy in the air. A heron calls in the distance and you hear the deep, plunging splash of a caiman tumbling in from the marshy bank. The musty scent of arrow arum wafts past as tall cypress trees rise up like arms to hold you. You are home.

But you see a new shape on the landscape, pale and curvaceous. A woman. Naked and lovely, soft white skin that strikes you as vulnerable in such a harsh environment. She is marked by the only real color in the gray-and-green film of the bayou—a pink hibiscus juts from her hair, the large petals shading her face.

Although when you look closer, trying to see more clearly, she somehow blends with the trees and foliage, hidden, gone. And in that silent moment you understand that vulnerable is the last thing she is. She is a chameleon in the forest, using her defenses with confidence and ease.

You scan the moss-draped banks, searching the low, gnarled branches and cypress knees, before catching sight of her once more, a vision of beauty tucked into your world as naturally as if she'd always been lurking, waiting to make herself known.

Dipping your oar into the water, you row toward her, hungry, anxious. The need presses on you as if it were a boulder weighing down your chest. You have to reach her. But as you approach the bank where she's been standing as still as another tree, she vanishes again, lost to you in the gangly greenery.

"Where are you?" you call out.

A hint of pink draws your attention and your next glimpse of her comes beside an ancient oak flung with Spanish moss—you spy the curve of a white breast, the stretch of a slender thigh. How can she merge and mingle so well with the trees and moss and earth here? How long has she been waiting, watching, thriving here, like some beautiful bird or rich, lush plant?

You row furiously in her direction—you have to have her, press against her—but one blink and she's gone, an apparition. Perhaps a thing you want so badly you've imagined her?

But then, no—

Because in an instant everything changes—

She is beneath you in the pirogue, all wild, welcoming flesh, and you are in her, deep, tight.

Her arms and legs curl around you, her body nimble and as eager as yours.

You thought it was hot in the bayou, but no climate could compare to the solid wall of heat rising within you, wrapping around both of you as you thrust into her warmth. You rain kisses on her glistening skin—mouth and face, neck and breasts—a man starved for what she can feed you.

You drink her in, soak her up, greedy, needing every last drop of her.

And only when you come inside her do you realize— this is home.

Chapter 4

The next morning, Stephanie resolved to put the previous evening behind her, sexy bartender and all. Her heartbeat skittered a bit at the memory of his warm hands, but she consoled herself by thinking, *What else would you expect? It's the first time you've been touched that intimately in a while, and the first time you've* ever *been touched by a man like that.* Dark. Dangerous. Another skittering heartbeat, damn it.

After returning from a hearty breakfast prepared by Mrs. Lindman, the sweet gray-haired proprietress of the LaRue House B and B, she moved to the small desk near her window. She tried to focus as she flipped open her laptop, but strangely, she found herself noticing things about her room that she hadn't before.

Fringed lampshades. The lush brocade of the armchair she'd pulled up to the desk. Vibrant purple throw pillows on the bed that she'd carelessly shoved aside last night when crawling beneath the sheets, so anxious to escape the night.

The light of day was making her realize that what had

happened last evening had left her more sensitized, aware. Of everything. Mrs. Lindman's sausage links had seemed spicier this morning, the orange juice tangier. The very act of eating had felt . . . bizarrely sensual.

What else have I missed? she wondered as she studied the bold colors and luxuriant textures surrounding her. *Is the whole world like this and I've just never noticed?*

Taking a deep breath, she murmured, "Get hold of yourself," and turned her attention where it belonged, onto her computer screen.

Her e-mail was filled with messages from Grable & Harding, the ad agency she'd temporarily left behind. Thanks to technology, though, one couldn't seem to leave much of anything *truly* behind these days. Most of the e-mail could be waded through later, but she opened the one labeled "Curtis Anderson." Curtis was, foremost, her boss, but also the man she'd been dating prior to her trip south.

S—

How's your sister? Hope she's well and that you're helping get her problems ironed out.

Also, have to inquire as to your return to the office. It's not me—Stan and the bigwigs are asking about your absence. He's worried about the phone co. campaign. You know Stan. He was his blustery self, asking how a major campaign can be pulled together with you there and the rest of your team here. So I told him I'd check with you.

And besides that, I miss you.

Let me know when you're coming home, and I'll plan something special.

C

Given its fairly short length, the message left her head spinning.

It reminded her of her lie, simply claiming Tina was in New Orleans and going through some personal problems. She recalled the way Curtis had tilted his head, his sandy hair never moving, but his eyes reaching. "What . . . sort of problems?"

She'd decided it was none of his business. Now she wondered if she'd simply been embarrassed. They were executives. Executives didn't have sisters who were prostitutes. "I can't really say."

He'd patted her hand to let her know it was okay. That was the kind of man he was. A hand patter. A giver of consoling smiles. A man who knew to open and close a message with personal concerns, sandwiching the real question in between.

And she couldn't blame Stan. Nailing the account for the long-distance carrier was huge, and so, naturally, the campaign had been assigned to Grable & Harding's most accomplished ad exec—and she'd promptly dashed off to the Big Easy on a leave of absence that was going to take longer than she'd promised.

She clicked on reply.

> *C—*
>
> *It's nice to hear from you.*
>
> *Please assure Stan I've got the pitch under control. Phil is working on the demographics and setting up focus groups, and Maria is handling the concept boards. I'll get the PowerPoint presentation rolling on my end.*
>
> *Remind Stan I've never pitched a campaign without winning the account, and I don't plan to*

*start failing now. Sometimes issues outside of
business must be dealt with, but I'm competent
enough to do that without jeopardizing Grable &
Harding.*

*My sister still needs me for a little while longer,
but I'll be home soon.*

Thank you for thinking about me. I miss you, too.

S

When she hit the send button, her stomach was tied in
a knot.

*I miss you, but I let a stranger touch me last night. I
miss you, but he made me feel more than you ever have.
Infinitely more.* Her thighs ached even now.

If Curtis's kisses had ever made any part of her ache,
she'd entirely missed it.

And up to now, she hadn't minded. Like so often in the
last ten years, she'd told herself she'd simply gotten too
mature for passion, that not all women could experience
the overwhelming desire you read about and saw in
movies.

But last night had proven she *could* feel it. Dear God,
she hadn't even thought about Curtis when she'd been
with the bartender, hadn't thought of him until just now.
Fortunately, she, too, knew enough to pad the bad news
with a lot of good, so he'd never have to know what he
didn't make her feel.

Next, she pulled up an Instant Message box to see if
Melody was online. Her heart lifted when she got a quick
answer.

TIFFANYSMOM226: *Hi—I was just hanging
out in the baby chat.*

A common occurrence. Melody's obsession with her six-month-old always left Stephanie amazed at such an about-face.

> STEPHGRANT: *I went to Chez Sophia last night. No success. No one knew her. What now?*
> TIFFANYSMOM226: *I wouldn't give up on Sophia's.*
> STEPHGRANT: *Why?*
> TIFFANYSMOM226: *There's a different crowd every night. Some girls only work there certain nights of the week.*

Stephanie hadn't thought of that. But she certainly didn't relish the idea of returning, for more reasons than she could easily identify. Which reminded her . . .

> STEPHGRANT: *You didn't tell me not to use my last name.*
> TIFFANYSMOM226: *Never crossed my mind. Some things in the business are just understood. Sorry.*

Stephanie only hoped there weren't a lot of other insider tips she was missing out on.

> STEPHGRANT: *Are there any other places to find high-end escorts?*
> TIFFANYSMOM226: *Afraid not. A couple of big-time madams were shut down in an FBI sting several years ago, and since then, things have been kept more on the down low. Sophia's third floor is the only place that wasn't affected, because the feds never found out about it.*

Stephanie considered her next move. To her dismay, she only saw one.

STEPHGRANT: *So you really think I should go back there? I was glad it was over.*
TIFFANYSMOM226: *I'm sorry it was difficult. Did you do what I told you?*

Sell it, feel it, flirt, smile, touch their arms, giggle, and only ask about Tina once you have them buying your act.

STEPHGRANT: *Yes.*

Except maybe the last one, with the bartender.

TIFFANYSMOM226: *I still think it's your best bet. Outside of Sophia's, I wouldn't know where to look.*

Stephanie sighed. She'd so hoped Melody would have something else to share.

STEPHGRANT: *Okay. I'll go back.*
TIFFANYSMOM226: *Good luck, and let me know. I have to run. Tiff is teething and she's getting irritable.*

"I'll go back," she whispered, staring blankly at the screen, "but how the hell will I face the bartender?"
And if he comes on to me again, how will I resist this time?

* * *

Shondra's stomach rumbled fiercely, but she was used to hunger pangs. So she looked down at the dollar bill in her hand and, instead of darting off to buy a day-old doughnut at the bakery on St. Ann, she stuffed it in her pocket. At the same time, she checked to make sure the five was still there. Damn, five dollars! That guy must be whack, giving away money like that. She'd been sure he wanted something, but she'd slept in peace on the old mattress. Best sleep she'd had in a couple of weeks.

Not that she trusted him. She didn't trust nobody. Trusting only got you hurt and she was too smart for that.

She leaned up against the cracked plaster wall in the hot little room with the washing machines, listening as two of them ran. "Other three's broken," the old woman in the flowery tent dress had told her a little while ago. "So ever'body's gotta fight over these two. Give you a dollar you stay and watch my clothes, don't let nobody take my washers. I got four more loads to do."

Money, just for watching washing machines? She'd said, "You got it," plucking the bill from the woman's wrinkled hand before she'd waddled away in canvas tennis shoes nearly as dirty as Shondra's.

If somebody had given her a dollar *yesterday,* she'd have thought, *Screw the damn washing machines,* and hit the street for the bakery. Afterward, she'd have taken out the paper cup in her backpack and sat in front of St. Louis Cathedral asking for quarters until the cops ran her off. But this wasn't a bad place and she wasn't gonna blow it. For all she knew, *every* fool who lived in this building would give her a dollar to watch their washers. She let her back slide down the wall until she rested on worn, pock-marked linoleum.

When a large shadow filled the open doorway, she

flinched. "Shit," she muttered, looking up to find the guy from last night.

He jolted, too. "What the *hell*?" Then he sighed. "What are you doin' in here, *'tite fille*?" He wore a white T-shirt and baggy khaki shorts. His dark hair was messier than last night, like he hadn't combed it yet today.

She glanced at the washers, then at the cracked old laundry basket he toted. "Hope you ain't plannin' to wash those clothes."

He blinked. "Why?"

"Machines are taken."

He tilted his head. "And who appointed you laundry police?"

"Mrs. La . . . somethin'."

"LaFourche," he said on another sigh. "Thinks she owns the damn laundry room." He rolled his eyes.

"She gave me a dollar not to let nobody mess with these machines. She's got other loads." She patted the front pocket of her blue jeans.

He raised his eyebrows, delivering a pointed look. "I gave you *five* dollars last night. What do *I* get?"

Was he taking back what he said? Did he want in her pants, after all? She pushed staunchly to her feet. "You said you was just bein' nice."

He plopped his basket on the floor. "Don't get your back up, *'tite fille*. I *was* just bein' nice. But what say we make us a little bargain?"

She crossed her arms, stood up straighter, tried to look mean. "Like what?"

He reached into his back pocket and pulled out a worn brown leather wallet, then held out a ten toward her. "What say you run down to the Café Du Monde and get us some beignets for breakfast."

She worked not to let her relief show. "It's too late for breakfast."

"Call it lunch then, whatever you want."

She glanced at the money, thinking some beignets sounded damn good. Wouldn't even cut into her six-dollar stash, either. Another hunger pang prodded her to take the cash, but she glanced to the machines. "What about the washers? I promised. For the dollar."

He tilted his head. "I'll watch 'em for ya."

She widened her gaze accusingly. "You won't steal 'em? Won't put your clothes in as soon as hers are done?"

He gave his head a solemn shake, which made her believe him. And she couldn't deny he'd kept his promises so far. "In fact, while you're there, get me three bucks' worth of quarters for the Laundromat. And get somethin' to drink with your beignets, too."

Shondra thought about saying thanks, but decided not to. Wouldn't pay to let her soft side show, even if the dude seemed straight up. "How many you want?"

"An order for me, and an orange juice. Get however many you want for yourself."

"For real?" She hadn't eaten since day before yesterday.

He gave a short nod before glancing to his feet, where a cute, furry little dog stood. It made her think of Rex, the boxer she'd gotten as a puppy for her tenth birthday— leaving Rex had been one of the hardest things about running away.

Just when she was gonna ask to pet his dog, he yelled at it. "*Vat'on*, scruffy old mutt! Get outta here!" He waved a hand to shoo the poor dog away.

"Don't holler at him," she said as the pooch ducked his head and tail, moping back out into the courtyard.

"Why not? Mangy thing just comes around to beg food and bother people."

Something inside her drew up tight at his words. Like the dog, she looked down at the cracked flooring. The air felt thicker than usual.

"Sorry," he said, his voice softer than she'd heard it before.

She risked a short glance up. "It's a'ight. You're cooler to me than you are to the dog, so what do I care?"

His eyes went a little softer, too, as he quirked half a smile in her direction. "I *like* you better than the dog."

"What's to like?" She hadn't felt very likable in a long time.

"Like I said last night, you're pretty funny." He glanced to the washers. "And looks like you're pretty dependable, too."

She rolled her eyes toward a saggy, water-stained ceiling. "Laundry guard. My claim to fame. You want my autograph?"

"See, you're a laugh a minute," he chuckled, then pointed toward the street. "But my stomach's growlin', so get goin' with you."

She nodded, moving past him out to the courtyard before stopping to look back. "What's your name?"

"Jake."

"I'm Shondra." She turned to go, but as she passed by the dog, now lying in a spot of shade just big enough to hold him, she couldn't resist stopping to pet his head. "He ain't so bad as he seems," she whispered to the dog, glancing back to see Jake disappear into the laundry room.

When she took off toward the gate again, the pooch trailed her. "Stay," she said, trying to sound firm but not harsh. She didn't want him getting into traffic. "Stay here and I'll be back soon," she said as if he could understand her.

Then she smiled to herself as she headed off toward the Café Du Monde. Jake would never know if she got an order of beignets for the dog, too.

Jake perused the bottles perched on the glass shelves behind the bar, taking inventory of the booze. It was a task he'd been putting off, but he'd come into work early, more energetic than usual.

The sun shining through the old scratched-up windows of his apartment didn't generally keep him from sleeping, but he'd found himself getting up early today, too. Late for most people, but early for him. He'd lifted weights—the equipment being among the few things he'd taken when he'd moved out of the little house near City Park. Then he'd even gone around the apartment picking up laundry. He wasn't sure where the burst of energy had come from, but it was good timing, since he'd run out of clean clothes.

He *hated* laundry. He couldn't seem to load clothes into a washer or fold towels from a dryer without images of Becky filling his head. She'd always taken care of their clothes with a merry little smile on her face, like she knew some secret about laundry that no one else did.

So he'd been almost thankful for the distraction the homeless kid had provided. Shondra. Daylight had revealed she was pretty, with long, wavy hair and smooth brown skin. No wonder she'd thought he'd wanted to get in her pants, then gotten so nervous again today. His gut pinched wondering how many men she'd already had to fear at thirteen or fourteen.

Despite himself, he was glad he hadn't let her stay on the streets. She wasn't exactly *off* the streets now, but at least he'd given her a safer place to sleep than most homeless kids had. He was glad he'd fed her, too.

He couldn't start going all soft, though. Girl would go and get herself hurt or worse, and then there he'd be, *feeling* it. The loss, the regret—the sense that he hadn't done enough and should have known better than to even try in the first place. Wasn't gonna happen.

Behind him, someone slapped the bar impatiently. "Bartender, give me a White Russian."

He turned to find Alan Cummings, a sharply handsome investment hotshot who he'd come to think of as a real asshole. For one thing, the guy had probably heard fifty people call Jake by name, but he stuck with "bartender," giving it enough of an inflection to make it clear he thought he was better.

"Sure," Jake said, hoping his tone conveyed his similar disregard for the man.

He poured the drink, finishing with the splash of milk that gave it color, and took Cummings's money. He didn't leave a tip.

"Hey Jakey," said Misti, a brunette raspberry daiquiri, as she sashayed up to the bar in a dress cut nearly to her navel.

Jake put on his workplace smile, but almost thought he preferred "bartender." Misti was giggly, silly, too youthful for the setting, and the very sight of her tonight, for some reason, made his gut wrench with disgust for Sophia's third floor. "Let me guess. Raspberry daiquiri?"

She raised her eyebrows cartoonishly. "How'd you know?"

Because people are predictable. He'd learned that at

the police academy and had since discovered how true it was. People liked patterns, especially in high-tension situations. They liked to reach for the familiar to give them some sense of control. "Just lucky," he said.

She tilted her head. "You know, I like when a bartender knows what I want to drink, or when a waitress remembers what I like to eat." Clearly a delightful new thought in her young mind.

You like it because it makes you feel you belong somewhere. Like somebody gives a shit about you in some way.

He was tempted to explain that to her, but didn't. Because he didn't care. Didn't care how young she was, or how foolish.

You're all just drinks to me. He thought of saying that, too, to remind himself as much as her. But he bit his tongue, kept on with the smile, and said, "You have a good night, okay?" He even added a wink for good measure as he pushed down the useless thoughts clouding his head.

With that, silly Misti eased down from the stool with her drink and disappeared into the lush surroundings, which had grown crowded without his realizing. He glanced at a little clock behind the bar. Ten-thirty on the dot.

As if on cue, one of the red curtains at the door was drawn back to admit a blond vision in black lace. Long legs, high breasts, creamy skin—this woman had the whole package. That's when he narrowed his gaze and realized who it was.

Stephanie Grant.

His chest clenched with a combination of desire and anger.

Damn it, she'd come back. After he'd warned her how dangerous it was. He'd thought she'd seemed adequately off balance by the time they'd parted ways, but now he wondered if maybe that was just from the touching.

The truth was, it had left *him* off balance, too, and though he'd done a decent job of not thinking about her today, now it all came rushing back. Her gentle sighs beneath him in the red room. The catch of her breath when he skimmed his fingers over that sinfully soft skin. That fast, he was fighting an erection. Peter, Paul, and Mary.

To his surprise, rather than try to duck him, she made her way directly to the bar.

Predictable? Not *this* woman, it seemed.

As she took the same stool as she had last night, he braced his arms on the counter below him and pierced her with his gaze. "Chardonnay?"

"Tequila sunrise."

Another surprise. "Hittin' the hard stuff tonight?"

"Just approaching the evening in a different way."

Yeah, he could see that. Her lace dress hugged her more snugly than the previous one, the skimpier fabric maximizing her cleavage and continuing to tighten his groin more with each passing second.

And like a bolt from the blue, his mind flashed to the dream he'd had last night. A woman in a pirogue, turning him wild with hunger. The driving feeling that he couldn't get enough of her, that he wanted to consume her. She hadn't been masked—in fact, she'd been as natural as the wild bayou itself—but he still had no more than a vague idea of her face. *This* hunger wasn't as overwhelming as *that* hunger, thank God. But it came close.

"What the hell you doin' back here?" he asked, squirting tequila in a glass.

Her voice came as even as his. "You won't help me, so I'll have to keep looking on my own."

He raised his gaze to hers, hoping no one would hear him say this to a "customer," but it needed to be said. "This is a stupid, dangerous, and I repeat, *stupid* way to do it."

Stephanie Grant shrugged her pretty shoulders, her hair falling across them tonight in golden waves. "I don't know how else to find her. And I *have* to find her."

"How the hell you gonna do that, *chère*?" He finished her drink off with grenadine and OJ, setting it on the bar. "You said nobody here knew her."

She spoke with far more confidence than on their first meeting. "There's a different crowd every night. Tonight I might get lucky."

Despite himself, he cast a wolfish expression. "Tried to help you get lucky last night, *beb,* but you turned me down."

Her cheeks flushed pink behind her heavy makeup, sending a thin shot of masculine satisfaction through him. He kept his gaze trained on hers, seeing the same memories as his floating in those pretty blue eyes. For a long moment, it seemed like nothing else in the world could possibly matter more than the heat they'd shared last night.

She finally glanced down to her drink, picking it up for a quick sip. "I . . . have to go," she said, starting to leave the stool.

He reached across the bar and grabbed her wrist. "You didn't hear a word I said last night, no? You can't be foolin' around with these people. You're not that good an actress."

She pulled in a deep breath. "I have to try."

He released her wrist—no other choice. "You got more looks than brains, *chère*."

"You're an ass."

"Maybe." He shrugged. "But an ass who's tryin' to look out for you."

She narrowed her gaze on him. "You tried to seduce me last night. That's how you define looking out for me?"

"Didn't plan it," he said with a frank tilt of his head. "But I'm a red-blooded guy."

Stephanie Grant withdrew her troubled glare from him to scan the room bustling with suits and curves, and when she met his eyes again, raw resolve filled her expression. "The rest of these men are *just* as red-blooded, and if whatever is so tempting about me worked on you, maybe it'll work on them, too."

He let out a sigh. "That's exactly what you should be afraid of."

Chapter 5

Stephanie had decided to face him head-on. Besides, he'd been the only truly familiar face in the room. What she'd forgotten was how the mere sight of the man affected her. It was like being dipped in a vat of hot lava. Now, as she walked away, her nipples rubbed against the lace cups of her scant dress, and the juncture of her thighs burned. For him. For more of what they'd started last night.

God, stop this! she yelled at herself.

She needed her wits about her, more than ever in her life. If what he'd said was true, her safety might depend on it. But more than that, *Tina's* safety depended on it. Each passing day, it felt as if her sister were slipping a little further away.

And yet, what was foremost in her mind as she strolled from the bar?

She remained caught up in *herself,* in the lure of sensuality, wondering if her sexy bartender watched the sway of her hips as she walked away. She wanted—more than she'd wanted anything in a long time—to take him by the hand and lead him back to that red room, then lock the door and forget the rest of the world existed. She wanted to get lost with him in all those lush textures. She wanted to get lost in *him*.

The insane desire remained as foreign to her as it had been last night, but also as potent. This man moved her in a way no man had before. Even having now remembered back to college, high school, times when she had indeed experienced true passion, she knew this was more than that. It felt almost as if those earlier times had been some kind of an introduction, but that *this* was the real thing.

And she was walking away from it. For more reasons than she could name.

But the most important reason, at the moment, was finding Tina.

She lectured herself with last night's mantra: *sell it*. Somehow tonight it was easier. Maybe because she'd figured out after last night that it wasn't going to be as simple as just walking into this den of sin and locating her sister. She had no choice but to be strong now, to figure out how to get these people to open up to her.

As the tropical tequila mix warmed her inside, she thrust out her chest slightly and licked her lips. Somewhere in the room, a man was watching—she could feel a hungry gaze making her skin prickle with awareness. The bartender? Or a piece of prey? That's what she'd decided the other men were. She wanted it to be the bartender watching, but *needed* it to be some rich man who might know her sister.

As she gazed toward the wide windows spanning two sides of the large corner room, she tried to look sexy and slightly aloof, for a man who enjoyed that little pretended bit of challenge. In her peripheral vision, she found a light-haired guy, handsome, mid-thirties, leering at her.

Prey.

She turned her head slightly, casting a soft glance, then a smile. *Sell it.*

She held his gaze and licked her lip once more. It was hard as hell to do, but she'd just discovered how. She pretended he was the bartender.

The handsome man wore an Armani suit and a lecherous smile as he moved toward her, closing the gap and stepping too close into her personal space. "What's your name, sweetheart?"

"Stephanie." Her stomach churning, she peered up into eyes filled with arrogance and lust. *Pretend he's the man behind the bar, the hot man who nearly seduced you last night. You can do this.*

Although as he made small talk with her, he slowly quit being the bartender and became merely a client, another client at another party. Only, just like last evening, she was selling *herself* instead of an ad campaign. And growing more practiced at it by the second.

"Why haven't I seen you here before, Stephanie?"

She gave her head a coquettish tilt. "Maybe you have and you just don't remember."

He chuckled deeply. "You're not a woman I'd forget." He punctuated the statement by reaching up to run his finger down the thin bra-like strap of her dress until he was nearly touching her breast. *Don't panic.* She smiled and turned slightly away so that he dropped his hand.

Without planning it, her eyes landed on the bartender— who watched from behind the bar. His look was clearly one of warning and she hoped he could read the defiance on her face.

It felt utterly strange shifting her eyes back to the letch she was pretending to seduce, knowing the real object of her desire spied her every move. The bartender was cramping her style, taking her head out of the game.

She reached to lightly touch the Armani's sleeve. "It's too loud in here. Let's go out on the balcony where we can talk."

The Armani grinned. "Excellent idea. After you."

Pushing through the nearest set of French doors was like escaping a nemesis. As soon as the darkness closed around her and her prey, she felt freer to begin probing for information. She leaned against a white wrought-iron railing and took a sip from her glass. "You seemed surprised you hadn't seen me here before. Does that mean you're a frequent customer?"

The Armani laughed softly and began stroking her arm with his thumb. "Now, sweetheart, what difference does that make?"

Her skin crawled at his caress, her body going cold despite the heavy air. *Keep selling it.* "Just curious. And the truth is, I *haven't* been here too many times before . . . but maybe you know my girlfriend Tina? She's here all the time."

He tilted his head. "Tina, huh? No, I don't think so."

She lowered her chin in teasing accusation. "Are you sure? Pretty blonde, twenty-five, gorgeous eyes?" Then she laughed. "Because if you're worried I'm the jealous type, don't be."

He flashed a lecherous grin. "Well then, maybe you should call her up and the three of us can have ourselves a little party."

Oh God. Talk about skin crawling. "No, *sweetheart*," she said, playfully echoing him. "I don't share."

"My loss," he said lightly before raising his eyebrows. "Or maybe my gain? Why don't we go to my place and you can show me just how possessive you are."

Now what? He didn't know Tina, or if he did, he

wasn't saying. And she'd as good as agreed to have sex with him, damn it. She'd gotten so good at selling that she'd forgotten when to stop. "I . . . need to visit the ladies' room first."

She kept her smile in place but immediately sensed that she'd made a faux pas. She'd hesitated too long when she'd been scrambling for an excuse to walk away.

"What if I don't want you to go?" He continued flashing a lusty grin as he slid his arms around her in a loose embrace.

She forced a laugh. "Why wouldn't you want me to go to the ladies' room?"

He gave his head a slight tilt, as if trying to read her eyes. "Just a funny feeling I've got. Not trying to get away from me, are you, sweetheart?"

She gazed up at him. *Pretend he's the man you desire. As much as you can.* "Why on earth would I do that?"

His expression went serious. "I'm not sure, but I'm not interested in risking it. I want you for the night. How much?"

Despite that wanting her for an hour was just as heinous, her throat caught. She'd never expected to end up in a mess this deep. She hoped like hell he didn't see her nervous swallow. "That depends."

"On?"

His touch grew more offensive by the moment, but she made herself giggle. "If you're going to be a gentleman and let me go to the bathroom first."

"How about a preview before you go? Something to keep me happy while you're away."

She laughed again, praying he didn't feel her body tensing. "I'm not going across the country or anything. It's the bathroom. I'll be gone two minutes."

"Even so, the customer's always right, right?"

He slid his hand from her hip up toward her breast—until she reflexively clamped her arm down tight against her body, stopping his progress. Even in the darkness, she could see the ugly tint suddenly lighting his eyes. "What's wrong?"

"Nothing." She shook her head, but damn it, her voice quavered slightly.

His eyes narrowed to thin slits. "Look, I don't know what kind of game you're playing, but I don't like it. I came here to find a willing woman, and I picked *you*. I want to start getting my money's worth, *now*."

Suddenly unable to endure his touch for even a second longer, the instincts of a lifetime kicked in and made her struggle against his tightening grip. Bad move. He anchored one arm around her waist and used his free hand to latch onto her chin, turning her face up to his. "I don't know why you're trying to get away from me, sweetheart—maybe you're new at this, I don't know. But I don't like being teased, so I suggest you be a good girl and give me what I want."

This was bad. Really bad. Her stomach lurched and her skin prickled. And in the midst of her personal terror, another ugly vision blinked through her brain. Tina, in the same situation. If you were an escort, what happened if you changed your mind? What were your options? Did anyone care?

As the letch reached down toward the hem of her short dress, she batted his hand away, hard. *"Get off me right now, you jerk!"* she said through clenched teeth. Adrenaline made her stronger as she pressed her hands against his chest in an attempt to free herself, but the arm locked around her still didn't budge.

So she clawed her fingernails deep.

"Hey!" he snarled, leaning back but still not releasing her.

Next, she would go for his eyes.

"Lady said no, asshole."

The deep, commanding voice stunned her until she looked up to find a muscular man standing outside one open French door, arms crossed.

The bartender.

Jake watched as Cummings loosened his grip on Stephanie Grant to look at him, bothered when the shithead didn't turn her loose completely. "What the hell business is it of yours? I suggest you go inside and mind your own business."

Jake held his ground, but narrowed his gaze on the slimy bastard. "Can't do that. *I* suggest you let her go."

When Cummings hesitated, Jake flexed one fist—a warning. At this, Cummings finally released her from his grasp, but appeared almost as angry as Jake felt. "She does this for a living, pal."

That's what you think. He couldn't help flitting his gaze quickly to Stephanie before looking back to Cummings.

Finally, the asshole stepped away from her, so Jake stood aside, leaving the man a clear path through the open door.

"You just lost your fucking job, pal!" he said, wagging a finger in Jake's face.

Jake reached up and caught it, like capturing a fly in his hand. "You get on outta here and maybe the lady won't file assault charges."

Cummings laughed. "Like anybody's gonna believe a whore." But at least he made the stinging comment his exit line, departing back into the glitz and soft jazz that did such a good job of covering the ugly reason why everyone was there.

Jake walked from the light streaming out the door into the shadows where Stephanie stood. "You all right, *chère*?"

"Yeah, fine." She was lying. Eighty damn degrees out here and she was shivering.

Instinct made him want to hold her, attempt to comfort her, but it was the wrong move. Women didn't like to be touched by strange men right after something like this. And best he keep his hands off this one anyway.

Even so, his gut stayed all pinched up. She was a damn stupid woman, but her blind stupidity hadn't stopped the inexplicable fear that had raced through him when he'd opened that door. Never mind that this wasn't his business and he shouldn't give a damn. Never mind that if Cummings really went to the top brass, over and above his easygoing boss, Danny, he might have just jeopardized the easy gig he had here.

He crossed his arms again and leaned back against the railing next to her. "You see my point now, no?"

The question earned him a sneer.

Good. Would be best if she was mad at him. "You can't handle this, Stephanie Grant. Now you best get on home to Chicago, back to your neat little life up there, and forget all about this place."

She stared blankly through the mullioned glass, the old panes distorting the colors and shapes inside. "I wish I could."

"Well, you can sure as hell try. And the sooner the better, you ask me."

She whipped her gaze to him, her ire suddenly returned. "I didn't ask you, and I meant I wish I could go home, not just that I wish I could forget this place. I *can't* go home. Not until I find my sister."

Jake let out a long sigh. This woman tired him. He pulled out a chair from a little white table next to the railing and sat down, resting his elbows on his knees as he loosely laced his fingers. "What am I gonna do with you, *chère*? I can't be chasin' you around all over New Orleans tryin' to keep you safe—I'm nobody's hero. But seems to me that if I don't, you're gonna keep on gettin' yourself in trouble you can't get out of."

"Look, I'm not your responsibility." Her tone was pointed, harsh. "I appreciate what you did just now, but you can consider yourself relieved of duty."

He shifted a sour gaze from his hands to her face to see that damnable determination *still* shining in her eyes, even after this. He simply shook his head. "How you expect me to sleep nights, *beb*?"

"You just said you weren't a hero. So what's it to you? I never asked for your protection."

But I just can't seem to stop giving it, can I? He wanted to accuse her of dragging him into this, but she hadn't. He'd made her problems his business by coercing the truth from her last night, and again tonight, by following her out here when he'd seen her leave with Cummings. "Tell me somethin', *chère*? Is there anything I can say to make you stop actin' like some crazy *couillon*? Anything I can do to talk some sense into you and get you *out* of Sophia's? And *into* some clothes?"

When she lifted her gaze, he couldn't help wondering what she'd look like without all that makeup. What was she like—out of this place, out of this situation, in her normal, everyday life? Softer, he thought. Softer, in a good way.

She crossed in front of him, moving to the other side of the table to the remaining chair. He made a point of staying bent over and went back to not looking at her, instead studying the grain in the balcony's wooden floor. It was easier that way.

"I don't even know your name," she said, her very tone relaying everything her words didn't. *I don't even know your name, yet you've touched me. I don't even know your name, yet you're asking me to listen to you.*

He couldn't help raising his eyes. "Jake Broussard."

She offered a soft nod in reply, then said, "It's like this. My ex-escort friend tells me this is the only place where high-priced escorts and their customers meet publicly. And Tina put herself in that category of prostitutes, unequivocally—it seemed important to her. Do you know of any *other* places high-priced girls work?"

"No," he agreed, still tracing the wood grain with his eyes. "Used to be more hot spots for high-priced hookers, but the feds came in a few years back and closed 'em down. The NOPD never quite understood—prostitution's against the law, but we had plenty else to keep us busy besides comin' down on the workin' girls. When the feds moved in, we were surprised they didn't have better things to do, too. Only thing we could figure is they were lookin' for somethin' bigger and didn't find it."

"Well then," she said with a nod, "I have no recourse than to continue asking around *here*. Someone *has* to know something about my sister—I just haven't found them yet."

He lifted his eyes to hers for the first time in a while. "Supposin' I said I'd ask around *for* you. Would that keep your pretty little butt at home a few nights?"

He saw her absorbing the offer, finally leaning across the table to say, "What more could we do? Where else could we search? If you're willing to help, surely there's more to be done than just snooping around this one place. As an ex-cop, you must know other avenues we could try."

A thin ribbon of weariness fluttered through him. "So you're sayin' that me askin' around here isn't enough for you?" He hiked a thumb in the direction of the party.

"I'm saying that if you're going to help me, why not use all your resources? Like I said, I can pay you whatever you like and the sooner we find Tina, the sooner I'll be out of your hair."

"I don't want your money, *chère*."

"What *do* you want?"

As their eyes met, he thought they both felt the heat the question implied. *I want to lay you down and touch you, glide my hands over each and every one of your pretty curves.* He gave his head a quick shake to jerk himself back to reality. "No payment required," he finally said, his gaze still locked on hers. They were so damn blue he thought he could go for a swim in them.

She sat up a bit straighter, her breasts thrusting forward with the motion. "So you're saying you'll help me find her?"

He let out a sigh. Was that indeed what he was saying? That he, a man who tried to care as little as possible about anybody or anything these days, was going to attempt assisting Stephanie Grant in locating her lost sister?

"Yeah, *beb,* sure. I'll help you find her."

He had to be out of his mind.

Chapter 6

Tina pulled the sheet up over her breasts, watching as Robert crossed in front of the bed, naked, disappearing into the bathroom. For a guy in his forties, he had a good body—he worked out every morning, and it showed.

She wasn't sure why she felt the need to cover herself. The sex wasn't horrible or anything. And whenever those weird feelings of *yuck* entered the picture, she just closed her eyes and imagined it was Russ making love to her, and that took any slight element of distaste away.

She sighed, sinking a little deeper into the goose-down pillow, watching the sway of her toes, back and forth, where they stuck out from the one-thousand-thread-count sheet. Screw Russ. She didn't need him. She only wished he could see her now—living in the lap of luxury. Robert had put her up in a house in the Garden District. Well, not a whole house—it was a grand old mansion that had been divided into apartments—but it was gorgeous, everything a girl could want.

She shifted her gaze to the window, overhung with draping vines. Outside stood a large trellis adorned in wisteria, and sometimes she opened the window, despite the heat, just to drink in the fragrance. Yet the really fabulous part was inside—high ceilings, crystal chandeliers, plush draperies, and big, majestic furniture that looked like it should be in a castle. "Your throne, m'lady," Robert sometimes said when escorting her to the dining-room table, so she knew she wasn't exaggerating the grandeur in her mind. Stephanie always said she exaggerated *everything,* but Stephanie was so wrong about her, in so many ways.

She wished Stephanie could see the place, too, but that was impossible. Her holier-than-thou sister would never approve of the way she'd ended up here.

"You're doing *what*?" Steph had said when Tina had called her a few weeks back. "An escort, as in . . . a *prostitute*?"

It was only sex. Sometimes she wondered if Steph even *had* sex with the men she dated.

When Stephanie had been in high school, she'd gotten in trouble for coming in late from a date more than once, and on one occasion Tina had spied her furiously making out with Tommy Rhodes on their front porch when she'd thought everyone was asleep. But somewhere along the way, Steph had changed. By the time Tina was old enough to start asking questions about guys, Stephanie had turned all prim and proper, all "Don't do this" and "Don't do that" and "Don't let yourself get talked into anything" and "You'll like yourself better if you wait."

"How long?" she'd asked once.

Stephanie had been packing her green tapestry suitcase, the one Tina loved because it looked so sophisticated, to go back to college after a long weekend. She'd been making neat little rows of underwear and sweaters and jeans. " 'Til . . ." She'd pondered slowly, unaware that

Tina watched her fingers with the perfectly-polished nails, admiring her every move as she packed so fastidiously. " 'Til you feel like you're in complete control of the situation."

Tina had hugged a throw pillow from Steph's bed to her chest. "You mean, like, being in love."

To her surprise, Stephanie had shaken her head. "No, more than that. In love with someone who loves you back and who you know would never hurt you or leave you. Ever. Someone truly worthy."

Tina could only guess her sister had been hurt by someone she'd slept with.

Well, so had she now—lots of times. Who hadn't? She'd learned long ago that sex was just part of life and that it was silly to think of it as some sacred act, like Stephanie did. Christ, she'd still be a virgin if she'd waited for a guy as perfect as the one Steph had described.

And after Russ's rejection, she'd determined—finally, once and for all—that a guy like that just wasn't going to come along. She'd grown tired of waiting around for something fabulous to happen, so she'd *made* it happen. And now she had it all. Sparkly cocktail dresses, diamonds dangling from her ears, a debonair man who was crazy about her, and best of all—a future.

She might not be as madly in love with Robert as she had been with other guys, but he was wild about her—and he'd proven it with all he'd given her.

Of course, Stephanie would probably drop dead on the spot if she knew her little sister was having an affair with a married man, but Robert had promised to leave his wife—as soon as his kids left for college next week, in fact. He just wanted to wait until they were gone, until he could explain to Melissa in a nice, civil way that he'd fallen out of love with her and into it with someone else.

Robert exited the bathroom fully clothed—only his plum-colored tie hung askew around his neck. When he smiled at her, the skin around his eyes crinkled in that George Clooney way, which made it handsome. She didn't even mind that his dark hair was shot through with bits of silver—it only made him look distinguished, like a man to be reckoned with.

"Leaving so early?" she asked. It wasn't that she couldn't bear the idea of being without him, but that she'd spent so much time by herself the last few weeks that she'd begun, for the first time in her life, to feel lonely.

He stood before the dresser mirror, knotting the tie—a perfect double Windsor—but glanced over his shoulder. "I'm sorry, love. But a late business meeting can only run so late." He winked.

"Do you still sleep with her?" she asked without quite planning it.

Finishing the knot, he came to sit on the elegant little bench at the foot of the bed, reaching over to play with her toes. "Do you mean sleep in the same bed with or have sex with?"

"Sex."

He smiled his warm, winning smile—the one that made her so sure of him, like Stephanie had said she should be. "Of course not, love. Haven't for a long while now."

"So when you tell her it's over, it won't come as a total shock. I mean, she knows the marriage is failing, right?" It wasn't so much that she cared about his wife, but on some level she did care what his wife *thought* of her. And what other people would think, too. She would eventually be taking Melissa's place, after all, socializing with Robert's friends, coming to know his children.

"Yes, darling, she knows. We've never discussed it, but it's clear."

"Do me a favor?" She let her eyes widen to moon at him in a way she knew he adored.

"Anything. Name it."

"When you tell her about me, don't tell her how we met." *That you paid me for sex.* "It's not that I think there's anything wrong with it, but some people are such prudes, you know?"

He nodded, his look assuring her that he understood perfectly. She loved that about him. "No worries," he said as he got to his feet and came around to the side of the bed, bending to kiss her forehead. She liked when he did that. And in time, she'd grow to love him the same way she loved Russ, but better. Because he was worthy. Like Stephanie said he should be.

"Is that all I get?" she asked.

He chuckled, smiling into her eyes, then lowered a long, deep kiss to her waiting lips. She wished she felt it inside more—she'd thought maybe she would this time. But that was okay.

"Good night, love."

"When will I see you again?" She sat up in bed as he walked away, still careful to keep the sheet over her chest and still not quite knowing why.

"I'll have to call you. Probably not tomorrow, but by the weekend."

She nodded patiently. She could take a little loneliness for what she got in return. A life of ease and luxury. And as soon as he left Melissa, he was going to let her start managing the ritzy boutique he owned in the French Quarter—so soon she'd have a career, too.

Maybe then she'd call Stephanie, and maybe even her

mom and dad. She'd invite them all down to meet her classy husband and see their fabulous home. And she'd tell them all how fulfilling she found the world of high-priced fashion.

She'd never been as smart as Stephanie, but at least she was pretty. And she'd finally found a way to make that work for her, a way to get everything she'd ever wanted.

Nearly twenty-four hours after leaving Sophia's private party, Stephanie strolled down a narrow, old French Quarter street toward the diner where she had agreed to meet Jake Broussard. In the mood to walk, she'd forgone a cab as well as the rental car she'd procured but had hardly used since her arrival, given that parking spots were minimal in the Quarter.

She still couldn't believe Jake had agreed to help her—it was a godsend, a new road appearing at a dead end.

"We'll go some places I know, ask around," he'd said. "You got a picture of your sister, *chère*?"

"Yes," she'd replied, still awestruck with fresh hope.

Now, that hope mingled with the return of worry—what if this didn't help? what if they still didn't find Tina?—and it also mixed with something else she couldn't deny. Ever since the moment she'd known for certain she'd be seeing him again, her body had hummed with anticipation. Wondering if there was any chance he'd take her in his arms and brush another kiss across her lips. Praying he wouldn't, even as she burned for his touch.

How had she gotten so hung up on this guy? Two full days after their first encounter, she still hadn't a clue. All she knew was that he was a gruff, arrogant, know-it-all stranger who felt completely justified in bossing her around . . . and who'd been there for her when she needed him last night, and was willing to help her again now. Not to mention that he was the sexiest man she'd ever come face-to-face with, without a shred of effort on his part.

People had so many sides to them, so many facets to their personalities.

She'd never noticed that so much until her immersion into the Big Easy, but suddenly it seemed an unavoidable notion. Her sexy bartender, so big and dangerous, yet unaccountably concerned for her well-being. Melody, a woman who'd once made her living having sex for money, now turned loving wife and doting mother.

And even Tina. Stephanie laughed to herself, remembering her silly, feeble attempts today at crocheting, a hobby her sister had somehow stumbled into. She'd been shocked when Tina had shown her the fabulous winter scarves and hats she'd been creating, her eyes glittering with pride. She'd never before seen her sister do anything so . . . domestic, tranquil. "I'm thinking maybe I could sell them at craft shows or something."

Stephanie had simply laughed then, too. She couldn't see restless Tina content to spend her weekends in gymnasiums with craft-making moms who drove minivans and baked brownies. And yet the truth was, Tina was versatile, adventurous—traits Stephanie admired in her sister. She bit her lip now, realizing she'd probably never told her that.

Tina had insisted on giving her a crocheting lesson, but such abilities were even less Stephanie's forte than Tina's, and she'd failed miserably. Yet, for some reason, when she'd been packing for her trip south, she'd tossed the little bag of yarn and crocheting needle into her suitcase, and she'd spent some time in her room today trying to pick up the skill. It suddenly seemed that if Tina found it a worthwhile activity that she should try to learn. She envisioned being able to show Tina a crocheted scarf upon their reunion. She could already see Tina laughing, amazed Stephanie had actually done it.

Her imagined joy faded, though, when she reached the Crawfish Diner, where a red crawfish blinked on and off in an old neon sign in the dingy window.

Jake Broussard was waiting inside for her. Like once before, her instincts told her to run, to just forget the plan and get as far away from him as possible. Any man who made her suffer such unadulterated want was surely trouble in her carefully managed world.

Why *did* she always forget people had more than one side to their personality—just because *she* didn't? Well, she didn't *think* she did. But she had a feeling that if she'd said yes to his proposition the other night, she'd have become . . . someone she didn't even recognize.

Taking a deep breath, she pulled open a heavy door and stepped inside the long, skinny restaurant that smelled of Cajun spices. To one side of the aisle stood a counter with stools, to the other a row of booths.

Before she could scan the seats, her attention was drawn to an old man in a dirty apron, who shouted at a middle-aged waitress in a bayou accent much heavier than Jake's.

The red-haired woman, wearing a pair of too-tight white slacks, rolled her eyes. "Arlen, you don't know your head from your ass—I called out an order for shrimp, old man, *shrimp!*"

The old cook muttered something in French as the waitress stomped away, a heavy tray balanced on one hand. She maneuvered the thin aisle with ease, stopping at a small booth crammed tight with four burly men. Just beyond them, Stephanie caught sight of Jake, and her pulse began to race.

She'd never seen a man who filled out a simple T-shirt so well. Tonight's was dark gray, and she knew without seeing that beneath the table he was poured into his jeans just as pleasantly. His dark hair was pushed back over his head, but as usual, a few locks dropped down above his eyes. Black stubble dusted his jaw and chin.

God, was it hot in here? As she worked her way toward Jake, she glanced to the kitchen, hoping like hell that it *was* hot, that she wasn't starting to sweat because of *him*. On the other hand, though, why did that shock her? Just like every other time she'd seen him, a mere glimpse turned her inside out.

His once-over slid from her head to her feet as she approached, and even as dressed down as she was tonight in a simple linen sheath, his look transformed her into that sexual entity she was getting to know better the last few days—against her will. She found herself *wanting* him to see her that way. Not an ad exec, or someone's big sister, but purely as a woman, with curves to be touched and lips to be kissed. Clearly, she'd gotten too good at her escort role, learned to "feel it" a little too well.

She slid into the cracked red vinyl booth across from him before meeting his eyes.

"Evenin', *chère*."

His slow Cajun drawl delivered in that deep voice seemed to reach way down inside her to someplace foreign. Foreign but . . . getting less so. She couldn't decide whether or not to smile, so she settled on the "pleasant look" she used in corporate dealings. "Hello."

"Find the place okay?"

She nodded, letting her hands settle in her lap—then,

feeling fidgety, she reached for the water glass that had already been delivered.

Around them, people talked and silverware rattled. From the kitchen came the clatter of dishes being heaped in a metal sink. The red-haired waitress called out orders of things to be fried and smothered. And Jake Broussard's eyes pinned Stephanie in place, making her weak and excited and nervous all in the same breath.

Say something. Anything. "So, you don't have to tend bar tonight?" *Please don't let my nipples be showing through my bra and dress.*

He shook his head. "Only work a few nights a week."

She tilted her head, caught her breath. Calm down. "What do you do with the rest of your time?"

He quirked his mouth into a half-smile. "I take it easy."

At her uncertain nod, he went on.

"Job pays better than you'd expect. Big tips from those rich guys—payin' me to keep their secrets."

"Oh." Made sense, she supposed.

The redhead suddenly appeared, slapping two plastic-covered menus on the table. "Evening, folks. Name's Ada. Be back to take your order in a minute."

"If you don't like the local cuisine," Jake said, "they have burgers and double-deckers, too."

Don't just nod this time. "What would you recommend?"

"You like shrimp?"

"Mmm-hmm." She tried not to look at him over her menu, but her eyes kept drifting up.

"How about onions, garlic, and peppers?"

"Mmm-hmm," she said again. *You're such a sparkling conversationalist tonight.*

When Ada returned, Jake handed her both menus, saying, "Two orders of shrimp étouffée."

"Shrimp, huh? Well, cross your fingers Arlen's cleaned out his ears by now or God knows *what* you'll get." With that, she rushed off, calling out, "Two *shrimp étouffée!* Got that, old man? *Shrimp!*"

Arlen muttered in French, and Stephanie couldn't help laughing lightly at the show they put on. "I'm not sure those two should work together."

"Have been for as long as I've been comin' here."

"I'm surprised they haven't killed each other yet."

Jake shrugged. "I suspect they like each other more than they let on, or they'd be divorced by now."

"They're *married*? To each *other*?"

He gave a nod. "Used to come in here for dinner a lot when I was a beat cop. You listen to people for a while, you figure things out."

She couldn't help forming the impression that he'd probably been a good cop. But that begged the question . . . "Why did you give up police work?"

He shook his head lightly, glanced down, and started playing with a salt shaker. "Heart wasn't in it anymore." Then he raised his eyes, so very brown and deep, directly back to her. His gaze seemed to capture her—she couldn't escape. "Tell me about *you,* Stephanie Grant."

"Nothing much to tell," she began. "I've lived a pretty ordinary life. I grew up in a middle-class family in a Chicago suburb. Two kids and a dog, block parties, that sort of thing." She wasn't sure why she'd reached that far back in her life to begin, nor why she'd sounded so self-deprecating. She supposed that compared to him—even knowing nothing about him—she just felt so "white bread." She had the notion his life had been anything but ordinary. "I'm in advertising now," she added.

"What do you sell?"

She lowered her chin slightly, letting her eyebrows rise. "Besides myself, you mean?" She wasn't sure why she said it. Perhaps to beat him to the punch?

The corners of his mouth curled into a slight grin. "I was gonna be a big enough man not to mention that, but since you did, yeah. Besides yourself."

She bit her lip, wondering if her job would sound interesting or boring. "I head up campaigns for major corporations—everything from cars to breakfast cereals to fast-food restaurants." Boring, she decided as she finished. Or maybe it was just this situation with Tina making everyday life seem insignificant.

"You like it? Happy doin' it?"

She considered her answer. She'd spent the years since college so concerned about her rise to the top of the corporate ladder that it wasn't a question she'd ever asked herself. "The corporate aspects of it are getting a little old," she finally concluded, "but I love thinking of ideas, trying to hit on the perfect slogan or image. What about you? Are you happy tending bar?"

"It's a paycheck."

"You weren't happy being a cop?"

He raised his eyebrows, looking almost amused by her willingness to press the issue—before his mouth straightened in a grim line. His voice sounded a soft warning. "You best leave that alone now, *beb*."

Her annoyance was squelched by Ada, suddenly plopping a couple of plates on the table. "Might be hot. Watch yourselves," she cautioned. "And check to make sure that's shrimp, will ya?"

Rather than use his silverware to look beneath the reddish stew covering the dish, Jake forked a bite into his mouth. "Yep, shrimp."

"Hallelujah, it's a miracle," she said, rolling her eyes in the direction of the kitchen as she hurried off.

"Dig in, *chère*."

At first, the spicy dish was a shock to Stephanie's taste buds, burning her throat, nearly making her eyes water. But she tried not to let it show, taking large drinks of water, and soon the heat wore down enough for her to realize the smothered shrimp was delicious.

"You like?" he asked.

She nodded yet again, this time because her mouth was full. Upon swallowing, she said, "Hot. But good."

"Arlen serves up good food. His jambalaya's the best you can get around here. Not quite as good as my *grand-mère* used to make, but close."

"Used to?" She tilted her head.

He dug his fork back into the plate of shrimp. "Died when I was eighteen. Best Cajun cook on the bayou, though."

"I lost my grandma around that age, too. She used to make the best apple pie in the world."

"Where you get your pie now?"

She shrugged. "No place special. Haven't really found any that lives up to hers."

"I know what you mean. Things like that aren't easily replaced."

Somehow, his eyes said he really did understand those sorts of little losses that sometimes felt big, and the sudden connection made her nervous. She bit her lip and smiled. "So now you come here for your Cajun delicacies."

He laughed. "Sometimes. It's easy. Other times I make my own. Well, I used to. Wasn't half bad in the kitchen, if I do say so myself."

"Used to?" she asked again, trying to hide her surprise that the sexy bartender was also a cook.

"No energy for it anymore."

"Why?"

He leaned forward across the table, his eyes twinkling. "You sure are a nosy little thing, Stephanie Grant."

"Sorry. I just . . ." She dropped her gaze, but then raised it again, summoning the courage to be honest. "I'm curious about you."

"Why?"

Because I want you so badly I can't understand it. She swallowed nervously and honesty fled the scene. "Because . . . you're being nice enough to help me."

He answered in a frank tone. "We best get somethin' straight. Me helpin' you isn't from the goodness of my heart. It's only because if I let you go on about this business the way you were, I might not be able to live with myself."

"Well, whatever the case, I appreciate it."

"As soon as we finish eatin', we'll head to a few places I know, show your sister's picture, see if we can get a lead. New Orleans is a big town, but not so big if you check the right places."

Again, another nod—she'd given up trying for anything better. Sometimes thoughts of Tina, being out there in this city-with-a-dark-side, simply stifled her thoughts, made it so nothing else could come in or out of her head. She might be slowly starting to grow used to the way Jake made her feel with just a glance, but her worries for Tina didn't operate that way. They didn't grow more normal or acceptable, no matter how long she dwelled on them.

"Listen, *chère,* don't worry so much."

She supposed it showed in her eyes, and she was about

to summon a response when he reached out to warmly cover her hand with his, where it curled loosely around the water glass. She froze, astounded at the strength of the desire the small touch sent racing through her limbs. Old—*ancient*—yearnings turned new, and even more powerful, beneath his fingertips.

She was sure if she tried to speak it would come out mangled and shaky, so in a bid for self-preservation, she finally drew her hand away, dropping her eyes to her plate, and resumed eating.

Conversation died then, which was at once awkward but not. He wasn't a highly talkative man, and it surprised her when he strung more than a couple of sentences together, so *that*, combined with her fear for her sister, somehow made the silence okay.

The next time she looked at him, they'd both finished eating and he was digging in his pocket, drawing out a roll of mints. He held it out, offering one, but she declined.

After putting a mint in his mouth, he shoved the roll back into his front pocket and his legs shifted slightly beneath the table so that their knees touched. Again, it was like a current of electricity, this time shooting up her thighs.

Pull your knees back. She didn't. Couldn't.

Neither did he.

She found the will to slowly raise her gaze.

His eyes were locked on hers, a silent affirmation of the sensual vibes passing between them.

What now?

Again, it should have been awkward, but instead, all Stephanie experienced was heat, raw and naked—no hiding what she felt, and at the moment, she didn't care. It went back to the red room, she supposed. There'd certainly been no hiding what she'd felt when he'd laid her back on that couch. They'd already been here once before.

"We should get started," he finally said. "Night isn't gettin' any younger."

"Right," she said, drawing her knees away.

But pulling back didn't squelch the sensations, her whole body throbbing for what she wanted. She wanted to have sex with Jake Broussard more than she wanted to breathe.

It was a startling admission.

At a horrible time.

She had a feeling it was going to be a very long night.

Chapter 7

Jake scooped the check up off the table and reached for his wallet.

"Let me get it," Stephanie said. "It's the least I can do, considering why we're here."

He simply shook his head and threw a few dollars down for a tip. "Not necessary, *chère*." Odd, he'd suggested coming here because it was loud and dingy and, therefore, perfect for a meeting he wanted in no way to feel like a "date," yet old-fashioned masculine pride wouldn't let him allow her to pay.

Damn, she looked good. He was trying like hell to concentrate on what they had to do tonight, trying to concentrate on passing the money to Ada at the cash register, trying to concentrate on *anything*—but it was as if Stephanie Grant had cast some sort of spell on him.

He supposed it had just been too long since he'd had sex. Good, all-night-long, touch-each-other-everywhere, kiss-each-other-everywhere sex. Had to happen eventually, he told himself as he held the door for her, following her out into the dark, balmy night. Had to come a time when he'd want that again, need it. But it didn't mean anything, he insisted inside. It didn't mean there was anything special about this woman. It was just attraction, chemistry.

It was the first time he'd seen her not dressed to seduce, yet she remained just as seductive. The plain pale yellow sheath covered a few more inches of thigh and followed her curves more loosely than the other dresses he'd seen her in, but that just made her sexiness shine through more naturally, seem more genuine. The reduction in makeup revealed a pretty face, and a pure sparkle in those bluer-than-blue eyes. Her blond hair fell softer around her shoulders now, bouncy. He had the bizarre urge to reach for her hand as they walked side by side down the old, uneven sidewalk.

Damn, what was *that* about?

Just Becky. Just missing Becky.

Probably the first time you've walked down a street with a woman since her—odd as it seemed. But it was true. He wrote off the urge to old habits.

Even so, what he'd feared was already materializing—it wasn't gonna be easy to locate her sister with all this heat between them. He'd indulge in it if she gave him half a chance, and judging from the look in her eyes across the table when their knees had touched, she might. He knew Stephanie Grant was a prim and proper lady in one sense, but he could feel something hot bubbling beneath her surface.

First things first, though.

As they turned up one of the Quarter's meaner streets, the sidewalks dirtier than most, the balconies sagging and the brickwork falling away from the walls in jagged chunks, he again fought the urge to take her hand. This time, though, it was about protection, putting her at ease in case she figured out this wasn't the best part of town. But he couldn't protect her—not really, and a handhold wouldn't change that. He'd learned the hard way that he couldn't really protect anyone.

"Where are we headed?" she asked, apparently noticing that the buildings had turned a little grayer, more neglected.

"In here," he said, gesturing to his right. A neon arrow of dulled blue pointed to the entrance of the Pirate's Den, a dive bar and cop hangout. Before pushing through the door, he tossed a glance over his shoulder at what was surely the prettiest sight to hit this street tonight. "Don't let any of the crusty old *couillons* in here make you nervous, *chère*."

"Okay," she said, already looking uneasy.

But he liked that about her—that being nervous didn't seem to hold her back, from anything.

A wall of smoke hit him as he stepped inside.

"Hey, *bougre*," said Shorty, the ancient Cajun bartender who had to be pushing eighty if he was a day. The wrinkled smile he cast at the sight of Jake brimmed with sincerity—he hadn't been in here for over two years. The greeting touched Jake unexpectedly.

He gave a brief nod, a quick grin. "What you say, Shorty?"

Other greetings sounded from around the bar as cops and old-timers recognized him. For some reason, he hadn't thought anyone would much notice his presence—maybe until now he'd forgotten it had been so long since he'd socialized with this crew.

"How's it hangin', Jake?"

"Long time, no see, buddy."

"Look what *fatras* de cat drug in." The last came from

Fat Eddie, a big Cajun from even deeper in the swamps than Jake. He'd worked more than a few cases with Fat Eddie back in the day and he stepped forward to shake his old compadre's hand. "And wid a *jolie femme* on his arm, too. Life treatin' you fine den, Broussard?"

"Good enough," he lied.

"Ah, listen to him," Shorty snorted from behind the bar. "Life's *gotta* be treatin' you good you got a woman like this with you. Come here now, *catin*," he said, waving Stephanie toward him, "and I give you a drink on the house. What's your pleasure? I'll show this old dog how to treat a lady right."

Next to him, Stephanie produced a sweet, blushing smile that, for some reason, nearly ripped a hole in his heart. "Um, okay, I'll have . . . a glass of wine. Maybe a Chablis?"

He couldn't help smiling inwardly. Still totally unpredictable.

"You ain't from around here, are ya?" Fat Eddie leaned around to ask. "You in de Big Easy now, sugar. Shorty, fix dis *femme* a hurricane."

Shorty drew back in mock warning before addressing her again. "I don't know 'bout that, *catin*. Awful strong drink. You don't wanna get drunk, let this fella take advantage of you now, do ya?"

Jake cast a soft smile down at her, sorry she'd been put on the spot by his old friends, but curious to hear her answer.

She returned a look of amusement, then focused on Shorty. "I'll take my chances."

Light laughter rose from the bar and Eddie looked to Jake. "Ah, now, dis one, she's a good one. I like her. You wanna keep her around."

Maybe he should have said something to make it clear they weren't a couple, but he couldn't quite find the words. He hadn't anticipated any of this, hadn't thought any further ahead than this being a good place to show Tina's picture. But his old drinking buddies seemed so happy to see him with someone else, it didn't seem necessary to let them know he was still in a bad way, and that not much had changed in his life since he'd left the force.

He made small talk with Eddie and a few other guys, some in uniforms, until Shorty passed Stephanie's drink across the bar. "Put it in a clean glass and everything."

She smiled, and Shorty handed Jake a bottle of beer, still remembering what he drank. When Jake reached for his wallet, Shorty stopped him. "Ah, no, *bougre,* your money ain't no good here—tonight anyway. You get comin' in regular again, *then* you pay."

They laughed as Jake nodded his thanks, then took Stephanie's hand, drawing her deeper into the bar. They were halfway down the narrow passageway between bar stools and tables before he realized he'd followed the urge this time—taken her hand. Despite himself, he didn't let go until they reached their destination.

Tony sat by himself at a table in the corner with a mug of draft. His light brown hair was messy, his jeans and loose T-shirt just as telling. "Rough day, pard?" Jake asked.

His old partner smiled up at him through tired eyes. "Rough enough. Better now, though."

Jake could read his thoughts with ease. Tony was happy as hell to see him acting human for a change, actually coming out to a bar, and with a new woman, no less. "Don't get too excited," Jake said, glad someone had put money in the jukebox—"I'm No Angel" by Gregg Allman half-drowned his words. "Not what you think."

"Why don't you pull up a chair for yourself and the lady, and fill me in."

"I'll pull up a chair, but the fillin' in can happen another time." He dragged two wooden chairs from the next table and gave Stephanie the least rickety. As they took a seat, he got straight down to business. "Have the picture, *chère*?"

Lowering her red drink to the table, she opened a little yellow purse that matched her dress. She passed him two photos—one a snapshot of a young woman in shorts and a snug tee standing on a wooden bridge, probably from a vacation, the other a professional portrait. "We both had these made for our parents' thirtieth anniversary a few years ago," she explained of the second shot.

He didn't know why it surprised him that Tina was a knockout. Probably because he hadn't quite believed she could be as pretty as her sister. Whereas Stephanie was a classic beauty, Tina struck him as the sort of girl most men would fall for faster—her eyes were filled with invitation, her clothing cut to garner attention.

He handed the photos to Tony. "Seen her anywhere?"

His friend studied the pictures. "Afraid not. Sorry." Then he raised his gaze. "Who is she?"

"An escort. Gone missin'." *Sort of,* he added in his mind. Jake still wasn't convinced the girl was missing at all, but if he wanted to find her, that kind of detail wouldn't help.

Tony handed the pictures back to Stephanie and looked to Jake. "Haven't heard about any missing girls lately."

"I called the police," Stephanie volunteered, "but they didn't seem concerned. She's my sister."

"I *am* the police," Tony informed her kindly, "but yeah,

they might brush off a missing person in that line of work quicker than not. How long has she been gone?"

"A few weeks."

Tony nodded, shifting his eyes to Jake. "I'll keep my eyes open."

"Thanks," Jake said.

"You might, uh, show those to Fat Eddie before you go."

"Oh?" Fat Eddie worked homicide these days.

"Girl down by the river last week." Tony spoke low, clearly trying to sound casual, and not saying the girl by the river was dead. Jake still thought it was pretty obvious, so he hoped Stephanie couldn't hear over Gregg Allman's gravelly voice.

"Listen, *beb,* I'm gonna show these around the bar a few minutes," he said, plucking the photos back out of her hand. "You sit here and drink your drink, chat with Tony."

"I wouldn't trust me with her if I were you," his friend quipped.

"I'm not worried." Friendly banter, his way of saying Tony was no competition. They'd once exchanged similar conversation over Becky. The memory made his gut clench lightly, and for the first time since walking in the door, he remembered there was a good reason he didn't go out, didn't see people—it still hurt too much. For now, though, he pushed away the recollections and focused on what he'd come here to do.

Approaching the bar, he placed his hand on Fat Eddie's shoulder. As always, the man wore a cheap suit and a tie with a spot on it. He held up the pictures. "Seen her?"

Eddie leaned in to look close, shaking his head. "A hot cookie like dat, I'd remember."

Jake swallowed. "Tony said you had a homicide down by the river."

Eddie looked again, then gave his head a solemn shake. "Girl we found was heavier, didn't look like dis at all."

Relief on Stephanie's behalf rushed through him. He wasn't sure when he'd gotten emotionally involved in this, but he couldn't imagine having to tell her Tina was dead. "You see a girl looks like this one, you let Tony know, okay?"

"You got it, pal."

As he started to walk away, Eddie grabbed his wrist and Jake looked up. "Really is good to see you, Jake. You should come around more, shoot de bull wid me."

Jake pressed his lips together tightly. It was good to see Eddie, too—but as for coming around, he wasn't planning to make it a habit. "Maybe," he said anyway.

Fat Eddie slapped him on the back and laughed. "Dat'd be good, real good."

After leaving the Pirate's Den, they stopped at a couple of other out-of-the-way haunts, but not places where Jake seemed as well-known or warmly regarded. He showed the pictures to one or two guys inside each place, still with no luck.

As usual with Jake, Stephanie found herself experiencing warring emotions. Her hope deflated a little at each shaking head they encountered, and at the same time she was shamefully overcome with an attraction to her companion that escalated with each passing minute. How could she be thinking about *that* at a time like *this*?

Each small touch of his hand, every meeting with those dark eyes, carried her a little deeper into desire. Such an unfamiliar territory. Unfamiliar, at least, for a very long time. It made her remember that as a teenager, she'd never really gotten hold of it, never reached a place where she could push it away with any success. And as an adult, she'd had no practice with it.

So when they turned a corner onto Bourbon Street, suddenly thrust into flashing lights and a street party that happened every night, she didn't flinch when Jake took her hand. She hated being unable to control her reaction to him, but at the same time she loved succumbing to it.

Although it was September, heat and humidity still soaked the air where people stood in clusters, drinking, laughing, eating. Open-air storefronts offered T-shirts, Mardi Gras beads, and frozen daiquiris in countless flavors, while music spilled onto the closed-to-traffic thoroughfare—rock, jazz, and Cajun all vying to be heard the loudest.

They passed a strip bar where two young women wearing skimpy bras and thong panties posed provocatively in the doorway. Just as she felt her face growing warmer with embarrassment, one of the girls smiled at Jake—and Stephanie wanted to kill her. Could she not see they were holding hands? And—

Oh God. This was it. She was losing her mind.

You and he are not a couple.

And the only reason he tried to seduce you the other night was to teach you a lesson.

"Where are we going now?" she asked, growing uncomfortable in the heart of the red-light district.

"Place just up ahead here. The Playpen."

She came to a dead halt, jerking Jake to a stop as well. He turned to look at her.

"Is that a strip club?"

He nodded easily. "Yeah. Why?"

She pulled in her breath. "Why on earth would we go to a strip club?"

Jake blinked, tilted his head, his look making her feel childish. But she couldn't help it—she couldn't imagine going into a place like that.

"*Chère,* you remember the last guy we spoke to, at LaFitte's?"

She thought back to the bar, and the guy—a handsome man in his late thirties with curling brown hair—then nodded.

"Danny Richards, my boss at Sophia's. He's a decent guy, I've known him a lotta years, and he's pretty familiar with the clientele on the third floor. What I'm sayin' is, he *knows* the high-end escort business in this town."

"And?"

"I mentioned Tina by name and showed her picture, and he's never seen her."

Stephanie's heart plummeted a little further.

"Makes me think we've exhausted our resources in the high-priced escort market," he said. "But what happens to some girls is—they try turnin' tricks, can't handle it, and take the next highest-payin' road, which is strippin'."

"Oh. Oh God," she murmured as the idea settled over her.

It shouldn't seem worse than prostitution, but she couldn't imagine taking her clothes off for a roomful of men. At least at Sophia's, there was some semblance of elegance. She shook her head. "I don't think Tina could be a stripper."

He narrowed his gaze on her, pointed but kind. "Did you think she could be a hooker?"

Another flood of ugly acceptance washed through her as she whispered her reply. "No."

"Then we best start checkin' some of these places out. The Playpen's the classiest in the Quarter, so if a girl knows anything about the business, she'd apply there first—and Tina's pretty enough to get hired on."

She began shaking her head. "Even so, I can't go into a place like that."

He lowered his chin, looked matter-of-fact. "Not a big deal, *chère*. There'll be other women inside."

"Naked ones."

When she least expected it, he laughed. "No, not just them. There'll be couples, groups of people. More men than women, sure. But otherwise, almost like any other bar."

"Really?"

He gave her a gentle nod, and only then did she realize he'd never dropped her hand and now stroked his thumb gently back and forth over the top, trying to comfort her. "Hate to tell you this, but it's not like on TV. Not just a seedy place where old guys in bad sport coats hang out. It's more like . . . a tourist attraction."

Unfortunately, his attempt at comfort couldn't override her shock. She opened her eyes wider, feeling as if she'd been born in some other universe and couldn't begin to comprehend the things happening in this one.

"It's like Eddie told you, *chère*—you're in the Big Easy now. Some things are just different here."

Not that she had the first idea what a strip club was like at home, either. She'd just assumed they were patronized strictly by men. She took a deep breath and looked into Jake's warm brown eyes. Despite herself, for some reason, she trusted him. "So you're saying men aren't going to gape at me if I go in this place with you?"

"Right, *chère*. You're not what they came to see. And I wouldn't insist so much, but you're gonna recognize your sister a lot quicker than me. Same reason I took you everyplace else, too. Figured there might be questions only you could answer, or that somebody might say somethin' I wouldn't hear in the same way as you—know what I mean?"

She nodded, the night air seeming to thicken still more around them. *You're in the Big Easy now—don't be a prude. Do what you have to do to find your sister.* "All right—let's go." Not wanting to give herself a chance to back out, she grabbed his hand and started briskly through the throng of Bourbon Street partyers until they reached the bright lights and cherry red awning of the Playpen.

To her surprise, the place was large, crisp, and clean-looking. Two men in suits stood at the open door. Between them, in the distance, she caught sight of a woman in silhouette, dancing around a pole. Her heart dropped to her stomach, but she worked hard not to hesitate, dragging Jake right up the red-carpeted steps.

This was even harder than going to Chez Sophia the first time. Perhaps due to the abject fear of walking through the door to see her baby sister swaying naked on a stage. If she'd found her at Sophia's, it wouldn't have *seemed* much worse than spotting her at a cocktail party. She suddenly missed the veil of dignity, however thin, that hung over Sophia's third floor.

"Good evening, folks," a large, bearded man said. "Welcome to the Playpen. Ten dollars for you, sir. The lady gets in free."

She watched nervously as Jake peeled a ten from his wallet, then placed his hand at the small of her back, gently propelling her onward.

Inside, red and pink lights swirled, but soon her eyes adjusted, revealing, to her shock, that the room possessed more than just the one stage she'd seen from outside. Instead, there were five, six, seven—a lot—each holding a girl in a different state of undress. Frightfully young girls. Baring their bodies on small stages all over the room. The sense of being surrounded by crude sexuality that had no relation to romance or love overwhelmed her instantly, tightening her stomach. On impulse, she turned and ran smack into the hard wall of Jake's chest. "Sorry," she murmured.

He gently curled his hand around her elbow. "You okay?"

"Yeah. Can we sit down?" Given that she was hardly the main attraction in the room, she felt strangely in the center of the action and experienced a burning urge to blend in.

"Sure, *beb*." Jake pulled her down into a small one-sided booth and she breathed a short sigh of relief. "Take a look around," he told her easily, "see if she's here."

What Jake had said was true; the room held a mixed crowd, both men and women. But she looked past them, scanning the various stages for Tina. Thankfully—or not, she couldn't decide *how* to feel—her sister inhabited none of them.

It felt unbearably bizarre to be watching strippers at Jake's side. Unlike the other couples in the room, they barely knew each other. The girls on the stages were impossibly thin and beautiful, peeling off scant dresses and lingerie, down to nearly nonexistent flesh-colored

G-strings. She watched in fascinated horror as they swayed with slow precision, tweaking their bared nipples, running their hands down perfectly flat stomachs and shapely thighs.

Soon enough, though, her eyes were drawn to the men in the room. Jake was right about that, too. Not a bad sport jacket among them. They were . . . guys she would date. They wore khaki shorts and golf shirts. They were corporate America after hours. But the most unsettling part was the expressions they wore.

She'd once gone to see the Chippendale dancers with some women from work. They'd giggled all the way through it, laughing at the costumes, at the forced sexuality the men worked so hard to convey. It had been, for all of them, a silly, crazy thing to do.

But this was not that. The faces of the men here shone with a raw, ugly lust she'd never quite witnessed before. Their eyes turned the girls into nothing more than animals in an obscene zoo.

"Any luck?" Jake finally asked, oblivious to all she was experiencing.

She absently shook her head. "No." Then uttered her thought aloud. "These girls look so young." Eighteen or nineteen, *maybe*.

"Yeah," Jake said, solemnly enough that she could hear a calm hint of concern in his voice. "College girls from Tulane or Loyola, most likely."

College girls. She almost laughed with horror. At nineteen, she'd been studying hard and hanging onto the last shreds of her virginity. Things *were* different here.

"Something to drink?"

Stephanie looked up to find another college girl, this one wearing a red sequined bikini top and a matching micromini. The coed smiled down at her as if they were chums.

"Chère?" Jake deferred to her.

She started to order a glass of wine, but felt desperately hot inside and, for the first time, realized Shorty had been right—the hurricane had made her a little drunk. "Just a glass of water."

"Bottle of Bud," Jake said.

"I'll have them right up," the cheerful waitress replied.

But as she started to walk away, Jake called her back. "Hang on a minute."

She smiled down at him. Still chummy, sweet, as if they weren't all surrounded by naked young girls and a lust that permeated the air. "Something else?"

He turned to Stephanie. *"Chère,* your pictures."

She scrambled to open her purse, glad for the brief distraction.

Jake held them up for the girl to see. "This girl work here? Name's Tina."

The waitress looked closely at each photo. "Pretty," she mused. "But no, I don't think so."

Jake nodded, murmured his thanks, and let her go on her way. *"Merde,"* he mumbled under his breath, passing the pictures back to Stephanie. "Thought sure I might be onto somethin' comin' here."

"What now?" She concentrated on getting the photos back in her purse without looking at Jake, somehow unable to meet his gaze given all the gyrating nudity in the room with them.

"Tempted to try talkin' to one of the doormen," he said on a sigh, "but I'd have to be careful—unless I give it the right finesse, they'll think I'm a cop and that she's in some kinda trouble. Let me think about it a few minutes."

At that moment, her eyes landed on a naked girl straddling a guy in a small, plush easy chair, undulating in time with the sexy music that played, her firm breasts swaying dangerously close to his mouth, his eyes gaping up at her, lost in vulgar desire. And somehow she saw the girl who writhed on a total stranger for money as Tina—and broke out in a cold sweat.

She couldn't stay in this room any longer. There was too much sin here, too much ugly lust. Just like at Sophia's, veiled or not—it was more sex for money. It was just harder to handle here because there was no jazz or expensive furniture to mask it. Here it was more raw—on the table for everyone to see. Shared, public sin.

"I have to get out of here."

Jake turned his eyes on her, clearly confused. "What?"

She swallowed past the lump that had grown in her throat. Her body had gone so tense that her chest ached. "I have to go. I can't be here. Let me up." The booth set against the wall and Jake blocked her exit.

He simply gaped at her. "What's wrong?"

She widened her eyes on him, wondering if she was going to have to climb over him. *"Please get up. I have to get out of here."*

Dark eyebrows knitting, he finally pushed to his feet, eyes puzzled. "You don't want your water?"

"No, I don't want my water." She thought she probably sounded a little hysterical, but that's how she felt, suddenly—as if it had all come tumbling down on her at the sight of that lap dance, twenty dollars for simulated sex.

She bolted for the door, not giving a damn if she *looked* hysterical, too—she had to get out now or she'd smother.

By the time she'd rushed past the doormen and hit the busy street, tears streamed down her face. She wanted to hide, but had no idea *how* in such a crowd. The scents of pralines and beer met her nose as she wove a jagged path across the street, desperately seeking someplace quiet, private.

Her eyes were drawn to a darkened storefront, big glass windows filled with junky-looking antiques on either side of a deeply receding doorway. She made a bee-line toward it, figuring the little alcove was as good a retreat as she would find.

She'd just reached it, turning to lean back against the peeling paint of the wide wooden door frame, when Jake arrived, hot on her heels. His expression remained baffled. "What's wrong, *chère*? What happened?"

She shook her head, unable to look at him, since she had no explanation that would make sense to most men. Not even some women, she supposed, since there'd been plenty of females inside the Playpen in addition to the strippers.

"Talk to me," he insisted.

She simply kept shaking her head. She wanted to be at home. She wanted Tina there with her. She wanted her safe life in her safe world, where she could keep everything under control. "I can't," she said.

"This guy bothering you?"

They both turned to find a tall, thin, dark-skinned man. Ironically, the guy trying to come to her rescue carried neon pink flyers for the Playpen. "No," she said, "he's fine. We're fine."

"You sure?" Concern colored his deep voice. For such a skinny man, he looked deadly bent on defending her. She supposed all he could see was a woman in tears racing away from the man chasing after her.

"Yes! Please. We're fine," she insisted.

The man offered one last worried look before finally going on his way, and Jake muttered, "asshole" behind him.

"He was trying to be nice."

"He thinks I made you cry."

"I know. I'm sorry." She peered up at him, guilty for making him look like a bad guy.

His eyes were fraught with worry as he gazed down on her. He stood only a few inches away, closing both hands warm around her elbows. "What is it, *chère*?" he asked, his voice softer. "What's makin' you cry?"

She shut her eyes, trying to squelch the flow of tears before meeting his gaze again. She could barely speak past the lump in her throat. "The girls in there . . . are like objects. Not people. I *felt* that."

He looked sympathetic, worried. His fingertips caressed her arms. "Not much different than at Sophia's, *beb*. It's not pretty, but surely it's not a surprise."

Yet that was just it. It *was* a surprise. She'd heard all her life about such places objectifying women, but she'd never really understood it so deeply as she did in this moment. "I just . . . somehow felt like an object, too. By default."

He glanced down, then raised his gaze again. She read in his expression how hard he was trying to understand. "I'm not sure I completely get it, but I'm sorry. I wouldn't have talked you into goin' in there if I'd thought it would upset you so much."

She could only look up at him and nod.

His hands rose to her face, his fingertips playing about her ears before skimming down onto her neck. His touch made her heart beat faster as he blotted away the wetness on her cheeks with his thumbs, then smiled gently into her eyes. "Let's dry up those tears now, *chère*, hmm?"

She nodded again, hating that she was crying in front of him. "I guess it's just . . . everything. Worrying about Tina. She's my little sister. When I imagined it being her in there, having guys look at her the way those guys looked at those girls . . ." She shook her head. "I'm sorry."

"Nothin' to be sorry for," Jake said softly, remembering a time when he, too, had held all women in such high esteem. Working behind the bar at Sophia's had hardened him to such emotions.

But no—it wasn't just Sophia's. It had happened before that.

He'd quit caring, or had tried like hell to and was still trying like hell, and maybe he'd come real close to succeeding—because this was the *first* moment he *got* it, really *got* it. Tina was her *sister. Her little sister.*

He'd never had a sister, but there'd been women in his life whom he'd loved, and the very thought of any of them having sex for money or stripping on a stage made his heart threaten to explode in his chest as he stood here before prim and pretty Stephanie Grant, who was getting initiated into this world the hard way.

He'd met her at the bar, masquerading as an escort—and yet even then he'd felt in her that primness, that sweetness that flowed so freely from her now. Maybe *that* was how he'd known she wasn't what she claimed.

It was the wrong time, he knew, but her face was so close to his, her lips so ripe and pretty, that he wanted to kiss her. Just to make her feel better. A comfort kiss. Hold her, kiss her, make the bad stuff go away for a minute or two—maybe for both of them.

It was more than the wrong time; it was a *terrible* time. She would think he'd gotten turned on in the club. But the dark arousal expanding from his gut was about so much more than anything he could see on a stage—it grew from someplace deep inside him he couldn't fully understand.

Which made it unstoppable.

Not a decision. A compulsion.

He bent his head, brought his mouth gently down on hers. A soft, sweet melding of lips.

When it was done, he leaned his forehead against hers. "Wanna make you feel better," he whispered.

He felt more than saw her nod. Heard her soft murmur. "I know." Her voice trembled. It made him need more.

Slanting his mouth back over her tender lips, he kissed her slow, deep, felt the power of it moving through him like a warm drink of alcohol spreading through his chest, arms, downward. *Just to comfort her, that's all. Just want to comfort her a little more.*

A lot more.

Don't think about the depths of it, where it's coming from, how much you feel it—it's only comfort. Simple comfort. Keep telling yourself that and it'll be true.

The next kiss was just as slow, but it went hot on him, too—gut-wrenchingly, uncontrollably hot. He felt it in his groin, a sharp bolt of pleasure. He let his mouth linger over hers, hungry, so tempted, wanting to devour her the same way he'd wanted to in the red room.

Her fingers curled into the cotton on his chest as he quit fighting the heat and lowered a scorching kiss to her responsive mouth. He wanted her so badly. Wanted to touch her, to taste her. Wanted to bury himself inside her and stay all night long.

His hand drifted lightly over her breast and she let out a ragged sigh just before he gripped her waist in a firm, slow caress. He needed to feel her curves, everything that was soft and female about her.

He pressed into her, hip to hip, the contact dragging a ragged moan from her lips. She'd turned him rock hard and he wanted her to feel it, crave it, the same way he craved her. His fingers curved around her ass, pulling her tight against him, and she began to move, grind, press the soft juncture of her thighs against the solid stone between his legs. He tried not to groan at the sensation, not wanting to attract the attention of anyone on the street, and wishing they were someplace else, alone.

When he dropped his kisses to her neck, she arched for him, inviting his mouth lower. He kissed a line down the pale expanse of skin to her shoulder, then let his lips travel downward, along the neckline of her dress. He yearned for it to be cut lower, hungry for a taste of the feminine flesh he knew hid underneath.

In response to his craving, he skimmed his hand upward, to the side of her breast. She trembled harder at the intimate touch, her arms locked around his shoulders, her hands in his hair, her breath labored above him. He pressed gently on the malleable flesh until the top curve of her breast swelled from the neckline—beneath his kiss. *Mon Dieu*, yes.

His erection thickened, his chest throbbing with hot desire. He rained a trail of kisses across the soft ridge, knowing that if they were anywhere else, he'd be tempted to just rip the damn dress off her, straight down the middle.

By the time his kisses returned to her lips, he felt ready to combust. He stroked his tongue deeply into her accepting mouth, loving the tiny whimper that escaped her, then pulled back to look at her—sweet, prim Stephanie Grant, who was responding so eagerly to his every touch and kiss.

She bit her lip, appearing spent and passionate as she gazed up at him.

He kissed her again, quick and hard, on impulse, because the very sight of her mouth had made him need to feel it under his once more.

"My place isn't far," he breathed. "I want inside you. Wanna make you come."

Chapter 8

Stephanie was drowning. High school, college—no passion she'd ever experienced had been like this. Utterly consuming. Her breast pulsed at Jake's touch, her sex ached at the heavy sensation of his hardness there, their bodies fitting together like puzzle pieces. Her flesh turned liquid in his grasp, even as her skin sizzled at each point where he kissed her.

The way they moved together was as steamy as the night itself and nothing mattered but the searing pleasure that begged for more. His words echoed through her. *I want inside you. Wanna make you come.*

It was the red room all over again, but not a game this time. What was it, then?

To think of where they'd just been was like a hook scratching at her heart. Was this happening because they'd just watched women dancing out of their clothes? How had they gone from that to *this*—pressing against each other in a dark doorway in this dark city of debauchery that seemed so adept at turning her into something she wasn't? It didn't seem real, couldn't *be* real. She couldn't be straining against this sexy man she barely knew, her body taking over her thoughts.

His lips still whispered across her skin—her neck, shoulder. His hand closed gently over her breast, making her gasp. He murmured something French, and despite not having any idea what he'd said, she pooled with wetness just from the sounds.

His kisses rose, skimming up her neck like an electric current until he nipped at her earlobe, his teeth capturing the sensitive flesh with a searingly tender bite that made her release a rough, hot breath. "My God," she whispered.

"Come home with me, Stephanie."

Why did that sound so intimate it made her flinch? Because he was inviting her deeper into his world, his life? Because she wasn't sure she'd ever heard him call her by her first name before? Or was it just his hot, deep voice delivering the words in that sexy Cajun accent that seemed to reach inside her and twist her soul into something unrecognizable? Something hungry. Something lonely. Lonely for what this man could give her tonight.

She clawed at his chest, drinking in his musky scent laced with the softer odors of alcohol and Deep South perspiration. It turned him so human to her—no longer just the hot, unattainable man behind the bar who seemed to know all her secrets the moment their eyes had met. He was human, just like her.

His tongue pushed past her lips as he stroked his thumb across her nipple. "So good," she breathed without quite meaning to.

"Let me make it better, *chère*. Let me take you all the way."

Say yes. Let him show you exactly what "all the way"

could feel like. She knew instinctively it was a place she'd never been before, and she wanted to go there with him.

His hands sank to her bottom as he pushed against her in a slow, ancient rhythm. She'd never felt more captured by a man, enclosed by all he was—and she'd never dreamed such an experience could be so fraught with pleasure.

"I wanna sink deep into you, *beb.* Like this," he murmured, low, as he thrust slow and firm against her. "But no clothes, nothing between us." Each hot drive of his hips sent heat diffusing through her.

Say yes, her body begged her again. *Just say yes.*

Except then panic struck. Panic, reality; everything that existed outside this dark alcove where he'd nearly made her climax just from kissing and moving together. She pressed her hands flat against his chest, pushing him a step back. "We have to stop."

He didn't get it. "I know. Not here. Let's go." His voice was a warm whisper; his big hands still rested cozily on her hips.

Her next words came out shaky. "I can't."

He pulled back slightly to look down into her eyes—even in the shadows of their private doorway, she could feel the intense heat burning in them. "Why not?"

"I just can't." She shook her head, suddenly feeling unaccountably afraid. Not of him exactly, but of what she'd been so tempted to do with him.

His sigh of frustration weighed on her. "You got a husband I don't know about or somethin', *chère*?"

She bit her lip, made herself look up at him, and shook her head.

"A boyfriend then?"

She hesitated at that, but shook her head again. Curtis

wasn't the reason she'd said no. In fact, he was so far off her radar screen that now guilt pummeled her, too.

Jake's expression still brimmed with seduction. "Then what's wrong with you and me gettin' together?"

Good question. She couldn't explain it, even to herself. "I don't know. I just . . . can't."

He ran one hand back through his thick hair as another sigh left him. She thought of apologizing, but caught herself—reminding herself there was nothing wrong with turning a man down for sex.

Even if you want it just as much as he does?

Confusion, frustration—too many indecipherable emotions swirled in her head. "I should go."

"Where?"

"Back to my room." She broke away from him and started toward the street.

He caught her wrist. "Where's that, *chère*?"

"The LaRue House, on Esplanade."

"You can't be walkin' that far by yourself."

"Why not?"

He looked dumbfounded by her protests. "I'd think a big-city girl would have the common sense to know you don't walk on dark streets alone at night. And you especially don't do it in the Quarter, *beb*. I'll walk you."

"No." She yanked her arm away, too hard, and he stared. She just . . . needed to be away from him, right now. She met his gaze and tried to act as if she hadn't just done something uncalled for. "I'll get a cab. I'll be fine. Really."

He tilted his head. "You don't seem so fine."

No, she seemed like a woman who was afraid of her own shadow, afraid of a man who'd done nothing but make her feel good. *Too* good.

"Look," she said, trying to sound more rational than she felt, "things just . . . went too fast for me. And I'm worried about my sister, more now than I was before. I just want to go back to my room and unwind."

Their gazes met and she was sure he knew there was more to it than that, but after a long moment he simply said, "Okay."

She bit her lip, a hint of regret rolling over her because she was peering up into those incredibly sexy eyes of his, where temptation still beckoned.

That meant now would be a good time to go, so without further delay, she turned and started up Bourbon, headed back to where the streets weren't closed off and she could find a taxi.

She plodded quickly, her low heels clicking on the pavement as she wove through the decadent crowd, and she breathed a sigh of relief when she turned a corner to find a cab sitting curbside. She opened the door and slid in, then grabbed for the door handle, only to find Jake's imposing body in the way.

Utterly shocked, she flinched. She'd been walking so fast that she hadn't even realized he'd followed her.

"Where we going, miss?" the elderly driver asked in his rearview mirror.

"The LaRue, on Esplanade."

"I'll do some more work on locatin' your sister, *chère*," Jake said, still leaning in the open door. "I'll call you at the LaRue."

She blinked, gazing up at him. "You're still going to help me find Tina?"

"I said I would, didn't I?"

She simply nodded, amazed. Somehow she'd been sure his help was over—because he'd tried with no luck, and because she'd just let him kiss her senseless before haring away from him like a madwoman. "Thank you."

"Nothin' to thank me for yet. You can thank me when we find her. And *beb*?"

"What?"

"Don't do anything stupid like go lookin' on your own again. Wait to hear from me."

She drew in her breath, tempted to argue, but then remembered the ugly scene on the balcony at Sophia's. "All right."

With a short nod, he closed the door tight and stepped away from the cab. As the car started up the narrow street, she found herself peering out at him until he faded into the darkness of the French Quarter.

It was like a replay of two nights ago. She lay in bed, aching for Jake Broussard's touch. She was an idiot to have denied herself the pleasure she knew he could bring her.

She was thirty years old, old enough for a night of casual sex if that's what she wanted. And yet, as things had grown more heated, as she'd grown more lost to his hands, his lips, the hard planes of his body, something unexpected had risen within her. Apprehension.

It was akin to what had made her push him away in the red room, but at least then, she'd had a reason—he'd thought she was a prostitute.

Now, though, there were no misconceptions or lies standing between them. And she'd been sure she would give in if they got close again. Yet as she'd gotten danger-ously near to saying yes to all he had to offer, something had injected that irrational fear into her head. What was she so afraid of?

Was it him? This sexy Cajun ex-cop who wouldn't tell her why he wasn't a cop anymore? There might not be lies between them now, but secrets still existed, and maybe that was a good reason to worry. The possibility still existed that he'd done something wrong and been kicked off the force—maybe he'd even committed a crime. Underneath his gruffness, he seemed like a decent man, but what if that was just one part of him? Hadn't she just been telling herself people had more than one side to their personalities? What if Jake had a *dark* side? What if he was capable of doing something truly wrong? *Maybe your instincts are holding you back; maybe some sixth sense is telling you he* isn't *a good man.*

All of that made sense as she lay in the darkness, watching the shadows of thick tree branches dip ominously through the pale moonlight shining in the window. And even as frustrations continued to rack her, it made her glad she'd had the strength to resist him.

Except that one other possibility hung in the back of her mind, and she couldn't not ask herself the question: *what if you're just afraid of the things he makes you feel?*

In the beginning, he'd been a stranger. But now she knew him better and she trusted him more. She kept telling herself she barely knew him, but here in the darkness, she realized that was only a wall she was erecting between them, a reason to say no. If he was the good man her heart told her he was, well . . . it would be more than just two strangers grappling around in his bed. It might not be meaningful and lasting, but he was no longer just "the bartender." So why did it feel as if having sex with a man she deeply desired would be some sort of betrayal to herself?

What are you running from, Stephanie?

* * *

Jake headed south on 56 through the heart of Terrebonne Parish behind the wheel of the old pickup his father had driven when Jake was a boy. Amazing the beat-up Ford still ran, but despite all its clunks and rattles, it got him where he was going. After Becky was gone, he'd traded in the new Camry they'd bought together, leaving the old truck—which had been parked behind his mother's little shotgun house—for him to get around in. It was enough—other than heading to the bayou, he didn't go anyplace that required a vehicle.

He flipped on the radio to hear a static-filled version of Matchbox Twenty's "Bright Lights" asking him who would save him from all he was up against in this world? Unlike the girl in the song, though, Becky couldn't come home. The sad strains added to his general melancholy, which had grown worse over the last couple of hours.

He could still smell Stephanie Grant's soft floral perfume, still feel the softness of her breast in his hand. The memory made his fingers itch and he curled them tighter around the steering wheel. He'd wanted her—badly. And he still wasn't sure why she'd said no. Of bigger concern to him, though, was why it had bothered him so much, actually leaving him with hurt feelings and a sense of rejection he hadn't felt in a long time.

So he'd walked home, changed clothes, and started toward the old house. He needed to get away, even if just for the night. He'd planned to spend his days off there like he did every week, but if he didn't come back tomorrow, Stephanie would surely get herself into trouble and he couldn't risk that.

There you go again, trying to save somebody, even

when the song on the radio just reminded you—you *need saving as bad as anyone.* He hated himself for giving a shit about the woman or what happened to her, but maybe that just showed how truly weak he was. *Can't even quit caring about women you don't even know.*

Yet there was something about *this* woman, he thought as he turned onto a gravel side road. She was so different from him—so prim, and yet so haphazard when it came to finding her sister. And something about her kept calling him back for more.

Although she could wait a day while he unwound a little and got his bearings back. That's what the bayou house gave him.

It was the only place where he felt truly safe, from everything, and when he thought he couldn't survive one more day, he came here, and listened to the sounds, and let the moss-covered trees close around him—and he survived. Just enough to make himself go back to the city and survive a little longer there, too.

The end of the winding road appeared, the dark bayou waters ahead glinting in the moonlight. He parked the truck and walked toward the lean-to where he and a few other locals kept pirogues. Slipping a key in a lock so flimsy that anyone with a notion could break through, he dragged his boat down to the water's edge, overhung with ancient willows.

Pushing off into the water, he let the soothing qualities of the bayou fill him. Becky had always thought the bayou was "creepy," and as he drifted along the dark surface, he supposed he could understand what she'd meant. But since she'd been gone, it had become exactly what he needed—a place to close himself off from everything.

By the time he'd traveled a quarter of a mile downstream and paddled the pirogue into an even narrower tributary, he already felt a little better, a little . . . emptier. For Jake, empty was good. Empty meant emotions were held at bay. Empty meant feeling as close to nothing as possible. The dark water calmed him, made him feel almost as if he were easing down into it, letting it swallow him in its blackness.

A few minutes later, the old house came into view on the bank, flanked by clusters of enormous cypress on both sides. The back porch served as a dock, where he tied off the boat.

Stepping inside, he didn't bother turning on any lights. Didn't want to disturb the sweet, consuming darkness that made it feel like he was in a dream. Well, he amended with a wry chuckle, not the kind of dreams he'd been having lately, all fiery heat and sizzling sex—but the vague dreams that came with good sleep.

"You're beginning to heal, Jake," Tony had said when Jake had told him the dreams were better—no more nightmares—and the sleep was getting more restful.

Yet Jake had only laughed. If this was healing, it was a hell of a weak remedy. Better than nightmares and nagging, gnawing despair—but he hardly felt like his old self. He could barely remember that person, in fact— could only see him in shades and shadows of memory, in old photos it hurt to look at. He didn't think he'd *ever* heal. The way he saw it, he was just doing his time for another thirty, forty years, until they buried him, too.

Despite the lack of light, he could make out the under-construction state of the kitchen—the counters currently torn out, the new one leaning against the back wall. Beneath him, the new subfloor he'd started putting in a couple of weeks ago. Maybe he'd devote a couple of hours to it before heading back to the city tomorrow. Stephanie could wait that long.

Stephanie. Writhing against him. Pushing that softest spot of her against his hardest.

Quit thinking about her.

It was easier out here, in his private world. He succeeded in forcing thoughts of her away, even if he remained half stiff behind his zipper.

He looked around the room, wondering for the hundredth time why he was bothering to rebuild the place. To save this one safe haven from his childhood? Or just because pounding nails into boards took his head away from real life, gave him something simple and solid to concentrate on?

"You build somethin' wid your hands, boy," his father had once told him, "and you got somethin' to hold on to, somethin' that lasts. You can look at it, say, 'I made dat. Widout me, dat wouldn't be here.'"

On that particularly steamy summer day, it had been the back porch, built out over the water on thick pilings to keep it from sinking into the soft, volatile earth beneath the bayou. Back when this, his grandmother's house, had just been a place to visit on the weekend; back before he'd come to live here. But even on the weekends, it had felt like home. A place you didn't knock on the door, you just walked in, said, "*Mamère,* I'm here," and she'd come scuttling from the kitchen, wiping her hands on a dishtowel, smelling like herbs and bayou water and all things warm. She'd laugh and say, "You done growed a foot since I saw you, Boo," even if she'd seen him just a few days before. "Come on, den, and look what I made," she'd say, dragging him in the kitchen to show him something dark, ground up in a glass bottle or jar. "Dis wild bark take away de toothache," or "Dis some grigery for Mr. Dulac's sore hands."

Jake found himself wondering, had she been alive after what happened with Becky, if his grandmother could have mixed him up something to make him feel better, feel alive again. Yet he smiled sardonically, since he could almost hear her answering, "Ah, now, you need to see de voodoo lady for dat, Boo—I can't fix no heart."

Nobody could.

Sighing, he grabbed a beer from the antique refrigerator and walked out on the back porch he'd rebuilt a time or two since his father had first constructed it, settled in the old glider, and looked out into the darkness, trying to quiet his thoughts. *Just drink your beer. And feel home.*

When he felt himself drifting off into blessed sleep a few minutes later, he didn't bother getting up and heading for bed. A little trick he'd learned: sometimes moving killed it, that sweet, feel-nothing drift into sleep, so he'd taught himself to just stay put where he was and let it steal him away. Setting his beer on the wood below him, he leaned back his head and closed his eyes.

The red room feels even more red, more lush, than usual, like someone has put red bulbs in the lamps. But the one thing you see clearly is her. She stands naked, her back to you, her body a collection of pale curves that beckon in silent temptation.

You entered quietly, yet you know she feels you there, wanting her. Without acknowledging your presence, she drops to her knees and bends across a red velvet chair, her liquid movements a blunt invitation.

Drawing closer, a moth to a flame, you study the arch of her back, the roundness of her ass, adorned with a tiny tattoo of a simple flower, yellow center, five red petals.

"Come to me, lover," she says, her voice a husky whisper.

You're just as impatient, but as you kneel behind her, you can't help running your hands over her satin skin. Starting at her shoulders, you smooth your palms downward, molding them to her slender waist, then over her rear and down her outer thighs. You bend to deliver a soft kiss to her tattoo, which makes her sigh.

"Now," she says, so you grab firm to her hips and sink inside her, fast, easy. She is a soft, warm glove hugging you; you close your eyes at the profound pleasure. "Yes," she purrs, "yes," as you begin to move in her. Sweet. Slick.

Even with closed eyes, all you see is that same red glow, electric and hypnotizing, drawing you deeper and deeper into her. And in your mind, you see her amid that glow, but her face remains hidden by the color—she is only shadow, a silhouette.

Opening your eyes, you fall onto her, needing more. You press your upper body flat against her back, cocooning her; you rain kisses across her neck.

Somehow, even as you're having her, you still want—want to see her face, look into her eyes.

You want her to love you.

You want her to be the only thing in your world.

You want her to shroud you, protect you, so that nothing can hurt you, or her, ever.

And in this moment, you believe she can.

Chapter 9

Jake lay staring at a brown water stain on the ceiling, trying to focus on that and nothing else, as he lifted the barbell. He felt the welcome strain in his forearms, shoulders, chest, as he held the weight steady, despite the shakiness in his wrists.

Lowering it back into place, he let out a breath, glad for the burn in his muscles, but still seeing . . . the woman in the dream. Her back, her delectable rear. Over a full damn day ago, and still he felt it. He refocused on the water stain as if it were a cloud, or a Rorschach, something he could remold in his mind. He saw a flower in the stain.

Like the little flower on the dream woman's ass. He went hard. Damn it.

Not quite ready to lift the barbell again, he did it anyway—to dull the memory and accompanying emotions. Why did these damn dreams make him feel so much? And he always awoke with such an overpowering sense of guilt. He wasn't supposed to feel this much for anyone else—anyone besides Becky. Even if it was only a dream.

He glanced toward the scarred, secondhand end table across the room and caught sight of the framed photo of her taken in Audubon Park one spring day. Mardi Gras beads they'd found hanging from a tree on the St. Charles parade route draped her neck. His chest sank and he nearly dropped the weight on himself before letting it fall into the Y-shaped brackets with a clatter. *Merde.*

Maybe he should have just stayed out at the bayou house for his remaining days off—he was so much more at peace there. But he'd come back yesterday and spent the evening making phone calls to other old connections on the force, all looking to turn up some sign of Tina Grant. It had been emotionally taxing—having to make chitchat with old colleagues, hearing the requisite concern in their voices when they asked how he was doing— and it had led to nothing. It was as if the girl had vanished into thin air.

As for Stephanie, he'd picked up the phone to call her twice last night. To make sure she wasn't out doing something stupid. And . . . why else? Because he wanted to hear her voice? Because he was so tempted to try getting her to drop that barrier she'd put up when things had got too hot between them?

Maybe getting with Stephanie would bring an end to these haunting dreams.

Of course, he knew the woman in the dreams bore startling similarities to her—except he'd had the first dream before they'd even met, so . . .

Ah hell, give it up, Broussard. Since when was he the type of guy to sit around analyzing dreams?

He wasn't, so he refocused on the water spot and thrust the barbell up over his head again.

A hard knock sounded on his door. "Jesus," he

breathed, dropping the weight back in its rest. Pushing up from the weight bench, he strode to the door and yanked it open to find Tony on the other side.

His old friend gave him a long once-over, his eyes critical. "You look like you just ran a marathon. Or tried to and failed."

Jake glanced down at himself—his white tank was damp with sweat, and he doubted he'd raked a comb through his hair today, so it was probably pointing in all directions. "Liftin' weights," he said, realizing the activity had left him breathless. He'd been lifting for probably an hour or more.

"You're supposed to have a spotter for that, you know." Once upon a time, they'd traded the favor.

He only shrugged. He figured if that was the most reckless move he made, he was doing pretty damn good.

"You gonna invite me in or what?"

Jake stepped back and Tony came inside, heading to the little kitchen, where Jake heard him help himself to something in the fridge. "So about this beautiful woman you were with the other night," he called, "what's the deal?"

Jake plopped on his drooping couch. "Nothin' romantic goin' on, pard."

Tony eased down in an overstuffed chair across from him, popping the top on a beer, one of the few things probably *in* Jake's fridge. His friend's eyes urged him to say more.

"Just a woman I met at Sophia's."

Tony flinched. "She's a working girl?"

Jake laughed softly. "No. She was just there lookin' to find her sister, the girl in the pictures."

Tony nodded. "That's why I'm here. Might be nothing,

but might also be a lead. A guy named Rich, who tends bar over at the Crescent. I was there last night, so I asked about her, gave her name and a description. He said he'd seen a girl there a few times who could've been her, but she'd quit coming around."

The Crescent was an old hotel across Canal Street, beyond the Quarter, where more than a few prostitutes found business in the cocktail lounge. It had just never occurred to Jake to start snooping outside the "high-priced hooker zone" because Stephanie seemed so sure that was where her sister had set up shop.

"He couldn't say for sure her name was Tina, but he thought it was something like that."

"What else? Customers she hooked up with? Other girls she came in with?"

Tony shook his head, his expression a familiar one from their days on the streets—it meant *That's all I got.* "Guy pegged me as a cop and clammed up." He sighed. "But it's *something* anyway."

Jake nodded. It *was* something. The best and only lead of any kind he'd gotten. "Thanks, man. That's a help."

"But back to the beautiful woman," Tony said, a suspicious smile forming.

Jake just gave his head a short shake. "There's nothin' there, man. Just tryin' to help her out."

"Come on, dude," Tony prodded, raising his eyebrows. "She's pretty. You're horny. That combination's *gotta* go somewhere."

Jake lifted his gaze from his coffee table to Tony, smirking. "How do you know *what* I am?"

"You *gotta* be, man."

Jake just gave a cynical laugh. "Don't you know depression kills the sex drive?" It was a lie in his particular case, but Tony didn't know about his dirty dreams, and he didn't need to know what had happened between him and Stephanie, either.

His friend eyed him for a minute, as if trying to decide whether or not he was holding back, then shifted his gaze to scan the apartment. "Well, something must be going better for you. You did some laundry and the place doesn't look like quite as much of a pigsty as usual."

True enough, he'd had a little more energy lately. Enough to do the laundry *and* some dishes. But he wasn't ready to attribute that to Stephanie Grant. "Ran outta clothes," he said simply.

Tony let out another sigh, his lips drawing into a slight frown. "Well, whatever the case, it was good to see you out the other night. Everybody at the Den was glad you came in, glad to see you with somebody new." He chuckled. "Shorty spent the rest of the night wondering if you were getting lucky."

"Shorty's got a big imagination." He decided to change the subject. "What had you so strung out that night anyway?"

Tony lifted his can to his mouth and got a faraway look in his eyes. "Still can't get any closer to Typhoeus," he said, and the name made Jake's stomach clench. "We found a young Latino girl who we think was dealing for him. She'd overdosed and . . ." He shook his head lightly. "Just had me down, you know?"

Jake nodded, but his back had already stiffened, his throat grown tight, as he struggled to remain emotionless at the mention of the local drug kingpin. He remembered the day he and Tony had sat combing the Internet for clues to what this guy was about. They'd learned that in Greek mythology, Typhoeus was a giant monster—part human, part serpent. The story went that he was defeated by Zeus and imprisoned beneath Mount Aetna, but so far, in real life, no other gods had shown up in New Orleans and Typhoeus was wreaking havoc on the city at will.

"Don't suppose you have anything new on that for me?" Tony asked.

It was Typhoeus who Tony thought might be using escorts to filter drugs to wealthy clients on Sophia's third floor. On his good days, Jake tried to keep his eyes open for anything shady—but so far they had nothing but suspicion, and a handful of obscenely rich guys who seemed likely to be involved.

Jake *didn't* have anything new—because sometimes he let his guard down and didn't think about it, because sometimes it was easier that way. He'd been trying to accept that Typhoeus had beaten him already, and he'd been thinking maybe if he could just accept that, it would make things better, allow him to start moving on.

An hour later, Tony had departed and Jake wandered down the sagging stairs outside his apartment, into the courtyard. He hadn't seen Shondra in a couple of days, and when he crawled far enough out of his self-absorption to remember that, it made him feel like a shit. Not that he owed her anything. Not that he believed anything he could do for her would make any difference in her life in the end. But since he'd taken to coming out every day around lunchtime and giving her a few bucks to go get beignets, he found himself wondering what she'd done for food yesterday when he hadn't been around until late in the afternoon.

Making his way across the barren courtyard, he peeked under the stairwell where the mattress rested and found it empty—not even her backpack remained. His gut went hollow. She was gone. She hadn't seen him around and thought he'd abandoned her.

He straightened his spine, telling himself this was a *good* thing. He wasn't anybody's baby-sitter, and hell, maybe she was more capable of taking care of herself than he thought. Street kids got pretty good at that, pretty fast.

So she was probably fine. Just fine.

The words rang through his mind like an echo—*just fine, just fine*—but he didn't feel them as much as he would have liked. He let out a sigh, still staring down at the flimsy old mattress.

"Yo, you lookin' for me?"

Shondra watched as he turned to face her, and for the first time she realized how handsome he was. It caught her off guard.

"Where you been keepin' yourself, *'tite fille*?"

"Right here, mostly." She tilted her head, weighing her next words. "I was wonderin' the same thing about you." She swallowed back the lump in her throat, instantly embarrassed to admit she'd noticed his absence. She had to get tougher than that, once and for all. Just because this dude was being nice to her didn't mean it would last. He himself had told her that, so she sure as hell couldn't start depending on him.

His eyes dropped to the pooch at her feet. She'd discovered Scruff couldn't be trusted to stay where she told him—he followed her everywhere. He was pretty cool about not running into traffic, though.

"That mangy mutt still botherin' you?" Jake asked.

She narrowed her gaze vehemently. "Don't be dissin' Scruff."

Jake's chin lowered slightly. "Scruff?"

She shrugged. "Seemed like a good enough name."

He cast a disparaging glance to the dog. "Suits him anyway." Reaching in his pocket, he pulled out his wallet. "Up for beignets?"

She bit her lip and nodded, trying not to look too enthusiastic.

"You get by all right yesterday? I wasn't around."

She nodded again, standing a little taller. "Don't worry about me. I get by fine on my own." And she had. She'd been hanging onto her six-dollar haul and she'd used some of it to buy some day-old doughnuts to share with Scruff.

"Okay then," he said, sending her off.

Scruff followed behind, and as she walked down St. Ann toward Café Du Monde, she realized how much his gentle panting and the click of his claws on the concrete comforted her. She might get by fine on her own, but it was nice to have a friend. Maybe two. She just wasn't as sure of Jake yet as she was of the dog. She'd even let Scruff share her mattress these past couple of nights. When the only sound was an occasional siren, she felt a lot less alone with him by her side.

Reaching the café's outdoor window, she placed the same order she had on the other days Jake had sent her, glancing down at Scruff, whose tongue already hung out one side of his mouth. "Just stay cool a minute, then you can eat yours on the way back." *Had* to eat his on the way back, actually, so Jake wouldn't find out she was slipping pastries to the dog.

A few minutes later, they were headed to Jake's building, Shondra stopping every block or so to stoop and feed Scruff half a beignet. He ate the last of his order not long before they reentered the courtyard.

Realizing her hands were dusted with powdered sugar,

she reached into the white bag she carried and drew out a pastry, taking a big bite. It was only to cover for Scruff, but it tasted good to her hungry stomach. She'd gotten used to eating once a day or less, but when she did get to eat, it was like heaven.

Heaven must hold different things for different people, she thought, and after the past few months, she knew that heaven, for her, would hold food.

And dogs.

And her daddy.

Her mama and daddy together, like they used to be, like they were *supposed* to be.

When she and Scruff made their way into the courtyard, Jake sat on the half-rusted metal bench someone had parked in front of the dilapidated fountain that didn't work. He didn't see her coming—had his head leaned back toward the sun, his eyes shut, his muscular arms crossed over his chest, and his denim-covered legs stretched out, crossed at the ankles.

She lowered the bag and drinks to the metal slats at his side. "I'm back," she announced, settling on the other end of the bench.

When he opened his eyes, he looked amused. "Couldn't wait to eat with me, huh?"

"Hungry," she said past a mouthful of beignet; it wasn't a lie.

As he uncapped his juice, his eyes fell on Scruff and his happy expression disappeared. "Looks like somebody else had a nice breakfast, too."

Scruff sat at her feet, peering up at them, his little dog lips covered with white powdered sugar. Uh-oh.

She bit her lip. "He must've, uh, gotten into a trash can at the Café Du Monde."

"Those cans are a little tall for him, no?" He gave her a come-clean-with-me look.

Finally, she sighed. "What? I'm supposed to make him watch us eat without givin' him none?"

Jake's eyes scolded her. "So you're tellin' me I been buyin' breakfast for all three of us these past days?"

She shrugged her shoulders and waited for him to come down on her.

Instead, though, he just leaned over and shook his finger in Scruff's furry brown face. "You best thank your lucky stars you got her lookin' out for you, dog." Then he shook his head, letting out a short laugh. "Damn dog needs to learn to wipe his mouth if he wants to keep a secret."

Shondra breathed a sigh of relief, laughing, too.

As their laughter faded, though, the merry mood seemed to die with it—and he turned to pin her in place with his dark gaze. "Tell me somethin' else, *'tite fille*. What are you doin' here?"

She blinked, nearly choking on the thick dough and hoping he couldn't tell. "Here?"

"You know what I mean. On the street."

Her face heated in a way that had nothing to do with the hot French Quarter day. She peered down at the white bag in her lap, fiddling with the edge. "Just, you know, gettin' by." Her voice hadn't come out as strong as she'd intended.

He sighed. "No, I mean really. Why aren't you at home?"

She gave a little shake of her head, wishing he hadn't asked. Things had been going so good—her, him, Scruff, beignets—and now this.

"Why'd you run away, darlin'? You can tell me."

She raised her eyes at the unexpected endearment. But he was wrong; she *couldn't* tell him. She couldn't tell anyone. "Just . . . couldn't deal."

"Bet your folks are real worried."

She glanced down, trying to ignore the empty feeling in the pit of her stomach—it wasn't about hunger. Closer to loneliness, even with Jake and Scruff right here. "My mama don't care. Probably glad I'm gone."

"What about your dad?"

She let out a snort of sarcasm. "He ain't even around no more. Don't even know I left."

He stayed silent so long she felt her own words hanging in the air. On a good day, she didn't think about home, didn't even let it cross her mind. At the moment, it seemed the biggest part of her.

"You know, there are places you can go that can help you work through your problems, give you a better place to sleep than that old mattress."

"No," she said, and this shake of her head came with vehemence. "Joints like that just wanna make you go home, and I ain't goin'."

"What was so bad there?" His eyes on her, looking perhaps kinder than ever before, seemed to drill some sort of hole into her that the truth might leak from.

But no, she *couldn't* give voice to what had made her run. "I don't wanna talk about it."

"I'm just tryin' to help, you know."

"I know," she said on a nod. "And I'm down with the food, and the place to sleep. But that's the only help you can give me." Then she reached down one powder-laden hand to the fur at Scruff's neck, giving a gentle scratch and letting his warmth comfort her again.

* * *

Jake walked the three blocks to Esplanade, worrying.

Worrying about Shondra, wondering what terrible secrets she had.

Worrying about Tony, wondering if his ex-partner would ever realize that no matter how hard you worked as a cop, you couldn't win. There would always be more bad guys stealing your hope, showing you how mortal you were.

Worrying about Stephanie—who he was on his way to see right now. How would she deal with it if they never found her sister? What if Tina Grant *was* in trouble, and what if it was already too late to do anything about it?

He spotted LaRue House, a historic mansion-turned-B and B, not long after starting northeast on the divided boulevard. Its Greek architecture, wrought-iron trim, and moss-covered trees were steeped in elegance, but his respect for the place dropped when he stepped inside asking for Stephanie Grant and the old woman behind the desk said, "She's in number five, around back," directing him outside toward the private entrance room he found with ease. He could be someone who meant her harm, yet the woman had pointed him right to her. Just one more reminder that no one was safe anywhere.

He knocked firmly on the crisp white door, and when he didn't hear any stirring, tried again, hoping like hell she'd just gone for dinner and wasn't out trying to track down Tina in another sexy dress.

He'd just about given up when the door opened. Stephanie stood before him in a little pair of flannel shorts and a tight white tee, no bra. The sight nearly took his breath away.

When she realized where he was looking—he was a

guy, he couldn't help it—she crossed her arms across her chest, going red-faced. It didn't help—in fact, it only thrust her breasts higher. "I . . . wasn't expecting you."

He swallowed. It was bad enough that the last time he'd seen her, they'd been making out like maniacs, but now this. It was all he could do not to grab her and kiss her. He finally managed to wrench his eyes from her chest, moving them to her prettily blushing face. "Who *were* you expectin' that you answered the door like this, *chère*?"

She shook her head, looking flustered. "I . . . fell asleep, wasn't really thinking when I opened the door."

Ah. That explained how sexily mussed she looked. Like she would look, he thought, if he ever got her in bed.

"Wait a minute," she said, walking away to return a moment later wearing a white cotton blouse over her sexy little T-shirt. He missed her breasts instantly.

"I came by to bring you this." He held out a Styrofoam container.

"What is—" She took it and opened the latching lid to reveal the slice of pie inside. "Oh."

He wasn't sure why he'd done it, but . . . "From a little bakery on St. Peter. Don't know if it'll hold up to your grandma's, but it's the tastiest apple pie in the Quarter."

She lifted her gaze to his, her eyes gone soft and pretty. "That's nice, Jake."

He played it off with a shrug. "I also came to tell you I might have a small lead on Tina."

She tensed visibly and he regretted not prefacing the news with a warning.

Better late than never. "Now, don't go gettin' your hopes up—it might be nothin'. It's a very *light* lead."

Her eyes remained wide and blue on him. "Well?" Blue as pictures he'd seen of the Mediterranean.

It distracted him for a second, until he got his wits back. "You remember my friend Tony?" He explained what Tony had told <u>him</u> that morning about the Crescent's lounge. "I just never thought of lookin' there since it's a whole different league of prostitutes than you'd find at Sophia's."

"Maybe Tina . . . exaggerated about the elegant part," she said quietly, clearly thinking out loud. "Maybe she thought that made it sound better." Then she turned anxious. "So what do we do with the information?"

"*We* don't do anything, *beb*," he said, looking pointedly into those ocean-colored eyes. "*You* stay here and do whatever you *been* doin'—go back to sleep if you want. *I'm* gonna go check it out. I'll stop by later and let you know if I've found anything new."

"But if the guy made Tony for a cop," she said, using the language he had when explaining, "won't he do the same thing with you?"

He shook his head. "First thing, I'm *not* a cop—anymore."

"That didn't stop you from worrying the doormen at the Playpen would think you were."

"True enough. But second thing, now that I'm wise to them bein' on guard for cops, I know how to approach the situation."

"How?"

"Like I'm one of her customers, lookin' to get with her again."

"Oh," she said, her body seeming to deflate a little.

She didn't like that, he thought, unduly pleased. Didn't like even the pretense that he could be with her sister that way. But maybe it was a little quick to get arrogant—maybe it was just the idea of *any* man being with her sister, under the circumstances.

"Maybe I should go, too."

He let out a sigh. "Why would *you* need to go?"

"The same reason you took me along the other night. I might hear something in a different way than you. He might drop some bit of information only I can recognize."

"Normally, I might agree, *beb,* but guys seekin' female company don't usually bring a date."

She smirked, taking on a forlorn look he'd seen her wear before. It gave him the urge to wrap his arms around her and just hold her.

Only problem with that was—he didn't think he was capable of simply holding Stephanie. Holding would bring on kissing and touching, and he was already half hard just from being around her, just from seeing those dark nipples jut through that white fabric, just from remembering how hot they'd gotten together a couple of nights ago.

"I still think I should go," she argued, but she spoke more softly now as she peered up at him, and he wondered if she was recalling the same thing he was. "I just . . . feel like this is a whole new playing field, and like *I* need to investigate, too."

"We had a deal, *chère.* You remember it, no?"

She nodded somberly. "You'll only help me if I do what you say."

"Right. And right now I say you stay put. Watch TV. Eat your pie. Call a friend. Whatever you want. If I need you to get involved, I know where to find you."

Stephanie sat on the bed trying her damnedest to crochet. She'd been trying for two days, but she had to face facts: she had zero skills with needle and yarn. Still, learning took on more importance to her with each day Tina was missing. She let out a wry laugh at the insanity of her compulsion. This whole situation was pushing her so far outside her usual boundaries that she feared she was starting to lose it a little.

Case in point, Jake Broussard. Every time she saw him, she craved him more. Getting so intimate with him in the Bourbon Street alcove had left her wondering what it would be like to get even *more* intimate with him. And wondering why she couldn't.

If you're ever going to have a wild, hot, hedonistic affair in your lifetime, this is your opportunity. Her inner voice whispered the words, begging her, pleading with her not to let this man and everything so sensual about him pass her by.

Yet something continued to hold her back.

Even now, after he brought you pie? She'd already eaten it, torn the whole time between thinking he was sweet and horrible and everything in between.

Because even as thoughtful as bringing the pie had been, he'd ruined it by demanding she stay home and twiddle her thumbs while he was out searching for Tina. She should be out there looking, too, no matter *what* he said.

In a fit of frustration—multiple kinds—she flung the crocheting needle down to the bed. She walked to the desk, to her laptop, and—ignoring an e-mail from Curtis—pulled up an Instant Message box to see if Melody was online. When Melody didn't respond, she went through her saved mail file until she found the one she sought—containing Melody's phone number.

She'd been keeping Melody up to date on her progress—or lack thereof, and the other woman had said if she needed to reach her and couldn't do so via computer that she could call her cell phone. She'd done it once before, and feeling a little frantic, she decided to do it again now.

"Hello?" Utterly refined and sophisticated—it all came through in that one little word.

"Melody, this is Stephanie. Can you talk?"

The other woman hesitated. "Um, yes. But hold on just a moment." She heard Melody tell her husband that it was one of the other mothers from the play group, and that she was going to take the call in the den. "I'm back now, Stephanie."

"I'm sorry to have caught you at a bad time."

"No, it's fine. Is there news about Tina?"

Stephanie explained what she'd learned, asking, "What can you tell me about the Crescent?"

The other woman's voice went lower. "I didn't know girls still worked there. When I was in the business, the Crescent was crawling with cops and became considered an off-limits place. But it's possible that's changed."

"Do you think some of the same girls who work Sophia's work the Crescent? Or could I find a whole new set of escorts who might know Tina?"

"The Crescent is . . . a big step down from Sophia's, I'm afraid. And while most of the girls at Sophia's work under a madam, the girls who worked the Crescent were more the type who worked strictly for themselves. More freedom, but less protection. For what it's worth, they might be more open with you than the girls at Sophia's. Whenever I met any of the lower-paid girls, they seemed to think we were all *sisters,* if you know what I mean. They trust each other in a way high-end escorts don't."

After they disconnected, Stephanie plopped back on the bed. She'd promised Jake she'd stay put, but there might be women at the Crescent who would know Tina. They might tell her something they wouldn't share with Jake. It felt absurdly like going back to square one, and yet how could she not?

Picking the phone back up, she called for a taxi and slipped into a dress designed to entice. The timing was bad, but Jake hadn't turned up any leads other than this one, so she *had* to explore it to the fullest. She simply couldn't sit on her hands when she might be able to do something constructive. She knew there were dangers, but Jake had made her feel useless when it came to locating her sister—and she didn't like giving up control that way.

She'd be careful tonight—she wouldn't talk to men, only other girls. And as for Jake, well . . . who cared what he thought? In fact, why had she let him tell her what to do in the first place? Bottom line, she had to find Tina. Even if it meant breaking the rules.

Chapter 10

The Crescent lay a couple of blocks outside the tidy grid of the French Quarter, and as Stephanie passed a ten-dollar bill to the cabdriver and stepped out into the night, she noticed the area lacked the charm of the historic Quarter, giving off more of a this-could-be-any-city feeling. It looked like one of a hundred streets she might find at home in Chicago, with clumps of small, older buildings squeezed between cold skyscrapers.

The Crescent was one of those older places, nothing glossy or glamorous about the dark, squat hotel—and as she walked through the door, she felt more like what she was pretending to be than she ever had at Chez Sophia: a hooker.

That should have horrified her, but maybe she was becoming more seasoned—or desperate—about this whole business. She was no less intimidated than she'd been that first night—she was just getting better at handling it. *Sell it,* she told herself as she moved through a plush but dated lobby. Tonight, though, it wasn't an urgently needed pep talk, just a simple instruction. The transformation came easier.

This is Jake's fault, she decided. He'd loosed something inside her, from the very first time she'd met his gaze—something brazen she couldn't quite stuff back in the box it had oozed out of.

Even as she moved across slightly worn carpet toward the double doors beneath a sign that read CRESCENT LOUNGE, her body ached and yearned for him. It was insane and uncontrollable—and she couldn't think about that right now. *Sell it,* she whispered inside as she reached for a big brass door handle.

Inside, dark wood beams saturated the room with a certain dullness. Lights burned low. Clusters of people mingled beneath a layer of smoke hovering near the ceiling. A baby grand piano, as dull in sheen as the rest of the lounge, sat in one corner and an old man with thin, greasy hair played a jaunty tune from the crooners' era. Stephanie felt like she'd stepped back in time.

Thankfully, the place was kept dark enough that no one seemed to have noticed her entrance. Three girls drinking martinis and wearing sequins caught her eye—her prey this evening. She spotted Jake, too, sitting at the bar, but at least his back was turned. *Arrogant, bossy, even-if-you-are-gorgeous man.* Her skin burned, part attraction but also part irritation at him for making her feel so . . . *helpless.* As if she could do nothing to aid their search. Well, she *could,* and she was going to prove it.

She would have liked a drink—both for the nip of courage a little alcohol could deliver and because she felt empty-handed approaching the escorts without one. But since Jake hadn't seen her yet, she didn't want to go to the bar. So she took a deep breath and sauntered toward the young women, ready to conquer her task.

"Hi," she said, and all of them looked her way—wary,

skeptical. "I'm sorry to interrupt, but I'm looking for a friend. Maybe you know her. Tina Grant?" Damn it, she'd just used their last name again, automatically.

A pretty redhead, who was managing to chew gum even as she drank a trendy appletini, spoke up. "Tina?" She looked to an exotic Latina brunette in red spangles. "Was that one girl's name Tina? Raven's friend?"

Thrilled to the core at this quick nibble, Stephanie hurriedly dug Tina's pictures from her tiny beaded black purse, passing them to the redhead.

The girl nodded. "Yeah, that's her."

"You know her? You're sure?" She struggled to keep the excitement from bubbling in her voice.

"Only met her a couple of times," the Latin girl said. "She was new. Real green. Barely knew the business at all."

Stephanie nodded. "Yeah, that sounds like her. Do you know how I can get in touch with her?"

Both girls gave vague head shakes, while the third—a petite blonde—lit a cigarette and blew smoke toward the layer already floating above their heads. She said, "I'm gonna get to work, look for a trick," then set off into other parts of the cavelike room.

"It's really important," Stephanie said to the remaining two, her stomach churning. "What about the friend you mentioned—Raven, was it? How can I find *her*?"

The redhead shrugged. "Haven't seen Raven in a few weeks."

Stephanie's hope dropped further, but she couldn't give up. "Do you know where Raven lives? Or"—God forbid—". . . maybe you know which guys Tina . . . hooked up with, and you could put me in touch with *them*?"

The girls stared at her. Her desperation was showing.

She needed to explain herself. "It's just that . . . I haven't heard from her in a while, and I'm worried about her. We're . . . close."

The Latin girl cast a skeptical look. "Honey, you seem pretty green yourself. Too nosy."

"Yeah," the redhead added. "This ain't a job for asking a lot of questions. People get the wrong idea about you." She glanced toward the door, where a tall, handsome man who appeared too sophisticated for his surroundings stood looking about the room. "Oooh, one of my richest customers. Gotta go."

So much for Melody's claim that these girls would be nice. But on the other hand, they'd told Stephanie enough to make the trip completely worthwhile.

"Sorry, buddy, I don't know the girl you're talking about, and even if I do, I don't know where to find her."

This guy, Jake thought, was no help at all. Every sentence out of his mouth contained a contradiction. Probably a not-real-bright guy's attempt to cover up now that Tony had made him think the cops were looking to bust the Crescent.

"I hooked up with her here before," Jake lied. "Sure you don't know if she comes in regular?"

Rich, a thirty-something guy with receding blond hair, braced his hands on the bar. "Look, pal, I don't know what to tell you. But you want a blonde so bad, there's a hot one waiting to get picked up right over there."

Jake turned to look where Rich pointed, his eyes landing on a knockout in a sexy black dress. *Stephanie.*

An unprecedented rage rose in him until he felt like a volcano about to blow. Never mind that she looked absolutely stunning, the flowy material of the low-cut dress hugging her breasts, their round swells creating enough cleavage for him to drown in; never mind that his heart pinched oddly at the sight of her. He was gonna kill her.

Without another glance at Rich, he slapped some money on the bar for his half-finished drink and crossed the room. She stood alone, so he didn't have to worry about niceties. "What the fuck do you think you're doin'?" he bit off.

Her back went rigid, but she didn't shrink beneath his tone. "I'm coming at it from another angle."

"Are you deaf or somethin'? Did you not hear me tell you to stay put? Are you tryin' to drive me out of my mind? What is it with you and simple instructions?"

She started to respond, but he wasn't listening, because no matter what she said, it wasn't good enough. He latched onto her arm and pulled her toward an exit that opened into a dank alley. It was only as he was dragging her toward the street that she wrenched away from him. "Would you let go of me?" she snapped, her blue eyes wide and luminous beneath the streetlights.

He grabbed her hand tight and proceeded forward again. "No way, *beb*. Seems if I don't keep hold of you, you run off and get yourself in trouble." Upon reaching the sidewalk, he flagged down a taxi with his free hand.

"I wasn't in trouble, for your information. I wasn't going to talk to any men, just the escorts," she argued as he delivered her into the car. "Melody said they'd be more open with another hooker than with a guy."

He climbed in behind, shoving her over on the seat to make room for him.

"And why on earth are you going with me? Why aren't you going back in there and grilling that bartender some more?"

"LaRue House, on Esplanade," he told the driver.

"You might think I'm totally incapable," she went on snippily, "but I can certainly get myself back to my place without your help."

"I know you can, *chère,* but I got no confidence that you *will.*"

"Look, I'm sorry I *disobeyed* you, *Master,*" she said, rolling her eyes at him. "But I knew there might be information out there about Tina and I had to try." The cab crossed the wide thoroughfare of Canal Street, then dipped into the French Quarter, the buildings on either side closing in darkly around the car. "And if anything had happened, you were there," she added with a brisk take-that nod.

"Damn good thing, too, because in case you didn't notice, nobody lifted an eye, let alone a finger, when I manhandled you out of there. If somebody had wanted to hurt you and I hadn't been there, Stephanie . . ." He was peering at her in the darkness, seeing only the shadowy shape of her, but feeling her warmth pressed up against him—and he found himself unable to go on because his throat was closing up at the very idea that some guy could have hurt her. Some guy could have hurt her and he might not have known, or might have been gone by then. Some guy could have hurt her and there wasn't a damn thing he could have done to stop it.

"What?" she whispered, shaking her head softly when he didn't go on.

Unwanted emotion clogged him up inside. It seemed to stretch like a physical thing from his throat down through his chest, then into the depths of his gut. He couldn't look at her anymore, even in the dark, so he focused on the back of the cabbie's head—a dark, greasy ponytail. Finally, he took a deep breath and spoke slowly, choosing his words carefully. "I just can't *help* you if I have to *worry* about you at the same time."

"Then don't worry. I'm a big girl. I can take care of—"

"No, you can't," he snapped. "I already had to rescue you once, and I thought you understood then what the deal was."

"But listen, Jake." She grabbed his wrist, her hand warming his skin. "I showed Tina's picture and found out she *has* been there before. The girls I spoke to haven't seen her in a few weeks, but they said she has a friend named Raven. They haven't seen Raven, either, but it's *something*. Another *name*. A place she's actually *been*. Did you get anything from the bartender?"

He sighed. "No." And he hated to admit it, but maybe she actually *had* done them some good. Raven was a lot more uncommon name than Tina. It was another piece of information to give Tony, a name he could drop at Sophia's.

As the cab pulled to a stop on Esplanade, Jake paid the driver, then took Stephanie's hand as they exited the car. Realizing he still held it once they reached the sidewalk, the taxi speeding away behind them, he let it drop, but automatically lifted a palm to the small of her back to propel her down the brick walk to her room. The gnarled oaks and their moss-draped boughs provided a canopy overhead.

"You have to admit that's helpful information, right?" she asked.

"Yeah, *beb,* you did good work tonight, but"—he stopped and turned her to face him, taking her hands in his—"you can't keep doin' this, understand?"

Their gazes met in the night, a sliver of moonlight

fighting its way down through the trees to make her eyes sparkle, and Jake's desire for her rose yet again. Had it ever waned since he'd set eyes on her this evening? Her hair was simple, falling over her shoulders in the same soft waves he'd seen earlier, only tamed now. Her filmy dress, its two wide swaths of black fabric tied behind her neck, made him think of old Hollywood glamour and sophistication. He caught sight of her nipples pushing against the fabric, and he wanted her naked, wanted to see her, touch her, explore her in a leisurely way he hadn't done with a woman in a very long time.

Since Becky, of course. Everything always led back to her. A more stinging guilt than usual bit at him with the knowledge that he didn't want to think about her right now. He only wanted Stephanie. No one else.

Finally, she turned and walked ahead on the path, digging a key from her fancy purse. "Well," she said, "looks like you managed to get me home safe and sound. I guess you can go now."

"No," he said, and as she stepped inside, he followed, shutting the door behind them. He heard a click as a dim lamp lit the room, which was filled with antique furniture and thick, elegant fabrics.

"I'll stay here this time, I promise. My work for the evening is done." She sounded far from contrite, though—more like pissed.

Well, that was too damn bad.

He watched as she dropped her purse on the bed, before reaching to undo the bracelet that sparkled at her wrist, tossing it carelessly on a dresser. When she turned toward him, he stepped up close to her. "You still don't get it, do you?"

"Yes, yes, I get it. While you search for my sister, I

have to trap myself in this room, stare at the walls, and feel powerless, all because you think I'm defenseless."

"Damn it, Stephanie!" His voice raised without his intending it to. She flinched beneath him and he locked his gaze on hers, needing to make her understand. "I don't want you to get hurt, for God's sake!" he shouted, then tried to speak more gently. "That's not so hard to understand, no?"

But for Stephanie, it *was* hard to understand. Who was he? The gruff ex-cop who was all business? Or the softer man she saw only tiny hints of, hints so small that she wasn't even sure if they were real or simply in her tortured imagination? The answer mattered, a lot—because wouldn't it be easier to let herself sleep with him if she thought he cared for her?

He stood over her, his eyes filled with some combination of fury and tenderness so profound that she leaned back against the wall in an attempt not to wither and faint beneath his stare. She hated all the uncertainty, hated not knowing where she stood, not being in control of it. "What do you care?" she finally barked at him.

He shook his head. "What do you mean?"

"What do you care if I get hurt? What's it to you? You barely know me. You're only helping me because you think I'm a danger to myself, some stupid little waif playing private detective. And you couldn't really care less if we find my sister—except maybe to get me out of your hair so you'll never have to see me again."

As she'd spilled the indicting words, she'd watched his face tighten still more fiercely, aware that his shoulders were set tensely and his fingers curled into fists at his side. "You got one thing right, Stephanie Grant," he growled.

"What's that, tough guy?"

His hands closed on her shoulders and his expression appeared positively tortured. "If I never saw you again, it would make my life a hell of a lot easier." With that, his mouth came down on hers, hard and demanding, his kiss feeling as if he were attempting to wrench something out of her.

Her entire body responded, her breasts tingling, wetness pooling between her thighs. Their mouths struggled together, their tongues sparring hotly. And in that heated moment, she didn't care *why* he was kissing her, didn't care if he hated her and never wanted to see her again. She only wanted to take what he had to give, and wanted to give him whatever he needed. And *clearly* he needed. *Something.* No man had ever kissed her so powerfully.

His arms closed around her and she moved against him without hesitation, needing the sweet, hot friction, needing to feel his very maleness against her curves. Her lips felt bruised beneath his, but she didn't care. She clawed at his back, grabbed onto his hair, kissed him as feverishly as he was kissing her.

When one of Jake's hands sank to her butt, she clenched at the pleasure and unthinkingly lifted one leg, curling it around his thick denim-clad thigh. His erection pressed insistently between her legs, forcing a low moan from her throat. Oh God. Oh God. She closed her eyes as the heat licked at her inner thighs, the small of her back. She was lost to him, lost to the weight of the desire pressing down on her.

Then, without warning, the passion turned slower—kisses still hard, but lingering. She heard them both panting as the heat of his body warmed her from shoulder to thigh. He tasted of cool mint. The kisses ended with his forehead pressed to hers in quiet, breathless recovery, but still their bodies writhed slowly together, as if they just couldn't stop.

"I don't want like this," he whispered hotly.

"Huh?" His voice caught her off guard, his words not quite making sense.

He hesitated slightly, and when he spoke, it came between heavy breaths. "I don't think I've ever wanted a woman . . . the way I want you. Since that first night . . . in the red room. The second I see you . . . I wanna sink so deep inside you, *beb.* Let me."

Let me have you.

Could she? Could she let go of whatever held her back each time? Now they were in her room—a private, comfortable, safe place. *Let go,* she told herself. *Just let go and feel him the way you want to.*

He pulled back just enough to look into her eyes. "Tell me you want me, *chère.*"

"You know I do," she whispered.

They went totally still in that moment, no movement—just the connection of their gazes and the insistent beat of her heart against her rib cage.

She said it again, even softer this time. "You know I do."

His next kiss came shockingly gentle, swallowing and sweet; their tongues licked at each other, tasting deeply. Good, delicious kisses, the best of her life. She thought for a few moments that maybe she'd be content just to stand here and kiss him all night long. Her fingers curled in his thick hair and the musky, sexy scent of him permeated her senses. She wanted to crawl inside him.

When he slowly skimmed one hand to the side of her breast, her knees buckled, but he was there to catch her, his other arm anchored securely around her waist. The stroke of his thumb teased the outer curve, touching skin to skin, thanks to the bareness of her dress. Her breath grew more labored until she realized she was kissing him harder, pulling him closer, thinking, *Touch me, please touch me,* feeling sure that if he didn't, she would die. *Please, Jake.*

But she was careful not to voice her wishes out loud. That would be too much, giving away every last ounce of control—and she had to hang onto *something,* didn't she?

When his thumb passed over her nipple through the dress, she went weak again, but still he held her, drawing back to look at her from beneath shaded lids. "You get me so hot, *beb.*"

She could only sigh, her breath trembling, glad when his kisses returned, because she was better with that, with simply being swept away, than with having to acknowledge her passion with words.

As his hand closed full around her breast, inside the dress, she let out a low groan and locked her arms tighter around his neck so she wouldn't fall. His tongue delved deeply into her mouth as he slowly kneaded her, his thumb and forefinger teasing the hard peak. Harsh pleasure spiraled through her.

When his kisses trailed away from her mouth, over her cheek, to her neck, shoulder, she could do nothing but acquiesce, leaning her head to one side. Her breath grew shakier with each inch he descended, his mouth getting closer and closer to where his thumb and finger played.

Yes, yes. Kiss me there.

She never realized his other hand had left her waist until she felt the smooth, light tug at the back of her neck—he was untying the top of her dress. *Oh God.* Her knees trembled and she fought not to let them give way.

She'd had sex with enough men that this part wasn't foreign. Yet it still felt new—with Jake. He pulled back slightly and the top of the dress slipped like satin over her breasts, falling away to leave her bared to the waist.

He studied her unabashedly, his gaze making her even hotter. "So pretty, *chère*," he whispered, slowly lifting his brown eyes to hers.

She felt lost. Free. Trapped. Confused but wild, and growing hungrier with each passing second. "Kiss me there," she murmured. It was an accident—words never meant to leave her lips.

But Jake didn't hesitate. Stepping up close again, he curled both hands over her breasts, massaging deeply as he delivered a long, slow kiss to her mouth—and then lower. Her neck. The hollow of her throat. The upper curve of plump, pale flesh. Then his tongue flicked over the dark pink tip.

She gasped and the juncture of her thighs spasmed. Her own thready breath was the only sound.

More. Please. This time she held it inside, didn't beg, thank goodness—but it was almost as if he'd read her thoughts anyway, because his warm mouth closed over her distended nipple, his tongue swirling around it in wet, intoxicating circles.

Thank God she had the wall to lean against or she'd surely be on the floor by now. She moaned and sighed, drinking in the pleasures from his mouth and hands, still caressing her breasts, molding, shaping, making her crazy with the hot joy of it. *God, yes.*

When he switched his ministrations to the other breast, licking and teasing with tongue and teeth, a tiny bite that seemed to reach all the way into her panties made her cry out. She held his head there, ran her hands through his thick hair, and peered down to find him looking back, his tongue raking across the moistened peak as his brown gaze seared her.

She wanted desperately to look away because his eyes made her so wild inside, made her simply want to rip his clothes off, push him to the bed, do everything she'd ever dreamed of—and *never* dreamed of. Her wildest dreams had never been as wild as *he* turned her.

But control, control. You have to keep at least a little control. She'd never felt comfortable giving that up—especially when it came to sex.

Just when she was sure there was nothing he could do to make her any more deeply aroused, he bent even lower to kiss the smooth plane of her stomach. Her whole body seemed to flutter at the light assault.

And before she could think, he was dropping to his knees, slowly skimming his hands down the fabric that covered her hips. He gazed up, heat rushing from his eyes as his hands closed around the backs of her legs.

"Wh-what are you doing?"

"Want to kiss you *here* now, *chère*," he rasped, then lowered a chaste, tiny kiss to the black filmy fabric that lay across the juncture of her thighs.

Chapter 11

She gasped at the pure pleasure radiating through her. "Oh . . ." she breathed.

His gaze rose to meet hers as his hands slid up the backs of her thighs, to her bottom, taking the soft black fabric with him.

"I never . . ." she whispered without meaning to.

"Never what, *beb*?" His voice was a deep purr from below.

Never felt such hot wanting. Never felt so on the edge of truly letting go.

He blinked, peering up at her. "Surely you've been kissed here before."

She nodded. "Yes, but . . ." *It was never like this.*

"But what?" he asked, lowering another soft kiss through the dress.

An unstoppable shiver rushed through her, leaving her unable to answer. Why had she even started talking at all? Words seemed ridiculously inadequate in summing up the intense heat surrounding them. He still looked up at her, waiting for a reply, but she only shook her head, beseeching him with her eyes to go on. And just in case he didn't get the message, she eased one high-heeled foot to the side, parting her legs a bit farther.

Kiss me again.

His eyes seemed to deepen a shade before he lowered them back to the part of her body so close to his mouth. His hands slid from her rear around to her knees, pausing just long enough to gather the fabric in front and push it up, higher, higher, until he held it bunched at her waist. She couldn't stop the trembling that assaulted her, but he seemed undaunted.

"Want to make you feel so good, *chère.*" His voice fell over her as dark and soft as a shadow just before he kissed the front of her black silk panties, openmouthed, deep and passionate, as if it were a part of her that could kiss him back. Warm pressure and heat—his tongue—permeated her most sensitive spot, and without planning it, she began to grind against him. Maybe she *could* kiss him back—this way.

She closed her eyes, melting, thrusting—softly, softly. She pressed her palms flat against the wall behind her for support, then found her fingers curling, clawing at the slick wallpaper, reaching for purchase as she sank deeper into his ministrations.

She heard her own whimper as his fingers curved over the top edge of her panties. *Yes. Take them off me.*

Grabbing onto one side with both hands, he gave a rough tug and the thin elastic band snapped, leaving the underwear to fall away.

"Oh!" She drew in her breath.

Too much. This was too much. Too much pleasure, too much abandon.

Damn it, no—it was happening again, her body tensing sharply. And like everything else with this man, it was beyond her control.

Her legs snapped together tight as she tried desperately to quell the hungry sensations inside her. "I can't," she blurted out.

Still kneeling before her, he raised his gaze. "What?"

One glimpse of the disbelief in his sexy eyes and she couldn't continue to look at him. She tried to close her legs still tighter, but it wasn't possible. "I'm sorry," she whimpered, "so sorry. But I can't."

"You can't," he repeated, somber, bewildered.

"I'm sorry, Jake. I just . . ." She shook her head. Maybe she should tell him about Curtis. She didn't officially consider him her boyfriend, but maybe that's what this was about, some kind of guilt. God knew it would be easier if she had some sort of concrete reason to give him. Yet even without speaking the words, it sounded like a lie to her. "I'm sorry," she said again.

He let her dress fall back down her thighs as he rose to his feet. Shutting his eyes, he ran his hands back through his hair and let out a heavy sigh of frustration. Feeling like the worst sort of tease, she remembered she was still half unclothed and began fumbling to grab up the front of her dress.

Casting only one last look of disappointment, he started for the door. "I'd better go."

"Wait."

He paused, his hand on the doorknob, to look over his shoulder. Like always, his eyes nearly buried her.

"Wh-what about Tina? Do you think you'll be able to find her now that we know her friend's name?"

He looked dumbfounded that she could be talking about *that* at a time like *this*—and at the moment she couldn't blame him. She asked too much of him.

They stood like that for a long, tense moment, until finally Jake gave his head a quick shake. "I can't do this anymore."

He turned to go again and impulse made her rush forward. Still using one hand to hold her dress up in front, she latched onto his wrist with the other. "What do you mean?"

Shaking free from her grip, he took a step back, looking more dark and forbidding than usual. "I can't be near you, Stephanie, without wantin' you. And if I haven't been able to locate your sister by now, I seriously doubt a girl's name is gonna make a difference. I can't help you." He shook his head again. "I can't keep doin' this."

With that, he stalked out the door, pulling it firmly shut behind him. The slam drove home for her how alone she suddenly was. She stared at it blankly, feeling as if she'd just lost . . . everything that mattered.

Idiot, idiot, idiot. Ten minutes after Jake left, Stephanie's fear of sleeping with him had faded, but her desire remained in full swing, pulsing through her body like something trying to get out. *Idiot.*

Pushing up from the bed, where she'd let herself collapse a moment after his departure, she stripped off her dress, changing quickly into a pair of blue jeans, a gray tank top she usually wore to the gym, and her comfortable leather sandals.

Locking the door behind her, she headed for the customer parking lot. Jake had once told her—only because she'd pried—that he lived in an old building on Burgundy.

That's all she knew about where to find him other than Sophia's. So if she had any chance of finding him *tonight,* she needed to beat him home, see him walking down the street. Finally, a use for the rental car she'd kept just in case her search for Tina led her beyond the immediate vicinity. Even driving, she'd still have to hurry, and still might not locate him.

She pulled out on Esplanade, heading toward the French Quarter. Passing Burgundy—a one-way going the wrong way—she turned onto Dauphine, speeding down several blocks before circling back to Jake's street again. That quickly, though, it seemed futile. Too many doorways. Too many balconies and windows and gates and shutters. He could be behind any of them. She briefly considered the phone book, but quickly concluded that a guy as secretive as Jake would be unlisted, even if just as a holdover from his days as a cop.

She crept up the street in the midsize sedan, studying the few people she spotted on the sidewalk, but none of them were Jake. Until, that is, she spied a man crossing toward an old blue pickup truck parked along the curb. Her stomach lurched at the sight of him.

She slowed to a stop, hoping he wouldn't realize it was her—although she wasn't sure why.

She'd been trying to tell herself she'd come to plead with him about not giving up on Tina, since he was the only person in this town willing to help. But the much bigger truth was that she'd come to apologize, because she was so sorry for what had happened back at her room, so sorry she'd said no. Something had compelled her to seek him out and make things right.

And yet now she hid within the safe confines of her rental car, just wanting to watch him, see what he did, where he went. He never gave her any answers about himself—maybe if she followed him, she'd finally learn more about him.

She flipped on her turn signal, as if waiting for his parking space, then watched the truck's taillights blink on before it rumbled away from the curb. Hanging back, she killed the turn signal and proceeded behind him.

She followed him up a maze of streets that led deeper into the city. Maybe this was childish, maybe it was downright stupid—but her heart beat faster wondering where he was going and what it would tell her about him. Within a few turns and stoplights, the blue pickup veered onto an expressway ramp, leading her onto Interstate 10.

Once on the open road, Jake drove fast and she struggled to keep up without him noticing. As they crossed the Mississippi, she found herself asking: *Where does a man like Jake Broussard go at a time like this?* To another woman, someone who wouldn't heat him up just to turn him down? Her stomach tightened at the thought. Why was sex so difficult for her? She wanted so desperately to explain it to him, but she didn't know the answer herself. She pressed on the gas a little heavier, lest she lose sight of the truck.

Soon they were on a more desolate, empty road and she was careful to stay back a reasonable distance, just barely keeping his taillights in view. The farther they got from the city, the darker the air became. She saw only the low-lying road directly in front of her. God, where on earth was he going?

If you had half a brain, you'd turn around and go back. Leave the man alone.

Yet she'd come so far, and to head back to New Orleans now would only leave her all the more curious and frustrated. Despite herself, she simply . . . wanted to be close to him, wanted to be wherever he was.

But an hour into the trip, she let out a huge sigh, thinking he might never get to where he was going. And dear God, what was that on the side of the road? She only caught a glimpse, but was fairly certain she'd just passed a small alligator.

Following more twists and turns, Stephanie found herself pursuing Jake down a two-lane road labeled Route 56 and knew instinctively she was in the heart of bayou country. For some reason, it made her heart beat painfully—it somehow seemed dangerous and a little eerie to be out here in the middle of a deserted area she knew nothing about. Keeping up with Jake had turned into a safety measure as much as anything else—she no longer even cared if he figured out she was following him.

After ninety minutes of driving, Jake slowed and took a left. When she reached the turn, she nearly missed it, even knowing it was there—the narrow one-lane gravel road wasn't marked, and pulling onto it felt like crossing some sort of invisible line, some point of no return.

She crept slowly along the bumpy, winding path, afraid she'd come upon Jake's truck if she rounded a bend too fast, and also hoping she didn't end up driving into a swamp.

Around a curve and through thick trees, she spotted Jake's truck stopped beneath a single light pole, a dim beam illuminating the area. She pressed her brakes, bringing the car to a stop as she shut off the lights, then struggled to peer through the tall trees.

She could barely make out Jake's shape as he walked to a shanty-type building beneath the light, then pulled something long and narrow, bigger than himself, from the lean-to. She squinted as he moved back past the trees blocking her view to realize he was dragging a small boat. They must be at the water. And he was going to get in the boat and float away from her after all this?

Flipping the headlights back on, she gave it some gas. Only—damn it!—her tires were spinning. She'd gotten the car stuck—in a pocket of mud or something. "Oh, please, no—don't let this happen," she beseeched God or anyone else who might hear.

Taking a deep breath, she released the gas pedal, then slowly, patiently tried again. Nothing but spinning wheels and a horrible whirring sound that multiplied her fears. *This can't be happening.* After another deep breath, she asked herself what her father would do in this situation. Surely they'd covered such things when she'd been learning to drive. *Put it in reverse,* she told herself. *Ease back and turn the wheel to let the tire find something new to bite into.*

Voilà—a second later, the front wheel backed out of the mud, and Stephanie let out a huge sigh of relief as she drove around the hole and sped to where Jake had parked.

Yanking the keys from the ignition, she practically leaped from the car and raced to the shore, but saw only a pale wake that told her which way he'd headed. *Damn it.*

Looking around, her eyes came to rest on the shack Jake had taken the boat from. Jogging to it, she tried the wide door only to find it padlocked. Could *nothing* go her way?

Again, she lectured herself that anyone with any sense would get back in the car and head back to the city, where at least you could see the danger coming at you, where at least there were other people around if you screamed for help. But despite the insanity of it, she found her gaze dropping to a little boat turned upside down on the ground beside the weather-beaten building. Bending, she mustered the strength to turn it over, toss the accompanying oar inside, and begin dragging it toward the gently sloped bank.

She was moving on autopilot now—she didn't consider the risk of such an act, she didn't let herself think about getting lost in the bayou—she only knew she had to hurry if she was going to follow Jake's wake, and she hoped like hell the moon would provide enough light to show her the way.

"You can do this," she told herself as she climbed in, her bottom landing on a hard wooden slat of a seat. She took a deep breath and lowered the paddle into the dark water. "You can do it."

Besides the fact that she regularly used the rowing machine at the gym, she'd competed in many a canoe race at summer camp, and had even gone on a number of canoe trips with friends over the past few years. So this wasn't *entirely* crazy.

Probably no crazier than pretending she was a high-priced hooker.

Probably no crazier than following him this far already.

And she'd come too far to turn back now.

She ignored the painful beat of her heart as she labored to steer the boat, thankful she worked out three times a week—or at least she had before she'd come haring down to New Orleans and watched her whole world turn on its end.

Dim moonlight fought its way through Spanish-moss-covered trees, and—*thank you, God*—gave her a glimpse of the ripples Jake's boat had sent spreading across the water. She worked to calm her breathing, even as she paddled harder, trying to gain on him. The moonlit bayou seemed otherworldly, almost iridescent somehow, ancient tree stumps and drooping moss becoming giant stalagmites and stalactites, making the swamp a primeval cavern, the star-dotted sky overhead nothing more than a dark ceiling. *A place as mysterious as he is,* she thought.

No wonder he'd come here. Already, she had the sense of him blending with this landscape, belonging to it. It all felt so surreal, she actually found herself hoping he didn't somehow just dissipate, fade into the cypresses and dark water until there was nothing more for her to follow.

Floating along the isolated waterway was almost serene—if she hadn't been tormented by thoughts of never reaching him, of losing sight of his wake, of not being able to find her way back to the car.

She came upon a fork in the bayou and followed the rippling water to the right. Ahead, trees blotted out the light enough that she still saw nothing of Jake or his boat.

That's when the water rushed around her toes and she looked down to see that the floor of the boat had filled with water, at least half an inch deep. Half an inch that hadn't been there when she'd departed, because it had been upside down until then. Her boat had a leak.

Don't panic, she lectured herself. But the ache in her chest grew sharper as she realized just what a foolish decision she'd made. *You're going to die out here. You're going to die and no one's ever going to know what happened to you.*

Or maybe they would. They'd trace the car back to her, and Jake might help the authorities figure out that she'd followed him and set out in a boat after dark without a clue where she was going. Death by stupidity.

She paddled faster, desperation driving her.

Was the water around her shoes getting deeper quicker now or was that just her imagination? Exactly how many alligators lived in the average bayou? And did they aggressively attack humans dumb enough to end up in the water with them?

"Jake!" she yelled with every ounce of energy left inside her. Her heart was going to beat right through her chest soon. "Jake! Are you out there somewhere?"

Just then, a light came on in the distance, Jake's shadow within its beam. He stood on a dock, peering out over the dark water. She rowed furiously toward him, thinking, *Thank you, God!*

"Jake, it's me!" she yelled again, getting nearer.

"What the hell. . . ?" she heard him mutter, squinting.

"It's Stephanie!" she said, the dock just a few yards away now—and shit! She was about to float right past it!

She reached out and grabbed onto the canoe already tied to the pilings, but her boat kept going, until she was pulled off her seat, her butt sloshing in the water, her back slamming painfully into the rear concave panels of the vessel. She yelped in pain as Jake said, "Jesus," and held out another paddle to her. "Hold on to this."

She used one hand to grab the offered oar, the other to raise herself back onto the seat and hold steady. He pulled the opposite end of the paddle until her boat came flush against the moorings behind his—then he stared down at her, wide-eyed.

"Boat has a leak, *chère.*"

She didn't have to glance down to see the water was up around her ankles now. "Thanks for the newsflash."

"Well, get the hell up here," he said, dropping the oar on the dock and reaching down to her. There was a ladder, but she clung to his arm and he pulled her most of the way up without her having to climb.

When they stood face-to-face, he simply shook his head, his expression one of pure disbelief. He asked her the same exact question he'd posed earlier at the Crescent. "What the fuck are you doin' here?"

"I followed you."

Only this time she feared he might be even angrier. *"Are you outta your mind?"* He peered down to the boat. "Floatin' around in a leaky pirogue on a dark bayou where you don't know your way? You tryin' to give Mr. *Cocodrie* a late-night snack?"

She shook her head, trying to get her bearings, never so glad to have something solid beneath her feet, but feeling just as close to collapse as she had back in her room a couple of hours ago when he'd been kissing her so intimately. "No—I was just following you."

His expression remained bewildered. "I heard you the first time, but I still don't get it. Why the hell would you do *that*?"

Again, she found herself shaking her head, having run out of words that made sense—if she'd ever had any. Exhaustion buffeted her. "I just needed to apologize. For everything. For not doing what you tell me in regard to finding Tina. For . . ." God, this was hard. She looked at his feet, then made herself meet his gaze. "For not being able to . . . you know . . . *be* with you. The way I want to."

He gave his head a slight tilt. "From where I stand, seems I'm the only one really wantin' you to be with me. But that aside . . ." He shook his head and ran a hand back through his hair, focusing on her again with those captivating brown eyes. His voice came softer, nearly drowned out by the night sounds of the bayou. "You're a mess, *chère*. Come inside and let's get you cleaned up."

It wasn't until he took her hand, then pushed through a door, that she comprehended there was a small house attached to the dock. And as he led her through a dwelling that seemed to lie somewhere between old and new, in flux, she already felt the very essence of him here, and she knew this was where she'd find out the things she wanted so badly to know about Jake Broussard.

Chapter 12

She might be a mess, but she still looked damn fine. Which was why he consciously averted his eyes as he led her through the kitchen, into the bedroom, finally into the tiny bathroom where an old sink ran a dribble of water that would have to do.

Her hands were scratched and dirty—pricks and thin lines of red that needed to be cleaned. He drew them under the faucet, making sure not to look at the swell of her breasts rising from the low neckline of her tank top or the way those jeans hugged her curves. He'd never imagined Stephanie could be so casual, nor tough enough not to complain about what she'd just been through, with hands that had to be stinging and a back that surely ached from the tumble she'd taken in the pirogue.

Having held her hands too long, he let go of them abruptly, passing her a bar of soap. "Wash up real good," he instructed as he turned away to find a towel, echoing words his grandmother used to impart.

He shuffled through the little linen cabinet, automatically seeking the least worn and raveled of the old towels he'd never gotten around to replacing. But his mind traveled back, unwittingly, to the sight of her soft, round breasts, to the sensation of kissing between her thighs, to how lost in her he'd been, and how hard it had been to stop when she'd clamped her legs together.

He'd headed out here to get away, from everything, just for the night, but now here she was—she'd *followed* him, for God's sake. For a conservative woman, he was starting to think Stephanie Grant seemed pretty foolhardy.

Pulling out a small green towel, he turned back, silently watching her lather her hands, and felt how close he stood to her in the tiny room.

He couldn't stand the silence for another second, especially when he thought of the danger she'd put herself in by coming out here. She was beautiful, and tempting, but he was starting to wonder if she had any common sense at all. *"Peter, Paul, and Mary, do you have any idea how goddamn stupid that was?"* he exploded. "Do you realize how lucky you are you didn't get lost, and that you didn't *sink* in that damn pirogue?"

He waited for her to come right back at him, to defend her actions like usual, but instead, she only raised her head slightly and nodded, swallowing visibly as a look of regret washed over her. Her answer was an acceptant whisper. "Yes." She turned off the water and took the small towel from his hand.

He suddenly felt like an ogre, yelling at her, unable to take his eyes off her—unable to look away from her quiet strength. "Thank God nothin' happened," he heard himself mutter—then he pulled her into his arms for a crushing hug.

She was so soft and warm, smelling now of his soap and the sweet, lush scents of the bayou. He bent over her, sinking his face into the silk of her hair. Her breasts pressed against his chest, her curves molding to him, and he was struck with stirrings that had just finally begun to fade with the horror of finding her in the bayou in a leaky boat.

So just as suddenly as he'd embraced her, he pushed her away and reached for a tube of disinfectant cream on a shelf behind him, shoving it into her hand as he squeezed past her out of the bathroom. "Put this on your hands. I'll be outside," he said over his shoulder, too brusquely.

Passing through the kitchen, he grabbed a beer from the fridge and, as an afterthought, reached for a second. Heading out to the old glider, he thought, *I can't keep seeing her, I just can't.* Because the truth was—part of him had been *glad* she'd turned him down earlier. It had alleviated the guilt, sending him home frustrated but free. Free of that nagging shame that battered him upon acknowledging how much he'd felt with her—again.

What had taken place back at the LaRue House wasn't just sex. It was about giving her apple pie to help her feel close to her grandmother. It was about holding her hand as they walked down the street. So many little things twined together in his heart when he was with her, making it so that he simply wanted to be with her *more.*

And at the same time, what had happened in her room had been *all about* sex. He'd been driven by something so deep in his soul he could barely understand it. He'd desperately wanted to give her something she needed. Something he needed, too. He'd forgotten about everything—*anything*—else in those moments. There had only been him and her and a raging desire that felt palpable, like it was wrapping around them, propelling his every action and emotion.

So it was pure hell that she was here now—in the one place that was his alone, where he could escape and not think, not feel.

He'd tell her she had to go. Then he'd take her back up the bayou himself and see that she got on her way. It was that simple. He'd break it to her as soon as she came out.

As if on cue, she pushed through the door and he silently offered the can of beer he'd been unsure she'd drink. Taking a seat next to him, she accepted it without reaction—as unpredictable as always, his Miss Chardonnay.

He stared out over the dark waters that usually brought him so much peace, listening as she popped the top and took a sip. "Drink your beer and then I'll take you back up the bayou."

He felt those blue eyes piercing him, but didn't turn to look at her. "I need to talk to you."

Something in his stomach pinched, yet still he stared straight ahead into the swallowing night. "So talk."

"It's about what you said back at my room. That you couldn't help me anymore."

He blinked, tried not to feel her nearness. Tried to push away the wanting that seemed to pluck at every pore of his skin. "What about it?"

"I'm desperate, Jake. You know that."

Her gentle sigh wafted over him, but he cut her off at the knees. "We've had this conversation before. If you've got anything new to say, get to it."

She stayed silent for a long moment, before speaking softly. "I *don't* have anything new. And maybe that's the point. Tina's still out there somewhere and I have to find her. But I know I can't do it alone. You're my only friend here. And you're also my only hope. Maybe Tina's only hope, too."

Finally, he turned his gaze on her, only in order to drive his words home, since they must not have sunk in back at her room. "What makes you think I have any more chance of findin' her than you do? I've already looked under every rock I know and no sign of her. What makes you think havin' my help makes the slightest difference at all?"

"For all I know, maybe it doesn't. But . . . you're all I have here. And I know you didn't want to help me in the first place and that I really have no right to ask, but I'm asking. I'm asking you not to desert me."

I can't do it.

Tell her that. Say the goddamn words.

But something prevented him from it. He'd made the mistake of looking into those earnest blue eyes and his chest had tightened, his stomach shriveled.

"I happen to think we make a decent team," she went on. Yet when he narrowed his eyes in doubt, she added, "Although I'll do whatever you say if you keep helping me. I promise."

"You've promised before, *chère.* Tonight, for instance, you said you'd stay put, no? But then there you are, back in a slinky dress, puttin' yourself in harm's way. What reason do I have to take you at your word?"

She bit her lip, then took a page from *his* book—staring out into the black bayou. "Because I'm at rock bottom," she said frankly. "Without you, I truly don't have a clue what to do next." She turned to look at him again. "But I think you know me well enough by now to know I *will* do *something.* And I don't want to be stupid about it."

He tilted his head. "Too late for that."

"Then I don't want to *keep* being stupid about it."

He withdrew his gaze once more. Talk about being

between a rock and a hard place. The rock was the knowledge that she would eventually do something dumb enough to get herself hurt if he left her to her own devices—the same reason he'd agreed to help in the beginning. The hard place was behind his zipper, and he didn't know *how* the hell he was gonna keep dealing with that.

"What do you say, Jake? Give me one more chance?"

He still wanted to refuse, but he didn't have it in him. *Face it, son, you was born to help folks,* his mother had told him not too long ago. Stephanie. Shondra. That stupid, mangy dog. Jesus, what did they think he was, some kind of superhero? But no, not even close. Superheroes got the job done. He just *tried* to—and it didn't usually work. Becky could attest to that.

Finishing his beer, he calmly crushed the can in his fist and lowered it to the porch. Finally, he took a deep breath and focused on her again. "Let's get somethin' straight here. I keep lookin' for your sister, I do it on my own—there's no 'team' about it. Got it?" He didn't give her a chance to answer. "I do this on one condition and it's that you do *nothin'* independent of me, understand? I find out you did and that's it, I'm done, you're on your own. You give me the pictures of your sister and you're not involved in this anymore, other than hearin' what I find. Is that *perfectly one hundred percent clear?*"

She looked contrite, but far from beaten, as she firmly replied, "Yeah, it's clear."

"Good."

"Any other concerns?" she asked with a slightly sarcastic bite to her voice.

"Yeah," he said. "What about the other part?"

She blinked. "Other part?"

He pulled in his breath, crossed his arms over his chest,

and peered out over the water. "The part about me not bein' able to keep my hands off you."

The admission, though one he thought pretty obvious, hung between them for a long moment. Long enough that he grew restless, uncomfortable. He reached in his pocket and pulled out a roll of mints, popping one in his mouth.

Finally, her voice came soft, almost drowned out by the sounds of insects, but not so low that he didn't absorb each and every word. "Believe it or not, Jake, I don't *want* you to keep your hands off me. I . . . definitely want them on me."

"Coulda fooled me, *chère*."

She glanced down at her beer can, fiddled with the ring on top. "I know. I'm sorry. I . . . can't explain."

He'd stopped trying not to look at her. "I wish you'd try."

Slowly, she raised her blue gaze, looking nervous and sad. Then she blinked and turned away. "I just have this thing about . . . not liking to lose control." She drew in a sharp breath and met his eyes once more. "And you make me lose control."

His chest began to sizzle. He hadn't seen that coming. Maybe he should have, yet it still struck him hard—and good. His muscles tensed with heat as he went stiff in his pants. But then again . . . "Not completely, though. You always manage to stop, no?"

She looked emotionally spent. "I try to let go with you, Jake, but . . . no man has ever made me feel like you do."

"Which is?"

Her lips trembled slightly, yet she didn't break their gaze. "*Wild.* Like I don't even know myself. Because I want to do *everything* with you."

Jake leaned closer, without planning it, and lifted one

hand to her cheek. "Tell me what you want to do with me, *beb*."

"Things I . . . don't even know about." She shook her head lightly. "Just . . . everything. *Everything*."

He moved still nearer, bending over her. "Think you'll ever be able to let go completely and let me have all of you?" His voice was a dark whisper just before he lowered a soft, slow kiss to her lips.

Stephanie gave in to the moment without thought or decision. She couldn't resist Jake's kisses. From the first one he'd swept across her lips to this deep, tender meeting of tongues, she was lost to him when his mouth covered hers. Heavenly sensations reverberated through her entire body until the kiss finally ended and she murmured, "God, I hope so."

"Mmm, me too, *chère*." A small grin softened his strong features when she least expected such tenderness.

She returned the gentle smile, repeating the same words she'd already spoken a few minutes ago. "What do you say, Jake? Give me another chance?"

He pulled in his breath, his eyes going darker with want, as his gaze settled on her mouth. His answer came in the form of another kiss, his tongue warmly seeking hers. He felt impossibly good—his hands gently cupping her cheeks, his mouth seeming to drink of her, the warmth where their bodies touched. Risking her life in the dark swamp had been worth it, for this.

His kisses grew shorter, but still tender, and as always, he tasted of mint and masculinity. She loved the very bigness of his body, the hardness of his muscles as she ran her hands over his broad shoulders.

When he laid her down on the glider, pain arced through her. "Ow! My back."

"Mmm, from your spill in the pirogue. You'll have a couple of nasty bruises come mornin'." He reached behind him for the vinyl cushion he'd been leaning against, sliding it beneath her. "Better?"

She relaxed, testing it. "Yes."

"Good." He lowered a gentle kiss to her forehead before bringing his mouth back to hers. She wrapped her arms around his neck, wanting him closer, wanting to feel the weight of his body.

When one hand covered her breast, she sighed with pleasure and instinctively arched deeper into his palm. His low growl fueled her, and as for any trepidation, it was—blessedly—nowhere in sight. There was only him, and her, and this dark, private place that seemed a world away from anything bad. His thumb gently stroked her nipple through her top and bra.

"These are so pretty, *beb*," he murmured, his breath warm at her ear. Shifting to his side next to her, he bent to lower a delicate kiss to the curve of feminine flesh exposed by her top. "I loved kissin' 'em earlier, loved how hard your pretty nipple felt on my tongue."

She whimpered, turned on by his erotic talk, and also because her nipples weren't the only things that were hard—his erection pressed like a column of stone against her thigh.

When his hand slid from her breast to the denim between her legs, she sucked in her breath, moving involuntarily against his touch. "And down here—mmm, I wanted to taste you down here, too, *chère*."

She shivered in his arms, despite the heat, then rolled to face him, wanting to feel his hardness where she yearned for it most. But when his hand eased onto her bottom, he pulled back, chuckling. "Your jeans are all wet back here. Why didn't you tell me? Want me to find somethin' for you to change into?"

"It's okay," she murmured. "No big deal."

He reached for the button in front, deftly undoing it before sliding her zipper down. "Why don't you just let me take 'em off you," he whispered.

Let him take your jeans off and God knows what *you'll do.*

Lose control? Definitely.

Get that horrible shriveling, shrinking feeling that always seemed to strike at the most critical moment? Probably. In fact, the first hints of it were stealing into her already, replacing passion with a tinge of prickly nervousness.

She shut her eyes. *Why does this have to keep happening?*

"Uh-oh," Jake said. Only then did she realize she'd gone completely still.

She raised her gaze, her lips trembling not from passion now but embarrassment. "I'm sorry."

He smoothed his fingers back through her hair, his eyes earnest. "It's okay."

She shook her head. "No, it's not. I don't like this any more than you do."

He shifted to lay his head next to hers on the thick cushion, bringing their faces incredibly close. "What is it that makes you stop exactly?" His voice remained as gentle as the still water beyond. "What are you feelin' right now?"

She thought for a long moment and summed it up in one word. "Just . . . nervous."

"Nervous how?"

She closed her eyes, unable to keep looking into his

and summon an answer at the same time. And as for that answer, she'd never truly examined the emotion before now—she'd always been too busy running, trying to escape from the situation. "I guess maybe I'm worried . . . it'll hurt."

"Hurt?"

"The sex. The penetration."

His eyes narrowed. "Why do you think that, *beb*? Is it always like this?"

She shook her head against the vinyl. "Not with other men. But . . . this is different. When I'm with other guys, I always stay . . . in control. They don't make me feel . . . you know . . . *wild* for sex. But you do, and somehow I worry that if I'm not careful . . . that if I'm not fully in charge of the situation . . ."

"What?"

She shook her head and pushed back an unpleasant memory before it quite made it to the surface of her mind.

But he must've seen it flit through her eyes. "What are you thinkin' about? Tell me."

She shook her head again. "Nothing, really. Just something that happened a long time ago, but I don't like thinking about it, so it's . . . nothing."

He lifted his palm to her cheek. "Sounds like *somethin'.*" Again, she shook her head, but he pressed her. "Tell me, Stephanie. What's this 'nothin'' in your mind?"

She swallowed fretfully, uncomfortable at dredging up the recollection.

"Please," he added.

That was the part that got to her. When Jake went all tender, he was *impossible* to resist.

"Once," she began softly, somehow thinking that if she spoke quietly the memory might not seem so real, "I drove home from college a day earlier than my parents were expecting me. I came bouncing into the house in a great mood—it was Christmastime, end of the quarter. It was nine or ten o'clock at night and Tina wasn't home—spending the night with a girlfriend.

"I walked in, about to shout hello, when I heard my mom and dad arguing." Her throat seized a bit, threatening to close up, but she pushed on. "So I stayed quiet, and I listened, and what I heard was . . ."

"What?"

"My mom was . . . crying . . . and telling him she didn't want to, because it hurt . . . and he was . . . making her anyway."

"Mon Dieu," Jake breathed, his eyes gone starkly sad.

She girded herself, just as she had that night so long ago. "So I walked back to the front door, and I made a lot of noise like I was just coming in, and I yelled out, 'I'm home!' Anything to stop it, you know?"

He nodded softly.

"A minute later, they were both in the kitchen listening to me explain how I got out of classes early, and my mother was getting out cookies and milk . . . and it was over." She took a deep breath. "But I've always had to wonder, ever since, how often it happened that way." Sighing, she shook her head. "So you see why I don't think about it. I just *can't*." She leaned her head back to look at the stars, seeking out the crescent moon as a distraction. "I don't know why that passed through my mind right now—it just does sometimes, but I kind of . . . block out the thoughts." She feared she sounded a little manic.

When she lowered her gaze back to Jake, he spoke gently. *"Chère,"* he began, pushing her hair out of her eyes with warm, gentle fingertips, "don't you think this probably has somethin' to do with why you're afraid to have sex? The kind of sex that makes you lose control?"

Dear God. She thought about arguing, but his words made perfect sense. Or sort of perfect anyway. She was no psychologist, but . . . when had she become so dense? "I . . . I never thought about it that way before. I mean, since I hardly ever let myself think about that night." She lowered her eyes, planting them on the front of his light gray T-shirt, studying the hard planes of his chest where the cotton lay snug against him. "Before that happened, I was a virgin. But I wanted to have sex—badly. And then I did, once, with the guy I'd been dating for a long time . . . and it hurt."

"Oh," Jake said, sounding sad for her.

Upon returning to DePaul after Christmas, she'd had that one night with Jason, when he'd tempted her past the point of no return. It had started out so good, but ended terribly. Afterward, she'd no longer been interested in sex—in fact, for a while the very idea of it had simply made her ill. And maybe it had made her think of her parents, too, stirring up the memory she'd wanted so desperately to forget. She'd been unable to explain any of this to Jason and they'd broken up by Valentine's Day. "Since then, I've never let myself lose control during sex—I just couldn't give that power up to a guy."

"Because of the pain?"

"And . . . I guess maybe never wanting to let a man have that kind of freedom with my body—like my dad had with my mother."

"Have you, uh, *had* much sex?"

"Some. But I've always controlled the situation, never let it get too wild, always kept it very mild—boring, actually. Up to now, it's always just been"—she shook her head, embarrassed, but still trying to be honest—"a thing that happens sometimes at the end of a date. Because I wanted to feel . . . normal. But I've never been with a guy since college who made me really *want* it again, who made me feel . . . you know."

His eyes widened slightly, hopefully. "Like *I* do?"

She nodded, whispered. "Yeah."

They stayed quiet for a moment, until finally Jake lowered a tender kiss to her forehead. "I'd never hurt you, *chère*. I'd never let you feel any pain."

She looked up into his eyes. "I guess, logically, I know that. You've been nothing but patient, and"—a sigh of pure longing escaped her—"sexy as hell."

He grinned, clearly pleased.

"It's just . . . hard," she said. "To let go. To trust somebody that much."

He nodded and said, "Then what about this? What about we don't have sex, you and me?"

Despite everything, disappointment barreled through her. "Huh?"

He smiled softly at her confusion. "How about we just fool around? No sex, no pain. And there's plenty you can do foolin' around."

She blinked. "And . . . that'll be enough?"

"We'll make it be enough. Trust me."

Chapter 13

As Jake scooped her into his arms, she bit her lip and laced her fingers behind his neck, thrilled to her very core. That was the one saving grace of her horrible affliction—it never seemed to outlast her desire for him. Not even close.

She looked up at his strong face, his stubbled chin, as he carried her through the door and to the bedroom. Lowering her to the bed, a massive piece of furniture she'd failed to notice the first time she'd passed through, he stood back and stripped off his T-shirt, tossing it on the floor.

The sight of him in nothing but well-worn blue jeans nearly stole her breath. And if the bulge at his zipper was any indication, he remained delectably hard. She wondered why that excited her so much if she wasn't going to have sex with him.

Kicking off his shoes, he stepped toward the bed and relieved her of her wet sandals. "These may not recover," he told her, studying one before letting it plunk to the floor.

"I'll live," she replied, just watching him, absorbing him in a way she'd never quite given herself permission to do before now.

Jake padded across the room on bare feet to an old record player in a little suitcaselike container, where a stack of albums lay on the turntable—he lifted them up on the center spool, setting them to drop and play. The room's windows were pushed open wide, admitting the same scents and sounds that had punctuated the air outside, and a ceiling fan spun above, sending down a surprisingly cool breeze. A few seconds later, though, those sounds were blotted out by the dreamy sound of Etta James singing, "At Last."

The utter sensuousness of the old song swept Stephanie away that much further as Jake joined her atop an old quilt. He lay beside her, propped on one elbow, his hand sliding to rest on her stomach. "We'll go as slow or as fast as you want, *beb*—you just let me know if I do anything wrong."

"*Wrong* isn't the right word for it." She owed him this, at the very least. "Nothing you've ever done to me was wrong. It was just . . . too much for me, that's all."

He leaned closer, skimming his hand upward, across one breast, to gently caress her cheek. His forearm stretched up the center of her chest. "Then you'll tell me what's too much, no?"

She nodded, the spot between her thighs tingling.

"Good," he whispered, bending to kiss her.

He hoped like hell it wasn't too soon to do that again, but it was pure impulse driving him; he needed to feel her supple lips under his. They exchanged soft, sweet kisses for a few moments, and it felt almost easy to Jake—like maybe just kissing was enough, like maybe it wasn't going to rip his guts out not to sink himself inside her sweet body the way he'd been wanting to since they'd met. He knew it wasn't true—soon enough they'd get to the gut-ripping part—but he'd do his best not to let his torture show. Her story about her parents had pulled at his heart, and he wanted everything that happened tonight to be exactly what she needed. He wanted to take away her fears.

When their kisses ceased, he nuzzled his nose against her silken cheek. "How's that?"

She smiled. "You taste good—*always* taste good. Minty."

"Mmm," he purred, dragging the tip of his middle finger slowly down the side of her neck and onto her shoulder, then under her tank top to play with the strap of her bra.

"Why is that?" she asked gently.

He gave a soft chuckle. "I gave up smokin' a few years back. Now I'm addicted to mints instead."

"Ah." She tipped her head back into the pillow. "Well, as addictions go, that's not a bad one."

He'd quit smoking for Becky—both her parents smoked, and she'd hated it. He'd been sorely tempted to pick it up again after she was gone, but something had kept him from it—to this day, he didn't know what. But this one little conversation made him glad he'd persevered.

Stephanie's eyes sparkled on him in the low-lit room—giving him a reason to decide it must have been fate that had kept him from replacing a burned-out bulb in one of the lamps. He watched her studying him, her eyes traveling down over his jaw, cheek, and lower. Seeming to realize she'd been caught exploring, she bit her lip. "You have an incredible body."

He liked this honest side of her. Smiling playfully, he leaned to kiss her neck. "I like yours, too, *beb*." He slid his hand to her ass, reminding him her denim was soaked. "But we really gotta get you out of these jeans. If we're not havin' sex, no good reason to put up with a wet spot in the bed."

She laughed and didn't protest, and he checked her eyes to make sure they still twinkled. Conveniently, her jeans remained unzipped from out on the porch, so he sat upright, reached for the waistband, and said, "Lift up."

With a little tugging—her grabbing onto white cotton bikini panties to keep them on—the jeans came down around her thighs. He pulled them the rest of the way off, shucking them on the floor, and a few seconds later, he was molding against her close, letting his hard-on rest at the crux of her thighs as he slid his arms back around her.

"Underwear's just as wet, *chère*," he said when his hand returned to her rear. He couldn't hide his teasing grin. "I think we should take those off, too."

Her widening eyes came with a chiding laugh. "No, those stay on." She lowered her voice. "For now anyway."

He let another small smile unfurl. "For now," he repeated. "I can live with that. Even if it means we're doomed to havin' a wet spot without the usual perks."

She laughed and batted playfully at his chest. "You want perks, buddy—I'll give you perks." With that, she rose up onto her knees, facing him, then reached down to the hem of her sexy tank top, arms crossing, and pulled it off over her head.

He watched in awe. Her bra was conservative white lace, just as simple as the cotton panties, but everything about her was lush and sensual, from the curves and rises of her body to the sexy look of daring on her face.

Yet then she bit her lip and seemed to sink a little.

He tuned in immediately. "What's wrong?"

She shook her head, casting a sweet, sheepish expression. "I'm just not sure where to go from here. This isn't usually me—taking off clothes, making suggestions."

"Not a problem, *beb*. I'll be happy to take over for you."

She tilted her head, a lock of blond falling across her face, and looked so pretty he could have died.

"Lie down with me," he said, all playfulness fleeing the scene. "Let me make you feel good."

She lowered her head back to the pillow and he rolled to his side to look down on her. When he'd first seen her soaring toward him in that leaky old pirogue, he'd felt intruded upon. He'd never wanted to share this place with anyone—it had belonged to him alone. But now that he peered down on this woman, at once so sensitive and so damn determined and strong, he was glad he wasn't alone anymore.

Dropping his gaze from her eyes to her chest, he gently skimmed one hand up her smooth, pretty stomach and onto the lower curve of her breast. He played lightly with the hard bud of her nipple jutting through the lace before bringing on more kisses. Tender at first, then infused with a deeper passion than he'd meant to set free. He wanted to kiss her senseless, wanted to kiss her until neither of them could think. He wanted to lose himself in this lush body.

But whoa, slow down. You've got all night. And you've got a woman who needs you to be tender. Even so, his breathing hitched when he tried to soften the kisses. "You doin' okay, *beb*?" he whispered, their faces an inch apart.

"Mmm, yes, good." Her voice came high-pitched, fluttery, aroused.

He sighed his relief, glad his little loss of control hadn't taken her anyplace she didn't want to go. "You get me so hot," he breathed as he began raining kisses over her throat, chest. *You make me want you more than I've ever wanted—*

But no, he couldn't go there; he successfully stopped the thought midway through. *Don't think, damn it. Just feel.*

He kissed his way onto the lace that covered her, loving the rise and fall of her breasts, her breath audible and lovely. But that quickly, he couldn't bear having the lace between them anymore. Memories of earlier kisses to her bared flesh made him slip his fingers beneath the bra strap, then whisper, "Can I take it off?"

Her eyes glazed with pleasure even as her lips trembled. "Yes."

Reaching behind her, he deftly unhooked the bra with one hand and slowly eased it away. Tossing the lace aside, he swallowed at the delectable sight. "Just as pretty as I remember, *chère.*"

Like earlier, he started out just kissing her there, delivering gentle licks, but soon he was suckling. Her sighs came faster as she arched her breast upward, deeper into his mouth. Her responsiveness aroused him more than it would have with any other woman because this was Stephanie, sensitive Stephanie, Stephanie who was afraid of sex. Afraid, but so damn sensual at the same time. He loved drawing it out of her, loved making her want more, making her *need* it.

Only he had the sneaking suspicion he wasn't responsible for *that.* He thought she'd probably *always* needed it. Just like the woman in his dreams. Wanted it, needed it—but could only get it from him. She *was* the woman in his dreams. He'd known that, of course, just never let himself fully accept it—because it added to his guilt, and it also begged the question: how the hell had he dreamed her before he'd met her?

His hands left her breasts to roam and explore, wanting to learn every inch of her. His touch gently skimmed her neck and shoulders, the curve of her waist, the swell of her hip, the lushness of her thigh. It was pure instinct that led his hand onto the cotton between her legs until he was cupping her warmth, molding his palm to her, kneading softly.

Her breath grew more labored and her eyes fell shut, color suffusing her cheeks.

He couldn't *not* go further.

Easing his hand beneath the elastic below her navel, he grazed his fingertips across the smooth, satiny skin that led through a light thatch of hair, then down farther. He groaned as his fingers sank into her, gently beginning to stroke. Her sigh was one of abandon. He couldn't have asked for more.

Nipping lightly at her breast, he eased up near her ear. "You're so wet for me."

She only moaned in reply, lifting to his touch. His fingers dived deeper. He wanted to swim inside her.

When he curled his fingers into the elastic at her hips, she rose automatically and he drew the panties down her thighs and over her knees.

If he'd thought she looked lovely and passion-filled earlier, against the wall at the LaRue House, it was nothing compared to how utterly erotic she looked now, naked on his bed, thighs parted so he could kneel between. "You take my breath away," he whispered into the warm night air, then bent to lower a kiss just above the clump of hair that shielded her most intimate parts.

She whimpered needfully, sounding impatient, and he couldn't help grinning as he peered up the soft planes of her body, into her eyes. "Goin' slow for you, *beb*. That's what you wanted, isn't it?"

"Yes, but . . ."

"But what?" He blew on the moist flesh just below his mouth.

She shut her eyes, looking tortured. "But . . . God, please."

"Tell me you want me to kiss you there, *chère*."

She nodded wildly against the white pillowcase. "Yes," she moaned. "Please, Jake. Kiss me. There."

Her words echoed through him hotly as he raked his tongue through her sweetness. *Mmm, yes, so good.* Even better than earlier, because something had changed since then. Hell, a lot of things. He knew her so much better than he had just a few hours earlier.

She moaned in response, and he dipped back for more, soon dragging the tip of his tongue over the swollen nub he knew lay at the center of her sensitivity. She sighed, lifting to him, and though he'd had every intention of taking this slow, making it last, giving her a gradual rise to climax—he couldn't hold back.

He let the taste and scent of her fill him as her body jerked reflexively. Her hands curled in his hair and she let out a small, heated cry at every stroke, her sounds driving him.

He instinctually pushed one finger inside her warmth. A heavier sob met his ears, but she kept moving with him, and soon he slid in a second, eliciting a hot whimper. "Oh God," she breathed above him. "Oh God."

The ceiling fan whirred above them, cooling his back, and Dusty Springfield crooned "Son of a Preacher Man" from one of his grandmother's old records, and he gave himself over to pleasing her completely. No thinking. No planning. Just doing. Just getting lost in her warmth, in her soft, sexy noises.

"God, Jake, God," she said, louder.

Yes, beb, *come for me.*

Her wild moan had her convulsing around him, thrusting, thrusting, climaxing against his tongue and fingers— and when she stopped moving and only the music remained, he stayed very still, too.

He couldn't quite believe it, but he knew if he moved a muscle, he'd explode in his pants. And that just wasn't good enough here. Even if it meant falling asleep with a hard-on, he didn't want to spend himself this way. Just in case. In case she wanted it for herself. He didn't think she would—he knew he was damn lucky to have taken her this far without her retreat. But even so, if he came tonight, he wanted her to be fully aware she was making it happen. Otherwise, it seemed empty. And he just couldn't abide that—not with Stephanie.

When the threat of eruption had passed, he moved from between her legs to crawl up beside her on the quilt. Their eyes met, hers filled with the last embers from the flames. "Good?" he whispered.

She bit her lip, casting a coquettish smile. He'd never seen such a sexy look on her face. "Amazing."

He returned a soft grin, leaning in for a slow kiss.

"Thank you."

He spoke deeply. "My pleasure."

"No," she said. "The pleasure was definitely mine."

"A different kind of pleasure on my end, *beb*. The pleasure of tastin' you, hearin' you, watchin' you."

She flushed slightly, her cheeks going pink in the pale

light. "I'm just so glad . . ." She blinked prettily and met his gaze. "Glad I didn't . . . do what I usually do. Glad I didn't make you stop."

"Mmm—me too."

She looked around the room, seeming to take it all in. "I feel a world away from New Orleans," she said, and he knew what she meant. When he was here, it seemed as if no other place existed. It was just him and the water and the cypress trees.

"This bed is extraordinary," she said, looking up above them at the thick headboard of dark pine.

He barely noticed it anymore, but her words reminded him that when he'd first started coming back out here a couple of years ago, it had struck him the same way, as if he'd never even seen it before. "When I was a kid, my dad and me made it for my *mamère*."

"Your *mamère*," she repeated slowly, trying out the word.

He delivered a soft smile. "My grandma."

She sat up, turning to study the wood. His dad had gotten the heavy pine in trade for repairing somebody's car in Houma, where they'd lived at the time. *You gonna help me make your* mamère *a pretty bed for her birthday, boy. Gonna make her somethin' nice*, he'd said, slapping his hand flat on the wood. He'd been pleased his father wanted his help, and together they'd spent hours, his dad teaching him the right way to hammer a nail and operate a jigsaw.

"I can't believe you made this, Jake." She ran her hand over the hand-carved design in the center of the headboard.

He laughed. "Not me alone, *chère*. Like I said, my dad and me. Mostly him."

She looked him in the eye. "Tell me about this place. Where are we?"

"My *mamère* lived here all her life—the place was built by her *père*." He stopped to laugh at his tendency to think everyone understood him. "Her father," he translated. He paused to look around the room then, same as Stephanie had been doing, wistfully recalling all the ways this little house had become such a large part of his life. "My dad left my mother and me when I was twelve, so we came to live here with *Mamère*."

He appreciated the sadness that filled her expression. "Where . . . did he go?"

"Don't know. You've heard the old story—went out for cigarettes one day and never came back? That's exactly how it was. Haven't seen him since. Over twenty years ago."

"I'm sorry."

He bent to lower a soft kiss to her smooth stomach, summoning an acceptant smile for her. "Not your fault, *beb*."

"Where's your mom now?"

"She lives in a little shotgun house in the Ninth Ward. Cuts and sets old ladies' hair in her kitchen and drinks too much. I used to try to take care of her, but . . ."

"But what?"

He shook his head and wondered when the hell he'd decided to open up to Stephanie Grant. "It's . . . not easy. She tells me she's gonna quit drinkin', then I go over and find her drunk 'cause some old guy she was datin' did her wrong. I get where I can't handle it." He'd been in the can't-handle-it mode for the last two years, only going over when his hair got so long it started bothering him or when she got on a kick to call him day and night because she wanted to make him a pot roast and act like the two of them were a normal family, when they were anything but. "All I know is there's nothin' I can do to make it better," he added without quite meaning to.

Merde. What was he doing spilling his guts to this woman? Usually, he was real good at keeping his troubles to himself—something Tony claimed was "part of your problem, man, part of why you can't move on." But he liked keeping things to himself just fine, and decided to go back to doing that, starting now.

Time to turn the focus back to what he wanted from Stephanie, and what he knew Stephanie wanted from him. That was easier. Well, in a way—if only she didn't make him feel so damn much.

But it felt too good to push that part away right now.

He dropped his gaze to her body, enjoying the simple fact that there was a naked woman lying beside him in bed. He bent to nibble at the taut peak of one breast. "Enough about this old place," he murmured, blowing coolly on her nipple and watching her bite her lip at the sensation.

She rolled to her side, her breasts swaying with the movement. "But I *like* this place. I . . . *feel* you here."

"Even so," he said with a grin, "I'd rather get back to feelin' *you* here." He ran one hand over her bare hip, letting it rest in the valley of her waist. Then he leaned close until they were chest to chest, her beaded nipples raking teasingly at his flesh.

He rolled to his back, taking her with him, so that she lay atop him, the crux of her thighs nestling his erection through his worn jeans. Anchoring one arm around her and lifting his other hand to her cheek, he reached up for a kiss—and instinct made him slide his hand from her back to her ass, pressing slightly, bringing her closer against him. A soft moan escaped her, washing over him in a wave of warmth. "Want me to make you come again?" he whispered.

She replied just as low. "No."

"No?"

"*I* want to make *you* come now."

He blinked his surprise, taken aback. But then he remembered—she was the least predictable woman he'd ever met, constantly catching him off guard. This one topped the heap of things he hadn't expected from her, but the deep pleasure of anticipation settled into his bones as he lay back and smiled. "Won't take much, *beb.*"

Stephanie's heart beat a mile a minute as she raised off him to kneel at his side. Her body still reeled from orgasm—hell, she was reeling from *everything,* the whole night. And now, here she was, hovering over him, wanting to do things she'd never wanted to do before.

Somehow, when she'd least expected it, things had turned easy with him.

No, not easy. Scary as hell, in fact. But her want truly overrode her fear tonight, and the pleasure he'd brought her was beyond anything she'd ever experienced. Now she wanted to please him, too.

The truth was, though, she barely knew how. She was more accustomed to being a recipient than a giver of sexual favors. But she was going to follow her instincts. She bit her lip, staring down at the thick bulge in his jeans.

She felt him watching her, studying her every expression and move. It should have increased her worry, made her feel she'd been placed in a spotlight—that's how it usually was with her and sex, when she deigned to have it. But with Jake, his penetrating gaze only made her want to please him that much more, made her want to be some sort of sexual vixen for him.

"Don't be afraid, *chère*."

She took the words to heart. *Don't be afraid, Stephanie. Not now. Just follow your instincts.* And tonight, she realized happily, there was no selling it, no asking herself to be something she wasn't, no masquerade of any kind. Tonight, it was real—she was a woman who wanted to be with this man, in every way.

Reaching down, she undid the top button on his Levi's, hissing in her breath as she drew the zipper down to reveal white cotton straining from what lay within.

She touched him through his underwear, let her fingers close gingerly around the large columnar shape. Big. He was big. She gasped softly and prayed he hadn't heard since he was watching her hand now, his eyes gone glassy, his breath heavy.

She was probably the only woman on the face of the planet who took a man's pants off hoping he was small, but the realization made her understand: Jake was so right about what scared her, that the night she'd heard her parents arguing made her fear pain. And Jake was probably bigger than any man she'd been with.

That's okay. Because you aren't going to have sex. He said so. Just fooling around. That's all you're going to do.

And like before, it was that affirmation that allowed her to push every ounce of trepidation aside and relish him.

Glancing from his erection to his face, she said, "Lift," and he did, allowing her to lower his jeans. Underneath, he wore snug boxer briefs that barely contained him, his stiffness stretching the top edge of the underwear. Next, she reached for the elastic and he rose up, helping her push them down. Her womb contracted with need at the sight of him.

She didn't bother taking his jeans and underwear the rest of the way off—just reached down and ran the flat of her palm up his length, letting his gasp of pleasure fill her. She slowly began to stroke him, thinking how amazing the male anatomy was. But wait, no, not every male. *This* male's anatomy was amazing, moving her in ways she'd never expected to be moved. How could he feel like satin and steel at the same time?

She lowered her mouth, kissing his tip.

His groan traveled the length of her body and made her want to give him more, so much more—so she followed the unfamiliar urge to sink her mouth onto him.

She moved slowly, feeling her way, sensing his pleasure. His hand wove through her hair, holding it back from her face. He murmured deeply in French and she savored knowing he watched her.

She was not a virgin at this, but it was the first time in her life she'd ever *wanted* to do it, ever felt the urge to give a man that gift without any prodding on his part. She hoped he could sense what it meant to her, how freely she gave, and as their gazes met, she believed he could. "Mmm, *ça c'est bon, beb. Oui.*"

She wanted to take him where *he'd* taken *her,* to utter ecstasy—and within a few moments, his labored breath had turned to moans, until he uttered, "Now."

She rose off him, wishing he were inside her, wanting to feel him there—but before she could even weigh those thoughts, his rough groan permeated the air and his warmth splashed across her stomach.

She gasped, looking down, and he reached for her, kissing her wildly, his tongue plundering her mouth as he pulled her tight against him. *"Mon Dieu,"* he whispered breathlessly between kisses. "Mmm, *merci, chère. Merci.*"

A moment later, they lay unmoving, her body still plastered to his, when he kissed her forehead and offered a soft, sexy grin that nearly turned her inside out.

She smiled back. "You speak French a lot more when you're excited."

He arched a devilish brow. *"Oui."*

She chuckled, drinking in the mannish scent of him, and of sex that hadn't quite happened. And yet, even without the act of sex, she felt so close to him. He rolled them so they lay face-to-face on their sides, bodies still crushed together. She bit her lip and met his gaze. "What I did just now . . . I don't usually do that."

He tilted his head against the pillow, those chocolate eyes seeming to bore into her soul. "That makes me a very lucky man, no?"

She smiled. "Yes."

His grin faded, their faces still close, his embrace loosening only slightly. "Why'd you do it, *chère?*"

"Because I wanted to. I just . . . wanted to. I can't explain it," she said, then laughed, thinking how many times she'd said that to him in their short acquaintance. "I can't seem to explain *much* when it comes to me and sex, but . . . I wanted to make *you* feel as good as you'd made *me* feel. I wanted to be . . . as intimate with you as I could."

His next smile came more warm than playful. "You succeeded. And some guys would say that's better than sex anyway."

"Some guys," she repeated. "What about you?"

"Don't get me wrong, what you just gave me was . . . *incredible.*" He flashed a quick grin. "And I'll be happy to oblige anytime you feel that urge. But," he said, grin fading, "for me, nothin's quite the same as bein' inside a woman, as sharin' that ultimate connection. Know what I mean?"

Despite how meaningless that connection had seemed for most of her adult life thus far, she did know what he meant and she wanted that with him so, so badly. "I wish I were braver," she said softly, almost hoping the fan would suck the words out of the air, even as she spoke them. She didn't like admitting her weaknesses.

He pulled back slightly to look at her. "You're about the bravest woman I ever met, Stephanie Grant."

She flinched. "Me?"

He quirked a light smile. "I don't know any other woman who comes runnin' down to a strange city, ready to move hell and earth and high-priced prostitutes to get what she wants."

She swallowed and gave her head a short shake. "That's not bravery, Jake. That's . . . having no other choice."

"No, *chère*. That *is* bravery. I promise."

She lowered her gaze. "Well, then, I wish I were braver about sex."

"You're doin' just fine, *beb*." He winked. "Do you see either one of us lyin' here frustrated?"

"Well, not anymore, but up to now . . ."

"You act like somewhere along the way you became obligated to sleep with me."

"No, not obligated. But I *wanted* to. I *really, really* wanted to. From the first moment I saw you on the other side of the bar, I wanted to be with you. And when you came into that red room and things started up between us, and you were kissing me and touching me . . . God, Jake, it nearly killed me to say no."

"Really?"

She spoke with sureness. "You knew. You *had* to know."

"Okay, I knew in the red room. But I didn't know at the bar."

He kissed her then, warm and sweet, and she feared she'd been too honest, but she didn't care anymore—so far, tonight, honesty had taken them to some wonderful places. "From the first time I looked into your eyes," she admitted.

And he was kissing her again, deeper now—nothing sweet or casual, all heat, his tongue moving against hers, making love to her mouth as his thigh slid between her legs.

As they shifted in the bed, she felt the wetness not quite dried on her stomach and said, "Did we make a mess on your grandma's quilt?"

He laughed softly as he rubbed his thigh against her. "I told you, we're doomed to have a wet spot. But fortunately for us, *Mamère* wasn't real picky about that sorta thing."

"About you having sex on her quilt?" she said, giggling.

He grinned. "No. About things bein' kept perfectly tidy. She thought things should be used for what they were made for, and if they wore out or got messed up, it meant they were servin' their purpose."

"Just the same," she said, "I'd feel better if we pushed the quilt down. It seems . . . kind of sacred or something, especially if she made it."

"She did," he said, sounding a little more reverent, and together they lifted and shoved until the quilt lay scrunched at their feet and only soft white sheets spread beneath them. "Speakin' of grandmothers, how was the pie?"

She grinned up at him, remembering. "Good. A hint more cinnamon and it would have rivaled Grandma's. Definitely the best I've had since hers."

He cuddled against her. "I hope it maybe made you feel . . . a little like she was still around or somethin'. Like I feel when I come out here."

Her heart warmed as she reflected. "Yeah, for a few minutes, I guess maybe it did." Then she reached up to touch his chest. "Thank you for that."

He just shook his head. "Nothin' big, *chère*." But she wasn't so sure she agreed.

"Tina crocheted," she said unthinkingly, just wanting to tell him.

"Hmm?"

"She crocheted. Winter scarves. I couldn't believe it—she's not normally the crafty type—so when she showed me this beautiful scarf she'd made, I was stunned. She gave it to my mom, but now I kind of want to get hold of it and pack it away, keep it pristine and perfect, you know."

"*Mamère* wouldn't have approved of that—and I don't know your sister, but I bet it'd mean more to her if the scarf kept your mom warm come wintertime."

Stephanie swallowed, soberly remembering just what had brought her to Louisiana. Her lost sister. "Tell me the truth about something, Jake. Do you think we'll find her?"

He nodded softly, surely. "We'll find her, *beb*. We'll find her. I promise."

Chapter 14

A few minutes later, Stephanie stood in the tiny bathroom and peered at herself in the mirror, unable to believe she was in a house on some dark bayou, in bed with a man she'd just met, while her sister was missing. And she couldn't recall the last time she'd felt so safe.

When she exited to the bedroom, she found Jake sitting up, still wonderfully naked, a sheet pulled to his waist.

"Not going shy on me, are you, Mr. Broussard?" she asked with a smile.

He arched one eyebrow. "You're not serious?"

She laughed. "No."

"Good, 'cause you'd be sorely disappointed. I don't do shy." With that, he whipped back the sheet and drew her onto the bed until she found herself straddling his lap. She pulled in her breath and glanced down to find him erect again, pressing against her center. Jake was looking, too. "Neither does he."

It was her turn to raise an eyebrow. "He?"

"The little guy down there."

She tilted her head. "I . . . wouldn't call him little."

He slid against her in a smooth and utterly arousing stroke as the corners of his mouth quirked into a smile. "That makes him like you even better."

She couldn't help rubbing back, all amusement fading as passion returned full force.

"That feels so damn good, *beb.*" His voice was a low growl.

She let out a breathless sigh. "For me, too."

"Playin' with fire, though. You gotta know that."

She nodded, unable to think clearly. "Kiss me," she said, and he braced one hand behind her neck, pulling her closer, delivering a series of hot, short, sexy kisses that nearly buried her.

He gazed down at her breasts before bending to capture one in his mouth. She locked her hands behind his neck and leaned back to offer him better access, unable not to press against the column that stood so powerful between them. Instinct led her into soft, rolling gyrations.

"Guess you're not afraid of fire, huh, *chère?*" he asked, breath labored.

"Not at the moment," she managed, unable to believe how badly she wanted him inside her, how much she yearned for that ultimate connection. Although she'd thought she'd grasped it completely before, she suddenly gained a deeper understanding of what he'd just said a few minutes ago—there was nothing like actually doing it, actually bringing your bodies together that way. She'd never felt that before with a man, but she felt it now.

Their kisses turned rougher, more needful. His hands roamed her—breasts, back, rear, before his fingers slid down over her bottom, into her wetness, making her move against him harder.

She found herself rising—without thought or decision—until she was poised atop his erection, teetering on the edge of heaven, and ready, so very ready. Fear be damned.

"Ah, *beb*," he breathed, his dark eyes filled with longing. "Does this mean you want me inside you?" His hands rhythmically kneaded her backside.

She nodded, lost in desire. "Yes." Then she bit her lip. "Do you have a condom?"

"*Merde*," he muttered, leaning his head back in frustration. "I can't believe this, but I don't."

She gasped. "I can't believe it, either." She was so close to sinking down on him, taking him into her, and her words came out sounding breathless. "No offense, but you seem like a guy who'd have reason to carry a condom with you at all times."

He managed a grin, even through ragged breath and what she thought incredible restraint. "I do, at least lately. But when I went home, I changed into old jeans for comin' out here in the pirogue, and forgot my wallet in my other pocket."

She sucked in her breath. Her breasts ached and the crux of her thighs yearned to be filled. "That's . . . horrible." Especially given that she didn't know if she could stop now. She *needed* him inside her.

"If it helps, I've only been with one woman without usin' one—and I was her first, her only—so . . ."

"I'm on the pill," she said, "and always careful about condoms."

She saw him swallow, his eyes glazed over with how close they were to doing it. "It's your call, *beb*."

She placed her hands on his shoulders, curling the tips of her fingernails into his skin, peering at him intently. "How badly do you want this?"

Trembling, he appeared barely able to speak. "I'm about to self-destruct."

She drew in a quivery breath. "Me too."

Only one answer existed—nothing left to do but surrender.

She sank down.

That hungry part of her began taking him in, slow, deep—and he was so sweet, staying so very still for her, the heat in his gaze branding her heart. From the old stereo across the room, Solomon Burke wrenched out the soulful "Cry to Me," and the jolting rhythm prompted her motions. The song was an old favorite of her mother's, but as she made love to Jake to the searing notes, they moved her in a way they never had before. The music drove her to arch against him, lean her head back so he could kiss her neck.

"Hurt?" he whispered between little nips at her throat.

Their eyes met. It *should* hurt. He was so big. But it didn't. She simply shook her head. He let out a low growl of satisfaction, accompanied with a sexy smile as he met her next thrust.

"Mmm," she purred, their hips meeting in perfect unison to the beat of the song.

He pushed into her in long, smooth strokes, his hands in her hair, hers wrapped around his neck. "Ahhh, *oui, beb.*"

Their movements stayed slow, intense—and except for the moments when passion drove one of them to let their eyes fall shut, they gazed at each other the whole time, so that when she moaned, she was looking into those warm brown eyes. When she cried out from the overwhelming pleasure, she was looking into those warm brown eyes. And when the heat began to rise inside her, as her breath went thready while she bucked softly against him, she was still looking into those beautiful warm brown eyes.

The spasms of release racked her body, drove her harder against him, made her moan, and moan, and moan with each amazing pulsation. She was still coming, their gazes still connected, when he rasped, "*Mon Dieu,* me too."

He emptied himself in her with a powerful groan, wrapping corded arms around her as they both panted their exhaustion.

"Sorry," he whispered in her ear when it was done.

She drew back slightly. "For what?"

"Long as it took us to get there, I shoulda made it last a little longer."

She was dumbfounded, letting a satisfied smile take her as she said, "Jake, that was the best sex of my life."

Their faces still close, the corners of his mouth turned up into a smile. "Then this is your lucky day, *chère.* 'Cause there's plenty more where that came from."

He lay next to her, the sheet pulled to their waists, his head propped up by one elbow. "I'm glad it didn't hurt." She was sure she'd never seen him look sexier than he did just now, naked in bed, eyes half shut, chin covered with a day's dark stubble.

She gazed up at him, listening to the night sounds. The records had all dropped and played, and the only remaining music came from the bayou. "Me too."

"Has it hurt . . . other times? I mean, since the college guy?"

"A little, I guess," she said, swallowing. "But . . . . you're bigger than the guys it hurt with, so I don't know . . ."

"You explained this yourself before, *chère.* It's 'cause

you weren't hot for them—your body wasn't ready. To-night, it was."

"Was it ever," she said on a heady sigh.

As he shifted, she noticed the tattoo on his arm. Inked in muted black and gray, the size of a fist, it looked too complex for her to easily make out the picture. She reached up to touch it. "What's your tattoo?"

"St. Michael, the archangel."

She looked closer to see a winged angel brandishing a sword and stepping on the head of some kind of demon.

"The patron saint of police officers," he explained. "He's castin' Satan into hell. It's a good-triumphin'-over-evil thing. We pray to St. Michael to protect us."

We, he'd said. As if he were still a cop.

"Does it work?" she asked.

He rolled to his back, put his hands behind his head, and peered up at the brown slatted ceiling. "Tricky question, *chère.* Depends on what you consider protection."

She turned onto her side to look down on him. "Were you ever wounded?"

He shook his head. "Guess Michael took care of my body okay. My mind, my heart, not so much."

The sexy, seductive Jake from earlier seemed to have faded slightly, making room for the other side of him she'd seen sizable, even if inexplicable, hints of. Some-thing had hurt him—badly. She could almost feel the pain oozing from him like perspiration in the warm night air.

"Tell me why," she said. "Why aren't you a cop any-more?"

He gave her a long, somber look she couldn't read. Her heart hurt for whatever secrets he held inside. "Lost too much to keep doin' it," he finally said.

"What'd you lose?"

He shook his head and looked back to the slow turn of the ceiling fan above. "Stuff I don't wanna talk about."

She swallowed, trying to decide how much to pry. She didn't want to ruin what they'd shared tonight. She didn't want to dampen the sense of security she felt lying in his arms. "Remember, earlier, when I told you about my parents?" Her stomach pinched a little at the thought, but she pushed away the emotion and stuck to the facts. "I didn't want to think about it—but you kind of . . . made me. And that turned out to be a good thing, in a way. Don't you think?"

He shifted his brown gaze to her. "It got to the bottom of a problem you were havin', *chère.* I got no problems that can be fixed by thinkin' about unpleasant things."

She drew in her breath, wondering what had hurt him so much that he'd give up his career. A man who had the patron saint of police tattooed on his arm clearly cared about his job, considered it his *life.* It made the fact that he'd given up that part of himself in order to make a living serving drinks to hookers more monumental than she'd ever realized before. *What did you lose that was so dear, Jake?*

The question burned in her heart—she longed to ask it. She'd been right when she'd suspected that following him tonight would open up his world to her, and now that they'd made love, she wanted to know every thought in his head, every secret in his soul.

God, *that* was sobering. And bad—really bad.

Because this was sex—*casual* sex. That's what it was supposed to be anyway. All the more reason not to pry any deeper into what he held back, no matter how much she wanted to know. The greatest sex of her life aside, this would be a bad guy for her to get attached to—a guy who lived a thousand miles away from her, a guy who had troubles that probably ran deeper and blacker than the bayou outside. A guy who came from an entirely different world. Yes, this was sex and nothing more. And despite his patience and tenderness tonight, she had no illusions that he felt any different, and she knew he'd be glad she had the sense to take it for what it was.

"Besides," he finally said, flicking a glance her way, "I've got better things to think about right now." He rolled back onto his side and slid one hand beneath the white sheet to her hip. "Like this pretty body of yours."

The blatant sexuality flashing in his gaze made her summon a teasing smile. "I hope you're going to do more than just think about it."

He quirked a sexy grin. "And what exactly is it you want me to do?"

"Surprise me."

With that, he pulled her to him, chest to chest, thigh to thigh, hip to hip. A hot column of rock pressed against her abdomen. "Is *that* a surprise?"

"That's a very *good* surprise." Even better than earlier, now that she knew she could handle what he had to give. Peering into his eyes, she bit her lip and impulsively slid her arms around him, planting them on his firm butt.

"Mmm," he growled, doing the same. At which point he got a peculiar look on his face and said, "*You* don't have any tattoos I haven't noticed, do you?"

She pulled back slightly to laugh. "Me? No. I'm not really a tattoo sort of girl."

He chuckled at her reply, then pulled away and rolled her onto her stomach. Hand still on her bottom, he seemed to be inspecting it.

"What are you looking for?" She smiled over her shoulder.

"Nothin'," he said, shaking his head lightly. "Just checkin'."

"Checking what?"

He raised a grin to her. "Just seein' if your ass looks as good as it did in those blue jeans."

"And the verdict is?"

"Guilty as charged, *beb*."

A white room is filled with stiff, colored netting, like on a bridal veil or a ballerina's tutu. Pink, lavender, blue the color of the sky. Yards of it stretch back and forth across the space—and on the other side of it all, you see her.

Only her face is clouded by the netting, and the colors cast thick shadows. The one thing you can make out clearly is the vibrant tulip she holds, the shade of an amethyst—she stretches out her arm, offering it to you.

You push your way through the curtains of sheer fabric, hacking through it with outstretched arms like machetes helping you fight your way through a pastel jungle.

She beckons with one long, tapered finger that curls toward her, silently saying, Come here. *But it seems no matter how many layers of netting you push past, more grow in your path and you never get closer.*

Your heart beats like a freight train and you're determined to reach her, so hungry for what she has to give you. Not the tulip—everything else. You hope she sees how hard you're working, trying to carve your way to her. You hope she knows how desperately you want her.

Finally, only one last layer of blue net stretches taut between you. Through it, you see her lovely flesh, pale curves, welcoming smile. The tulip is gone—her arms are spread open, waiting for you.

You gather the netting in your fists, tighter and tighter, but then . . . the bunched swath of blue is covering your eyes. Just when you could almost see her without any barriers, your vision is fogged again by a blue blindfold.

Her small hands come firm on your arms, pushing you backward, and you wait to hit the floor, but instead you land on a bed, and you feel her climbing, crawling to straddle you, thighs stretched across your stomach. You still see her only in shadow as she pushes your arms over your head, holding you down, taking control.

You don't fight, though, because why would you? You want her to do everything she's doing—you want her to run her fingernails lightly down your chest, to lower her breasts to your mouth, to sheathe your hardness with her softness, connecting you to her warm and tight.

You want her to moan and writhe on top of you. You want her to kiss you hard and whisper your name in jagged breaths.

You want her to scream her pleasure. You want her to buck against you and make you feel every ounce of her joy. And you want to let it all push you over the edge until you come inside her, emptying all your desire into her accepting body.

When it's over, you want to hold her, feel her snuggled against you.

Only when the netting leaves your eyes and you strain to focus on the woman nestled at your chest, you still can't see her clearly, and despite the warm connection, you feel strangely alone.

Chapter 15

The warm night wind whipped through Tina's hair as Robert's vintage 1957 Thunderbird zipped along I-10. As they traveled the causeway across Lake Pontchartrain, the moon cast a silver glow on the water. She hummed along with the Tubes to "She's a Beauty" and clutched tight to Robert's arm while he drove.

The whole night had been beyond dreamy. They'd just shared a fabulous dinner at a ritzy plantation house out in the country and she'd felt like a princess. She wore an elegant dress he'd picked out for her, and earlier tonight he'd added a diamond tennis bracelet to the diamond necklace and earrings he'd already given her.

Now he sang along with the radio, too, occasionally turning for a quick kiss before refocusing on the road.

It was getting better, kissing him, having sex with him. Maybe not as good as with Russ, but that would come over time. And moments like this—just being with him, laughing, having fun—wasn't that what a relationship was *really* all about?

"I love you," she said, curling her free hand over his Armani-clad thigh.

"Mmm, I love you, too, darling."

A familiar thought edged into her mind: wouldn't Stephanie be surprised to see what a class act she'd become? The musing, though, made her a little sad. Despite herself, she missed Steph. She was tempted to call her when she got home, just to tell her—tell *someone*—what a fairy-tale evening she'd had.

But no, you can't. Not yet. Not until Robert was free of Melissa. It sounded much better to say you were dating a man who was in the process of a divorce than one who was still living with his wife. It would be a mistake to call Stephanie while it was any less than perfect, while there was still any ammunition her sister could fling at her. She loved Steph, but her approval was hard to come by.

"Can you spend the night?" she asked.

He cast her a you-know-better look. "You know I can't, love."

Yes, she knew, but for some reason it still stung, taking a little of the "perfect" out of the evening. "I can't wait until it's not like this anymore, until you can sleep beside me each night."

She hadn't always minded his leaving so much, but now she found herself getting lonely, and depending more and more on Robert for her happiness. As for the *I-love-you*, the words fell from her lips easier lately as well. The more time she spent with him, the more *real* it seemed that this man's life was becoming *her* life, that he wanted her to share in it. So maybe it wasn't as good as with Russ in terms of pure romance, but there was something about Robert, something so established and sophisticated—she wanted to belong in his world, and she wanted to be the sort of wife he could be proud of.

"Couldn't you make up some excuse, some business problem that ran all night long?"

Next to her, he laughed. "Not if I want her to believe me."

Does it really matter if she believes you? The question weighed on her instantly, making her wonder why he even cared about Melissa's reaction if the marriage was over. But she didn't want to ruin the night. She sighed. "When are you leaving her?"

"Soon, love. Soon."

"And then I can manage the boutique?"

"Of course."

"I'm going to do such a good job, you're going to wonder how the place ever got by without me."

He flashed a debonair smile. "I already do, darling."

The reassurance shot straight to her heart. Soon everything would be perfect. "I love you," she breathed again. Saying it helped make it more true.

"Why don't you show me how much," he suggested, reaching down to cover her hand with his. He moved it higher up his thigh, between his legs.

"When we get back to the apartment," she cooed.

"No, love. Now."

The light air of demand in his voice caught her off guard, and her stomach tightened. She spoke soft and sexy in his ear. "I'd rather wait. It won't be long. And it'll give you something to look forward to."

He only chuckled. "There'll still be plenty to look forward to. We can just call this an appetizer." He pressed her palm harder into him—without her realizing it, her touch had frozen in place. Lifting both hands to the wheel, he leaned back against the headrest, and said, "Unzip me."

She didn't want to. She wasn't sure why . . . except that maybe this seemed like something you paid a whore to do, not something you insisted on with the woman you loved if she wasn't into it.

His eyes shifted from the road to her, his smile persuasive. "Do I ask so much, darling?"

No, he didn't. That she couldn't deny.

And why was she making such a big deal of this anyway?

He gave her *everything*—and asked for very little in return. Just her love. And her sex. She'd been working hard to meld the two together the past few days—that made it all real, made everything all right.

She swallowed. This would be okay. It didn't mean he still thought of her like a prostitute.

"What are you waiting for?"

"Nothing," she whispered, then unzipped his pants. And told herself this made the night no less dreamy. Everything would still be perfect in the end.

The next morning, Jake rowed his pirogue up the bayou, Stephanie seated across from him. Hers had sunk during the night.

He loved the bayou in the early morning. Before the heat of the day pervaded, the sights and sounds around the water made him feel like the world was fresh, being born all over again. Lily pads sporting white blooms sprinkled the water to one side of the boat; duckweed, rimmed by elephant ears at the shoreline, floated on the other. A snowy egret soared past near the bank and drew Jake's attention to a caiman stretched out in the mud by the shore.

"Little *cocodrie*," he said, pointing, for Stephanie's benefit.

She tensed slightly, and he chuckled.

"No worries, *chère*. No leaks in my boat."

She cast a sheepish smile, tilting her head. "I thought Louisiana had alligators, not crocodiles."

He nodded. "But my ancestors didn't know the difference, started callin' 'em *cocodries* and it stuck."

"Mmm," she said, seeming to relax, turning to study the small, dark caiman where it rested still as a statue. Never scared for long, his Miss Chardonnay.

They'd had sex twice more before falling asleep last night—the same slow, sensual sex as the first time, but with each liaison she'd grown a little more daring, planting her hands on his ass to pull him deeper inside her, once wrapping her legs around his back. Common fare for most people, but not for Stephanie—he knew without her saying so. He felt like she'd been a closed-up little flower and last night he'd watched her begin to blossom, stretching her petals a little wider each time they connected.

And she had a lovely little bottom, but that wasn't really why he'd been checking it out last night. For some reason, even when she'd said no, he'd had to see for himself that she didn't have a flower tattooed there—like in one of the dreams.

One more sign you're losing your mind, once and for all. He gave his head a short shake with the realization that life had seemed a little off-kilter since the moment Stephanie Grant had arrived. Then again, life hadn't exactly been *on*-kilter before that, so maybe he was just imagining things.

The second time they'd made love had been after his little examination of her rear. The third time after he'd woken from the dream—in total shock.

Because why the hell was he still having erotic, needful dreams when he'd just gotten the satisfaction his body had clearly needed so damn bad? He'd been sure it was simple lust causing the dreams, that they'd been nothing more than wishes in the night, because he couldn't have her. But now he *could* have her, *had* had her, so the dream had left him feeling more disturbed than usual.

After dreaming of sex, it had seemed natural to reach for her. The room had been dark, the lamp extinguished, only a thin ribbon of moonglow lighting his way. And like the dream—God, how the need had struck him, like something new and overwhelming. He'd been glad they were both half asleep, glad her sighs of pleasure came with closed eyes, glad she couldn't see the emotion surely dripping from his face. He still didn't understand it and it was damn unsettling.

A blue dragonfly buzzed, flitting in between them in the boat before darting away, and the silence began to bother him. He was normally content to go hours without speaking, even if he was with someone, but he supposed this was just part of feeling uncertain about last night. "You're quiet," he said.

"Tired," she replied softly, offering a smile. "You wore me out."

His own grin escaped, unbidden. He liked the idea of having caused her exhaustion. They'd definitely had that hot, slow, all-night-long sex he'd been thinking about lately.

"Tell me about the house," she said.

He raised his eyes to her—she was pretty in the morning, even sans makeup and hairbrush, high pink color lighting her cheekbones. "Already told you about the house."

"No, about the work you're doing on it. The new floor

in the kitchen and the new sink. Are you going to move back out here or something?"

No, just run away to it whenever I can. "It's just a weekend place for me now," he said instead.

"And you're doing all the refurbishing yourself?"

He nodded. *Hard physical labor makes it so I think less and sleep better. It fills the days when I have nothing else to fill them.* "It's cheap that way."

She looked down at the boat they floated in and said, "How do you get the materials out there? Surely not in this?"

He laughed softly. "No, *beb.* There's a road leads up to the front of the house. But if I'm not haulin' anything, takin' the water cuts the trip by half."

"You love it there." Not a question, a statement.

"Yeah, it's . . ." *Safe. Private. Far away from the bad stuff.* "It's home."

She glanced down at her toes for a minute, then met his gaze. "I'm glad I followed you last night."

He let the corners of his mouth turn up just slightly. "Me too, *chère.*" *Much to my surprise.*

Up ahead, a clearing split the elderberry bushes and willows that hugged the shore. The landing came into view and Jake angled the boat toward it.

Five minutes later, he'd locked up the pirogue and was shutting her into her car. Her window lowered immediately and her blue eyes pierced him. "I wish I could ride back with you."

He didn't know what to say to that, so he stooped next to the sedan, rested his bent arms on the door, and gave her a warm—but short—kiss.

She tilted her head, offering a soft laugh. "That was a horrible thing to say. It sounded so high school."

"Not so horrible," he admitted. Even though he thought it was probably good for them to be parting ways now. Because no matter what he'd felt with her last night, it still didn't—*couldn't*—mean anything. Good sex. *Great* sex. That was all. "You'll need to follow me back, make sure you don't lose your way."

She nodded. "But can you slow down a little, Speed Racer? I had a hell of a time keeping up with you last night."

He laughed. "Sure, *beb.* I'll make sure I keep you in my rearview 'til we get back to town."

And then? She didn't ask, but the question hung in the air.

"I'll drop by to get Tina's pictures from you later, or tomorrow sometime."

She nodded. And he relaxed a little. He'd added the "or tomorrow" part so she'd understand he wouldn't be sharing a bed with her again tonight. He couldn't say he wouldn't be doing it again *sometime,* but he had no plans to let this become an every-night thing.

Even so, when she said, "Good-bye, Jake—and about last night, thank you for being so patient with me," impulse drove him to lean through the window for one more kiss, this one complete with tongues and her soft sigh, shooting heat straight to his groin.

"No, *chère,* thank *you.*"

They exchanged a quick last look that spoke of fresh desire and propelled him away from her and into his truck before he did anything stupid like open her door and drag her into the backseat. What they'd shared had been damn hot, but the guilt was beginning to set in now.

Starting the old truck, he reached down to shift gears, then circled around Stephanie's car and headed up the gravel road away from the bayou.

Being with another woman was one thing, but being with another woman and experiencing so much emotion, that sense of attachment—*that* felt like betrayal. Even if Becky wasn't around to feel betrayed anymore. As he braked at the end of the unpaved thoroughfare, it felt almost as if Becky sat next to him in the truck, knowing what he'd done—knowing how bad he'd wanted Stephanie, and how good it had all felt . . . in more than just a physical way.

That was it—he was losing it. Ghosts in the Quarter, that was one thing. But ghosts in the damn truck with him? He had to be out of his mind. Becky wasn't here. The sad, still-painful truth was . . . Becky wasn't anywhere.

But he had to move on, didn't he? Wasn't Tony always saying that? His mother too. "She'd want you to be happy," his mom always said—most recently over fried chicken at the tiny table in her little kitchen, the place still smelling of peroxide and perm solution.

"If she could have what she wanted," he'd replied, "she'd still be here with me." They would still live in the little house he'd been refurbishing, she'd still be teaching second grade at the little school nearby. Life would still be great.

Jake shook his head. Sometimes that life seemed a world away, like something he'd made up, or just dreamed. He'd never expected to find someone like Becky, someone who'd made him feel so good about himself, someone who'd had enough goodness for both of them—she'd made him a better man than he'd been before her.

Other days, he woke up still not quite believing it was all gone and that he'd sold the house and traded in the car and moved into a shithole because it didn't matter where he lived anymore.

Shake this off, man. Stephanie had made him feel so good last night—why couldn't he just be happy about that?

You have to try.

He wasn't sure where the words came from, but it was as if they'd been whispered in his ear. He knew they were true. He had to believe it was okay to have had astounding sex with Stephanie. Mostly, he had to believe it was okay to do it *again*—because even as anxious as he'd been to get in his truck and put that little bit of distance between them, he already wanted more.

He had to believe something else, too. He had to believe he could find Tina Grant. Because he *had* to now. He had to give Stephanie her sister back. He didn't think he could bear it if he let her down.

Just then, he remembered she was following him and glanced in his rearview mirror. Damn—he could barely make out her car a good distance behind. He stepped on the brake and berated himself. *You're thinking about the woman so much you forgot about her.*

Within thirty seconds she came speeding up behind him. He slowed to a crawl so that she came up even closer, then rolled down his window and hung his head out to yell, "Sorry, *beb.*"

"Good thing you're not still a cop," she yelled in reply, "or you'd have to give yourself a ticket."

He smiled at her in his mirror, saw her smile back. Felt it warm his heart. And the insides of his thighs. After which he pressed the gas pedal, because he was already starting to think it would be easy just to stop here, just pull off the quiet roadway and relieve that ache with her one last time before they headed back to the city.

But he already had enough guilt eating at him—he didn't need any more.

"Bye for now, *chère,*" he murmured in the mirror, then tried to concentrate on what else he could do to look for Tina as he headed back toward New Orleans.

Stephanie pushed through the door to her room feeling like a new woman. A satisfied woman. A woman who finally understood what the fuss over sex was all about.

She fell onto the bed, giggling like a teenager after her first kiss. Hugging a velvet bolster, she lay staring at the ceiling, reeling in the wonder of it all. Oh God, it had been so good! The memory made her let out a sexy little growl. And Jake had been so patient, so sweet—and so utterly *incredible.*

She wished she could tell Tina. Her sister popped to mind instantly—the only female Stephanie was close to who she knew, beyond a shadow of a doubt, would *get* this, and would think it was as wonderful as she did.

Where are you, Tina?

On impulse, she tossed the round pillow aside and reached for the bedside phone. She dialed her own number in Chicago, keying in the code to retrieve messages as she did every day, just in case her sister had left something on her answering machine. But still no Tina.

Dropping the phone back in its cradle, she went to her laptop. She doubted Tina would e-mail her—mainly because she doubted Tina was anyplace where she had computer access. Yet she longed to talk to her sister so badly right now that she couldn't help checking every possible method of contact.

Nothing in her e-mailbox looked promising, though,

and her stomach churned at the sight of all the new messages from Grable & Harding. *Yech.* Clenching her teeth in distaste, she opened the first to find one of her coworkers just needed a quick answer on something. She typed in a response and sent it off. The next message, however, wasn't as simple and would take some time. Nor was the next. Or the next.

The last message was from Curtis. She grimaced at seeing his name.

> S—
> *Bad news. Things are getting sticky with the phone co. campaign. Rod Hartman there is wondering where you are and seems shaky about dealing with anyone else. Can you call him and put his mind at ease?*
> *And while you're at it, can you call ME and put MY mind at ease, too? I really miss you, and feel awfully out of touch. Would like to hear your voice and know you're okay. Hate that I don't really know what you're doing down there, even as much as I respect your privacy. Will wait to hear from you.*
>
> C

Stephanie leaned back in the desk chair, sucked in a deep breath, and let it back out. Talk about a killjoy. What timing.

But the truth was, she'd been neglecting her job. She hadn't thought about Grable & Harding in a couple of days, in fact. That was so unlike her she could scarcely believe it—but somehow things that had seemed of dire importance a week ago had faded into the background for her now.

Time to settle down and put on her work cap. Although

she didn't look forward to phoning Rod Hartman—and first, she should call Curtis at the office. She didn't especially want to do that, either.

But she forced herself to pick up the phone and dial his direct line. This would be the hardest part of her day, so she might as well get it over with.

"Curtis Anderson." His all-business tone.

"It's Stephanie." Did she sound different? she wondered. Would he hear the same soft lilt in her voice, left over from sex, as she did?

His response was one of relief. "Stephanie, thank God. I was getting worried."

She glanced back at her computer screen to see his message had arrived yesterday morning. "Sorry," she said, attempting to swallow her guilt. "I was . . . busy with the Tina situation all day yesterday."

"Any chance you could fill me in on exactly what Tina's situation *is*?"

The question rubbed her the wrong way, his attitude implying her sister was a bother. And that was probably *her* fault, because before all this, she had likely painted Tina as immature and reckless, but that didn't soften the sting. She pulled in her breath and tried to speak calmly. "Look, the situation is just . . . that she followed a boyfriend down here and I want her to come home."

"And it's taken this long?" When she didn't answer right away, he kept talking. "Listen, Stephanie, I hate to be the bad guy, but your leave of absence isn't coming off well. People keep asking me what's wrong, and I don't have any answers. They end up thinking you're having personal problems, or health problems—God forbid. And yesterday Stan asked if I thought you were coming back *at all* or if this was your way of leaving the company."

That should have alarmed her. Should have had her packing her bags—now. At the very least, it should have her ready to call Stan Grable and convince him of her intense loyalty to Grable & Harding.

But instead, it only pissed her off. "This is the thanks I get for pouring my blood, sweat, and tears into this company for the past nine years? Why don't you ask Stan if he knows how many vacation days I've never used, or how many times I've dragged myself into the office sick because I thought I should be there. This is the one thing I've ever asked of Grable and Harding, and if they can't give it to me, they can just go to hell."

Curtis simply stayed silent, finally saying, "Are you done?"

"I suppose."

"Don't think I haven't been singing your praises and trying to convince people everything's fine, because I have. I've watched you come a long way in this company and I don't want you to lose it just because you feel the need to control your sister's life."

She gasped. He sounded just like Jake—in the beginning. A part of her wished she could tell Curtis the truth about Tina's disappearance and see if he thought she was just being a controlling older sister *then*. But it was none of his business. "There's more to it than you know," she said simply.

"I miss you."

I slept with another man last night and had the most mind-blowing sex of my life. "I . . . appreciate that." Under the circumstances, she couldn't return the sentiment.

"I see." Which meant he'd noticed.

She let out a long sigh, not knowing what to say. "I . . . should go."

"Are you going to smooth things over with Rod Hartman?"

"*Yes,*" she snapped. She shouldn't be so offended—she'd just admitted to herself that she'd been neglecting her work. Still, everything about this phone call had irked her.

"Stephanie," he said, his voice going softer.

"Yeah?"

Damn, a knock on the door. Probably Mrs. Lindman delivering fresh towels. She walked over, stretching the phone cord, as Curtis said, "I'm sorry if you're mad at me. Being apart is hard on our relationship." She opened the door as he said, "Tell me things are okay between us, will you?"

Jake stood on the other side.

She sucked in her breath, still holding the receiver to her ear. "Hi," she breathed, wondering how horrific her expression was. She suddenly felt like she'd been cheating on *both* of them, even though she didn't think it true in either case.

"What?" Curtis asked.

"Um, hold on." She covered the mouthpiece and looked up at Jake expectantly.

He lowered his chin. "Catch you at a bad time, *beb?*"

The worst. Curtis seems to think I really care for him and wants to hear me say it. "Not at all." She shook her head. "Just talking to work."

"I came for Tina's pictures. Turns out I'm meetin' Tony for lunch—thought it might be a good idea to have 'em in case anything new comes up."

"Oh. Of course." She looked around and found the evening bag she'd carried to the lounge last night still lying on her dresser. Setting down the phone, she snapped it open, drew the photos out, and returned to the door, wishing like hell she could pick the phone back up and cover the mouthpiece without it seeming weird. "Here. And thanks."

"I'll be in touch soon," he said, his brown eyes half shut and sexy as hell as he leaned in, curled one hand around her neck, and bent down for a searing hot tongue kiss.

As he turned to go, she stood there breathless, wondering if it was possible to hear a kiss over the phone. One like *that,* she thought, *maybe.*

She bit her lip as she picked up the receiver. "I'm back," she said, thinking she sounded ridiculously breathy. "Sorry," she tried to say louder, clearing her throat.

"What's happening there?"

"Just had someone at the door. Nothing important." *Except hot and heavy desire.*

"*Is* everything okay between us, Stephanie?"

She closed her eyes and wished the question away. It didn't go.

She'd have to tell him the truth, but not now, like this. When the hell had Curtis started thinking this was more than casual dating? "Everything's fine," she said. "But I'd better get to work. Talk soon. Bye."

Chapter 16

"So what the hell brought *this* on?"

Jake lowered his po'boy to the plate and looked across the table at Tony. "Huh?"

"Lunch," Tony clarified.

"I gotta eat, no?" He picked the sandwich back up and took a bite.

Tony only laughed, and Jake understood why, but he feigned ignorance since he didn't have an explanation. He and Tony ate lunch together at least once every couple of weeks, but always at his friend's insistence, and he usually made Tony pick something up to bring to his place so he wouldn't have to go out. Today, he'd called Tony's cell and left a message to meet him at a greasy spoon near the French Market.

"Well, whatever the case, it's good to see you getting out a little. Although you could've put on some clean clothes." He gave Jake a critical once-over.

"Slept out at the bayou house. Didn't get around to changin' when I got back." He purposely left out the part about being up most of the night making a beautiful woman whimper and moan. That was getting difficult enough to accept as the hours passed anyway.

But he'd decided he knew why he'd had the dream again—and the reason was equally as disturbing as the sex. As much as he'd wanted Stephanie, as much as he'd even let himself have her, he knew in his heart that he hadn't truly *let himself go* with her, the way he would have if he'd met her seven or eight years ago. He hadn't let go of the stuff inside him. He thought maybe the dream was telling him he *should* let go of the guilt pummeling him; maybe it was telling him it was all okay.

Jake Broussard, dream analyst. He rolled his eyes, glad Tony had been late and was now distracted with the menu—he hadn't noticed Jake looking downcast. Not that Tony wasn't used to seeing him downcast, but anytime he could escape a lecture, it was welcome.

And it wasn't anything Tony could help him with anyway. He felt torn inside—ripped down the middle. He wasn't even close to being ready to care for another woman, and where all that tenderness had come from, he hadn't a clue. He hadn't known there was anything like that left in him after Becky. And he couldn't help it, he felt like he'd forsaken her. He'd never expected to share anything like that with a woman ever again—and he couldn't help thinking he *shouldn't* have.

After Tony placed his order and shoved a laminated menu back behind the napkin holder, he said, "Anything happening at Sophia's?"

Jake shook his head. "I've been off the last few nights, but nothin' unusual comin' down lately."

Jake would have worked harder to get to the bottom of the drugs-at-Sophia's theory if he'd still been a cop. Or if he thought bringing down a couple of midlevel pushers would really make a difference in anyone's life—because he felt *that* was the best they'd ever do; they'd never get to Typhoeus.

As it was, he only kept his eyes open at Chez Sophia for Tony's sake, out of friendship. And anytime old instincts kicked back in and made him feel like a cop on the prowl, hungry to bring somebody down, he reminded himself that in the big picture it didn't matter, and it didn't pay to care.

"Do me a favor," Tony said, then asked him to keep an ear to the ground on a couple of third-floor regulars, explaining they'd ended up on his radar because "they have more money than they should," even though one had a high-paying job and the other ran a successful car dealership. "It has to be coming in from somewhere else."

"I'll see what I can do," Jake said, "but I need you to return the favor."

Tony raised his eyebrows until Jake whipped out a color copy he'd made of Tina's photos, side by side, and underneath he'd written down her vital information. "I need you to keep lookin' for this girl."

Tony gave a nod. "Having the pictures will help."

"Also got another sightin' of her at the Crescent's lounge. Some girls there IDed her from the photos. Seems she has a friend named Raven—but neither's been around for a while."

"Friend a hooker, too?"

Jake nodded. "Seems so."

The corners of Tony's mouth edged slightly upward. "You going to tell me why finding this girl is so important to you?"

"Told you the other night. Her sister's worried, couldn't

get any assistance through conventional routes, and I'm just tryin' to help."

Tony's expression spread into a cautious, accusatory smile. "And you still want to claim there's nothing romantic going on between you and this pretty Stephanie?"

"Yep." Short. Simple. And true.

Because it *had* to be true. Nothing else made sense for him—at least not yet. And as for what he felt when he was with her . . . he couldn't decipher that, but he couldn't deal with the reality of it, either, so he was just going to push it aside. God knew he had experience at pushing down his emotions. This should be simple. And it should start right now. From this moment on, screw the dreams and whatever they might mean—from this moment on, she was a pretty woman and he was a hungry guy, and that was all there was to their attraction. Hot sex. Nothing else.

Even if his blood was itching with wanting to see her again, even now.

Rain raked in sheets across the empty courtyard and Shondra hugged Scruff tight, despite the smell of his wet fur, which was really no worse than the wet mattress she sat on. Her jeans were soaked. Her hair too. No matter how hard she leaned into the old concrete foundation, she and Scruff still got wet.

The dog whimpered, so she scratched behind his ears. "I know it blows, but this is the best we got tonight."

That's when she remembered the po'boy. She hadn't gone to the Café Du Monde for beignets today, or shared lunch with Jake as usual—in fact, she'd been sitting around wondering just where the hell he was when he'd come strolling into the courtyard with a brown paper bag in his hand. "Ate lunch out today, *'tite fille,* but got you some."

"Thanks," she'd said softly, unable to meet his eyes when she took the bag. There was something different about *him* bringing *her* food—maybe running the errand every day made her feel like she was earning it, like it wasn't pure charity. Today *was* pure charity, but she'd taken it anyway. She had her pride, but sometimes hunger won out and her stomach had gotten too used to being filled since she'd met Jake.

"Why the frown? You like a nice roast beef po'boy, no? Got fries, too."

The food sounded so good that her stomach had nearly jumped for joy. "Thanks," she'd said again, less timidly this time. "A lot."

She'd shared the thick potato wedges with Scruff, scarfing them down quick, then ate half the sandwich and decided to save the rest for later. Now seemed like a good time for something that would cheer them both up, so she reached for her backpack and unwrapped what remained of the po'boy. She pinched off a bite of roast beef and gravy-soaked French bread for Scruff—who'd learned to be real patient once he'd understood she always shared—before taking a big bite herself.

A few minutes later, though, the food was gone and the rain still fell, and even when it didn't slant up under the gallery, her skin stayed just as clammy. She held out the wrapper to let Scruff lick it clean, then wadded it into a ball, wishing she'd been smart enough to bring a windbreaker when she'd run away.

If I had it to do over again . . .

Would she have stayed? Nope. It made her skin crawl just to think about it.

If I had it to do over again, I'd pack better.

And I'd find a way to get some money off that bastard.

When a door closed somewhere in the courtyard, she flinched, pulling her shoes up under her, trying to make herself as small as possible. Nobody had ever bothered her here, but she still liked being as invisible as she could, especially at night.

So it was all she could do not to panic when the shape of a man came jogging toward her across the courtyard, ducking under the overhang directly in front of her.

She only breathed again when she saw it was Jake.

"You tryin' to scare the shit outta me?"

He only laughed. "Always good to see you, too, *'tite fille.*"

She swallowed sheepishly, sorry for biting his head off. "What do you want?"

"Thinkin' maybe you oughta come inside."

"Huh?"

He glanced toward the rain pouring a few feet away, then to the mattress she rested on. "Your bed's soaked. So are you."

She stayed quiet, searching for a reply and wondering if she looked nervous. She wasn't afraid of Jake that way anymore, she really wasn't. Still . . . old worries tightened her chest.

Finally, he sighed. "It's a dry place to sleep. You want it, take it. I'm goin' back in now."

Just as he started back out into the rain, she said, "Can I bring Scruff?"

He took a step back, dropping a disdainful gaze to the dog before finally rolling his eyes. "Fine. Follow me."

Looping her backpack over one shoulder, she gathered the dog in her arms and scuttled across the uneven brickwork behind Jake until they were under cover again, then followed him up the stairs she'd seen him come down so many times. She didn't put Scruff down, even though he weighed a ton, afraid he might do something to make Jake mad before she could get him inside.

She followed Jake into a living room with once-white walls that were now yellowed, the old linoleum on the floor scratched and torn. A sagging couch was strewn with newspaper, the beat-up laminate coffee table laden with a basket of laundry and an array of empty cans.

"But that mutt better not piss on the floor," he said, pointing to Scruff as she set him down, his claws tapping on the linoleum.

She took another look around. " 'Cause you take such nice care of the place?"

Jake just looked at her for a long, hard moment—then laughed. The rich sound of it reverberated through the space until he finally said, "*Mon Dieu,* you're a funny kid. I keep forgettin' that."

Feeling lighter inside now, she pointed to the broken-down couch. "This mine?"

He nodded. "Just shove the newspaper on the floor."

"Or I could put it in the garbage." A glance revealed it was from last week. "You *do* got a garbage can, don't ya?"

"Yes, I have a garbage can," he replied with a hint of sarcasm. "By the kitchen counter."

As she wadded the newspaper, her eyes stuck on a framed picture on the end table. A pretty white woman, dark brown wavy hair, light freckling across her nose. Her arms were crossed, sunglasses pushed up over her head. Colored beads hung around her neck. "This your girlfriend?"

He stuck his head around the corner from the kitchen to look, his eyes clouding over a little. "No."

"Who then?" she asked as he disappeared back through the doorway.

"My wife."

Whoa! "You're married?" She walked to the end of the couch and peered through the wide, arched opening to see him closing up a heaping garbage bag.

He glanced up at her briefly before looking back to his task. "Not anymore. She died."

It felt like all the blood drained into her feet. He wasn't old enough to have a wife who'd died. It explained . . . a lot. "I'm sorry," she said softly.

He plunked the full bag against an ancient refrigerator, cans and bottles rattling inside, and still didn't look at her. "Don't gotta be sorry. Everybody dies sometime."

She just nodded, even though he wasn't watching, and took a seat on the couch. Scruff jumped up beside her and she shoved him back to the floor, knowing Jake wouldn't want wet doggy paws on his couch, no matter how saggy it was.

Good thing too, because he came back in just then and sat down at the opposite end. Scruff stood at her feet, tongue lolling over one side of his open mouth, and she pressed on his furry back until he melted toward the floor to lie across the toes of her tennis shoes.

"I'm thinkin' maybe me and you need to talk," Jake said. He stretched one muscular arm across the back of the couch, the sleeve of his dark blue T-shirt stretching taut on his forearm.

She lifted her gaze. "What you wanna talk about?"

"Where'd you run away from, Shondra?"

The use of her name stunned her—he'd never called her by it before. But she still stayed quiet.

"Here in the city, somewhere outside town, somewhere different altogether?"

When she finally spoke, her voice came out meek. "I ain't sayin'."

"Why?"

She took a deep breath, let it back out. "'Cause you'll try to make me go back there, and I ain't goin'."

"What was so bad for you to run away?"

"Told you. Just couldn't deal."

He tilted his head. "What's that mean?"

Her stomach clenched, just like always when she thought about why she'd left. She'd tried to tell before. Tried to tell Grandma Maisy once. And tried to tell her best friend, Donya, at a sleepover. But each time, her throat seemed to close in on itself.

Despite all this, though . . . to her surprise she found herself slowly beginning to tell *Jake*. Maybe just to see if she could. "My father left a couple years back."

Jake's brown eyes narrowed. "That's rough."

She instantly went defensive, maybe because his reply sounded so clichéd. "What would you know about it bein' rough?"

"My dad left my mom and me, too. When I was twelve."

Her ire died, her stomach settling a little. "Oh. I was fourteen when mine took off." She looked away, down at her knees, before lifting her gaze again. "You miss him?"

"I missed the hell out of him. Kept thinkin' he'd come back—for years."

"Did he ever?"

He hesitated, then shook his head. "Nope. Still gone."

She swallowed and tried not to let it kill her hope that her father would come back. Not that she'd know, of course, not being at home anymore. She'd never thought about that before—about having no way to know if he ever came home himself.

"Anyway," she went on, "my mama hooked up with some white dude." She flinched slightly at her own words and added, "No offense."

He cast a soft smile. "None taken."

"They can't get married 'cause Daddy ain't been gone long enough, but he lives with us, same as if everything we got is *his* more than it's *ours*. He thinks he's all that, and he's always . . ." She glanced down, stomach churning again. "He's always . . . botherin' me."

"Botherin' you how?"

The heat of the obvious answer suffused her face, making her look away, back to her blue jeans. She reached out to fiddle with the hole just above her right knee, pulling lightly at the thick, frayed thread.

She hadn't actually gotten much more out than she had with her grandma and Donya, but she somehow knew he heard her; he understood.

"I'm sorry," he said, his deep voice more comforting than she'd ever heard it before. "I won't make you tell me any more."

"It's cool," she lied with a shrug, even though she still played with the threads of denim, running her fingers over them again and again. "It's just . . . whack, you know?"

"I know," he said. But he thought she was putting it lightly. His stomach was tied in knots and he only wished she'd tell him where the guy lived, so he could go rip him a new asshole. Maybe the mother, too. Peter, Paul, and Mary. No wonder she'd been so nervous around him in the beginning.

And damn, she was . . . what? Sixteen? He'd never have guessed her a day over fourteen and was glad he hadn't known as it would've made him even more hesitant to have anything to do with her, let alone invite her into his apartment. *Merde,* if anyone found out about this, he'd look like the kind of guy Shondra's mom had hooked up with.

To break the awkward moment, he said, "You want somethin' to eat?"

She nodded enthusiastically, and as he pushed up from the couch, he pretended he didn't see her wiping a tear away as she bent over to the scroungy dog.

He headed into the kitchen and checked the fridge. Beer, margarine, ketchup, and the last of a fruit salad Tony had forced on him a week ago. Turning to open an overhead cabinet, he found a box of Rice-A-Roni and some Pop-Tarts.

"You keep a well-stocked kitchen, don't ya?" she asked from behind.

He turned on her with a sarcastic smile before leaning back against the counter to cross his arms. "How about pizza?" It was late—he'd gotten home from Sophia's just a little while ago—but he hadn't eaten dinner, so it sounded good to him, too.

Her eyes lit up. "For real? You mean it?"

He'd had no idea pizza would excite her so much. "Yeah, sure."

"Can we get extra cheese?"

"Whatever you want."

She looked down at the dog, now sitting at their feet, staring up at them. "Hear that, Scruff? We're havin' pizza!"

He thought about saying the dog was *not* eating their pizza, but hell—let the mutt eat. Still, he arched one eyebrow. "Just don't let him make a mess with it."

She glanced around the kitchen. "Because you keep—"

"I know, I know—such a nice place. You're a smart-ass, you know."

She smiled. "Yeah. But you like me."

"Tony might have a lead on Raven," Jake had said to her over the phone a few hours ago. "I'm meetin' him at a bar on Bourbon at midnight, after work—place called LaVeau's. Thought you might want to join us."

"Of course," she'd replied, wondering if her enthusiasm was more about getting one step closer to Tina or just about seeing Jake. Ribbons of anticipation had curled through her at the mere thought.

Now Stephanie traveled Royal Street by taxi, her heart beating harder than it probably should. Especially given that she'd spent all day yesterday and most of today being a good little executive soldier, giving Rod Hartman his reassurance call, catching up with her other team members by e-mail and phone, and working on the pitch for the wireless company. Basically, she'd told herself, she was getting her priorities straight. One night of sex didn't mean she didn't have to care about her job, her future. All it meant was that she was a normal, red-blooded woman and Jake was a normal—okay, hotter than normal—red-blooded guy and they were having an affair.

God, she thought as she exited the cab on Toulouse, a block from Bourbon, *I hope it's an affair.* She hoped he would want her again . . . and again . . . and again. And upon recalling that kiss at her door yesterday morning, she decided she had nothing to worry about. It *was* an affair. There *was* more to come.

When she returned to Chicago, she planned to let Curtis down gently. Now that she understood how she was supposed to feel with a man, she knew she shouldn't waste her time with guys she experienced no real connection with. She should move on to the men who *did* thrill her. At the moment, she couldn't imagine being as turned on by anyone as she was by Jake, but wasn't passion always like that? She'd known little of it, but had to assume that was the case.

And another thing, she'd decided. No more sappy lines like *I wish I could ride back with you.* No matter how gentle and patient he'd been, she instinctively knew a man like Jake wasn't looking for a relationship. This would end when they located Tina. And that was okay.

Even if her stomach churned at the prospect.

Okay, so maybe she was feeling some tender emotions about the guy, but that was natural, given the sexual freedom he'd helped her find the other night. Not a problem, she promised herself. This was just an affair.

Her *first,* she thought with just a hint of I'm-a-liberated-twenty-first-century-woman pride. Her first real this-is-all-about-me affair. Jason didn't count, because that had been first love, and it had only happened once. And none of the other men she'd slept with counted, either, because there'd been no true passion involved. So as she reached the Bourbon Street party district, she experienced a pleasant little tingle between her thighs that came with the thought *I'm going to meet my lover.* Her first real, true, bona fide lover.

Darkness had fallen hours earlier and crowds of people moved up and down the small street, in and out of bars, restaurants, and open-air souvenir shops. On all sides of her, Stephanie sensed the night coming alive—people stood in clusters talking and drinking every colorful concoction imaginable. As she'd noticed the last time she'd been on Bourbon at night, some wore Mardi Gras beads.

Bars of every kind beckoned to passersby—offering jazz, karaoke, hurricanes, and *sex, sex, sex*. As she passed by the Playpen, she couldn't help revisiting her conflicted emotions on the night she and Jake had gone inside. Revulsion and . . . passion—with Jake. She shifted her glance to the storefront across the way where he'd kissed her senseless.

By the time she found LaVeau's, situated in a typical French Quarter brick facade, she was burning to see Jake. And praying she hadn't imagined his ardor at the door yesterday.

Music echoed through the open entryway, a song sung in Cajun French. Inside, she found a small dance club, generic except for the decor: Mardi Gras masks of every shape, color, and material wallpapered the place. That one aspect somehow turned LaVeau's lush and mysterious in a way that seemed to reach out and grab her as she worked her way through the people gathered at the bar.

"Stephanie."

At the rich, deep sound of Jake's voice, her heart nearly stopped. She turned to find him sitting with Tony at a small table near the back. As she moved toward them, her stomach felt as fluttery as when he kissed her.

When their eyes met, his hot gaze instantly transported her away from the music and the people, back to the little house on the bayou where he'd shown her sex was nothing to fear, but something to be reveled in, so long as you had the right person to revel with.

That quickly, though, she nearly gulped back the thought. The *right person,* she quickly amended, meaning only someone who truly excited you and . . . someone you trusted. Somewhere along the way she'd truly started trusting Jake, in so many ways.

"Find the place okay?" he asked as she took a chair next to him.

"Yeah, no problem," she said over the music.

Tony leaned slightly across the table. "I'm meeting a date here in a little while, as soon as she gets off work at a restaurant around the corner. If I'd known Jake was inviting you, I'd have chosen someplace quieter."

She smiled. "It's fine—I like it here. Seems fun."

Although, admittedly, on the inside, what she really liked here was the sexy man seated next to her. His muscled arms extended from one of his usual well-fitted dark-colored tees, the bottom half of St. Michael peeking from beneath the sleeve. His ebony hair lay just slightly over the shirt's neckband in back and a few locks drooped across his forehead. His eyes looked sinfully warm tonight, and when his knee touched hers beneath the table, his smile seemed laced with still more of that sweet, hot sin.

"So, about your sister's friend Raven," Tony said.

She blinked, shifting her gaze from Jake to Tony, drawn from her sensual preoccupation. "Yes?"

"I did some asking around and found out she bounces around a lot, but seems to work mostly in the CBD."

"CBD?"

"Sorry," Tony said. "Forgot you aren't from around here. The Central Business District—across Canal Street. A lot of big hotels that host conventions, tall office buildings, and a casino—the girls there work the big spenders from out of town, plus the locals that hang out at the few seamier places tucked between the high-rises."

She nodded.

"The Crescent is in the CBD," Jake pointed out.

"I figure Jake and I can hit some of the hotter spots in

the area," Tony continued, "ask about both Raven and your sister, show your sister's picture to some bartenders, that sort of thing. It's not much, but it's something."

Fresh hope bloomed in Stephanie's heart. "It's a step in the right direction, and I can't tell you how much I appreciate it."

Tony shrugged. "Just my job, really."

Yet she shook her head. "It's a lot more than I got going through the official routes. And it sounds like a substantial lead to me—at least a lot more places to look."

Jake slipped an arm around the back of her chair, leaning in close. "But you'll be a good little girl and stay put and wait to hear from me, no?"

She thought of arguing that three people could cover the area easier than two, but thought better of it, given how many times they'd been down this particular road. So she simply pursed her lips and nodded, feeling almost contrite.

At Tony's puzzled look, Jake explained, "Miss Stephanie here likes to play PI, but I'm helpin' her only on the condition she take that particular job title off her résumé."

She couldn't resist rolling her eyes, a little embarrassed in front of Tony. "He exaggerates. I was just trying to help."

"Gettin' yourself in trouble is what you were doin' and you know it."

She flashed Jake a chiding look, so he returned it. But along with his annoyance he experienced a healthy dose of want, and even as he narrowed his eyes on her in derision, he remained fully aware of the points on his body that touched her. His hand, resting atop the back of her chair, edging into her shoulder. His knee, pressed firmly to hers beneath the table. Frissons of electricity radiated through his body from those two little spots.

As usual, she looked gorgeous. Tonight she wore a formfitting, stretchy little blouse of lavender above a pretty flowered skirt that stopped a few inches above her knee. Her blond hair fell straighter than usual, tucked back behind her ears, showing off beaded earrings that matched the bracelet circling her slender wrist.

"Can I get you a drink?"

They all looked up to see the same twenty-something brunette who'd already brought him and Tony tall glasses of beer. He watched Stephanie tilt her head, considering. "I'll have a sea breeze."

He couldn't help chuckling.

She noticed and said, "What?"

"Nothin'," he replied as the waitress walked away. "Guess I just get a kick out of hearin' what you order. Never the same thing twice."

She shrugged. "They say variety's the spice of life."

He allowed a soft grin to sneak out. "I like a woman who's a little unpredictable."

"And I qualify?"

He nodded shortly. "You never stop surprisin' me, in fact."

She returned his smile and he supposed she knew he was thinking about the other night, about the sex they'd had right after they'd agreed not to have sex, the way she'd so warmly sheathed him with her body just when he'd finally accepted the fact that it wasn't gonna happen. The hottest surprise he'd ever received, by far.

As a Zachary Richard ballad came to a close, a more lively tune took its place. "Dance with me," she said.

"Huh?" he asked, then shook his head. "I don't really dance, *beb.*"

"Neither do I."

"Then why . . ."

"Because you like a woman who's a little unpredictable."

She pushed to her feet and took his hands in hers, and the last thing he heard before he let her pull him onto the dance floor was Tony, whose presence he'd almost forgotten, saying, "Nothing romantic, my ass."

No, Jake didn't dance, but there he suddenly was, in the center of a small but crowded dance floor, moving to an easy, bluesy beat with Stephanie Grant. She smiled up at him as they both found the rhythm without too much trouble; she still held both his hands. His heart felt lighter than it had in . . . God, he couldn't even measure how long, and he didn't really want to, either. He just wanted to be in the moment with her—no past, no future, nothing but this.

He soon found himself stepping up closer, resting his palms on her hips, swaying to the music, pelvis to pelvis, as she circled his neck with her arms. Through the speakers, he heard Los Lonely Boys wondering how far it was to heaven, and he couldn't help thinking she made it seem pretty damn close sometimes.

Before the song ended, their legs had become intertwined, creating perfect friction as they moved together, and his hands eased farther down, onto her ass. He couldn't help drawing her even closer as she smiled up into his eyes to say, "Is this what they call dirty dancing?"

He chuckled, squeezing her rear lightly. "If it's not, it oughta be."

When she slowly ran her tongue over her upper lip, he watched it grow slick and shiny, then took the invitation to lower a slow kiss to her pretty mouth. He skimmed one hand to the small of her back, wanting to feel every contour of her body against his.

"Missed you, *beb*." He heard the words leave him, as unplanned as the low rasp in his voice.

"I missed you, too," she purred, her face close, her hips still swaying sexily against his.

"Wanna get outta here?"

Her eyes sparkled with heat. "Your place or mine?"

"Yours."

She laughed. "That was decisive."

"Well," he began uncertainly, "there's . . . sort of a sixteen-year-old girl at my place."

Her face dropped as she went stiff in his arms—and he realized exactly how bad that sounded. He drew her closer, eager to reassure her. "A runaway," he explained. "She was havin' a rough time with her mom's boyfriend, so she took off. I found her on the street one night—same night I met *you*, in fact. I've been helpin' her get by, makin' sure she has somethin' to eat every day, and last night when it was rainin' so hard, I let her sleep on my couch. I tried to talk her into goin' to a homeless shelter or a runaway center, but she wants nothin' to do with it—and I just don't have the heart to put her back out now that I've invited her in."

He couldn't read the look on Stephanie's face, had no idea what she might be thinking of him, but barreled ahead with a thought that had hit him earlier in the evening when he'd been watching Shondra standing at his sink, washing the latest pile of dirty dishes to accumulate there. "In fact, I was thinkin' maybe you could help me with somethin'. I wanna buy her some new clothes. As kind of a surprise—since sometimes she seems to have trouble takin' a straight handout, so I doubt she'd just let me take her shoppin'. She mentioned maybe tryin' to get a job, somethin' to get her on the road to bein' able to take care of herself, only right now she's in holey blue jeans and—"

Without warning, Stephanie pulled him down into another kiss, this one firm and sharp and needful.

After, he dared a small grin. "Is that a yes?"

She nodded. "You are . . . the sweetest man, do you know that?"

He laughed uncomfortably, looking away. Then he caught sight of Tony, chin perched on a fist, studying them with a gleam in his eye, so he turned back to her. "Isn't about bein' sweet, *chère*. Just didn't think I could live with myself if I left her on the street."

Her smile widened as her gaze turned piercing and sexy. "Let's get out of here."

He raised teasing eyebrows. "In a hurry?"

She nodded profusely. "I want to reward you. Want to show you just how sweet I think you are. Unless, of course, you still insist you're not sweet."

He grinned. "Okay, on second thought, maybe I *am* sweet. Maybe I'm the sweetest damn guy you ever met."

Curling his hand into Stephanie's, he led her off the dance floor and back to the table. She grabbed her purse from her chair as he said to Tony, "We're takin' off."

Tony only grinned as he pointed toward the tropical-looking sea breeze and Jake's nearly full glass of beer. "Don't want your drinks?"

Jake yanked his wallet out and dropped a twenty on the table, no longer trying to hide his ardor for the woman at his side. "Not thirsty anymore, pard," he said with a quick wink.

As he took her hand again and whisked her from
LaVeau's out onto Bourbon, he heard music blaring from
every door, people laughing, and saw scantily clad strippers tossing beads from a balcony to hungry-eyed guys
below. But he didn't give a damn about any of that as he
led her through the crowd, making a beeline for the nearest open thoroughfare where they could get a taxi. The
only party he wanted to have tonight was with the beautiful, unpredictable, sexy blonde whose kisses made him
tremble inside.

Chapter 17

Heat ascended his spine as he endured the short cab ride to LaRue House. They sat close, thighs pressed together, his fingers caressing her inner knee. She was peering up at him in the near darkness, saying how nice it was for Tony to help them out and how she felt in her heart that Raven would lead them to Tina. And he was peering down at her, thinking how soft her lips looked, and how warm and wonderful she was, and thinking, *I want you,* beb. Mon Dieu, *how I want you.*

Finally, he leaned to whisper warmly in her ear, "I'm afraid I can't hear a word you're sayin', *chère.*"

She blinked up at him. "Why not?"

Still gazing into those pretty eyes—midnight blue beneath the dim, passing streetlights—he reached for her hand and pressed it flat over his raging hard-on.

She sucked in her breath, her gaze going wide with shock—and longing.

She bit her lip, then squeezed lightly. He had to shut his eyes against the pleasure, lest he moan and inform the cabdriver something was going on in the backseat.

"Feel good?" she whispered near his ear. Her breath tickled.

He could only nod, forcing his eyes back open. Her face was so close he couldn't resist a short, firm kiss. "Wanna kiss you everywhere," he murmured.

"See how sweet you are?" she said in a playful tone.

"*Sweet* doesn't describe what I'm gonna do to you once we get in that room, *beb*."

She gave her lower lip another sensual nibble and looked ready to let him keep that promise.

"LaRue House," the elderly cabbie said, announcing their arrival.

Jake hurried to pay, then grabbed her hand. She led the way down the dark walk with him following close behind. While the other night he'd been willing to be patient and go slow for her, tonight it was all he could do to make it to the damn door.

As she dug for her keys, his hands found her hips and he leaned into her from behind. He kissed her neck and pressed his erection warm against her until she moaned softly, her keys dropping to the brick walk with a jangle. Instead of stooping for them, though, she turned into his arms, her eyes wild. Impulse led his palms to her rear until he was picking her up, nailing her to the locked door with his body, until her legs wrapped tight around him, small heels gouging at his butt.

They kissed feverishly, like long-parted lovers, and he couldn't get enough of her mouth, her soft skin, the kisses soon grown short and frantic to match their rhythm below.

"Put me down," she said, breathless. "We have to get in the room."

His own voice came just as choppy and labored. "Why not do it right here?"

She shook her head, still panting, and managed a small smile. "Because I like this place, and I don't want Mrs. Lindman to kick me out."

He looked around the quiet garden area. "Nobody here but me and you."

"Inside," she purred, but he liked that she didn't seem to have the strength to disengage from him on her own, that her legs remained folded firm around him.

He was more than a little tempted to reach for his zipper, but feared he'd drop her if he let go. He growled with frustration, lowering her to the ground, where she hurriedly scooped up her keys. She jammed one in the door, twisting the knob until it came open, both of them nearly falling through.

Once shut inside, Jake took the purse from her hand and tossed it on a desk as he backed her against the dresser, pure instinct driving his every move. Had he ever *needed* sex as badly as he needed it with this woman? Had he ever truly experienced this can't-make-it-to-the-bed feeling?

"Do you have any idea how beautiful you are, *chère*?" His hands curved over her full breasts, then down the slender arc of her waist.

She went still in his grasp, looking up at him as if he'd just said something amazing. "No," she said, her voice soft and low. "Or . . . not before you anyway. No man has ever made me feel that the way *you* do."

It was true, Stephanie realized with a hint of shock. No one had ever looked at her like Jake did. Even if it meant nothing, was no more than lust—the affair she'd acknowledged on the way to meet him tonight—he gazed at her as if she were the most exquisite woman ever born, as if he needed her more than he needed air to breathe, as if he

would climb any mountain for her or cross any desert.
Maybe that was why she'd been able to open her body
to him.

"Turn around," he whispered.

Somehow things had slowed. The same intense desire
still swam through her veins, yet their words had placed a
gentle hush over the passion.

As he guided her to face the cheval mirror in the corner
of the room, he softly whispered, "I want you to see. Want
you to see just exactly how beautiful you are."

Their eyes met in the glass, the small lamp she'd left on
providing just enough illumination that she could study
them both in shadow.

"Look at this perfect body," he murmured as she
watched his splayed fingers roaming her—hips, stomach,
breasts, thighs. "Look at how lovely you are from the top
of your head to the tips of your toes."

Stephanie stayed quiet, absorbing his words. Before
that quiet moment in time, she would have said her forehead was a little too wide, her breasts a bit saggy, and her
thighs far too flabby. She would have wished for a better
complexion, to have higher cheekbones, thicker hair. But
as she looked at herself through Jake's eyes, as she heard
the genuine sincerity in his voice, she swallowed back all
those old, vague wishes and felt as if she were exactly
what he'd said: perfect.

"Thank you," she whispered.

"For what?" His big hands still slowly explored, one
stretched across her stomach, the other pulling aside the
collar of her blouse so he could lower a kiss to her
shoulder.

"Making me see it. Feel it."

"That you're perfect?"

She nodded in the mirror.

"I just thought you should know. Thought you should see what *I* see when I look at you."

Leaning her head to one side to accept more of his spine-tingling kisses, she watched in the mirror, studying the sensual sight they created. Her inner thighs ached for more and she almost wished she'd let him make love to her outside, against the door. But she hadn't wanted to rush—there was so much she wanted to do tonight, so much inside her ready to burst free. She wasn't even sure exactly what lurked in there—only that she sensed she was on the verge of finding out. At the bayou house, she had learned to trust, to give her body over to him. Tonight, she wanted to go much further—she wanted to *give up* control, she wanted to *take* all control, she wanted to indulge her darkest desires.

Jake's grazing touches grew more demanding, his erection pressed into her from behind as he nipped at her earlobe to send vibrations of heat skittering inward. "Remember how patient I was the other night?" he whispered hotly, their gazes meeting in the mirror.

Both his hands closed firm over her breasts and she lifted her own hands to cover them, pressing his palms hard against her. "Mmm, yes."

"And you'd have to agree that these last few minutes, after what almost happened against the door, I've shown commendable restraint, too—no?"

She laughed softly, even as he lowered a kiss to her temple. "Yes. Definitely."

His face rested directly next to hers in the mirror, his eyes brimming with quiet insistence. "Well, *beb,* that's all gone. I'm afraid you've taken all I had, and I don't have one more ounce of patience to give you."

Her breath caught, wondering what it would be like when *he* wasn't patient and *she* wasn't saying no. When both of them were giving, and taking, and needing, and demanding. And from somewhere deep inside her, one word rose: "Please."

"What?"

"Please. Everything. Now."

"Mon Dieu," he breathed, then grazed his teeth down her earlobe to leave her trembling. Because she was giving it all to him, all control. Because she trusted him that much.

Their gazes met in the mirror as his fingers closed around the placket on her blouse—both hands yanked and the stretchy shirt burst open. She gasped, stunned at the sight of her blouse hanging askew, her breasts rising from the cups of her lacy lavender bra.

He began to knead one aching breast, and as she bit her lip at the pleasure, he skimmed his other hand up her inner thigh, under her skirt, until his fingers stroked between her legs. He caressed her over her lace panties as his fingers dug in the cup of her bra. "I wanna touch you 'til you come," he growled, soft and low. "I wanna watch you feel it."

She pulled in her breath as his fingertips edged beneath the elastic at her inner thigh, his touch coming flesh to flesh, sinking deep into her folds. She bit her lip and heard her own moan leak free.

"Open your eyes, *beb*."

She hadn't even realized she'd closed them, but on his command she eased them open and the erotic sight before her urged her to move against his hand. Her breasts had been freed from her bra, and with his other palm he caressed and molded, gently pinching the pink tip between two fingers.

She'd never seen herself in such sexual disarray—
never known desire so raw and fierce. "So pretty," he
murmured. And though she'd never imagined such half-
dressed abandon could be pretty, she saw it—what *he*
saw. She loved his ability to view things so honestly, to
make this rough, urgent sex so perfectly lovely. Not like at
the Playpen, where *raw* and *blatant* had meant revulsion
to her. Not like the unpleasant act she was forced to envi-
sion between her parents. Up to now, sex had fit only into
two categories in her mind: blatant and ugly, or more
refined but mundane. This—she and Jake in the mirror—
was something new. Raw, and real, and *good*.

"You *make* me pretty," she murmured on a hot rush of
breath.

She caught his sensual smile in the glass and knew he
understood what she meant—that this *un*refined sexual
version of herself was as much a product of him as her.
The two of them, together, made her this way.

His hand curved soft and gentle around her breast as his
touches below grew quicker, harder, driving her closer to
ecstasy. She felt herself reaching, reaching, working her
way toward that promised release, his fingers seeming to
know exactly what she needed at every step of the journey.
In their reflection, his eyes never left her—he studied her
as if she were some rare work of art, some erotic statue in a
park. And it was his gaze as much as his fingers that had
her panting, writhing, stretching—then dropping, dropping, plunging in a wild free fall through time and space
and pleasure, her hot, high sighs echoing through the room
as every limb of her body went weightless and tingly.

She nearly collapsed when it was over, except that he
was holding her up, one arm looped firm around her
waist.

The second she got her strength back, she spun in his grasp, lifted her hands to his stubbled cheeks, and pulled him into a kiss. Nothing gentle or warm—more like when he'd ripped her blouse open. She needed to feel his lips, his teeth, his tongue. She needed to feel his strength— nothing held back.

As they exchanged hard kisses, she jerked at his T-shirt, and he helped, stopping the connection of their mouths only long enough to yank it off over his head.

She reached for his belt and he assisted with that, too, not quite getting his jeans open before pulling her onto the bed with him, crossways, him beneath her. There the struggle reensued, leaving Stephanie so lost in the rough heat of pure passion that she couldn't make decisions. Undress him or kiss him? Kiss him or explore him?

She rained kisses down his darkly dusted chest, her hands shifting frantically between the breadth of his shoulders and the zipper at his crotch. He seemed to wrestle the same problem, his hands tangling in her skirt one moment, moving up to mold her breasts the next. Soft, teasing kisses cooled her nipples beneath the slow turn of the ceiling fan as he rolled her to her back. Then the kisses became little bites that made her cry out. The sensation pulsed between her thighs just as keenly as at her breasts, and despite her orgasm, she desperately needed more.

The next time his hands pushed their way up under the jumbled skirt, his fingers curled around the lace edge of her matching lavender panties, and his kisses skimmed downward, over her stomach, past the fabric bunched at her hips.

"Pretty panties, *chère*," he breathed, and their eyes met roughly over her breasts as he ripped the lace above one thigh. It dropped freely from her hip.

"You're hell on my underwear," she managed through ragged breaths.

"They keep gettin' in my way."

"I don't mind," she admitted. She'd never imagined something so urgent could please her. "It gets me hot."

He hovered above, peering darkly down at her. "Mmm, show me how hot you are, *beb.*"

Stephanie bit her lip, stared up into those sexy brown eyes that had all but paralyzed her the first time she'd ever seen them, then found the courage to truly do what he asked, to turn loose all her inhibitions.

Planting her palms on his chest, she rolled them both until he lay flat on his back, her on top. Lifting one knee over his hips, she towered above him as she reached to the panties still curving over one hip. Grabbing onto the swatch of lace, she followed his lead and ripped it further apart so that the tattered undies dropped away completely.

Next she went back to work on his blue jeans, lowering the zipper, spreading the denim wide, and freeing him from black cotton underwear. She trembled, looking down, and when she ran the flat of her hand over the hard ridge, he shuddered, too, and it raced through her like electricity. Who'd have ever thought that she, Stephanie Grant, would have power over a man like Jake Broussard? The very knowledge was exhilarating, and she bit her lower lip to quell the sensations crashing through her.

It didn't work, of course, and she didn't really want it to.

She wanted to thrill him. She wanted to thrill herself as well.

Easing her way up his body, she bathed his erection in her sex, raking slowly over his hardness to make them both gasp.

She leaned, lowering one breast to his waiting mouth as she continued moving against him, and she thought she could come that way—that fast, again—but she wanted more, more of that intoxicating power he was granting her. A whole different kind of control than she'd ever known—control that came from the very *loss* of control. So even as excruciating as it was to leave such intense pleasure behind, she rose higher, moved her knees up farther, past his shoulders, until that most sensitive part of her hovered over his mouth.

"Mon Dieu, chère," he growled, his warm breath assaulting her inner thighs as his hands curled like gentle vises over her rear.

A hot, trembling cry left her at the impact of his tongue. After that, all thought was gone—nothing remained but the heated circles she moved in and the selfless pleasure he delivered. The limpness of her limbs, the heat of his mouth. The raging sensations, climbing higher and higher, like flames inside her . . . until she combusted. The pulse of pure pleasure forced her to abandon her senses for a long, smoldering moment, until finally she collapsed next to him on the bed in complete exhaustion.

Jake, however, clearly was *not* so exhausted, and when he rolled onto her—and into her, easily—she cried out at the joy of being filled with him. He murmured in French as he moved inside her, delivering hot tongue kisses between his sexy whispers.

"You feel so good in me," she heard herself utter. "So good in me."

His eyes, shut in passion, opened on her, looking like she'd just given him a gift, and she knew her words meant more than if they'd come from any other woman, because having a man feel truly good inside her was such a new thing. *He'd* given *her* the gift.

"I don't think I can hold back, *beb.* Too excited by you."

"Come in me. I want you to."

The long, hot groan escaped him almost instantly as he pressed her to the bed with one deep stroke. Her arms folded around his shoulders as his breath warmed her ear.

And when his pleasure eased and she opened her eyes, she tried to think of something to say to express her emotions or capture the moment, something clever or witty or sexy that might make him remember this for a very long time—but his expression told her she didn't have to say a thing. Just the connection of their eyes was enough.

Jake lay in her bed, looking around a room that, by all rights, should make him a little uncomfortable—fine antiques, expensive fabrics, Old South luxury. Yet he'd never felt so relaxed in his life, or at least not for a very long time.

The rectangular shaft of light shining from the half-shut bathroom door made him hope she'd be back next to him soon. He let out a sigh at the memory of Stephanie being so aggressive, so wild and hungry. So much . . . like the dream woman.

There wouldn't be any more dreams. Couldn't be. She'd just fulfilled them.

More than just her actions, though—she'd made *him* feel exactly like *he* always did in the dreams, too. So much. Too much.

Don't think about that right now. Just don't think about it.

Easier thought than done. He shouldn't want her back in his arms so badly right now. Shouldn't want so desperately to feel her soft nakedness against him under the sheets. Shouldn't hunger so deeply to fall asleep in her arms, to wake up to her smile.

"Miss me?"

He opened his eyes to find her crawling beneath the covers. She pressed warm and sweet against him, nestling in the crook of his arm.

He answered her question with a kiss, then lay back, glad the bathroom light was off and the desk lamp extinguished. He tried to pretend that seeing her only in the shadows somehow lessened his emotions. He tried to let the darkness take him away to someplace else.

"What are you thinking?" she asked.

"That there are angels in the room."

She shifted against him, her hair tickling his chest. "What?"

"You know when you're in a dark room and every now and then you see an odd little spark, a tiny flash that's probably some sort of electricity in the air or the glint off a drawer handle, or maybe even just your eyes playin' tricks on you, but you're never quite sure?"

"Yeah," she said thoughtfully, as if she knew what he meant but maybe hadn't ever thought about it before.

"My *mamère* used to say those little lights were angels in the room, watchin' over us."

"You miss her," she whispered.

He continued watching for the flashes of angels, thinking of his grandmother. "She was my rock. The one thing in the world I could depend on, always. Especially after my dad left. *Mamère* was strong as a fortress, afraid of nothin'." *She was the one person I never had to worry about, knew nothing bad would ever happen to her, never had to take care of her—because she took care of me.*

He was glad he'd shut up before uttering that last part. He was growing sleepy, careless. And somewhere along the way, Stephanie had gained the ability to make him talk too much.

"You remind me of her, *chère*. So strong," he murmured, sleep threatening to swallow him at any moment.

"Me?"

He nodded, despite the darkness, despite that—already—he was talking too much again. "Maybe you don't see it, but you are." Slumber drifted nearer. "And just like her, you're always keepin' me in line, bendin' me to your will. I don't let women push me around too often, but for you . . ."

"Yeah?"

"I can't seem to resist."

The room is dark as night, but you stumble toward the prize that awaits you within. You sense her presence—you can almost feel her lush curves in your empty hands. You're painfully stiff and only she can ease that ache.

You could be in a French Quarter bordello or a Park Avenue high-rise or a country farmhouse—you have no idea where she's drawn you, only that you'd follow her to the ends of the earth if that's where her path led. You're in her world now. It's warm there.

Warm, but you're getting frustrated. "Where are you?"

Soft arms slip smoothly around you from behind. You don't hear as much as sense her answer. "Right here, lover."

Your head drops back, eyes closing, as she slides one palm down over the bulge in your pants. Mmm, yes.

"Is this what you want?" Her hand molds around you, begins to knead.

"Oui, beb. Oui."

A second later, your clothes are gone and she's kneel-

ing before you. You still can't see her—she's only a slender shadow below—but there's no mistaking the feeling when her mouth slides over your cock. You gasp, can barely breathe. Her soft lips, moist mouth—you feel every nuance so intensely that it's almost as if this is the first time a woman has done this to you. Not so, but nothing has ever felt this good. You sink your hands in her hair, whisper, "Merci, lover. Oui."

As her ministrations continue, your pleasure rises higher and higher until your eyes are shut and your panting breaths are the only sound.

But when next you open your eyes—there is light! And color! Fields of flowers. A hot sun beaming down from a bluer-than-blue sky.

Then, like the shift of a kaleidoscope, the colors transform, the fields fade away, the flowers grow into tall buildings painted in vibrant hues, towering over you, making you small.

And that quickly, it all shifts again, another turn of the kaleidoscope, and the ocean sparkles aqua in the distance, and seabirds fly past, an impossibly bright white.

You look down on her, but can only see her hair, your fingers still tangling in it.

Yet you need not see her face to understand she can take you anywhere, everywhere, turn your night to day and your darkness to light.

And she can make you come—mon Dieu, can she make you come—because the rough pulses of pleasure strike then, without warning, and you hear your own groans crawling up from deep within, and you know she owns you now. Funny, you're not a man who likes the idea of being owned, but in this moment it's the best feeling you've ever experienced.

Only when you next look down on her, she's gone. Nothing before you but a pale, sandy beach.

She owns you, but she's left you. You've never felt more alone.

Chapter 18

He awoke with a start, then realized she still lay in his arms. A blanket of relief dropped over him.

Damn it, why did he keep having these dreams? What more did his body—or mind—want?

His eyes adjusted to the darkness enough to see the shape of her head on his shoulder. He listened to her breathing. For now, the dream didn't matter—all that mattered was that he *wasn't* alone, and he was so damn glad. He bent to kiss her forehead and she stirred slightly. So did what lay between his thighs.

"*Merde, beb,* I want you," he whispered in desperate frustration. He didn't *want* to want her at this particular moment. Sleep would have been easier for them both, even at the risk of another dream. But he wasn't that strong. Reaching beneath the sheet, he found her hand and gently moved it until it covered him. *Mon Dieu,* so good.

"Oh Jake," she murmured in sexy half-sleep, then wrapped her fingers sweetly around him.

"I want inside you again."

"I want that, too." Her breathy assurance turned him even harder as she slid one bent knee across his thighs until she was poised perfectly for entry, the tip of him easing into her moisture. "You're wet," he whispered.

"Since the moment I met you."

The words drove him up into her sweet warmth and they both moaned at the impact. He thrust hard and deep, forgetting to be careful, forgetting her body might not be quite ready yet for everything he yearned to give her. But by the time he remembered, she was letting out heated, sexy cries and he knew she wanted to feel all of him. "Harder?" he asked.

"Mmm, yes."

She began moving on him in hot, tight circles, soon whimpering, whimpering, then yelling out. Even in the dark, he could see the hot convulsions take her—the sway of her breasts, the arch of her back—and within a few seconds, he was saying, "Me too, *beb*. Me too."

A minute later, she rolled off him, laughing softly.

He arched an eyebrow. "Somethin' funny, *chère*?"

"Just thinking I'm being . . . awfully loud."

He turned to face her on the pillow, hoping she could see his smile. "I like you loud." He pushed her hair back behind her ear. "Lets me know I'm doin' a good job."

She giggled. "Also lets Mrs. Lindman know you're doing a good job."

"Afraid she'll be jealous?"

"Afraid she'll kick me out."

"Mrs. Lindman got a husband?"

"She's a widow. She's about seventy-five."

"Sounds like we need to find Mrs. Lindman a good man."

They laughed for a moment more, until Jake asked,

"So what's the chance of us gettin' a bite to eat from Mrs. Lindman's kitchen?"

Stephanie shrugged. "She gives her guests keys to the kitchen, so I could probably go find us something."

"What—I can't go?"

"Ahem," she said, propping up on one elbow. "You seem to keep forgetting—if we haven't already alerted Mrs. Lindman to the fact that there's a man in my room, I'd like to keep it that way."

He grinned up at her in the shadows. "Come on, *beb*, live dangerously."

"I think I *have* been."

His mind flashed on Miss Stephanie playing high-priced prostitute, and also on Stephanie giving herself over to him out at the bayou house and again tonight. "So why stop now?"

"Good point," she conceded, reaching to a bedside lamp. They both flinched slightly from the light as she said, "Come on."

Jake stepped into his jeans and Stephanie tossed his T-shirt over her head—it hung well down onto her thighs. She led him out to the brick pathway that circled La Rue House, and when she stopped at another door, the word "Kitchen" written in neat script above, he couldn't help wrapping around her from behind. "Pretty dangerous, *chère*, walkin' around outside late at night with no panties on. What would you do if somebody came up behind you and did this?" He dipped one hand between her legs, his middle finger stroking into her.

She leaned back against him, practically purring. "I guess I'd melt into his arms."

He lowered a kiss to her neck and murmured low in her ear. "What would Mrs. Lindman think if she knew you were such a bad girl?"

She laughed. "She'd probably be as shocked as *I* am." She extricated herself from his grasp with a sexy grin over her shoulder, then unlocked the door.

"*I'm* not shocked."

Stepping inside, she turned on an overhead light to reveal a long table and chairs surrounded by cabinetry lining most of the walls. "No?" she asked, turning toward him.

Damn, she looked fine standing there in his T-shirt, her nipples poking at the cotton, her hair tousled. "I saw it in you all along, *chère*."

She tilted her head, messy locks tumbling over one shoulder. "Really?"

"Not that much of a stretch when you think about it. You were pretendin' to be an escort."

"But you saw right through me."

"You were a little too polished, and a little too innocent. But at the same time, I had a feelin' you'd be an animal in bed."

She straightened slightly. "An animal? I'm an animal?"

He grinned. "Don't worry, it's a compliment."

A slow, self-satisfied little smile unfurled on her pretty face. "I know. Although I think it's safe to say you're the first man who's ever accused me of being an animal."

"'Cause I'm the first man you've been an animal *with*."

Her expression edged into something more serious, soft, as they stood gazing at each other in Mrs. Lindman's breakfast room. Familiar emotions welled in him and he gently reached out for her hand, lifted it to his mouth, and delivered a tender kiss. All was quiet but for her pretty sigh, and his stomach twisted with affection.

Affection that he'd best quit indulging.

Spying a cookie jar in the shape of a cartoonish French

chef resting atop a sideboard, he pointed and said, "Um, let's check that out," in order to lighten things back up.

Stephanie nodded, her eyes saying she was making the same effort as she plucked off the chef's hat and peeked inside. "Chocolate chip," she announced with a smile that put him back at ease that quickly.

"Homemade?"

"Mrs. Lindman's specialty."

"I'm sold," he said, and together they collected a plate of cookies before Stephanie disappeared into the next room, returning with two glasses of milk.

As they made their way back to her room, it occurred to Jake that this was one of the first times he'd actually cared very much about something to eat . . . in a long while. Sure, he went through the motions, ate whatever was handy when his body let him know he was hungry, but only lately had he truly started *enjoying* food again— beignets, shrimp étouffée, the greasy good po'boy he'd eaten the other day with Tony, the pizza with Shondra, and now his mouth was practically watering for cookies.

They soon sat in Stephanie's bed, sharing them. "I hope Mrs. Lindman doesn't mind crumbs in her bed," he said.

"Why? Are you thinking of kicking me out and inviting her in?" She'd delivered it without missing a beat, face totally straight.

He lifted his gaze. "Anybody ever tell you sometimes you got a wicked sense of humor, Stephanie Grant?"

She shook her head and smiled. "No, actually."

He quirked a grin. "Must be somethin' else I bring out in you."

From there, conversation flowed easily. Jake asked her about little things he found himself wanting to know: what movies she liked, what music she listened to, her favorite flavor of ice cream. Stephanie soon regaled him with stories from her suburban upbringing—tales of slumber parties and hanging out at the mall, and the night she'd walked out the front door to go to her first formal dance only to be caught in an out-of-control lawn sprinkler.

"Shoulda grown up on the bayou, *beb*." Jake laughed. "No sprinklers there."

After that, they moved on to friends, Stephanie admitting she'd had close friends in high school and college, but had mostly lost touch with them now. She asked Jake how he'd met Tony, and he explained that they met on their first day at the academy and had hit it off fast despite their differences. But then he quieted—just wanting to hear more about *her.*

For some reason, though, Stephanie's animated smile immediately disappeared to be replaced with a thoughtful stare.

"What?" He shouldn't have asked, of course, and knew it the moment the word left his mouth, but there it was—an invitation to whatever serious thought suddenly swirled in her mind.

"I was just thinking that it feels like you know so much about me, and I still know so little about you."

He swallowed uncomfortably and hoped she didn't see. "You know plenty about me. You know about the bayou house and *Mamère,* you know about my dad leavin', you know things about my mom. Hell, *now* you even know I'm harborin' a runaway. Fact is, *chère,* you know more about me than *most* people." *These days anyway.* Once upon a time, he'd been an open book—it had only been the last couple of years that he'd changed into someone so quiet and gruff.

"All that's true, but I still don't know the one thing I've wanted to know about you since the night we met. I still don't know why you're not a cop anymore."

He flashed a look of warning. Same look he generally gave Tony during his lectures, his mother during her attempts at comfort. Same look he'd given Stephanie every time she'd ever asked him about this.

But she didn't back down. "Look, I've opened myself up to you in ways I never even knew I could. And I just . . . want to know what you're thinking about when you get that faraway look in your eye."

Could he tell her? he wondered. Could he get the words out—all of them?

Most people who knew him already knew what had happened, and they also knew not to bring it up. Even so, it was the reason he'd avoided everyone from his past as much as possible the last two years—because he couldn't face it, and dealing with people who knew the whole damning story somehow meant facing it. And he just didn't know how to—still. It was easier to wallow in guilt by himself.

Even his mother and Tony knew better than to ever say it out loud. Both were bold enough to skirt around it, talk about what they thought should happen now, how he should move on—but they never spoke the ugly truth aloud.

And neither did he. Never had. He'd never had a reason to.

Yet Stephanie's gaze bore into him, and again he asked himself: *Can I tell her? Can I get through it? Do I dare?* It was a world away from haywire sprinklers.

He swallowed again, this time past the lump that had grown in his throat. He glanced down at the sheets, the crumbs, the little flowers in the checked print, the remaining cookie on the plate in his lap. "I used to be married."

She hesitated, and he supposed that piece of news alone was enough to catch her off guard. Finally, she said, "Really?"

"Her name was Becky."

"Was?" He heard the dread in her voice and thought, *Ah, chère, you don't even know the half of it.*

"Was," he confirmed, lifting his gaze to hers just briefly. To those blue, blue eyes. But he discovered he couldn't look at them right now, so he lowered his back to the bedcovers, slouching down until his head met the pillow. "She died."

"I'm . . . sorry," she murmured, her voice gone soft and pained for him. But how sorry for him would she feel when she found out *why* Becky had died?

"It was my fault," he said in more of a rush than he meant to. He stared at the white ceiling, wishing the lights were out like earlier, that he could look for angels in the room to distract him from the truth.

"H-how? How was it your fault?"

"I was workin' undercover," he began, thinking, *Get through this. Do it quick, then it can be over.* "Tryin' to infiltrate a local drug ring. She didn't want me to do it," he remembered aloud, swallowing again past that damn lump blocking up his throat. "Thought it was too dangerous. But I was . . . so *fearless.* Thought I was the king of the fuckin' world or somethin'. I told her I *had* to do it—it was my job. I thought I was gonna save people, all the people who'd buy the drugs I was gonna get off the street.

"The plan was that I'd pose as a low-level, independent dealer, then get hired on by the organization. Our target was the kingpin, identity unknown, except to his closest associates. The guy goes by a code name—Typhoeus.

"I'd spent a couple months at it and was gettin' somewhere—buildin' trust, movin' up the ladder—when I got pulled out. Tony was workin' the case from the outside and got wind they'd found out I was a cop.

"I was pissed about all the wasted time and effort, but once I was out, we figured that was the end of it. We hadn't gotten Typhoeus, but we'd come at him from another angle sometime down the road.

"Then one night . . ." His stomach clenched and he felt close to retching, just thinking back to it.

Stephanie reached out to hold his hand, and he took a deep breath and tried to go on. "One night I took Becky out to dinner. We went to Arnaud's, in the Quarter—her favorite place. My idea, my little way of celebratin' that the job was over, celebratin' for *her,* 'cause it made her so damn happy. And while we were at dinner . . ." He stopped again, cleared his throat because something was clogging it up even more. "At dinner she told me she was pregnant. We hadn't been tryin', but we hadn't been *not* tryin', either. Still, it came as a shock. In a good way. A better-than-I-expected way."

Damn it, this was so hard. He closed his eyes against the emotions. *Don't feel. Don't feel.* He'd been telling himself that for two years, though, and what good did it ever do?

"On the way home, we stopped at a light on Canal Street and another car pulled up beside us . . . and by the time I saw the gun, it was too late."

Next to him, Stephanie flinched. *"What?"*

"Guy shot her," he said, his mouth feeling numb, his mind too. "Was goin' after *me,* but she got in the way."

"Oh Jake." Stephanie's voice wrenched with a pain he knew all too well. "Oh God, Jake."

"She just looked at me," he said, remembering it like a dream. "And I kept sayin', 'It's gonna be all right, honey, it's gonna be all right,' but there was so much blood, Steph. . . ." He glanced up at her, somehow needing to feel her presence now. "So damn much blood. In my heart, I knew it was useless. I was tryin' to get to my cell phone, callin' 911, at the same time tryin' to cover up her neck—that's where the bullet hit her—tryin' to cover the hole, stop the blood, but it was everywhere."

He let out a shaky sigh. "That's what I remember the most. All that damn blood. Like it could soak the entire world. And her eyes were so panicky—she knew she was dyin', but I just kept lyin' to her, and I guess I was tryin' to lie to myself, too. Just kept tellin' her it would be all right. But it *wasn't* all right."

He went quiet then, his body going hollow, his limbs too light. Somewhere during the story, Stephanie had sunk down next to him, so that when he turned to her, their faces were only inches apart. "She was dead by the time the ambulance came," he whispered. "And it was my fault."

Stephanie shook her head profusely, her eyes racked with sorrow. "No, Jake, there was nothing you could have done. You can't blame yourself."

"I *do* blame myself. For bein' a cop. For takin' an assignment she asked me not to take. For bein' so god-damn arrogant as to think I could take my wife out to dinner like normal, knowin' I'd just been made for a cop by a drug ring, too stupid to realize Typhoeus would want to make an example outta me. I shoulda laid low." He sighed. "Shoulda done a *lotta* things different."

She ran comforting fingers back through his hair, and her touch . . . helped.

That was a hard thing to grab onto and acknowledge, because it was the first time *anything* had *ever* helped.

But it didn't take away the sting of the truth. He'd brought about Becky's death; if it wasn't for him and his job, she'd be alive today, and they'd have a kid, and life would be fine. Better than fine.

The thought wrenched his stomach even harder when he remembered he was lying naked in bed with another woman. A woman he kept having some damn intense feelings for, whether or not he chose to admit it to himself.

He'd just never thought he'd care about anyone else in that way. He'd thought sex now would be an occasional one-night stand, or a one-*hour* stand, for all he'd cared—he hadn't wanted anyone new in his life. He couldn't believe he'd *let* someone into his life.

He couldn't believe how good the sex was, how often she made him smile, how much she lightened his heart. And that made him hurt for Becky—it brought that same familiar sense of betrayal closing in.

"You made her happy," Stephanie said.

He lifted his gaze. How did she know? "Yeah, I did. I made her *damn* happy. Then I got her killed." He looked away. "So now you know—why I act like a bastard half the time, why I don't give a shit about anything, why I quit the force. Because I spend most of my time feelin' guilty about her, and about our baby." He shook his head, incredibly tired. "My life felt like it pretty much ended with hers."

"You don't."

"Huh?"

"You don't act like a bastard so much. Maybe when we first met, sometimes, but not lately."

He gave a short, somber nod against the pillow. It was true, he supposed. Like caring about food again. The food thing was small, but the not-acting-like-a-bastard part was bigger. He'd been happier lately.

"You'd have liked her," he said without planning it, the notion just entering his head. He could see the two of them being friends.

"I'm sure I would have."

"She was a lot more . . . genteel than me. Raised in a big house in Metairie, rich parents, country club—but she was the most down-to-earth person you could ever meet. And she kinda . . . pulled me up, made me believe I could be more than I thought I could."

"What do you mean?"

He cast her a glance. "Despite my *mamère,* I grew up pretty tough. When I was a teenager and started gettin' in trouble—fightin', raisin' hell—*Mamère* said I should use the roughness in me for good and become a cop. She made me promise on her deathbed that I would, so I did." He stopped, swallowed, remembering the guy he'd been in those in-between times—after *Mamère,* before Becky. Trying like hell to be good, but still bad to the bone inside. Too angry over his father, his mother, the loss of his grandma.

"So I was already a cop when I met Becky, but she made me a *good* cop. Until then, it'd been a job, a way to feel important, shove my weight around. But Becky turned me into a better man, somebody who wanted to help people and believed I could. Truth is, I guess Tony had a hand in that, too. But it was mostly Becky. Wantin' to prove to her I could be the person she thought I was."

"And now?"

"Now what?"

She touched his arm. "*I* see that man in you, Jake. Even when you *do* act like a jerk, you still help me. But I'm just not sure. . . ."

"What, *chère*?"

She let out a sigh. "I guess I'm still a little puzzled about why you traded in being a cop for tending bar at Sophia's. I mean—you're so much more than that, and at Sophia's, you're only . . ."

He didn't make her finish, didn't make her tell him what a worthless existence he led now, because he already knew. "It's because I don't care anymore. Don't give a damn, about *anyone* or *anything*. Because carin' only gets you kicked in the *couilles*."

"Always?"

"For me, yeah—always. You care about somebody and they either die, or they die *inside*—like my mother, or they let you down. Carin's a lost cause."

Her sigh said she thought he was wrong, but she hadn't been where he'd been—she didn't know. They stayed awkwardly silent for a few minutes, until she said, "How did you end up working at Sophia's anyway?" He suspected it was an attempt to alleviate the tension now permeating the air.

He could go for that, too. "My friend Danny, who manages Sophia's—he knew me when I was a cop, and he knew I was down and needed an easy way to pay the bills."

"So no one at Sophia's cared that you used to be a cop and now you're serving drinks to people who are doing something illegal?"

"Nobody knows. To everybody on the third floor, I'm just a bartender named Jake."

"They didn't recognize you from—" She stopped

abruptly, then let out a heavy breath, not quite meeting his eyes. "Well, I'm guessing Becky's death made the news."

He couldn't quite meet hers, either, now that they were back to *this*. "The media was good enough to keep my face out of it—they'll do that for cops sometimes in especially hideous situations. And I had a beard and longer hair at the time, for the undercover work—just hadn't gotten around to takin' it off."

From his peripheral vision, he caught the inquisitive tilt of Stephanie's head. "And there's nothing inside you that *cares* about the girls at Sophia's, nothing that thinks what happens there is wrong?"

He turned to look at her again, surprised. He'd just spilled his guts to her about causing his wife's death, and she was questioning him about the girls at Chez Sophia? "What are you gettin' at, *chère*?"

She lifted her gaze. "When I first met you, you didn't seem like someone who would care about that sort of thing. But now . . . now I can't help but think that, deep down, you do. You must. You're too good of a man not to."

He blinked, wondering if she'd caught him in a lie, another lie to himself. He pushed the question away. "Losin' Becky taught me one thing, *beb*. It's that you can't save anybody, take care of anybody. It's useless to try."

"You're taking care of the runaway girl," she said softly.

He shrugged, sorry to be reminded. "I shouldn't be, if I had any sense. Because in the end, it won't matter—I won't be able to help her. She needs more help than I can give."

"Every night you keep her off the street *matters*, Jake."

He just shook his head, feeling resolute, and wondering exactly when he had started this business again of taking care of people, of thinking any good could really come from it.

"And you're helping *me,* too, with Tina."

Ah—*that's* when it had started. With Miss Chardonnay. "Only so you wouldn't get yourself—"

"I know," she cut him off. "In trouble. But you're helping me in other ways, too." She reached out to touch him, her hand skimming across his chest, down his stomach. "I've never had this with a man before. You know that."

They'd had this discussion a number of times, yet something in the words made him feel a little panicky just now; he suddenly heard them a whole new way. "Never had what exactly, *chère*?"

"Great sex."

Relief filled him. Thank God that was all she said, nothing more.

And that was exactly what they had.

Even if his heart argued there was more to it. Even if it beat harder than it should right now, each pulsation reminding him that—like it or not—he had feelings for her. Feelings that assaulted him in his dreams, and feelings that were assaulting him just as brutally *outside* the dreams.

Overwhelming guilt pummeled him with a brand-new fear, one he'd only admitted to himself this very second. What if he was falling in love with her? With another woman he couldn't allow to depend on him too much. Another woman who wasn't the woman he'd promised to love and take care of forever. Another woman he'd let down in the end if he allowed his feelings to go any further.

"Thank you, Jake," she said.

He met her eyes, hating in that moment how damn pretty they were, the way they always drew him in. "For?"

"Telling me."

He shouldn't have. He scarcely knew why he had.

Because you're falling in love with her.

No. No fucking way.

"We should sleep," he said.

"All right," she whispered.

He made sure not to touch her as slumber took him. Safer that way. Safer for him. Safer for her. This couldn't be love. He wouldn't let it.

Chapter 19

Sun glancing through the curtains forced Stephanie's eyes open. She knew without even peeking over that Jake lay next to her—she felt his massive strength; she drank in the musky, manly scent of him.

When he'd first told her he'd been married, her first reaction had been instant—and insane—jealousy. To think he'd had a wife. That deep connection, vowing your life to someone. It had made her feel like nothing, a tiny blip on his radar screen.

But when he'd told her the rest of it, her heart had broken for him. Dear God, no wonder he'd seemed so angry when they met. And to think he held himself responsible for Becky's death.

Impulse drew her closer to him. She simply leaned up against him, taking in his warmth, studying St. Michael busy vanquishing evil on his arm.

He stirred, sliding that arm around her, pulling her against him. She went willingly, her stomach swirling with how good he felt, how she wished she could somehow press herself into him, be a part of him, find a way to diminish his pain.

Their eyes met in the morning light, his sleepy but warm as he leaned to kiss her forehead. He spoke softly. "I shouldn't have told you all that."

"Why not?"

"I shouldn't have dumped it on you. It's too much."

"I don't mind. I'm glad I know. And I kind of twisted your arm."

He sighed. "You're sweet, *beb,* but even so . . . me and you, *this,* it's just . . ."

She bit her lip, waiting, tensing, praying he didn't feel her body go rigid.

"It's . . . fun, easy. I like things the way they are, and I shouldn't have muddied it up with such serious shit."

"I've told you some pretty serious shit, too."

"True. But what *you* told *me* enabled us to have some really good sex, so it doesn't count against you." He winked.

She smiled at him, but didn't feel it inside, because even though she *knew* what they had had was only fun, easy, casual sex, there were moments—like every time he looked in her eyes, every kiss, certainly every time he was inside her—when it felt like more. Just now, wanting to be so close to him—it was a nearly overpowering need.

Could easy fun be so intense? She didn't know. Maybe she was blowing this out of proportion. But while last night on the way to meet him she'd been able to smile about having an *affair,* and a *lover,* this morning the words didn't hold such grand appeal. They sounded far emptier than what she felt when she looked into his eyes.

Relax. Your body, your muscles. She couldn't let him know she was going schoolgirl and romantic on him. To turn it into something it wasn't would only make her look foolish and ruin everything good they'd shared. She had a feeling Jake Broussard didn't *do* romantic.

Except maybe with his wife.

She couldn't deny it—she'd heard the gentle cadence of true romance in his voice when he'd spoken of her. Hence the irrational jealousy.

Was that the problem here? Now that she knew Jake *could* do romance, she suddenly wanted that with him?

"Help me shop for Shondra today?" he inquired, eyebrows raised slightly.

She blinked. "Shondra? Oh, the runaway? Of course." Her heart warmed at simply being asked, just as it had last night. *You're a silly, silly woman, Stephanie.*

"Now," he said, "a much more important question. How do you think Mrs. Lindman will feel about you bringin' your lover to breakfast?"

There it was again, *lover.* Sexy-sounding, especially coming in his deep drawl, but still—suddenly—she wished the word meant more than "guy I'm having sex with." Damn it, she'd been doing so well with the *affair* concept—yet maybe this was inevitable. Maybe it was impossible not to feel something serious for the first guy since college to inspire real passion in her. It had been easy to be worldly and mature with *other* men, who made her feel so little, but this was the opposite end of the spectrum.

She smiled anyway and forced herself into the moment. "I think it's breakfast in bed for us today."

He grinned. "Suits me just fine."

She eased out from under the covers, still in his T-shirt. "I'll go grab us some muffins or something."

"Don't forget to wear panties." He winked. "The indiscretion might be a little more obvious in the light of day."

She laughed—for the moment, drawn back into the easy, fun part. "I'll have to see if I can find any you haven't ripped to shreds."

He put his hands behind his head and watched her as she dug in a drawer, and she liked feeling his gaze burn through her. "Maybe while we're out shoppin' today," he said, "we'll buy you some new ones."

"These." Jake held up a tiny pair of flesh-colored thong panties.

She cast a skeptical smile. She liked nice lingerie, but she'd never worn a thong before. "That looks a bit like a torture device. Don't suppose I could ask you to look for something more comfortable."

"Fact is, *chère,* I've heard they aren't as uncomfortable as they look."

She laughed. "Surveyed the girls at Sophia's, have you? Or is it a more personal study?"

He raised a wicked grin. "Let's just say I'm a connoisseur of fine panties and leave it at that." He leaned closer then, and spoke low. "Although I wasn't thinkin' about comfort when I picked these out. I was bein' far more selfish—thinkin' about how hot you'd look."

Her whole body went warm as she snatched the panties from his hand. "All right—for you, I'll wear them."

He bent for a quick kiss, his eyes so sexy that for a second she couldn't believe she got to sleep with this gorgeous man. "Only two more to go," he said, switching his gaze to the 3 FOR $20 sign.

Lowering her shopping bag to the floor, she began rifling through stacks of underwear on the same table Jake continued perusing. She liked that he wasn't one of those guys who stood around Victoria's Secret with his hands in his pockets, looking sheepish. It thrilled her to let him pick out something sexy for her.

It was to be their last stop at the Riverwalk Marketplace, as they'd already bought Shondra a bag full of clothes from both The Gap and Abercrombie & Fitch. Stephanie had enjoyed picking out cute shorts and summery tops for the girl, as well as finding a simple black skirt and low-heeled sandals that would work for job hunting. They were guessing at sizes, but figured some exchanging could be done if necessary since the mall that hugged the Mississippi was within walking distance of Jake's place.

Within a few moments, each of them held up another pair of undies. Stephanie's were lavender, while Jake's were black and predictably ultraskimpy. So skimpy that she laughed when she saw them. "Do they even serve a purpose?"

He blinked. "Of course. Pleasin' your lover."

There it was again, that word. God, it did sound sexy rolling off Jake's tongue. And that—being his lover—would have to be enough. It wasn't as if she really had a choice anyway. She'd have to view it as she had in the beginning, and as Jake undoubtedly did—as a pleasant way to pass the nights while they searched for Tina.

She smiled, taking them from his hand. "All right. With my pair, that makes three."

In response, he grabbed away the lavender panties and held them up, looking at the regular bottom as if it didn't quite meet his approval.

Giggling lightly, she snatched them back. "These are very much like the ones I was wearing last night. And I didn't notice you complaining about those."

One corner of his mouth tilted upward. "You're right, *beb*. You look real pretty in *anything* you wear, or in nothin' at all." He reached for her hand and lowered a slower, more lingering kiss to her mouth. When it was through, leaving her stomach filled with happy butterflies, he spoke softly. "We'd better go get lunch before I'm tempted to have my way with you right here."

She bit her lip. "That makes lunch sound pretty boring."

When had she become this woman who wanted to be ravished in the middle of a mall? she wondered, laughing. When had she become this wild thing eager to squeeze into naughty lingerie for her man's pleasure?

Mmm, this *was* fun. Easy. Just like Jake said.

Keep it that way, she warned herself.

"Oooh, *chère*," he said, reaching past her for a hanger holding a transparent, flesh-colored negligee trimmed in bits of mauve lace. "You look pretty in anything, but you'd look damn fine in this."

She bit her lip, studying it. Much more revealing than any of the standard lingerie she'd ever owned. Imagining how it would feel to have Jake's eyes on her when she wore it—and Jake's hands peeling it off her—made her tingle. "I think so, too," she said, gazing up at him.

"Now, that's what I like to hear," he purred before taking the handful of undies from her fist and heading toward the cash register to pay.

When an earlier conversation had revealed to Jake that she'd not yet tried a po'boy, he'd put that on the menu for lunch, so they soon settled at a table with a river view after grabbing some sandwiches from Messina's, to which Jake added a side of red beans and rice. View or not, though, Stephanie couldn't quite take her eyes off Jake as they ate and chatted.

"Have to work tonight, *beb*," he said. "And after that, I'm drivin' out to the bayou house for a couple days."

For a moment, Stephanie forgot to breathe, but at least she didn't gasp. Given all their sexy talk while shopping, she just hadn't envisioned . . . But she held in her sigh and tried not to be hurt. "Guess my sexy new panties will have to wait." She only hoped she sounded as natural and unaffected as she wanted to be. *Easy and fun. That's what this is. Get that through your head.*

He gave her a slow smile, enough to bury her in desire if she let it. "Gives me somethin' to look forward to," he said, then changed the subject to a topic much more important than her sexual urges. "I'll check with Tony before I go, though, and let you know if there's any news on Tina. And I'll give him your number at the LaRue in case he needs to reach you. Otherwise, I'll get down to checkin' out some spots in the CBD myself when I get back. Think you can stay put 'til then?"

Despite wanting to be totally cool about his departure, she took a saucy attitude. "Frankly, you're testing my patience. What am I supposed to do with myself for these days you're away?" *And these nights, too.*

He gave her a chiding grin. "Go see a movie. Go to the aquarium. Take the ferry over to Algiers—you'd like it over there, real quaint. Just do anything besides what you know you're *not* supposed to do."

She sighed. She'd promised, and she'd truly intended to *keep* the promise this time. But New Orleans sounded dreadfully boring without him. "You're a tease," she accused.

He rubbed his knees against hers under the table as he cast an apologetic smile. "Even so, you'll be a good girl while I'm gone, no?"

"I guess I could do some work while I'm waiting for news on Tina." Although the truth was that she no longer even *cared* if they got the phone company account. Trying to make one long-distance service seem better than the next had somehow ceased to seem important. The only thing motivating her at this point was her sense of responsibility, the fact that other employees depended on her, that her work reflected on her entire team.

"You, uh, don't sound too excited about that, *chère.*"

"I suppose my work doesn't hold the thrill it used to."

He tilted his head. "That surprises me. You seem like a woman who'd be all *about* work."

"I suppose worrying about my sister has made the corporate rat race seem . . . a bit like a rat race," she said on a soft laugh. So much so that the revelation startled her. Whereas a few weeks ago her job had been everything to her, she realized that she didn't miss going into Grable & Harding every day—at all. She didn't miss her power suits or her power meetings, she didn't miss the high-tension atmosphere, she didn't miss all the glad-handing and executive fakery that was part and parcel of that world.

"Well, no rat race down here for you, *beb.*"

You can say that again. The life she'd led since coming to the Big Easy, and the things she'd done with Jake, both in search of Tina and in bed—it was like having entered an entirely new universe. And it was suddenly hard to imagine that old world seeming like *enough.*

On the way toward the mall's exit, Stephanie stopped in front of another lingerie shop, this one featuring bath products in the front window. "I bet Shondra could use some new underwear, too," she said, the idea just striking her.

He gave her a look of caution. "Uh, no—I'm not buyin' the girl underwear. She's a cool kid, but she's a little skittish sometimes about me bein' a man, and . . . just . . . no way."

She bit her lip, smiled up at him, and proceeded into the store anyway, knowing he'd follow.

"What are you doin'?" he asked over her shoulder as she quickly grabbed up two pairs of good cotton panties—pink and yellow—as well as a bottle of peach body wash.

"What size bra do you think she might wear?"

He blinked at her disbelievingly. "How the hell do you think I'd know somethin' like *that*?"

She laughed. "You're right. Sorry. Guess we'll have to forgo that item." Then she headed toward the checkout, laying her purchases on the counter.

"Didn't you hear me, *beb*? I'm *not* givin' her panties."

She smiled up at him as the sales associate wrapped the undies and body wash in yellow tissue paper, placing them in a dainty matching shopping bag. "Just tell her this bag's from me. She can open it privately and you can pretend you have no idea what's inside." When he still looked skeptical, she peered up into his eyes. "A girl *needs* these things, Jake." The truth was, just since mentioning Tina's name over lunch, she couldn't help but wonder if her sister had fresh underwear to put on, soap to wash with, wherever she might be. Making sure another down-on-her-luck girl had them was the least she could do. "Just tell her a . . . lady friend helped you shop and wanted to add this."

He gazed down into her eyes, his expression going warmer, until he said, "You know something, *chère*? You're a pretty damn sweet lady friend."

The truth was, he didn't want to go to the bayou house after work. He wanted to stay here, with Stephanie. He wanted to make love to her 'til they were both breathless.

But good sense had prevailed. He couldn't get in any deeper with her. Didn't mean they couldn't keep getting together while she was here, but it couldn't be every night, and he sure as hell couldn't go confiding any more secrets in her. He had to keep it light, casual, fun—just like he'd made a point of mentioning this morning in bed. That had to be enough.

He'd decided not to panic over whatever it was he felt for her. His thoughts while falling asleep last night had been . . . well, crazy, that was all. An example of what great sex, bad memories, and exhaustion could do to you.

Yes, he felt something for her that turned him warm every time she came to mind—but he just wasn't ready for anything more than what they already had. Having fun with a woman, that was good. Sharing hot sex—also good. Definite steps in the right direction for getting his life back on track. That very concept had seemed impossible until just a few days ago, so being with Stephanie wasn't something he would deny himself. He just had to keep her at a certain distance. And putting some miles and time between them would do that—help him put all this in the right perspective. Then, in a few days, he'd come back to town and they'd be together again.

Sounded like an eternity.

Too damn bad.

The apartment was quiet when he came in. He lowered the shopping bags to the floor just inside as Shondra's mutt came trotting across the old linoleum to meet him, furry tail wagging, tongue lolling.

"You keep forgettin' I don't like you, mangy dog," he said as he bent to give the pooch a quick scratch behind the ears anyway. "But don't be lookin' to me for anything to eat. If I know little miss Shondra, she's keepin' you well fed."

Speaking of which—where was she? He made his way down the hall, pausing in the doorway when he found her asleep on his bed. He didn't wake her, knowing she was used to sleeping during the day.

When the phone rang, he hurried to grab it. "What's up, pard?" he asked when he heard Tony's voice.

"Slow day, so I started checking around for leads on this Raven girl. Quite a few people in the CBD seem to know her, but nobody's seen her lately. And I found another guy who might have seen Tina, too."

"No shit?" In a way, Stephanie's sister had begun to seem spectral to him, a ghost of a girl who would never turn up.

"Doorman at the Courtview, little old hotel that caters to businessmen traveling cheap."

"I know the place," Jake said—he'd once broken up a fight there back in his early days in blue. "What'd he say?"

"Didn't remember her by name, but the pictures and the association with Raven made him think he'd seen her pass through the lobby, looking for a pickup."

"How long ago?"

"A few weeks, at least. Said she and Raven were together, and it was probably the last time he'd seen Raven, too."

Jake nodded to himself. "Okay. That's something anyway." But not much. "Listen, I know I gave you Stephanie's number, but don't call her about this. No need to get her hopes up until there's somethin' more concrete."

"Got it."

"And by the way, I'm headin' out to the bayou house tonight, so I gave her your cell number, too—in case she wants to check with you while I'm gone."

"That's fine," he said, then slowly added, "About Stephanie . . ."

"Uh, what about her?"

Tony only laughed and Jake wished he were better at playing dumb. "I'm your best friend. Come clean with me."

"She's a nice woman who needs my help."

"Dude," Tony said, "you two looked like you were about to do it on the dance floor."

Jake couldn't help chuckling softly at the reminder. He'd sort of forgotten Tony had witnessed all that heat, and he supposed it made his lies even more useless. "Okay—yeah, we got together."

Tony stayed quiet for a moment, and Jake could almost feel his friend's smile. "So you got yourself laid by a pretty girl, huh?"

"I just said so, didn't I?" Jake grumbled, but neither of them would deny this meant way more than just some regular guy getting lucky. He knew Tony would see it as a return to the land of the living, and he couldn't refute it.

"Well, that's some damn good news, man."

"But it's just . . . you know . . . casual. Fun in bed."

"That's good enough, dude. I'm glad you're back in the saddle."

He laughed. "Yeah, me too. I mean . . . it's good." He was quick to add, "Only fun, but good."

He looked up to see Shondra enter the room with a sleepy-eyed yawn.

"Listen, pard, thanks for helpin' me out with Stephanie's sister, but I gotta take off. I'll call when I'm back." He hung up and gave Shondra a small smile. "Hey there, *'tite fille*. You finally wakin' up?"

She nodded, but looked sheepish. "Sorry I stole your bed. But it was almost morning, so I figured you wouldn't be usin' it."

"No problem—you were right."

She blinked, as if trying to clear the sleep from her head, then scrunched up her nose. "So . . . where you been? I mean, if it's 'cause I was here . . ."

He shook his head. "No such thing, *'tite fille*. I'm fine with you bein' here—I told you that. As for where I slept . . . well, my grandma had an old house out in Terrebonne Parish and sometimes I hang out there."

She tipped her head back slightly. "Oh. I thought maybe you were gettin' your groove on with some girl."

She said it easily enough that he thought, *Hell, what's the point of lying?* "Okay, well, actually, last night I *was* with a woman. Tonight I'm headed out to the bayou for a couple of days, though, so I'll leave a little cash on the dresser for food or anything else you need while I'm gone."

Her eyes opened wider. "You don't got to leave me money."

He sighed. *Merde*. If she was arguing over cash for food, how would she react to two shopping bags full of clothes? "Shondra, I want you to eat decent while I'm gone." The dog stood panting happily at her feet, so to drive the point home, he added, "Hell, I don't even mind if *he* eats good." Then he tried another approach. "In fact, you'd be doin' me a favor if you got some groceries in this place. Whatever you want—stuff that's simple to fix."

"What if you don't like what I pick?"

"I will. I'm easy."

"Speakin' of that . . ."

"Huh?"

She bit her lip. "Who's the woman? The one you were with?"

He drew back slightly, shocked, although with Shondra, he figured he shouldn't be. "Know what I like about you, *'tite fille*? You're direct as hell."

She shifted her weight from one bare foot to the other. "The reason I'm askin' is . . . am I crimpin' your style by bein' here? I mean . . ."

He shook his head. "Just the opposite, you wanna know the truth. She thinks I'm sweet as hell for lookin' after you some."

She relaxed a little. "Oh. Well . . . good." She dropped onto the couch, and glanced up at him, her interest suddenly seeming more girlish than worried. "What's her name?"

"Stephanie."

"You in love with her? Or is it just sex?"

He'd have been bothered by the first question if the second hadn't made him laugh at his world-wise little roommate. "Somewhere in between those two."

"But it ain't nothin' serious?"

He shook his head, perhaps a bit too hurriedly. "She's only in town temporarily. Be goin' back up to Chicago soon."

"She on vacation or somethin'?"

Given how world-wise she *was*, he decided to tell her the rest of it, to let her know bad stuff could happen to girls who ran away from home. "She's down here lookin' for her sister, Tina. Girl came down here, must've got into a rough crowd, and ended up turnin' tricks for a livin'. Stephanie hasn't been able to find her and she's worried somethin' bad happened."

He saw the mystery and fear pass through Shondra's gaze. "Do *you* think somethin' bad happened?"

A week ago, he'd have shaken his head. But somewhere along the way, he'd changed his mind. A girl didn't just disappear that easy. "I'm not sure, but . . . I'm worried, too." He tilted his head and used the easy segue for a question he'd asked her before. "Bet you got somebody at home worryin' about you, too—no?"

"I told you, my mama probably ain't even noticed I'm gone. She's too wrapped up in her big white lover boy. No offense."

He nodded, amused that she kept slipping up on that. "None taken. But besides your mom, I mean. Gotta be somebody else who loves you, Shondra, somebody we could at least call in order to put their mind at ease."

An answer burned in her eyes, but she stayed quiet.

"A grandma or a grandpa, maybe an aunt or an uncle, somebody you trust. Even just a girlfriend."

He watched as she slowly drew in her breath, then finally said, "Look, I know you're just tryin' to help, and you been real cool. But me and home . . . that's history. I'd rather talk about Stephanie some more. Is she nice?"

"Very." It made him glance toward the little yellow shopping bag at the door, as well as the others.

He didn't think this was gonna go over well, but there was no time like the present—especially since he needed to get to Sophia's soon and planned to leave town right after the third floor emptied.

Shondra followed his eyes. "What's in the bags?"

He got up, walked over, and carried them back to the couch. "Some clothes."

"Your Stephanie buy you some presents?" she asked

with a light, romantic little smile unlike anything he'd ever seen on Shondra before.

"Actually, we went shoppin' for *you*."

"Huh?" Her expression went blank with shock.

"Just figured you could use a few things is all."

She simply stared at the bags, her face turning a little red. He couldn't read her reaction, so he decided he'd best try to win her over quick. Plunging his hand in one shopping bag, he came up with a denim skirt Stephanie had promised him any teenage girl would "die for."

True to Stephanie's prediction, Shondra gasped.

He next got a handful of cotton, extracting two little teenybopper T-shirts from Abercrombie & Fitch. They earned another gasp and an "Off the hook!"

He raised his gaze. "You like 'em, no?"

"Like 'em?" She ran her hand across the denim stretched over both their knees. "I *love* 'em! They're slammin'!" He watched her study the tops and skirt as if they were the greatest treasures she'd ever beheld, and a fresh warmth filled his heart. *She likes the clothes.*

"Don't know for sure they'll fit," he said, digging out two pairs of shorts and another top, "but if they don't, we'll go trade 'em in for ones that do."

Her eyes were glued to the clothes filling their laps. "No, they'll fit. I'm sure!"

Next came a black skirt and white blouse. "I mentioned to Stephanie you wantin' to look for a job, and she said you could wear this. There are shoes down in the bottom here," he said, reaching in the other bag.

"Shoes? This is off the damn *hinges*!"

As he rose back up with the shoe box, he felt her touch on his shoulder and turned to face her.

"Thank you, Jake," she said softly.

He wanted to hug her. But he didn't—still didn't want to take a chance on scaring her that way. So he simply said, "You're welcome, *'tite fille.*"

"Why are you so nice to me?"

He shrugged. "You're a cool kid. Only kid I could feel comfortable tellin' I spent last night with a woman, that's for sure," he said on a laugh. "You're like hangin' out with a slightly miniature adult with bad taste in dogs."

"Hey!" she said, giving him a playful slug in the arm. "Don't dis Scruff."

"Scruff's a damn menace is what he is."

"Scruff's a good dog. Coolest damn dog I've ever known."

He pointed at her. "That reminds me. Don't cuss when you're talkin' to prospective employers."

"Why not, damn it?" she said, straight-faced.

He broke into laughter, then *he* gave *her* a playful punch—just as he remembered that one more bag remained on the floor. He reached down, grabbed the ropy yellow handles, and handed it to her. "This is from Stephanie."

She looked as awed by the pretty little bag as she did by the clothes.

"Said it was strictly from her to you and that you should open it in private. So after I head off to work in a minute, you can check it out."

Her face dropped slightly. "You're leavin' already?"

He nodded, feeling bad.

"It's no big deal," she said. "I just . . . ya know . . . like hangin' with you some."

"Yeah, I like hangin' with you okay, too."

Stephanie spent the rest of the day working . . . and not working. She caught up on e-mail and reviewed some files her team members had forwarded via computer—but her heart wasn't in it and she found herself drawn back to her crocheting. Somewhere along the way, she'd become determined to finish that damn scarf. Homage to Tina or whatever else it might be, she just wanted to prove to herself she could do one more thing outside her normal realm of activities. She liked all the new parts of herself she'd discovered since coming to this decadent city, and she didn't want to lose them yet.

She'd also exchanged a few e-mails with Melody—who, it seemed, had no other clues to give, adding, *I'm so sorry you haven't located her. I wish there was more I could do.* At which point she'd told Melody about Raven and her link to the CBD. Melody had replied with a list of places in the Central Business District that she'd once heard were frequented by hookers. Although, unfortunately, she didn't know Raven—*Since I stuck to the upper-class venues and never worked that area. Safer that way, you know.* Stephanie had thanked her for the list, planning to give it to Jake and Tony, and tried not to think about the CBD being a more dangerous place for an escort to ply her trade.

In between all this, her mind drifted repeatedly to Jake and all that had happened since last night. They'd had fabulous sex and he'd told her about his wife's tragic death. They'd had fabulous sex and they'd shopped for Shondra, and for her as well, and he'd been sexy and flirtatious and not at all a man who seemed mired in tragedy. They'd had fabulous sex and he'd told her he was heading to the bayou for a couple of days. And then there was the fabulous sex.

She went to bed early, feelings for him still badgering her. She'd once thought him an enigma, but now she thought of him simply as a man with a lot of pain inside, a man who—without knowing it—maybe needed someone to take care of him a little bit.

After tossing and turning for half an hour, she glanced to see the digital clock said it was only a few minutes after ten—prime time at Sophia's third floor. Sitting up, she switched on a lamp and looked across the room to the pretty pink bag containing the lingerie Jake had selected for her. Then she reached for the slip of paper he'd given her with Tony's number—she'd tucked it beneath the phone next to the bed.

Nerves bit at her as she dialed. She had no idea if this was the right thing to do, and maybe she should just forget it and hang up. Maybe she should do exactly what Jake had said—for once—and stay put until he got back.

"Hello?"

"Tony? This is Stephanie Grant. Jake's friend."

"Why, hello there, Stephanie." He sounded so merry that she decided not to apologize for calling so late. "What can I do for you?"

"I have . . . what might sound like an odd question."

"Shoot."

"You know Jake's grandma's house on the bayou?"

"Sure."

"Well, Jake is planning to head out there tonight after work and I was wondering . . . if you'd give me driving directions." No more leaky boats for her. If she was going to intrude on him there again, she was at least going to be sensible about it this time.

"Uh, yeah, sure, but . . . if you just need to speak with him or something, I have his number at work."

She took a deep breath and thought, *Oh, what the hell.* "Actually, the truth is, I kind of want to surprise him, at the house."

"I see." He still sounded happy, thankfully.

"Do you know if he keeps it locked?"

"Yeah, he does. But lucky for you, I have a key."

"Really?" she asked, not so surprised to hear he had a key, but that he was willing to give it to her, no questions asked.

"I used to do some fishing there. But I haven't gone out since Jake started heading to the house by himself so much." He paused, adding as if they were conspirators, "You know, don't you, that he usually goes there to be alone?"

"Well, he never told me that, but I presumed." Another deep breath, another truth. "I just . . . don't think he wants to be alone tonight as much as he might think he does."

She practically felt Tony's smile. "I like you, Stephanie."

Chapter 20

Jake pulled up to the house beneath a canopy of cypress and tupelo gum trees, surprised to see the front porch light on. *What the hell . . . ?*

He got out of the truck, but didn't slam the door—not wanting to alert whoever waited inside that they had company.

Merde. Who the hell could be in there? They'd had to break in—no other way to turn the porch light on except from the inside. And who on earth would break in and then announce their presence with the damn porch light?

Climbing up in the bed of the truck, he opened the toolbox mounted behind the cab and pulled out a hammer. No chance against anything that held bullets, but he felt thankful he had *any* sort of weapon—glad he'd driven instead of taken the pirogue.

He took slow steps toward the house when something crunched beneath his shoe. He looked down, squinting. Was that a . . . ?

Stooping, he found the remains of a round white mint crushed to pieces on the hard-packed dirt. He shook his head, figuring he must've somehow dropped it the last time he'd driven out here—but why hadn't some animal carried it off by now?

A few steps farther, though, and he discovered another mint on the ground. And looking ahead, he saw still more lying in a loose trail that led up to the steps and onto the rickety porch.

He wanted to be irritated as hell.

But instead he only smiled. And followed the trail.

Stepping up on the porch, he lowered his hammer to the sagging boards, then pushed through the unlocked door to find a line of mints dotting the floor that led through the living room into the kitchen. There, the mints lay among the debris of new flooring materials and tools, leading to the bedroom—where he was drawn by the familiar glow of a lamp still missing one bulb.

He stepped up to the doorway, crossing his arms as he leaned against the jamb. Stephanie lay on her side in bed, propped on one elbow. She wore the sexy, flesh-colored slip he'd bought for her today—it clung to every curve, and left her as close to naked as a woman could be with that much fabric on. The round globes of her breasts stretched the sheer slip prettily, showing off dark, erect nipples. At her hip, he saw the flesh-colored lace of the thong he'd selected.

"Mint?" she asked, holding out an open roll.

He grinned, motioning to the line of them that led to the bed. "Got some already, thanks."

Lifting her free arm from where it draped sexily at her waist, she curled one finger toward her.

He moved nearer, their eyes locking in the dim light, and kneeled next to the bed to bring them face-to-face. Leaning in, he delivered a slow, warm kiss—then gave a light laugh. "You taste minty."

"Well," she said with a teasing expression, "all the cool kids are doing it, so I tried it, too. Afraid I'm hooked now."

"An expensive habit," he replied. "At least seventy-five cents a day. Think you can afford it?"

"I might have to sell my body."

He glanced down at her curves showing so clearly through the meshy fabric. "*I* might have to buy it."

She bit her lip, somehow able to look both sexy and sheepish at the same time. "I'm . . . sorry I came out here like this. I was just . . ." She shook her head softly.

He let out a laugh. "Horny?"

She cast an indulgent grin. "No. Well, maybe. But I wouldn't have used that particular word."

"What word would you use?"

"Aroused, perhaps."

"By?"

"You."

"I wasn't anywhere near you, *chère*."

"Doesn't matter."

"I must not know my own strength." He spared another glance for the negligee, which looked even better on her than he could have predicted. "But I have damn good taste, no?"

"Yes, and it seemed a shame to let it sit in a bag all night long when we could be putting it to good use." She drew in her breath. "I . . . hope it's okay. That I came."

He smiled—and allowed himself to be honest. He was so damn happy to see her he could barely measure it. "It's more than okay, *beb*. Layin' in my bed like that, you look like . . ."

"What?"

He let his smile widen, even though she couldn't possibly know why. "A dream come true."

She leaned closer, her eyes sparkling with heat. "I want to *make* your dreams come true, Jake Broussard."

He ran a hand over her hip, lowering another lingering kiss to her moist lips. "You already do." Then he chuckled. "You have no idea."

She grinned. "Having dirty dreams about me?"

"Maybe a time or two." *Or ten.*

"Then I'm glad I came out here, so you can have the real thing."

"Speakin' of which . . ." He straightened slightly as a worrisome thought assaulted him. "You didn't take somebody's pirogue out here again, did you?"

She shook her head and he relaxed. "I drove. Tony gave me directions—and a key."

He grinned, imagining the kick his buddy must have gotten from this turn of events. "Where's your car?"

"I hid it. Parked behind some trees to the right of the house."

He arched a skeptical brow. "Stephanie Grant, PI, back on the job."

"A whole different kind of job," she said, her voice gone silky, sexy. She flashed a come-hither smile and he realized that, for a novice, Miss Stephanie did sexy *extremely* well.

Letting her expression seep into his bones, he pushed to his feet and stripped off his T-shirt. Below him, Stephanie reached up to press her palm over the ridge of his erection and he sucked in his breath at her heavenly touch.

"Tell me something. What if I'd come by pirogue? I wouldn't have found your mints."

She squeezed lightly and smiled up at him. "There happens to be a trail of mints in that direction, too."

With that, she shifted to her knees to work at his belt buckle, her moves brisk without being hurried, and watching her toil to get him undressed made his skin sizzle with anticipation. After unzipping, she pushed down the jeans and he helped her until they dropped to his ankles. She wasted no time in lowering his underwear as well.

"I want to make you feel so good, Jake," she whispered, her voice filled with a sweet, hungry desperation that nearly buried him.

He reached to cup her face, thread his fingers back through her loose hair. "You do, *beb. Mon Dieu,* you do."

She sighed below him, looking somehow bereft. "But . . . more than that," she said. "I want to . . . make you forget. I want to make it so . . . so there's only me and you. Nothing to hurt us. Nothing to hurt *you.* No painful memories. No guilt. Just good things."

He swallowed past the lump that had just risen in his throat with the realization that . . . "You do that, too, *beb.* You make me forget. When I'm with you . . ." How to explain? It felt so complicated inside him—and yet, so utterly simple, too. "When I'm with you, there *is* nothin' else."

She continued peering up at him from below as she licked her lips, then lowered her mouth over him. His breath went instantly ragged, his hands slowly kneading her hair and scalp. He had to brace his knees to keep from going down as spirals of sensation swirled through his torso, chest, thighs.

He watched her, her ministrations brimming with so much emotion—and *that* was what was burying him. He'd told her once that it was the act of connecting with a woman's body that moved him the most—but somehow, right now, he found himself thinking *this* was the most amazing sex he'd ever had. He knew no woman had ever given him more of herself.

When she reached for his hand and drew him onto the bed, he was more than happy to snuggle in close against the rise and fall of her body, their tongues mingling in slow, thorough passion. Part of him could have lain there all night, just kissing her, touching her. But he craved more, so he found himself moving south.

She sighed beneath him, soft and pretty, as he pulled the slip down over her breasts, the elasticized fabric catching on the underside. He drew one rigid peak between his lips, feeling each pull in the small of his back, the muscles of his thighs, and—of course—between his legs. He'd not thought to put on any of *Mamère's* albums, but Stephanie's sweet, tender moans mixed with the night sounds of the bayou beyond the window to provide the perfect music.

His kisses trailed down over her smooth stomach through the slip, past the shadow of her belly button, until he was pushing the fabric up over her thighs to her waist to bestow a firm, nipping kiss to the front of her new panties. He drew back, casting a wicked grin. "Pretty, *chère*."

She returned the sexy smile. "Happy with your selection, hmm?"

He replied with a slow nod. "Very." Then he whispered, "Roll over."

Slowly, she complied, drawing her knees up under her. Despite the heat, he shivered at the sight. Crazy, he knew—he'd seen women in thongs before. But this was Stephanie, his Stephanie, who'd loosed her inner desires for him, who'd turned his dreams to reality. Steep arousal drew his hands to her bottom to mold the round flesh—before he reached for the strip of lace above, easing it down until the thong dropped past her thighs. "Please," she whimpered.

Her need thrilled him. "Please what, *beb*? Tell me what you want."

"I want you inside me."

His need went as thick as the bayou heat. He bestowed one gentle kiss to the small of her back before easing into her. "How's that?" he asked, sliding deeper.

"Mmm, yes, perfect," she said through breathy sighs.

Within seconds, he was driving into her with an uncontrolled heat, and she met each stroke in that perfect rhythm, so ancient and impossible to improve upon—and no, *this* was the most amazing sex he'd ever experienced.

No, *every* union with Stephanie was amazing, *equally* amazing, *impossibly* amazing.

"Mon Dieu," he breathed helplessly—that quickly pushed over the edge of desire. And then the pleasure swept him away, up to the sky, down to the bottom of the deepest ocean. It made him think of the dream where he saw everything, every color, every world—and it was all about Stephanie. He rode out the pulses inside her until he slowly came back to himself, back to the bed, back to the woman who'd somehow started filling his world without him ever knowing it, and now she was almost all he knew.

He collapsed softly atop her, managing to lower an exhausted kiss to her neck. "I'm sorry, *beb*," he whispered.

"Sorry?" She sounded truly puzzled.

He couldn't help letting out a small laugh. Nice thing about a woman not real experienced at passion—she didn't realize he should have been able to give her a lot more. "Sorry I finished so fast." He stroked a hand through her hair, bent to nip at her earlobe. "I wanted to go all night in you."

She rolled from beneath him until they lay in a loose embrace, her body still sheathed in the clingy slip, stretched in beautiful, wild disarray across her skin. "I don't think I could take that all night, Jake."

Her smile warmed him, made him try to stay awake through the lethargy that came after climax. "Still, I wanted to give you more. I didn't even make you come."

She shook her head. "I don't think it's always about that for me. Remember when you told me your favorite part was the connection? Well, I think that's my favorite part, too. With or without an orgasm. I love the way you feel in me."

He buried his face against her shoulder and drank in her scent—something soft and flowery, remnants of the day's perfume. "I love bein' inside you, too." He lowered a kiss to her neck, but suffered a strange, soft wrench of his stomach. Had he just said too much? *Almost* too much?

He shut up, went quiet, just anchored his arm around her waist, pulled her close, and let the lure of sleep take him before he could worry anymore.

When Stephanie awoke, the lights were out, but the digital clock next to the bed said it was after three. The bed beside her was empty, yet the lulling sounds of insects reminded her Jake was probably out on the dock. She'd known instinctively from the first time she'd found him here that the bayou called to him in some way she'd probably never quite be able to fully understand.

Glancing down as her eyes adjusted to the darkness,

she saw the hem of her sexy nightie hovering at her hips and remembered the hot abandon of their sex, how it had at once been so easy—easy to want to do everything with him—and at the same time so intense. Each time she made love with Jake, the heat between them ratcheted up a notch. Her body warmed at the memory as she lay back against the pillow and smiled. If only everything in life was as easy as Jake made sex for her.

Sitting up on the side of the bed, she pulled down her negligee, then padded across the hardwood floor and over the last remains of old linoleum in the kitchen until she was quietly opening the door, stepping outside. Jake sat on the glider in black boxer briefs, looking like every woman's fantasy. But her reality. "Hey," she said.

He raised his gaze, then dropped it to her nightie with a sensual smile. "You runnin' around without panties again, *chère*?"

"What can I say? You bring out the wild woman in me."

He patted the seat next to him and said, "I know I do. Come here."

She joined him, curling one leg comfortably beneath her, and he put his arm around her, drawing her in for a warm, openmouthed kiss. "Mmm, still minty."

"You too."

He drew back slightly to look at her. "I wonder what Mrs. Lindman would think if she could see you now—runnin' around with barely anything on out on the bayou."

She laughed. "I also wonder what she would think if she realized I didn't sleep in my room every night."

"Like I said before, I think she'd just be a little bit jealous."

"If she saw *you*, definitely."

He grinned. "You think I could turn Mrs. Lindman on, huh?"

"I think you could turn *any* girl on."

He leaned in, bringing their faces close. "Lucky for you, you're the only girl I'm wantin' to turn on, *chère.*"

She kissed him again and it set her skin to tingling the same as if she were sixteen and on her first date. "Speaking of the barely-anything-I'm-wearing," she said, "did you give Shondra her clothes?"

He nodded, a slow smile reshaping his stubbled face. "She loved 'em."

Her heart warmed. "Really? Did they fit?"

"She hadn't tried 'em on yet when I left, but she thought they would. And if not . . . maybe you'll go with us? To trade 'em in?"

As before, the invitation touched her. "Yeah, sure, of course."

When they went quiet, Stephanie listened to the chirps and coos and calls around them, and found herself trying to pick out the individual noises that made up the cacophony of sound. The moon tossed a thin ribbon of light across the water, and the gnarled trees draped with Spanish moss were only dark shapes, sentinels that made the space feel unduly private, protected. "Tony told me you come here to be alone."

He looked down at her, his arm still wrapped around her. "Yeah. Mostly."

"It made me think twice about coming." She knew they'd had stupendous sex just an hour ago, but she still worried she was intruding somehow.

"Well . . . maybe I don't want to be alone as much as usual lately."

"Can I take that as a compliment?"

He pressed his forehead to hers and answered low. "Yes, *beb*. You can."

"Why are you rebuilding things? To have a better place to be alone?" She'd asked him about it before, but now had a feeling there was more to it.

He peered out over the black water. "Somethin' like that, maybe. Had this idea that someday I'd come out here to stay. That I'd have enough money to live a simple life here, just doin' a little fishin' to get by, or trappin' crawfish."

"You don't like living in the city?"

He glanced down at her. "Don't mind it so much lately, I guess. Minded it after Becky, though. Just couldn't see much there but trouble, and would've come out here permanently then if I'd had enough money. As it is, I make a lot for a guy who doesn't work much, and I don't spend most of it, except what I've put in to fixin' this place up. With an eye toward livin' here sometime down the road, like I said, and also . . . 'cause it's *Mamère*'s place. I just didn't want to see it fall apart. I feel her when I'm here, you know?"

She nodded, and leaned closer into him. Looked up into his eyes and hoped he saw the want in hers. His slow kiss said he did. "Come here," he whispered for the second time in a few minutes, but this time he pulled her up into his lap. She shifted to straddle him for a series of deep, openmouthed kisses, their tongues colliding soft and sweet.

As one of his hands curled around her bottom, the other worked in tandem with his teeth, lowering her negligee over her breasts again. "You know what I like about this nightie?" he breathed, his voice hot as the night. "I can get to all your good parts without you even takin' it off."

She giggled, shimmying her breasts lightly. "Are you saying these are my only good parts?"

Instead of laughing with her, he flashed a sexy-as-sin look and dragged his hands over her waist, hips, thighs, and slowly up her arms, onto her shoulders . . . neck . . . face. "Every single part of you is incredible, *beb*," he whispered. Only then did he chuckle softly and let his hands ease down to the sides of her breasts. "But I'd be lyin' if I said these weren't among my favorites."

He gazed up at her as he flicked the tip of his tongue across one turgid nipple, sending a bolt of pleasure and need straight to the juncture of her thighs. As he kissed her aching breasts, her hands sank between them, reaching to free him from the barrier that separated them. Their foreheads touched as she lowered herself onto him, their bodies meeting with slick ease, their ragged breathing seeming to drown out the bayou sounds.

He ran his thumb across her lower lip, his eyes riveted on her half-open mouth before he kissed her, the connection seeming as intimate and complete as their union below. As his kisses sank back to her breasts, turning their crests visibly wet beneath the moonlight, he said, "Sex might not always be about comin' for you, *beb,* but *this* time it is."

"How can you tell?"

He met her gaze, his dark eyes heavy-lidded with passion. "The way you move on me. I can feel you settin' the pace, pickin' the rhythm, makin' it happen."

He was right. She was only amazed that he could feel the subtle difference of the way she brought their bodies together, that sensual grind that was indeed lifting her to new heights.

She thrust harder, felt him deeper, moved closer to that

delectable precipice that meant ecstasy was a heartbeat away. Old words from the past came echoing back. *Let me have you.* Well, she was letting him now. Giving him every ounce of her. *This,* she thought, was dirty dancing. The dirtiest, sexiest dance two people could do. Except that nothing with Jake was dirty. Nothing.

The climax ripped through her hot and merciless, a pleasure so intense it was almost painful, a jagged ride that made her cling to him tight, made her breath tremble as she moaned—until she drooped limp and listless in his arms.

She bent her head to his shoulder. Felt his hands resting at her hips and his breath in her ear. "Are you okay, *beb?*"

"Mmm," she said. It was all she could muster for a moment. "That was just . . . intense."

"I know," he replied, "and if I move a muscle, I'll come, too."

She wanted that more than anything else. "Oh, come in me."

"*Ça c'est bon,*" he murmured just before thrusting deep inside her, nearly lifting her from his lap, a huge groan rising from within. She watched his eyes shut, watched his face clench, and reveled in making it happen.

"*Ça c'est bon,*" he said again, more quietly now, going still, touching his forehead to hers. "So good."

His eyes stayed closed, so she knew he couldn't see her smile, but she'd gotten what she'd wanted when she'd decided to venture out to the bayou tonight. She'd simply longed to make him happy. And she couldn't fathom feeling more for someone than she felt for Jake right now.

The next morning, Jake eased out of bed without waking Stephanie, pulled on his jeans, and made his way to the kitchen.

Given that the house wasn't in any pizza delivery zones and that a quickie mart didn't lie a block away, he'd been forced to keep more food in than he did at home, so he nosed around for some breakfast.

Cracking some eggs into a bowl, he sniffed at a milk jug, decided it was still good, and poured some in. Firing up his grandmother's old gas stove, he set one of her well-used frying pans on top and emptied in some frozen sausage links he'd found in the freezer. Heating another skillet, he poured in the egg mixture and stirred to make them fluffy. Odd, just standing there at the stove for the first time in a while made him think maybe he'd whip up one of *Mamère*'s specialties for Stephanie sometime soon, some shrimp gumbo or jambalaya.

"Mmm, breakfast."

He looked up to see a sleepy, tousled woman standing in the doorway in his T-shirt. He couldn't help liking when she did that—reached for his clothes to put on instead of hers—and at the moment, he didn't think he'd ever seen her look more beautiful. "Mmm is right," he said, arching one eyebrow.

Over breakfast at the old Formica table, they talked— about easy things: the bayou, the house, the condo she owned in Chicago, the job she was growing bored with. And about harder things: his worry over Shondra, hers over Tina.

He explained that homeless kids in New Orleans were screwed because they couldn't get a job without a birth certificate. But if Shondra found work, he was hoping to pull some strings among his connections to get what she needed.

He also broke down and told her about the last guy

Tony talked to who thought he might have seen Tina, but cautioned her she shouldn't get too excited. She told him her escort connection, Melody, had given her a list of places to check in the CBD and he promised he'd get them from her as soon as they headed back to the city. He'd planned to stay out here a couple of nights, but now he figured he'd follow her back today. The worry in her eyes when they discussed Tina dug into his heart, and wanting to make her smile, he promised her apple pie when they returned to the Quarter.

After they ate, Stephanie insisted on cleaning up— saying it was only fair since he'd cooked. He made the bed, then stepped out onto the dock to soak in the calm of the bayou before the sun rose too high and hot overhead.

A few minutes later, the door opened and she stepped out, still in his tee. He shook a teasing finger at her. "I've got a feelin' you're traipsin' around without underwear again, young lady."

"Guilty as charged, officer."

He grinned. "Take the shirt off and show me."

Her eyes flew wide. "What?"

"Take it off. I want to see you by the light of day, *chère*."

"It's the light of day that makes it a little more difficult."

"Nobody out here but me and Mr. *Cocodrie*. And he won't tell." He winked.

She looked around, out over the water. "What if a boat comes by?"

He shrugged. "Possible, but not likely."

She stood in place, her eyes twinkling with temptation, but didn't move.

He flashed his most persuasive smile. "Where's my wild woman? Where's my animal?"

She glanced down at herself. "Under the shirt."

He let his smile fade. "Take it off."

He watched his wild Miss Stephanie send a long glance up and down the bayou, then turn her gaze back on him before she pulled the tee off over her head. Just like last night, he felt sucked into a dream—his mystery woman in the bayou. Only then he couldn't see her. Now he could.

"Come here, *chère*. I've got somethin' for ya."

She moved on long, lithe legs until she stood in front of him. "What's that?" she whispered.

He answered by drawing her onto the glider to straddle him, but this time he urged her up onto her knees and he sank down in the seat to make wild, hungry love to her with his mouth.

Soon enough, he was telling her he had something *else* for her, down lower, and she descended eagerly onto his stiffness, leaving him to revel in her rhythmic movements, in her naked beauty, in everything about her, everything she became in his arms.

This *was* the woman he dreamed about. This *was* the woman who'd come into Sophia's looking ready to seduce. This *wasn't* the Stephanie who wanted but pulled away, who yearned but turned afraid. He hoped never to see that woman again. This was the woman he wanted to keep.

Hot, breathy whimpers sounded above him, and everything ceased to exist but his dream girl and the bayou.

Home. He was home. With Stephanie.

She came with long, beautiful moans, then sank slowly

into his arms, her soft breasts pressing against his chest, her lips against his mouth. "God, I love you," she breathed.

Jake froze at the words.

Everything inside him went cold.

And something good died.

Chapter 21

Oh God, what had she just done? Had she really just said *that*? Professed *love*?

Stephanie couldn't breathe beneath the weight she'd just dropped on them with a tiny slip of the tongue, words that had materialized out of nowhere. Jake had gone instantly still, and she knew she'd ruined everything.

"I'm sorry," she said. "I didn't mean to say that."

She couldn't look at him suddenly, letting her head drop. And when his arms fell away from her, she realized she was naked, and she *felt* naked. Heat climbed her cheeks as she scurried to the end of the glider to snatch up the T-shirt she'd dropped there. She rushed it over her head, pulling it down snug over her butt.

Somewhere, a plunking splash in the bayou. No other sound.

"Did you mean it?" he asked.

She searched her heart quickly and knew the answer. An answer she'd been pushing away because she'd known he didn't feel the same way. But it seemed stupid to lie. She stared out over the water, focused tight on a bird standing on the opposite bank. A heron, maybe. "Yes."

Still seated, Jake bent over, elbows on his knees, and ran his hands back through his hair. Confirmation. He didn't want this. Didn't want her to love him. Her heart crumbled.

"I'm sorry," she whispered. *Sorry you love him? How insane is that?* But she was—terribly, horribly sorry. This wasn't supposed to happen.

He stayed quiet another long, tense moment during which her throat threatened to close up, cut off her air. Her heart beat too hard and her muscles ached from going tense.

"I can't," he whispered softly. He still didn't look at her. Still held his head down, shaking it now. "I can't handle that."

Her voice trembled. "Why? Is it so awful?"

Another long stretch of quiet—only chirping insects, a day coming to life, heat setting in.

"I can't . . . love anybody but her," he wrenched out.

It was like a blow to her gut. After all this, all they'd shared, it was still Becky. Once more, Stephanie was reminded that this was nothing to him, that she was no more than an incidental speck on his shoe. Or maybe more than that, maybe a good lay, some pleasant laughs— she knew he wouldn't deny either. But the distinction meant less than nothing put up against the hard, cold fact that he had no love in his heart for anyone but his dead wife.

Taking a deep breath, she put herself on autopilot, pro- pelling herself into the house. *Have to get out of here, have to get out of here.* And she had to do it fast. She didn't want him to see her cry.

Since when did she *cry,* for God's sake? Over Tina, yes—a lot. It was worry. But she was usually so strong— a strong, in-control executive, the sort of woman people cleared a path for and worked hard to please. When had she quit being that woman?

She hadn't missed that part of herself, but at the moment it held great appeal. *Be strong now,* she lectured as she snatched up the small carry-on bag she'd brought. She dug inside, retrieving *sensible* white cotton panties, which she yanked up under the T-shirt, then hurried into her bra, khaki shorts, and a pullover.

She reached for her purse next to the bag, digging inside for keys. Damn it, where were they?

"Stephanie."

She stopped searching, glanced up. Oh God, he was beautiful. She felt it all through her. And couldn't look at him anymore, so dropped her gaze. *Love.* Why had she so foolishly flung *love* out between them when she'd known it wouldn't stand a chance?

"I'm sorry I can't . . ." he said. She sensed more than saw him shaking his head, looking lost. It came through in his voice.

"It's all right. My fault. I'm leaving."

At last, the keys were in her hand. *Stay strong. Stay strong. Do not cry.*

She grabbed up her bag, now empty but for a makeup case and deodorant, not bothering to zip it, certainly not bothering to look for the sexy apparel she'd greeted him in. She wouldn't need it anymore. She started toward the front door—but his hand fell onto her wrist, stopping her.

Just that—his touch—was almost enough to drive her to those dreaded tears. When the hell had she gotten in so deep here? When had she let herself fall in love? *You don't let yourself, it just happens.* She knew that, had always instinctively known it even when it hadn't been a part of her life. And God knew if she'd had any control over it, she'd have stopped it. She drew in her breath, still didn't look up at him, just waited to hear whatever he had to say.

"I'm really sorry."

He owed her nothing, she knew that. But his words were too damn simple to mean anything. Every intimate act they'd ever engaged in together came rushing back over her—empty now.

"So am I," she said a little harsher than she'd intended, jerking past him.

Tunnel vision led her out to the gravel drive overhung with Spanish moss and tall trees that kept the area dark and shaded, even now. She trudged past his truck, praying she correctly remembered where she'd hidden her car. His footsteps crunched in the gravel behind her. *Why are you following me? Just let me leave.*

She didn't stop until she located the car, nestled behind a dense enclave of towering cypress, Jake still on her heels. She struggled to find the unlock button on the rental's key chain, finally hearing the click.

"Listen," he said.

She opened the door, tossed her bag and purse toward the passenger seat.

"I wanna keep lookin' for Tina, wanna find her for you."

God, she hadn't even thought about that. It made her raise her eyes, but the shock of seeing his—so sexy and brown and no longer hers to look into—made her draw her gaze away just as quickly and climb into the car.

"But I need you to promise me you still won't do

anything stupid while I'm lookin', okay? It's still just as dangerous, and I won't be able to bear it if I have to worry you're puttin' yourself at risk."

"Why?" she shot at him through the open car door.

Their gazes met and locked. She didn't look away this time because she knew the answer. *He cared for her. He had to care.* She'd felt it in his touch, his kisses. It *had* been more than sex. If it was only sex, why would he worry so much that he wouldn't be able to bear it?

He only sighed, looked down. "Promise me."

Her lips trembled with indignation. "I'm a little too mortified right now to promise you anything."

"I don't want you to be mortified."

"Too late."

He closed his eyes, again ran his hands back through his hair. Met her gaze once more. Such dark, beautiful eyes. The memory of how they shone on her when they were making love was enough to paralyze her. Because now he only looked lost—and aggravated.

"I'm sorry, Stephanie, okay?" he bit out through clenched teeth. "I just can't have that kind of a relationship with you."

"I think you already were." Bold of her, and maybe she was humiliating herself all the more if he truly saw her as only a romp, a wild woman.

"No!" he shot back, his gaze glittering with anger, his voice harsher than she'd ever heard it. "It wasn't that! I'm sorry if I let you think it was!"

Oh. So she'd been wrong. She'd been nothing to him. "Okay," she said. "My goddamn mistake." She closed the door, jammed the key in the ignition, and haphazardly backed out onto the unpaved road next to where he stood. She pressed the gas pedal hard, throwing gravel, not giving a damn if any of it hit him. She hated him. She hated him for his tenderness. She hated him for his sexiness. She hated him for every sweet word he'd ever said, every warm kiss he'd ever given her, every moment they'd looked so long and hard into each other's eyes. She hated him.

Because she loved him.

Now that the tears could come, they did, hard and fast, so much that she could barely drive for trying to wipe them away, but she never slowed down. She wanted to get as far away from Jake Broussard as she could.

Jake hammered a nail into the kitchen floor, watching until it was embedded in the two-by-four. After, he picked up another nail, and another. He hammered 'til his arm ached, and then he hammered some more.

Hammer long enough, though, he discovered, and thoughts started sneaking in. That wasn't his usual experience—usually hammering and sawing and drilling kept thoughts and feelings at bay.

Goddamn it, why did she have to say that? Those three horrible little words. Words he just couldn't hear. Why didn't she get that? He'd told her about Becky—he'd somehow thought she'd grasped that what he'd had with Becky he simply couldn't have with anyone else.

Ever? That he wasn't sure about—at least not lately. But he knew he couldn't have it now. There was still too damn much guilt—it ran through his veins daily. Even if Stephanie *was* particularly skilled at making him forget.

But that, too, sent a whole new guilt thundering through him. When he'd been making love to Stephanie, he'd forgotten all about Becky. *She dies in your place and you forget her?* He couldn't do it. He could never forsake her.

And he surely couldn't betray her by falling in love with someone else.

Things would have been just fine if Stephanie hadn't come sneaking out here, turning him inside out with the sweetest seduction he'd ever known. He hadn't even thought of resisting—but he sure as hell should have.

He'd come out here for solace, peace—and space. Time and distance. But she'd closed the distance before he could even blink, and then, then—she'd announced that she loved him.

His stomach wrenched and he closed his eyes, fighting back a hundred different demons, all coming at him with spears of guilt and regret, love and hate, hope and despair, and everything in between. Where the hell was St. Michael when you needed him?

For that matter, where the hell had he been when *Becky* needed him?

He glanced down at the tattoo peeking from beneath his sleeve. St. Michael was on his arm—nowhere else. Protection was just an illusion.

In a few short moments, he'd gone so very backwards. Already, he felt the familiar emptiness returning. Didn't care if he ate. Never wanted to leave the bayou again. Just wanted to stay here, alone, hammering nails, until the day he died.

Chapter 22

As she peered into the mirror above Jake's dresser, Shondra thought life had been pretty damn fine the last day or so. "Check me out, Scruff," she said to the pooch, who stood at her side, seeming to smile up at her. She bent to pet the dog's head, then looked back to the mirror, liking what she saw.

A whole day on her own—not spent cowering or sleeping—had added to her confidence. After Jake had left last night, she'd ordered another pizza, tried on her new clothes—which had fit!—and she'd opened the present from Stephanie. The panties were simple, but real good quality, she could tell.

This morning, she'd gotten up, put on her new miniskirt and Abercrombie T-shirt, and walked to the little market around the corner with the rest of the money from Jake's dresser in her pocket. She'd toted home a bag full of groceries—and two cans of dog food. Scruff liked people food just fine, but she thought Jake would appreciate it if she tried to wean him off it.

After that, she'd microwaved leftover pizza for lunch,

gathered up her old clothes and a few of Jake's—which he'd left littering the bedroom floor—and taken them to the laundry room. Mrs. LaFourche wasn't hogging the washers today and one was free. Then she'd run herself a bath, where she'd used the fancy body wash from Stephanie. And somewhere along the way she'd started thinking, *I can do this. I can handle life on my own.* She missed Jake, but maybe it was good he was gone right now—it gave her a chance to try this out. Being an adult, buying groceries, having an apartment.

Afterward, she'd gotten dressed for job hunting—pleased that Stephanie had picked out a serious-looking skirt, like women on TV wore "to work." She wished she had a little makeup, but Mama and Grandma Maisy always said she had a pretty enough complexion without, so for once, she decided to believe them.

Taking a last look at the new adult her, she bent to take Scruff's furry face between her hands. "Wish me luck. It'd be off the hook if I could get a job before Jake gets back." She wanted to make him proud.

Locking up a few minutes later, she set out to find her future. High-class stores and shops, that's where she was gonna apply. Jewelry stores, boutiques, fancy antique shops, and art galleries—the Quarter was full of them, all crammed in between cheaper places that fell a lot further down on her list.

Her first stop was a small antique store. It was packed to the brim—she could tell even through the windows—but it looked like expensive stuff, so she went in. An older white lady with hair the color of the pearls circling her thick neck clasped her hands atop the glass counter between them and smiled. "What can I help you with?"

Shondra swallowed, nervous, then forced a smile and

gave the line she'd been practicing in her head. "I'm lookin' for a job, ma'am. Do you have any positions of employment open?"

The woman tilted her head in such a way that Shondra knew the answer before she gave it. "No, honey, I work here all by myself."

"Maybe you could use some help," she suggested. "I'd work real cheap."

The old lady smiled indulgently. "I'm sorry, but good luck. You have a pretty smile and I'm sure someone will have a nice job for you."

She tried to keep hope afloat as the little bell on the door chimed her exit back out into the heat. She felt sure if the woman had had a job to give, she'd have let her have it. An hour later, though, she'd lost track of how many times she'd been turned down—by jewelers, florists, boutique clerks, even a guy who sold nothing but semiprecious rocks. But she was determined to keep trying. She wanted to show Jake he hadn't been wrong to help her.

"Whas up, Miss Thang?"

She looked up to see a boy she knew from the streets, a kid called P.J. For some reason, though, it shocked her to see his clothes so dirty, his short Afro so nappy.

"You lookin' fine. What, you go and find yourself some sugar daddy? He buy you them fancy clothes you all ragged out in?"

Her cheeks warmed under his scrutiny. "I'm just gettin' up on my own two feet is all."

He gave a nasty chuckle. "Don't lie, girl—you done spread your legs and got yourself a sugar daddy to take care o' you." He was blocking her path and reached out to grab onto a lock of the hair hanging over her shoulder, twirling it between his fingers. "Sure wish I could get me some o' that."

She smacked his hand away and shoved past him. "You best get outta my way."

"Or what? You sic your man on me?"

She walked faster, praying he wasn't following. She felt people on the opposite side of the street watching.

"That's right, girl, you go run on home and give it to your man." Then he made disgusting slurping sounds, but at least his voice was fading in the distance. She didn't stop or look back for a full block.

When she finally paused to peek over her shoulder, he was gone. Slowly, her heartbeat returned to normal and her face cooled. She still felt shaky inside, but took a few deep breaths.

Damn that boy.

But no, wait, damn *her*. She'd gone way too soft. A week or two ago, she'd have given him what-for. She'd have said if he laid one dirty hand on her that she'd cut his prick off while he slept, or something else just as creative and ugly. It made her nervous to discover how quick her street-earned bravado had faded once she'd gotten back under a roof.

Shake it off, girl. Shake it off and toughen back up and get yourself a good job so you won't ever have to worry about fools like that again.

A few steps farther found her in front of a shop called Les Couleurs, whatever that meant. The front window overflowed with tailored ginger-colored dresses on headless mannequins, dainty rust-colored purses, and delicate brown shoes. Further back, she saw sections of pale yellow, warm olive, soft blue. Everything hung on fancy white racks or sat on sturdy white shelves. She bit her lip and thought, *I bet this is the kind of place Stephanie shops in.*

A bell on the door gently tinkled her arrival, but it was mostly drowned out by the soft classical music. She walked quietly through the pretty dresses until she reached the counter in back. She didn't see anyone, but heard a man on the phone behind a half-closed door. "Come on now, darling, you know I love you."

She pursed her lips, wondering if she should do something to let him know he wasn't alone.

"Soon," he said, "soon. You just have to be patient." He let out a big sigh and Shondra bit her lip and stepped back from the counter, pretending to look at a rack of red dresses, just in case he suddenly noticed her.

"Damn it, Tiana, I give up," he snapped. "I can't fucking please you."

Shondra shivered, glad she didn't have the dude mad at *her.* At least not yet. Maybe this wasn't the best time to ask him for a job.

"Listen, I'm at the boutique by myself, no one's out front. I have to hang up." Another huge sigh. "Yes, darling, I know you could be here helping me if only I'd let you, but I can't exactly do that while Melissa is still the manager, can I?"

Sounded to Shondra like he was getting more agitated, so she decided to leave. She started toward the door as she heard him say, "Enough of this. I'm hanging up." She walked a little faster and had almost reached the exit when he said, "Can I help you?"

He sounded a lot friendlier than he had to the woman on the phone. Tiana. Pretty name; she fleetingly wished it were hers. She slowly turned to face him. "If you're busy, I can come back."

"Nonsense." He was older than Jake, but real handsome for his age. He flashed a disarming smile that made his eyes sparkle. "What can I do for you, dear?"

She cleared her throat and said, "I'm lookin' for a job. Do you have any positions available?" It had come out softer than she'd intended—something about him intimidated her, smile or not. Maybe it was knowing he wasn't always so nice.

He tilted his head and gave her a long once-over, making her glad she had on good clothes. "Do you have any work experience?"

She gave a quick head shake. "But I'm a fast learner."

"And how old are you, dear?"

"Sixteen." She swallowed, wondering if he'd ask why she wasn't in school. If it seemed to matter, she'd pretend she could only work afternoons and weekends.

He didn't ask, though—just said, "Actually, my wife, Melissa, handles the hiring. But tell you what—leave your name and number and I'll pass it on to her with my recommendation. Next time she's looking for a new clerk, she might call you."

Shondra kept smiling as she stepped up to the counter and wrote her name and Jake's phone number on the slip of paper the man offered.

He peered down at it. "Shondra," he said. "Well, Shondra, good luck on your job search. I'm certain someone will have a job for a girl as pretty as you." He concluded with a wink.

"Thanks," she said, her smile growing more forced as she turned and walked out, glad to be gone. He'd been nice—*too* nice, *icky* nice; she could tell that fast. She wished Melissa had been there. And it was only as she walked away, leaving all the pretty dresses and strains of violins behind, that it occurred to her he'd been calling someone besides his wife "darling."

Jake came back late that afternoon, still pissed—at everything—but trying hard not to feel it. Trying hard to feel like himself, the slightly better self he'd been lately. He wasn't exactly sure how to do that without Stephanie in his life, but he still had Shondra at his place, and she didn't deserve to have him acting like a jerk.

He was surprised to find the apartment empty, except for Scruff. The ever-vigilant mutt greeted him at the door, jumping up against him like they were pals. "Mangy, no-good *couillon*," he muttered, scratching the dog behind one ear before he said, "Enough, get down."

He'd come back to keep searching for Tina. Now, more than ever, finding the girl seemed paramount. *Find her and Stephanie goes home.* Even if his stomach twisted at the thought, it would be best for both of them once she went back to Chicago.

He planned to start checking out the CBD tonight after dark. He'd decided not to call Stephanie for Melody's list—it wouldn't take rocket science to determine where the prostitutes hung out. He'd save himself some work, though, if he checked with Tony first, so he picked up the phone, dialed Tony's cell, and sat down in one of the old vinyl kitchen chairs.

"Hello."

"Hey pard, it's me."

"Why if it isn't Jake the Snake." Tony sounded too damn cheerful—he hadn't called Jake the stupid nickname for years, since back before Becky, during the immature time when they'd compared notes, bragged about conquests.

"Listen, I'm gonna hit the CBD later—look for our missin' girl. You hit any of the hot spots yet?"

Tony sounded more sober when he said, "No, actually. Been chained to my desk all day working a new case, so the CBD's wide open. Tell Stephanie I'm sorry I haven't had a chance to do any snooping yet."

Jake swallowed and figured he might as well get this over with. "You'll have to tell her that yourself."

As expected, Tony went on the alert. "Why the hell's that?"

"We're not . . . together anymore. I'm still lookin' for her sister, but that's it."

"Don't tell me you got pissed at her for coming to the house. Because if that's the problem, it was as much my fault as hers."

"That has nothin' to do with it." *Not exactly anyway.*

"Then what the hell happened?"

Jake took a deep breath. "Not your business, man."

"I don't give a shit—I'm making it my business. She's a *nice* woman, Jake. The kind you hang onto."

"Well, she's free now. You like her so much, call her up and ask her out yourself." He'd skin Tony alive if he actually did that, of course, but he had a point to make—that he and Stephanie were through.

"You exhaust me," Tony said quietly on the other end.

"I never asked you to care."

"My bad luck that I do, I guess." He sighed. "Damn it, I thought you were . . . getting better."

"Yeah, well, looks like a relapse."

"Sometimes I really think you're hopeless, man."

"I don't care."

"That's your problem. You need to *try* caring about something. Like Stephanie, maybe."

"Leave this alone, Tony. I mean it." He hung up the phone and let out the breath he hadn't realized he was holding, then shut his eyes. He was so goddamned tired. The safety of sleep beckoned, the safety of turning off the world and not *having* to care.

But sleep wasn't always safe. Once upon a time, there had been those godawful nightmares—Becky and blood. He'd traded them in, it seemed, for sex dreams. A whole lot sweeter, but . . . not someplace he wanted to go at the moment. He didn't want to see Stephanie in his dreams any more than he wanted to see Becky.

Heading to the living room, he reclined on the weight bench and started lifting. It was kind of like hammering. Took just enough concentration that nothing else polluted his head—usually anyway.

He looked over when the door opened, nearly dropped 250 pounds on himself, and struggled to get the barbell in its resting place. "You're home," he said, sitting up. Shondra wore the official job-hunting outfit, so he tried to find a smile for her, despite how lousy he felt. "Been poundin' the pavement?"

She nodded, but didn't look particularly happy, either. "No luck?"

Taking a seat on the couch, she let out a long sigh. "Nobody in the whole damn French Quarter needs any help."

"You covered the whole Quarter?" He arched a doubtful brow.

She replied with a shrug. "Felt like it." Bending down, she hugged Scruff against her leg.

"You'll try again another day." He braced his elbows on his knees. "Look real nice," he added.

This brought out a smile from his *'tite fille.* "Everything fits! I wore the other skirt this mornin'. I went out and bought some groceries, like you said. Oh, and I need to get laundry out of the dryer. After that, I'll make dinner. Hamburgers and some of those frozen French fries."

He grinned, shocked and amazed and . . . feeling utterly lazy. "You had a busy day."

"Straight up," she said, sounding happy, kind of proud.

An hour later, the sizzle of hamburgers sent a deliciously greasy scent through the apartment, and Jake was surprised to find he *did* still want to eat, and he hadn't had a good, homemade burger in a while. He sat in the living room, folding the clothes she'd washed, because it was the least he could do.

"What'd you say Stephanie's sister's name was?" she asked as they sat in front of the TV a little while later with plates in their laps. She'd changed into a pair of her new shorts and, at a glance, looked like any other teenager. Scruff scarfed down his own private burger, sans bun, from a plate between them on the floor.

Jake lowered his burger to the plate and turned to look at her. "Tina. Why?"

"Oh. Never mind. Just . . . a dude at a boutique I was in today was talkin' to some girl on the phone named Tiana. I thought maybe *that* was her name—couldn't remember. It sounded like he was gettin' busy with this Tiana 'cause he told me he was married to somebody named Melissa, but he called Tiana 'darling' before he knew I was there."

The wheels in Jake's mind began to spin slowly. "What boutique?"

"Less Cowl-ee-ers, somethin' like that. On Royal Street."

"Les Couleurs," he said. "I know the place. Means colors."

"Makes sense. All the stuff inside was arranged by color."

"Damn it," he said.

"What?"

He shook his head. "I'm sorry—not cussin' at *you*. Just figured somethin' out. Maybe somethin' important."

He couldn't be sure—but in another way, he thought, *How could I have been so stupid? How could I have thought Tina was using her real name all this time?* Of course, Tony had never suggested she might be using another name, either—but lots of escorts did. Hookers, strippers—they needed pretty, sexy-sounding names; it was part of what they were selling. Misti. Tawney. Bambi. All girls he knew from Chez Sophia and he was pretty sure they hadn't been using those names since birth.

Tina was awful damn close to *Tiana*. And he happened to know Les Couleurs belonged to a guy named Robert Nicholson, a whiskey sour who wasn't a regular at Sophia's, but he wasn't a rarity, either. One more middle-aged married guy who paid for it on the side. What if he was buying it from Stephanie's sister?

More than that, Nicholson was on the list of guys Tony thought might have a link to Typhoeus. Tony was watching some others more closely—since they suspected drugs were being siphoned through the third floor, it made sense to look at the regulars. But Nicholson made the list because he had more money than he should—too big a house and too nice a deluxe cabin cruiser on Lake Pontchartrain and one too many vacation homes in places like Vail and Palm Beach. He owned the upscale dress shop and had some real estate investments, but he seemed like a guy who was doing way too well. And if Jake remembered correctly, Nicholson also had a conviction for possession on his record. He'd been found with an ounce of coke when he was fresh out of college twenty-some years ago. It wasn't much, but it showed the guy wasn't adverse to drugs.

"What's so important?" Shondra asked.

"I'm just wondering if your Tiana could possibly *be* my Tina." He set down his plate. "I'll be back in a minute. Need to make a phone call." He'd nearly reached the kitchen when he turned back to point to the mutt. "And *don't* let that dog eat my burger."

Stephanie stood before the mirror in her room wearing the last of the sexy dresses she'd bought when she'd decided to search for Tina by pretending she was an escort. This dress was more casual than the others—sleeveless with a collar and buttons down the front, super short, and made of stretchy black fabric that hugged every curve. She wore a black push-up bra that thrust her breasts together for maximum cleavage, and she'd unbuttoned the dress to a point below her chest so that the bra showed in the center. Around her neck she wore a black choker, from her ear-lobes hung large silver hoops. Tightly curled hair, black strappy heels, and too much makeup completed the look.

She knew she was supposed to stay put and let Jake find her sister, but for all she knew, he was still out on the bayou—wasting time. And she'd wasted enough damn time with him, time that could have been spent scouring the streets for Tina. Besides, she hadn't promised him today when he'd insisted. And as for promises—who really cared? The way she saw it, Jake's eyes had made promises to *her.* His kisses and his hands had delivered promises as well. Broken ones.

What did she want with a guy like him anyway? He

was so screwed up inside that he clearly didn't know *what* he wanted. And his demons were just too big for her to slay. She supposed maybe she'd started thinking she was doing that, wiping out the things that haunted him—but now she knew she'd been nothing more than a pleasant diversion.

You wanted an affair, Stephanie. A lover. Well, you got 'em. Congratulations.

Part of her would always be grateful for the joys Jake had opened her to—but another part of her wished she'd never laid eyes on him. Life had been easier before she'd known true desire, back when it had just been a vague, distant memory of something she'd experienced when she was young and naive. Even now, her body pulsed with need, wishing like crazy Jake would walk through her door and take her into his arms.

But only if he loved her, too.

She couldn't, *wouldn't,* be a fool for him. She couldn't go back to merely wanting sex from Jake—now it was love or nothing, unfortunately.

And it looked like nothing had won, hands down.

"Bastard," she bit off through clenched teeth.

Deep inside, she was unsure if she had the right to hold him responsible for her feelings—but it was easier that way. She hadn't cried since she'd hit U.S. 10 late this morning, where she'd dried her eyes and vowed it was time to move on, time to find Tina and take her home where they both belonged. And to hope she never crossed the path of Jake Broussard—her lover, the man she'd fallen in love with—ever again.

She shut her eyes against the pain of that love. *Don't feel it. Don't feel it.*

Soon you can go back to your old life, your old self.

God knew that had been easier—boring dates, tedious sex, and all.

For now, though, you have to look for Tina again. You have to pretend again to be this thing you're not. Feel it. Be it.

To her surprise, that sounded a hell of a lot easier than it had been the first time, back before Jake. Now the rush of sensuality—the feel of the bra tight against her breasts, the awareness of the black thong under her dress—felt as normal as breathing. She'd worn the new panties, figuring that if she was going to feign being an escort again, she might as well. After tonight, she planned to drop them in the trash.

She called a cab and scooped up a little black purse, Melody's list inside.

I'm going to find her tonight. I have to.

The cab was due in less than five minutes, so she started toward the door, but stopped. She glanced back at the Victoria's Secret shopping bag next to the desk phone.

What if you don't find her? What if, instead, you find Jake? What if he discovers you're up to your old tricks again and this time refuses to help you for good? She liked to think she could do this on her own, but in the end, if she failed, she had only him and Tony to turn to. "Damn it," she muttered.

She walked to the desk and, against her better judgment, dialed Jake. If he was back in town, she'd give him a heads-up—that simple. If not, she didn't have to worry about being seen.

"Hello."

She closed her eyes as his deep voice melted through her. The voice of someone who was *supposed* to be in her life, but who had become a stranger—Jake was the stranger who'd made love to her just this morning. "I'm going to look for Raven in the CBD if you want to go."

"The hell you are."

"Try and stop me. If you want to go along, I'm starting at a bar called Antonio's, on Magazine Street. It's on Melody's list."

"Are you fuckin' crazy, Stephanie? Do you want some lowlife to attack you?"

She took a deep breath and spoke very calmly. "I want to find my sister. Once and for all. So I can get the hell out of this city."

On the other end, he issued a long, tired sigh. "Just keep a low profile 'til I get there."

Chapter 23

He'd called Tony about the possible Nicholson link. They'd been friends long enough that an angry conversation didn't have to be discussed afterward, so they hadn't alluded to their earlier talk—and Tony agreed the idea about Nicholson held merit. He'd said the problem would be tracking the guy down to question him about whether he knew Tina. Nicholson owned the boutique, but he didn't work there on a regular basis—he didn't exactly work *anywhere* on a regular basis.

"Now that I think about it, it makes the guy seem even more suspicious," Tony had said. "Even so, I don't have any cause—drug-related or otherwise—to go knocking on his door at home and interrogating him. If you really think this holds water, though, you might consider staking out his house, following him around for a couple of days and seeing where he goes." Since Tony couldn't do it, being a cop—but Jake could.

And he might just do that, but at the moment he was back to the drawing board in the CBD with Stephanie, who sat at the bar in Antonio's looking like a woman to be bedded. She was less high-class escort now and more hooker-too-beautiful-for-her-surroundings. Even a more dangerous disguise, which made him glad he'd come. He couldn't bear the thought of her going out like that without him there to look out for her.

At least she was quietly sipping her drink, not talking to anyone. He took the vacant stool beside her. "This is what you're wearin'?"

She raised a solemn gaze, her eyes outlined in black, her lashes long, her lips wet and red. "I dressed down. Now that we're not in the high-priced area anymore, I thought I might fit in better." She gave him a once-over. "*This* is what *you're* wearing?"

He had on a dark blue button-down shirt, black pants. "*I* dressed *up*. Figured I had to look like a guy who could afford you if I'm gonna be hangin' with you." His skin prickled with her nearness and his heart beat too fast.

But you have to ignore that now.

No, not just *now*. From now on. Like he'd told her, they *had* to be over. He couldn't deal with the guilt of caring for someone else this soon. Sometimes he felt like Becky had died just yesterday. He couldn't have Stephanie anymore.

"What'll you have?" a young bartender with a scruffy beard and an earring stepped up to ask him.

"Bud Light."

The bartender uncapped the bottle, setting it on the bar. Beside him, Stephanie twirled her finger through a lock of hair, tilting her head slightly. "Know a working girl named Raven?" she asked the bartender in a soft, sexy voice. The guy's attention riveted on her.

Damn, she was better at this than Jake had thought.

The guy shook his head. "Don't think so, sweetheart, but check with the girls at the other end of the bar. They get around a lot." He winked and she thanked him, and Jake just looked at her.

"What?"

"Nothin'," he groused.

"Who's going to ask them—me or you?"

"I'll do it." He didn't even particularly like the idea of her associating with prostitutes anymore. He stood up, grabbing his beer to take with him. "Don't talk to anybody while I'm gone."

"And if somebody talks to *me*?" She blinked, clearly irritated. "You'll be ten steps away."

She made a good point and he was too tied in knots by her to refute it. He just headed down to the girls in question, who were dressed a lot like Stephanie—but none of them could hold a candle to her. "Evenin', ladies."

They all perked up, stopping their conversations. A blonde stuck her chest out and a tall brunette said, "Hi, honey. Looking for some fun?"

He tried for a sheepish smile. "Actually, I'm . . . lookin' for a couple of particular ladies, and I was hopin' you girls might know where I could find 'em. Names are Tiana and Raven. Met 'em both here a few months back and they said they stuck to the CBD most of the time, if I ever wanted to get with either one of 'em again."

All four girls in the group exchanged looks, and Jake thought, *Pay dirt*.

Finally, the blonde spoke. "We haven't seen Tiana for a long time. And as for Raven, she's . . . uh . . . down on her luck right now." She lifted a hand to his shirt collar. "But *I'll* take real good care of you."

He sighed, trying to be patient, then dug for more information. "Raven's down on her luck how? 'Cause I'd like to help her out—if you can tell me where she is."

The tall girl sighed. "Look, Raven's on the street, man. Used to share a place with some girls we know, but they kicked her out. She's in a bad way."

Merde. "Any idea where she might be?"

She shrugged. "Sure, honey, but why would you want *her* when you could have one of *us*?"

"I just . . . need to find her." Time to pull out more ammunition. "It'd be worth fifty bucks to me if you can point me in the right direction."

At the mention of cash, both girls started to answer, but the blonde got the words out quicker. "Up at the projects, near St. Louis Number One." The city's oldest cemetery. "She can score drugs for tricks there. Probably a real mess, though."

He got out his wallet and peeled out a fifty. The blonde plucked it from his hand. "A pleasure."

"I imagine so. Thank you, ladies. You've been helpful."

He headed back down the bar, seeing red when he found Stephanie looking enraptured by whatever the bartender was leaning over to tell her. He plopped back on the stool. "I've got what we were lookin' for," he said loud enough to get her attention.

She and the earring boy parted and the guy went on his way, thank God. "What?" she asked. "They know Raven?"

He nodded. "I know where we can find her."

"Really?" She sat up a little straighter, her eyes gone wide.

He dropped some money on the bar. "Let's go." As he followed her to the door, he added, "Hope you won't miss your bartender friend back there too much."

"I won't. But *he* might miss *me*. Bartenders seem to have a thing for me."

* * *

They took a cab to his place, transferring into the pickup, Jake explaining that they were headed someplace where it wasn't wise to be walking around at night. He hoped they could prowl around in the truck and locate Raven along the street. Things between them remained tense, and Stephanie could barely decipher her own feelings. Adrenaline roared through her veins at the prospect of finding Tina's friend—and fear, too. Getting closer might mean good news or bad. And she continued to seethe with anger at Jake, trying to mask the ugly wound he'd gouged in her heart that morning. Acting tough with him was her best defense, but it wasn't easy.

Once in the truck, he said, "Listen, *chère*, you might want to brace yourself."

She turned to look at him across the long seat. "What do you mean?"

"I got the impression Raven might be strung out on drugs. At the very least, sounds like she's livin' on the street, so this might not be pretty."

Stephanie's stomach twisted, worrying she might discover the same fate for her sister. She just nodded and turned back ahead, not willing to let Jake see any more of her emotions.

"Somethin' else," he said. "I didn't want to get your hopes up, but I might have another link to Tina." He told her Shondra had met a man named Nicholson, who was having an affair with a girl called Tiana—and the guy was known to patronize prostitutes. Jake explained that sometimes working girls didn't use their real names. "Just never occurred to me before that Tina could be goin' by something else. Might be a dead end," he said. "But it also might not. I'll be lookin' into it."

Within a few minutes, they'd reached an area that reeked of depression. Stark, identical brick buildings lined a street where the sidewalks were cracked and littered with broken glass. They passed a small group of young black men standing in a tight circle and one of them looked up at the vehicle moving slowly past. The threat burning in his eyes beneath the streetlamps gave Stephanie the idea something shady was taking place, and her skin prickled.

A block later, as they drove along the white wall surrounding an old cemetery, they came upon a woman trudging up the street in a soiled white micromini and high heels that had seen better days. Jake pulled up next to her and rolled down the window.

Before he even spoke, she said, "Want me to get in your truck with you, mister?" Stephanie could see the light-skinned black girl had once been a beauty, but now her eyes were sunken and her skin sallow. Her halter top revealed shoulders of skin and bone.

"Is your name Raven?" he asked.

She didn't even look surprised, just tired. "That's right. You want some company?"

Stephanie supposed the girl didn't see her—or was too strung out to notice her.

"Raven, I'm lookin' for a friend of yours," Jake said. "Girl named Tina. But she might go by Tiana. Any idea where I could find her?"

Raven blinked. "Last time I seen Tiana she was with a dude named Nicholson."

Stephanie drew in her breath and Jake exchanged looks with her. What Shondra had heard confirmed Tina was still with this guy. Finally, a real break in her search, and evidence that Tina was alive and probably well!

"What you want her for?" Raven asked, suddenly looking suspicious.

Stephanie scooted across the seat and leaned up past Jake to the window, anxious to glean any more information she could. "She's my sister. I've lost contact with her and I need to find her."

"What can you tell me about her and Nicholson?" Jake asked.

"We met up with him at the Riverwatch Tavern a couple months ago," Raven said, pointing vaguely in the direction of the CBD. "He took a real liking to Tiana—dude was all over her, couldn't get enough. Last time I saw her, she said he wanted her for the whole weekend. She got in his fancy car and took off."

"And you haven't seen her since?" Stephanie asked.

Raven shook her head. "But I wouldn't worry none. That guy's rich. Knows how to treat a girl right. Fancy car, expensive suits—even gave her a diamond necklace before she went off with him."

Again, Stephanie made eye contact with Jake.

"Listen, Raven," Jake said, "this Nicholson—did you ever get the idea he was involved with drugs? He ever try to give you any? Or sell 'em to ya? Maybe ask you to pass 'em to somebody else?"

The girl just blinked, stayed quiet. Somewhere a siren rang out.

Finally, Raven turned and started walking up the street.

"Raven, wait," Jake said, easing the truck forward. She walked faster and he sped up. "Raven, listen to me. I'll pay you for the information. I'll pay you a lot."

The girl stopped and looked over her shoulder. Jake pulled alongside her again and she said, "How much?"

"How's two hundred bucks?"

The girl pursed her lips, looked down at the sidewalk, then raised her gaze once more. "I don't want to get in no trouble with Ni—" She stopped suddenly. "With nobody."

"This is just between you and me."

"You a cop?"

"No. I'm just somebody who . . . Well, let's just say I have a good reason for wantin' to find out who's runnin' drugs around here. They . . . took somethin' from me."

Raven let out a sigh, finally saying, "He didn't bring up drugs to me or Tiana . . . but I knew of him before, knew some girls who were selling for him. That was a few years back, but he was into it then, big time."

Jake's heart started beating faster at suddenly getting a leg up on answers that had evaded him two years ago and which, since that time, he'd tried to convince himself he didn't care about. He'd never looked for the people who'd ordered a hit on him—he'd been too lethargic, convinced it didn't matter because it wouldn't change anything. And he *still* wasn't sure it would change anything, but the mere possibility had his mind racing. "These girls—can you tell me their names?"

She hesitated. "That'd cost more."

"How much?"

"Another hundred."

"Done."

Raven looked a little taken aback, like maybe she hadn't expected him to agree so easily, but she replied, "Was a girl named Lena back then—skinny brunette, real pale white girl. And another one called herself Tori—red hair and wild green eyes."

"You know if they're still in the business?"

"Selling or whoring?"

"Either."

"See 'em both in the CBD sometimes looking to pick up tricks. Check in the hotels on Canal. But you didn't hear none of this from me."

"No worries—this is a private conversation."

"That everything?" she asked.

He nodded.

"Give me the money." She approached the truck, hand outstretched.

Jake dug in his wallet, counting out fifties and pressing them into her hand. She stank, and he hated to think about what she'd use the cash for—probably more of whatever drug she was on. It ate at his stomach. "Can I give you some advice?"

The girl shrugged. "Whatever."

"Get yourself in a cab and go to a motel tonight, and in the mornin', get yourself over to the Salvation Army on Claiborne or to a place called Bridge House on Camp Street. They can help get you on the road to gettin' well and havin' a better life."

This time she worked hard to look unconcerned and aloof.

"Think about it," he said. "Best possible thing you could do for yourself. Good people there who can help." He knew because he'd made a few phone calls when he'd hoped he might talk Shondra into going to a shelter.

Raven stuffed the money into the waistband of her skirt, taking care to make sure it was well hidden before turning to walk away. He wished she'd do what he'd suggested, but knew she probably wouldn't.

He'd just started rolling up his window when she said, "Wait."

He stopped. "Yeah?"

"You find Tiana, you tell her I said hey?"

"Sure," he said. "Anything else?"

She shook her head. "Just that. She was real nice. I hope Nicholson's giving her everything she ever dreamed of."

As Jake eased the truck away from the curb, Stephanie scooted over, away from him. "So if she's with this Nicholson guy," she asked, duly excited, "what now?"

"Next step'll be stakin' out his house, seein' if he goes to Tina when he leaves."

"Why not just ask him?"

He turned to look at her. "Go to the guy's house, where his wife and kids live, and ask him about the prostitute he's seein'?"

She looked belligerent and determined, as always. "I couldn't care less if his wife finds out he's a scumbag. In fact, I'd prefer it."

"Me too, *chère,* but as usual, you're ignorin' the danger factor. If this guy is big into the drug game—and he may or may not be, we don't know at this point—he's a dangerous guy. If he's in any way linked to the people that killed Becky, he's a *real* dangerous guy. The kinda guy we don't wanna piss off, especially since we have reason to believe your sister's doin' fine. The thing now is to be patient. We'll get to her, don't worry. In the meantime, I'll make some phone calls tomorrow, see if I can track him down some other way."

"If you find out where he is, you can't go without me," she said. "You have to take me with you."

He sighed. "It'd be better if I went alone."

"Why?"

"Because I'm havin' a hunch this is a *bad guy.* There's no need for you to be anywhere near him when I can go by myself and get the same information."

She wore a familiar look of desperation that her heavy

makeup couldn't hide. "She's my sister, Jake, and if she's with him—I can't be apart from her a second longer than necessary, okay? I've looked for her for too long and worried too much. I've felt too guilty that somehow this might be my fault."

Jake drew in his breath. Guilt. That he understood, far too well. "All right," he finally conceded. "I won't go lookin' for the guy without you."

"Okay." She sounded appeased.

Quiet filled the truck cab, making Jake relieved to reach LaRue House. Unfortunately, there was no free space along the curb to pull over, and one didn't appear until a block later.

Without a word, she got out and slammed the door.

Only when she heard his shut, as well, did she look back. "What are you doing?"

"Seein' that you get in all right."

She issued a sigh of disgust. "I'm fine, Jake. The B and B is right there." She pointed up the street, then walked on. "Go home."

"I'll go home once I see you're safe inside," he said, catching up with her. She took long strides that showed off her slender legs in that sinfully short dress. "And frankly, I'd feel better if I could lock you in the place. It'd be the only way I could be sure you won't do anything stupid."

She cast him a sideways glance. "I called you before I went out tonight, didn't I?"

"A shockingly smart move, *chère*. Still pisses me off that you had to go and take matters into your own hands, but I'm glad you called."

Reaching the brick walkway to her room, they turned off the street and headed into the shadowy garden area. "And *I'm* glad I took matters into my own hands. Do I need to point out that we found all this new information by going to the very first place on Melody's list?"

"Dumb luck."

She stopped, turning to face him, looking incredulous. "Would it kill you to ever give me credit for *anything*?"

He peered into her eyes, a warm deep blue beneath the lamps lighting the path. She was so damn beautiful, so much more than he'd even seen in the beginning. It was tearing him apart. *Everything* about this situation was tearing him apart. "No," he said softly. "You're right. Goin' to Antonio's turned out to be a smart move, *chère*."

"Thank you," she whispered before starting to head deeper down the path. He followed behind, watching the sway of her hips, thinking, *Why? Why do I have to want her so bad? Why does she have to turn me inside out?* His heart felt like it was going to beat right through his chest.

She was a few steps from her door when he grabbed her hand and spun her toward him. "I'm sorry, Stephanie. About this morning. About how things turned out." He shook his head. He owed her more than this, but it was *something* anyway, and it was all he had to give. "I never meant for things to get . . . so outta hand."

The look in her eyes told him what he already knew— the words were woefully inadequate. They'd never talked about what was growing between them, but for him to deny altogether that something *had* grown was just shitty.

And yet admitting it was . . . impossible. Because it was breaking a vow to Becky, a vow he couldn't let go of. He owed *her* a hell of a lot more than he could ever repay, too. And she'd loved him more than life. Sex with another woman, that was okay. But *love*? He swallowed back everything he knew he wanted with Stephanie because he'd *never* escape the guilt if he let himself have it all.

She stood there looking like the perfect sex kitten, waiting for him to say more. And he wasn't saying it.

The night air seemed to thicken, until she finally whispered, "I hate you."

She snatched her hand from his, and he grabbed it back—he couldn't let her go, not like this. "Don't say that, *beb*."

"Why do you even care?"

He swallowed back the unspeakable truth once more and said, "I don't want you to hate me."

"Well, you don't want me to love you, either, so what exactly is it that you *do* want, Jake?"

He stood looking at her, her eyes wild and beautiful, her chest heaving.

I just want you. I don't want to call it love, or need, or give it any name at all. I want it to be easy, and good, like before. I don't want words to mess it up.

"*Mon Dieu*, Stephanie," he uttered softly. He might not want to think he needed this woman, but there was no other way to describe what rumbled inside him, what yearned to get out, what yearned to take her in. He couldn't contain it a minute longer.

Lifting his hands to her face, he gave her a hard, slow kiss that ran through him like hot lava—especially when she began to kiss him back, firm and hungry.

Her fingernails clawed at his chest through his shirt and his breath came in heavy, rolling waves as his arms closed around her, pulling her to where he was hard for her. More desperate kisses followed, so rough he knew they were bruising each other's mouths, but he didn't care. Just had to have her. Had to feel her against him. They moved together in that timeless rhythm they always found with such ease.

He gathered the short hem of her dress in his hands so she could feel him better, closer, and at first, when he felt her bare flesh, he thought she'd left off panties. But then he realized she was wearing a thong—the other pair he'd bought for her. He kissed her even more brutally, wanted to make her feel everything there was to feel.

Her arms locked tight around his neck, and he never wanted the punishing kisses to stop—it was as if they gave him life, kept his heart beating, helped him breathe. Vague, distant street sounds filtered into their ragged breaths as he moved one hand to her breast, making her whimper against his mouth. More of her, he had to have more. He reached inside the open collar of her dress, freeing her breast from the black lace that held it, letting his touch close warm and firm over her softness, her beaded nipple jutting into his palm. Impulsively breaking their kiss, he dipped his head there for one brisk lick, her nipple sweet and turgid on his tongue.

"God, oh God, oh God," she murmured, her voice trembling. When he lifted his head from her chest, she lowered her hands to the front of his shirt, grabbed onto the placket, and yanked it apart. Buttons clicked and clattered to the bricks at their feet as she clawed her fingernails into his chest until he groaned.

They moved in perfect unison below, everything going quieter now, but just as passionate. He looked at her in the moonlight before kissing her again, and she kissed him back as ravenously as if she hadn't been kissed in years.

He knew she would come soon, just from the way they moved, and he pushed himself stiff against her. She met the pressure, and he pulled her tight, tight, to his body until she was whimpering, "Oh, oh, oh . . ."

Her hot cry of release followed, her head dropping

back, eyes falling shut. He listened to her breathe as she rode it out—and then—Peter, Paul, and Mary—he was coming, too. *"Merde,"* he moaned, too late to stop it, nothing to do but drive himself against her sweet, soft body and give himself up to the shock of pleasure he hadn't seen coming.

He rested his head against her shoulder for a moment after, even as his legs threatened to fold beneath him.

When finally he looked down at her, she was staring blankly, sadly, at his chest, as if she couldn't quite believe what they'd done. He shut his eyes against her pain—he couldn't quite believe it, either. "I'm so sorry," he said.

She pushed away from his embrace, hurrying to pull her dress together in front. "So am I," she said, still not looking at him.

He ran one hand back through his hair. "I never meant to hurt you, Stephanie."

Only then did she glance up. "You still are."

After which she rushed to her door, dug her keys out, and stuck one in the lock.

"Stephanie, please, let me . . ." He shook his head, so damn confused he didn't even know what he meant to say.

She stopped on the threshold and looked back. "Let you what?"

"Apologize?" He held his hands out in front of him.

"It doesn't help," she said, disappearing inside to slam the door.

He heard the lock turn and felt like a jerk. She had every right to hate him. He almost hated himself.

A shame, a little voice whispered in his ear as he walked up the street toward his truck. *Just when you were starting to like yourself again.*

You lie in bed at the bayou house. Cool white sheets cover you; the fan turns overhead. The window across the room is open, as always, but everything is cool—cooler than you've ever felt it here. Brisk and refreshing, like you imagine the first day of spring must feel someplace farther north. An old Sinatra album plays across the room, Old Blue Eyes crooning "Violets for Your Furs."

But you're not alone.

She crawls toward you from the foot of the bed, her face hidden by a white Mardi Gras mask—white sequins outline her eyes, and soft, downy white feathers curve around her face, so that you see only lush pink lips. She licks them, as if she knows you're watching them. You want to kiss her.

Long white gloves rise to her forearms and a white corset of satin and lace pushes her breasts high and curves down over her hips. Snow white garters stretch to sheer white stockings below. No panties.

"You runnin' around without panties again?" you ask. You know this is a dream, and you're thinking if she

answers the right way, it will prove this is her. *You* know *it's her, you always have, but still you're looking, reaching, for that little bit of confirmation. And if this is a dream, you should be able to control it, so you will her to answer.*

But instead she only smiles with those pretty pink lips, like she has a secret. You know this is a dream, but it doesn't seem to be yours to create.

They never have been, *a voice whispers in your ear.*

She straddles you, and you hiss in your breath, ready to embrace her, but suddenly she is stretching your arm up against the headboard, tying you to the bed.

As she ties your other wrist with a shiny white scarf, you wonder if this is punishment. But as she bends to rain kisses across your chest, you understand: This is a reward. Something she's giving you. Making it so none of the decisions here are yours, putting you at her mercy.

She kisses her way down your stomach, her lips leaving a trail of cool sensation when the fan blows over their path. Then she peers up at you, her eyes mysterious and playful and oh-so-blue through the mask, and you tremble because she's pulling the sheets down now, hovering above your erection, smiling at you as if to tease.

Her gloved hands run up your length, one after the other, caressing you with her silken touch, and your body convulses beneath her, making you pull at the satin ties, wishing you could touch her, hold her. Gift or not, it's not as easy as you thought to take without giving.

She no longer smiles when she lowers herself onto you, bringing your bodies together in that ultimate union. A low groan leaves you and everything inside you contracts.

She looks into your eyes as she makes love to you. You can't look away, don't even want to. You read what's in

*her gaze and you're not afraid of it. You can't not feel it,
too. And you can't hide it. She sees it. She knows.*

*She's waiting for you to say it. It's a dream, but you
know she's waiting for you to tell her what's in your
heart.*

*Yet, still, you can't—the fear is back, that quickly. It's
so hard to need someone this way. The last time you
needed someone like this, you lost her.*

So you simply say, "I'm sorry."

*And in an instant, she's gone, and you're alone. Music
no longer plays, and drenching deep summer heat pours
in the window to fill the room.*

Chapter 24

Jake stayed in bed late the next morning suffering a familiar feeling of not wanting to face the day. Sleep was easier.

But Shondra had risen early and returned from another trip to the market with ingredients for pancakes, and when he smelled them cooking, he couldn't bring himself to disappoint her, so he'd dragged himself up and into a pair of jeans he found on the floor, entering the kitchen with a forced smile.

Now she was gone again—off to buy Scruff a leash so she could take him outside without worrying he'd run into traffic—so he'd made himself shower and put on clean clothes and now sat by the phone in the living room, the local phone directory open in his lap. He supposed being prodded to get out of bed had motivated him a little.

He dialed the number for Les Couleurs and a woman answered.

"Hello," he said, putting on his best good ol' country boy voice, "I'm hopin' you can help me. Would Robert Nicholson by chance be there this mornin'?"

"No, I'm afraid he's not, but this is his wife. Can I leave him a message?"

"I'm an old buddy o' his from way back, in town for a few days, and was hopin' to get together. Wouldn't be anyplace I could reach him right now, would he? My schedule's kinda strapped after today."

"I'm not really sure of his plans today, but you might be able to catch him at home. Let me give you the number."

After hanging up, he tried Nicholson at home, but the answering machine picked up. He'd hoped Nicholson's wife might give him some other places to try, damn it, or a cell number.

Looked like he was back to the stakeout plan. Truth was, though, he wasn't sure he could pull it off. He was so tired the last couple of days, wrung out and on the verge of slipping back into a depression that seemed to come and go at will. A stakeout would mean getting up awful damn early, and he wasn't even sure he could talk himself into getting out of bed if the alarm went off in the middle of the night.

But maybe he *should* get up in the middle of the night. Might get lucky and avoid another one of those damn dreams. He was sick of them. They were incredible while he was having them, but he was disgusted with the after-effect, trying to figure out what the hell they meant. He was even more disgusted by what they made him wake up feeling— feelings he couldn't be having. He'd told her that, and God knew he'd told *himself* that—now his brain had to grasp it.

He couldn't love her.

And he wanted the dreams to be done.

"Five minutes," Tina told the cabbie, hauling her shopping bags from the car to the sidewalk. Almost more than she could carry, so she was glad to be home.

Although the apartment was beginning not to feel all that much like home. Old elegance and wisteria aside, suddenly nothing felt right.

She and Robert had had another explosive argument on the phone this morning, their third or fourth in as many days. To appease her, he'd suggested she go shopping, then to the spa. She'd ended up spending nearly a thousand dollars and had come home to drop off her bags before heading to her massage and facial.

Strange, she thought, teetering slowly up the brick walk, weighed down by her purchases. Before Robert, spending a thousand dollars on clothes in one day would have sounded impossible, but for him, it was merely a drop in the bucket. And, oddly, the spree hadn't made her feel any better. It didn't fix the problems standing between them. She doubted a facial would clear them up, either. *These are bigger problems than the ones you're used to.*

She sighed, wondering exactly how she'd got herself into this mess. Why had she turned to prostitution in the first place? *Devastation. You were in love with Russ. Maybe you still are.* Even so, it was hard to believe she'd been upset enough to start selling her body, selling herself. Just a culmination of *everything,* she supposed.

Doesn't matter, though. You're in it up to your neck now.

She was beginning to think Robert wasn't going to leave his wife. Both his kids had set off for the fall college semester yesterday, and he'd promised that last night he'd tell Melissa the marriage was over. This morning, of course, it had been a bunch of "it just didn't seem like the right time" crap, and in her heart, she had an ugly feeling it was *never* going to be the right time.

Worse yet, she actually thought she was starting to love the big lug. She felt more and more lonely when he wasn't around, craving his company and attention, feeling empty when she had to fall asleep without him. Was it possible to love two men at the same time? That didn't matter, either. She was beginning to suffer a familiar sense of desperation that—as she circled the luxurious mansion to her door in the back—made it easier to remember why she'd become an escort. She'd been running away. To something totally new, something that had seemed glamorous in some way. Or at least exotic. She'd wanted to be someone else. Tiana.

She finally pushed through the door, heaving all her bags through—to find Robert seated on the antique sofa with a pretty brunette wearing nothing but a lacy purple teddy.

All Tina's blood seemed to drain to her feet. "Who the hell is this?"

Robert looked up, not nearly as startled as she thought he should be. "I thought you were going to be out all day, darling."

Her stomach pinched to hear him use her favorite endearment in this damning moment. "I said, *who the hell is this? What's going on?*" Stupid question, though. She could see what was going on.

"Tiana, this is Amber. Amber, Tiana."

The bimbo in lingerie lifted her hand in an uncertain wave. Tina curled her hands into fists, unwittingly gathering the fabric of her skirt. She hated her life in this moment, hated *everything*.

"Well," Robert said on a sigh, "inconvenient that you should come home just now, but maybe we can make this work for us, hmm?"

"What?" she asked, still too stunned to do anything effective.

Robert gave his head a persuasive tilt, flashing a seductive smile. "Why don't you join us, darling?"

Bile rolled in Tina's stomach. She knew what she'd become—a whore—and she knew she was in the Big Easy, but she still couldn't quite believe what he was suggesting. "Are you out of your mind?" she uttered too quietly. She wanted to scream and yell, rant and rave—yet all she could seem to do was whisper.

"Come here, Tiana." He motioned her closer, but she stayed rooted in place. "This will help. Make you feel better. Make everything easier." He pointed vaguely to the coffee table, to a small mirror lined with what she presumed was cocaine.

She held in her gasp, but still felt breathless. She knew it was part of the scene she'd fallen into here, she knew her friend Raven had been into drugs. But Robert? She simply stared, agape. *I hate my life. I hate it. I hate it.*

"Don't be afraid, darling. Coke's not always in vogue these days, but I still like it. Try it with me. You'll like it, too." He held out his hand.

That was how he'd first invited her to be his for a night; also how he'd suggested she come live here. Something about the gesture combined with the power in his eyes was so alluring that she knew why she'd never turned him down for anything before.

Maybe it was time to start. "No."

Robert blinked, looked mildly displeased. "Tiana." The tone used on a misbehaving child.

"No," she said again.

He looked disappointed in her—an expression she was

too used to, and it made her stomach curl into a tight ball. *You're always letting someone down. Always.*

"Well, darling, there are two ways to go here," he said. "You can turn around and leave, pretend you didn't come home at an inopportune time, and we'll never have to speak of this again. Or you can come have some fun with Amber and me. I'd prefer the second, because I'd prefer for you to understand and respect my wants and needs— but the first will suffice as well."

Tina's mind spun. She just wanted some respect, and she'd thought Robert was the man who would give it to her. Fantasies of her future that, moments before, had been fading now vanished completely.

But wait. Maybe you can save this. If you stand up for yourself, show him you won't be kicked around, maybe you can change this into a victory.

"There's a third option," she said, her voice a little stronger now. "I have a cab waiting outside to take me to the spa. You can put Amber in it and send her home. Then you and I can talk this out, get back on track, and make some decisions about our future."

"I'm sure I don't need to remind you who pays your bills, darling," he said, his tone still bizarrely even and kind.

"No," she said, her hope crumbling. He didn't *want* her to stand up for herself. He wouldn't respect her, even if she earned it. He wasn't going to leave Melissa. This wasn't her home. It all became shockingly clear, and her strength diminished as she spoke from her heart. "I thought you loved me."

"I *do* love you."

You're sitting on our couch snorting coke with a woman wearing lingerie. "I guess you think I'm pretty stupid," she said on a hard swallow. *Don't cry. Don't cry.*

Robert gave her a long, scrutinizing look. "Stupid? No. But stepping beyond your bounds—yes. There are un-written rules to the kind of relationship you and I have. You need to understand that, once and for all. You've been far too demanding lately. Downright needy, if you want the truth."

She girded herself, kept herself from trembling. "Rules? Like that you get to do *whatever* you want with *whoever* you want, right under my nose, in the place you told me was my home?"

He looked unfazed. "Well . . . yes, frankly." When she didn't reply, he went on. "I take care of you, Tiana. I give you everything. Every stitch of clothing on your pretty back. Every scrap of food that goes into your pretty mouth. In return, I expect your obedience or, at the very least, your tolerance. Not much to ask for all I've given you."

From a technical standpoint, she couldn't argue it. And she supposed most girls in her position would shut up now and accept the situation—go to the spa.

One problem, though. She couldn't live like this. If she was with a man, she needed his devotion—that simple. And in that moment, she realized that as much as she loved all the material things Robert had given her, it had been his devotion she'd found most endearing, his devo-tion that had earned her growing love.

Now that she no longer had that—and realizing, in fact, that she'd *never* had it—she had nothing. Less, per-haps, than when she'd found him. "You're a bastard!" she spat, then reached for the nearest thing—an antique Chi-nese vase she knew he particularly valued—and flung it at him. It hit the wall above his head and shattered into pieces that rained down on him and Amber.

Amber gasped, putting her arms up to shield herself as Robert shot to his feet. "Have you lost your fucking mind?"

"No, *you* have—if you expect me to live like this! I'm outta here!" She spun, snatched up a couple of the shopping bags, and started to walk through the door.

But he crossed the room in a flash, grabbing onto her wrist, wrenching one bag free until it dropped to the floor. "Oh no, darling, that's not how it works. You leave, you leave with nothing."

She drew in her breath, then let it back out. "Fine! I don't need you anyway!"

She swung the other bag around, hitting him with it, and stormed through the door, thankful she had her purse and what cash was left over from her shopping spree. Not that she had any idea where she would go, what she would do. Oh God.

She ran back around the house and down the walk; she was shaking when she got back in the cab.

"To Jardin de Beauté now, miss?" the middle-aged cabbie asked, his eyes meeting hers in the rearview mirror.

He seemed like a nice man, but she didn't want him to see her fear, or her sadness. She didn't want *anyone* to see it. "Change of plans," she said, pleased she'd kept her voice from quavering.

"Where to then?"

"Um, just a minute—I need to think through the rest of my day." The rest of her day, and the rest of her life. God, where could she go? What should she do? She knew she could call her mom or Stephanie, and a certain comfort lay in that idea, but . . . Even if her fantasies of life with Robert had just turned to impossibility, she still couldn't give up and go crawling back with her tail between her legs. Maybe if she'd never told Stephanie she'd become an escort. Maybe if she hadn't heard Stephanie's nasty little sounds of disgust over the phone. She just wanted to do something on her own that would make them proud.

And she didn't *have* to give up yet—she just had to think. And right now she needed . . . not to be completely alone in the world—she needed to find Raven. Her only friend since hitting the city, Raven had shown her the ropes of the business. Raven wasn't happy doing it, either, so maybe together they could figure a way out of their problems.

So that's what she would do. She'd head to the CBD and find Raven.

Only, first, before anything else, she had a stop to make. "Les Couleurs on Royal Street," she told the driver.

Jake stood behind the bar at Sophia's, serving up drinks to the regulars, giving his well-practiced smile, keeping conversation to a minimum, and wishing the night would go faster. He felt like crap inside and wanted to be alone.

He couldn't believe what he'd done to Stephanie last night outside her door. He'd simply wanted her with a power he couldn't push down. And when she'd kissed him back, there'd been no stopping—for either of them.

Throughout the whole encounter he'd never once thought ahead to how she'd feel afterward. *Real nice, Broussard. Dump the girl, then force yourself on her.* He knew it had been mutual, but when he'd seen the abject hurt in her eyes afterward, he'd felt like the biggest scum alive.

The only thing to soften the emotion was the fact that it wasn't exactly a new one. In fact, it was real familiar. For a guy who'd once liked to think of himself as someone who took care of people, he sure managed to hurt the women in his life. In one way or another. *At least Stephanie's still alive.*

Damn, the power of that thought hit him hard, nearly had him reeling, making him glad he was leaning on the bar. Just the notion of something happening to Stephanie . . .

"Whiskey sour."

Jake looked up to find none other than Robert Nicholson standing across the bar, an experienced-looking woman he didn't know at the guy's side. "And a glass of your best Merlot for Dominique."

Jake's senses went on the alert as he poured the lady's wine and mixed Nicholson's drink. He scanned the room for Tina, but didn't find her. Setting both glasses atop cocktail napkins, he took Nicholson's money, saying low, "I need to speak to you privately."

Nicholson looked flustered at the request, clearly caught off guard, then told Dominique to go mingle and that he'd join her in a minute. Once she was gone, he said, "What is it?"

"I'm lookin' for a girl named Tina. You might know her as Tiana. Pretty blonde, last seen with *you*."

The man relaxed a little, looking more comfortable, and slightly smug. "What do you want with Tiana?"

"She's got a sister who's real worried about her 'cause she's been outta touch. Just tryin' to hook 'em up, that's all, and I heard you'd be able to help."

Nicholson looked around to make sure nobody was listening before he replied. "I suppose there's no harm in telling you—I gave Tiana a place to stay for a while. But she's not with me anymore. She left this morning."

Damn it, what timing. "Any idea where she went?"

Nicholson gave his head a casual shake. "Could be she's turning tricks in the CBD where I found her. And she's a clingy little thing, so if I were a betting man, I'd say she's likely with her friend who introduced us. What was her name?" He peered upward, thinking. "Raven. If I had to guess, I'd say that wherever Raven is, Tiana is."

Jake's stomach somersaulted. If he was lucky, Tina hadn't yet made it out of the CBD looking for Raven. But if she'd already tracked Raven to the projects—*merde*.

"Thanks, man," he said to Nicholson, even though the guy was a Grade A ass. And he might also be a big player in the drug scene, but Jake would have to explore that later.

Striding to the end of the bar, he called downstairs to Danny's office, informing him he had an emergency and had to leave. Next, he called LaRue House.

"Hello?" God, just her voice was enough to bury him. He felt it in his stomach.

"Stephanie, get in your car and pick me up outside Sophia's. I've got a lead on Tina and we need to look for her—now."

"God—okay," she said, and they both hung up.

He didn't want to scare her, but on the other hand, he had a bad feeling about this.

Tina peered out the window as the cab sped up Canal Street toward an address she'd gotten from a girl at the Crescent. "But you don't want to go up there, girlfriend. Raven's all strung out, and that's a badass neighborhood."

Yet Tina didn't care. If Raven was in trouble, she had to find her—then they could both deal with their troubles together. As soon as she located her, they'd grab another taxi and get a cheap hotel room for the night with the left-over money in her purse. Tomorrow, they could both start fresh.

God, this day hadn't turned out like she'd expected. It was supposed to be about shopping and spa-ing and then dinner and lovemaking with Robert. Instead, it had been about endings, and new—even if rocky—beginnings.

Her chest swelled with pride when she remembered her visit to Les Couleurs. Melissa had struck her as a friendly, likable woman, and Tina had actually found herself feeling sorry for her . . . even as she gently told her the truth. "Did you know Robert sleeps with hookers? And that he has an apartment in the Garden District where he puts them up? Did you know he promises he's going to leave you?"

Melissa had seemed wholly wounded, but not as surprised as Tina might have expected. She must have suspected there were big secrets between them.

"I'm not telling you this to hurt you. I'm only telling you because I thought you should know." *And because I want Robert's perfect little world to come crashing down around him just like mine did today.*

Melissa had thanked her, but then asked her to leave—which was understandable—so she'd headed to the shabby apartment she'd shared with Raven and two other girls for a few weeks. The place was quiet, though, no one home. From there, she'd headed to the Riverwalk mall, where she killed time and tried to think constructively about how to make a change in her life. Only when she'd headed to the Crescent a little while ago had she heard the disheartening news about her friend.

"Sure you want out here?" the cabdriver asked, pulling to the curb. He was young, kind of cute, and seemed sincerely concerned. She half-considered telling the guy her sad tale, watching for some glimmer of absolution or romance in his eyes, trying to make the miracle of a normal life materialize out of nothing in a New Orleans taxicab. Life didn't have to be fabulous or glamorous—just normal.

But even she knew the idea was insane, so she simply smiled and said, "Yeah, I need to find a friend here," then paid him and got out.

As the cab slowly drove away, she felt inexorably alone. *But you're going to be a stronger person, starting right now. No more Tiana.* She'd just be Tina from this point forward. And she'd help Raven, and together, they'd build a better life.

She walked briskly, wishing there were more streetlights as she peered behind Dumpsters and into alleyways looking for her girlfriend. *Where are you, Raven? Please be here.* She willed Raven to appear from somewhere, so they could get in another cab or a passing bus and get the hell out of this creepy place.

"You too fine to be a white girl."

She yanked her gaze from where she'd been searching the shadows and found three young black guys coming toward her. Before her days as an escort, she would have been scared, but she told herself she knew how to handle this. *Don't act afraid—act tough, like you belong here.* "You guys know a girl named Raven?"

One of them laughed. "Yeah, we know Raven. We know her real good." This elicited a chuckle from the rest.

"I'm a friend of hers. Do you know where she is?"

The first guy who'd spoken, wearing a dingy-looking T-shirt, baggy jeans, and a red bandanna over his head, came closer. He smiled at her as if she were prey, something he'd just caught. "Ain't gonna find no Raven 'round here no more. Done took off, went to some pansy-ass homeless shelter or somethin'."

She held her ground, even though he stood too close to her. "Do you know where?"

One of them shrugged, and the bandanna dude shook his head. "Don't care, neither. 'Specially now that *you're* here." He lifted his hand, stroking his fingertips down her cheek.

"Afraid I have to go," she said. "I have to find Raven. It's an emergency." She looked around, up and down the street—but damn it, not a cab or a bus to be seen. Nothing but one beat-up old car cruising past.

Bandanna leered at her with a grin. "Only emergency I know about's in my pants." His friends laughed. "You gonna take care of it for me."

Act like he doesn't repulse you, make a bargain with him, anything. She forced herself to lift *her* hand to *his* cheek. "Tell you what. As soon as I find Raven, I'll come back and we can have some fun."

But his smile faded. "Ain't gonna be no leavin' or lookin' for no Raven. You can make it easy on yourself or you can make it hard—don't make no difference to me. How's it gonna be? You givin' it up, or am I takin' it?"

Chapter 25

Oh God, Jake, that's her! That's her!" Stephanie felt ill as she watched Tina struggle against the guys attempting to drag her out of the light. "You have to get to her," she sobbed. "You have to do something!"

She'd let Jake drive, thank God, because she'd have wrecked the car by now. He squealed to the curb and lowered the window, yelling, "Police officer! Step away from the lady!"

The action on the sidewalk froze and Stephanie nearly fainted when Jake jumped out of the car and pulled a gun from his waistband. "Move away from her!" he commanded. "Now! Against the fence, hands on your head."

Finally, the young men let loose of her and Stephanie put down her own window and maneuvered herself up and halfway out of it. "Tina, it's me, Steph! Come get in the car!"

Two of Tina's attackers did as Jake said; the other fled. A second later, when the first two saw that Jake wasn't going to shoot or give pursuit, they sprinted off as well. It hardly mattered. All Stephanie could see was her baby sister running toward her.

She flung her door open and met her, arms outstretched, as Tina rounded the fender. As her sister came into her arms, it was as if Tina were a little girl again, running to Stephanie after a bicycle crash or a bee sting, or later, after a failed cheerleading tryout or a bad breakup. Stephanie held on to her as tight as she could, tears streaming down her cheeks into Tina's hair. She heard Tina crying, too.

"My God," Stephanie murmured. "We finally found you."

"How. . . ?" Tina asked, sniffling against her shoulder. "And why? I mean . . ."

"Ladies, I hate to break this up, but you both need to get in the car so we can get outta here."

Stephanie pulled back slightly, making eye contact with Jake over the hood. She loved him and she felt that love wanting to spill from her more now than ever before because he'd saved her sister. *Thank you,* she mouthed— not because it couldn't be said aloud, but because her heart was beating so fast and his eyes were so beautiful and dark that she couldn't get the words out.

He acknowledged it with a light nod, then said, more softly, "We gotta go. This isn't a good place to be."

On the ride back to Stephanie's place, Jake mostly kept his eyes on the road and listened as the two sisters talked and cried and blubbered to one another about how Stephanie had come to New Orleans to find Tina, and it was easy to see how much her concern moved the younger girl.

So, mission complete. Stephanie would go home now.

That was what he'd wanted and now it was going to happen.

And that was a *good* thing.

Never mind that it was ripping his guts out just to think about it. To know she'd no longer be a few short blocks away from him, to know he couldn't see her or talk to her at a moment's notice if he wanted.

But he swallowed back those emotions, because that's what he did, what he was about. And until Stephanie had come along, he'd gotten pretty damn good at it. Good at going through the motions and nothing more.

He could do that again. *Would* do that again. He had no other choice.

He pulled around behind the LaRue to the small lot where the guests parked, and as they all got out, he dropped the keys into Stephanie's hand.

She looked up at him, slightly surprised. "Oh—we probably should have dropped you at your place on the way."

Swell, she'd forgotten he was even there. Understandable, though, under the circumstances, so he tried not to let it bother him. He shook his head, spoke quietly. "No, I can walk. I feel better seein' you two get back here safe."

"Speaking of safe," she asked, "uh, where did the gun come from?"

He tried for a smile. "Don't worry, *beb*. Haven't been packin' heat the whole time I've known you. But we keep a gun in the safe behind the bar at Sophia's—just in case. I grabbed it on the way out."

Just then, Tina ingratiated herself between them. She was a beautiful girl, slightly taller than Stephanie, longer hair, thinner build, every guy's dream, so it was no wonder Nicholson had taken up with her. But already, on the quick ride from the projects, Jake had been able to see the little girl in her, and knew Stephanie had been right all along in worrying. He felt glad he'd done a little something to bring her home.

"Before you go, I want to thank you." She peered up at him with eyes nearly as blue as Stephanie's, but clearly younger and more immature. "Thank you so, so much for helping Steph find me. And for all you did back there."

He gave his head a short shake, playing off the praise. He hadn't done it for praise. He'd done it . . . for Stephanie. "Glad I could help."

The girl gazed up at him like he was some kind of hero, and he looked helplessly back, thinking: *One more female putting me on a pedestal, thinking I'm worthy, thinking I can save people.* But he didn't *feel* very worthy, even less so the last few days, after breaking Stephanie's heart.

"If you hadn't come along back there . . ."

Her breath started to hitch as she recalled what she'd just endured, so he rushed a reply. "It was a matter of good timin'. God watchin' over us, I guess." His own words caught him off guard—it had been a long time since he'd given God credit for anything.

When they reached Stephanie's door, Tina rose onto her toes to give him a kiss on the cheek. He looked down to find her eyes glassy with fresh tears. "Thank you again," she whispered. "And I'm sorry you got dragged into somebody else's problems."

It's my lot in life, he thought, holding in a cynical chuckle as he gently squeezed her hand. "Your sister's the one who really deserves your thanks. She wasn't gonna let anything stand in the way of findin' you. Just let Stephanie help you and things'll work out like they should."

She mustered a small smile through her tears and seemed ready to make a getaway so she wouldn't cry in front of him. "I'll say good night now," she said, pushing her way into the room.

Which left him with Stephanie.

Her eyes looked a little glassy, too, when he peered down into them.

I hate myself for hurting you, but I don't seem to have any other answers. "Well, *beb*," he said instead, past the small lump in his throat, "looks like we did what we set out to do."

She nodded, still gazing up at him.

"So I guess you'll be headin' back up to Chicago now."

Again, a nod. She looked so emotional it was killing him.

"Well, take care of yourself, and be careful. You'll do that for me, no?"

Her lips trembled when she said, "Wait here."

She disappeared behind the door of her room and returned a few seconds later cradling a mound of yarn in her arm, which—when she stretched it out—formed a scarf. "I finally finished it," she told him.

"This is what you were makin'," he said, remembering, "'cause Tina showed you how." She'd told him more than once of her attempt to pick up the skill.

She gave another nod. "And I know it's ugly, and it doesn't even get cold here, but"—she rolled her eyes and thrust it at him—"here it is. A thank-you present."

He took the soft swath of loosely interwoven yarn into his hand. "I thought you were makin' it to show Tina."

"I was." She stared into his chest instead of his eyes, seeming uncomfortable, embarrassed. "But I can make another one. This one I want to give to you, even if it's a stupid gift."

"It's not a stupid gift."

She raised her eyes to his, swallowing nervously. "I thought a lot about you while I was working on it, so it just seems fitting that it should be yours."

"Thank you," he whispered.

She blinked, her features pinching slightly, looking closer to tears, until finally she threw her arms around him, pressing to him tight. "No, thank *you*," she said softly into his chest, and he felt the warmth of her breath through his T-shirt as his arms closed firm around her. He took in the scent of her hair, the feel of her curves, one last time. "Thank you for helping me find my sister, and thank you for . . . helping me find a part of *me,* too." She pulled back, parting their bodies, and peered up at him. "Like it or not, I love you, and I'll always remember you for that." She looked at the scarf again. "Maybe you'll put this in a closet or a drawer and every now and then you'll see it and remember me."

He gazed down into her lovely blue eyes, already missing her embrace. "Despite what you might think, *chère,* I won't ever forget you. That's a promise."

She merely looked up at him, no response. He couldn't blame her. What a promise he'd just made. A promise of . . . nothing. She'd wanted so much more from him and there was a big part of him that wanted to give it to her—and still he was going to walk away.

"Take care of yourself, Stephanie Grant," he said, starting to take backward steps.

"You too," she whispered.

He shut his eyes to block the threat of tears, but opened

them to take one last look. She was wearing the same outfit she'd worn to the bayou house that first night they'd made love. He knew all the beauty that hid underneath it; he knew all the fire that burned in her heart. There was more he should say to her—words he hated, like "need" and "love." But he wasn't willing to back them up—he was only willing to run away. So that's what he did, turned and walked briskly from LaRue House, and as he forced one foot in front of the other, he felt his *own* heart breaking in two—again.

Although he heard a ruckus as he approached his building, he didn't really pay attention. He lived in a seamier area of the Quarter, after all, and it was late—and God knew he had a lot on his mind.

It was only as a low sob came from the street that he peeked around the cars parked along the curb and spied Shondra kneeling on the pavement. Scruff was stretched out in front of her.

"Aw, Jesus," he muttered, breaking into a run. He dropped down next to her on his knees. "What the hell happened?"

She looked up at him, her face wet with tears, lips trembling. "Car."

The little guy's new leash remained attached to his new collar—Jake could only guess he'd gotten loose from her somehow.

Bending over the dog, he pressed a palm to his furry little chest until he got a heartbeat. *Thank God.* "He's not dead," he said. "We need to get him to a vet."

"But . . . I thought you aren't supposed to move people when they're injured."

Poor sweet *'tite fille.* "He's not a person," he said

gently. "And we can't leave him in the street. I'll be careful," he promised, sliding his arms beneath the dog.

Once on his feet, he told Shondra to get his keys from his front pocket and open the passenger door of the truck, nearby. Just then, a cruiser came rolling slowly past, out on patrol. "Hey!" he yelled. "Need some help over here!"

The driver's-side window descended until Jake could see the face inside—a young guy he didn't know. "What's the problem?"

He motioned to the dog in his arms. "Know an all-night vet?"

"Uh, only place I know of is over in Metairie."

Merde. Jake knew the place, too—he'd just hoped there was someplace closer. "Thanks," he said, carrying Scruff to the truck. He laid the dog across the seat, then Shondra and he got in from the other side.

She cried the whole trip, releasing low sniffles and broken, heavy breaths. She stroked the dog's side as they traveled and every so often checked to make sure he was still alive, announcing it each time. Jake drove like a man possessed, but at the same time, tried to take it easy so he wouldn't jostle the dog.

Ten minutes after loading the dog in the vehicle, Jake carried him into the animal hospital. "Dog's name?" a lady asked from behind the counter.

"Scruff," Shondra said.

"Owner?"

"Shondra Walters."

"And who will be paying the bill tonight, Shondra?"

Jake stepped up. "Me."

The woman glanced back and forth between them. "And you're . . . her father?"

"I'm a friend."

The woman nodded, but Jake thought she still looked uncertain.

A few minutes later, Scruff was carried back to the vet. He and Shondra sat side by side in the brightly lit waiting room, where photos of playful puppies and kittens adorned the walls.

"Think he'll be okay?" she asked, glancing up.

He had no idea, of course, but nodded. "He's a tenacious little mutt—he isn't goin' anywhere."

She pursed her lips and he could see her trying to look strong. Funny, he'd never seen Shondra look scared—until now.

"Were you on your way home from work when you saw us?" she asked. "Or on your way home from Stephanie?"

"Work." *And* Stephanie. "Why?"

"Just . . . I thought if you had a late date planned with her after work or somethin', you should call her."

God, that stung. He would have loved to have a late date with Stephanie. He just gave his head a short shake. "No, no date."

"What's wrong?"

"What makes you think somethin's wrong?"

She shrugged. "You're just actin' . . . like you used to, at first. Like you're pissed at somebody. You and Stephanie have a fight or somethin'?"

He kept his gaze trained on a beagle puppy on the opposite wall. "We broke up."

To his shock, Shondra gasped. "Why?"

He peered down at her, deciding he should try to relax her. "Not that big of a deal, *'tite fille*. We just . . . couldn't work some things out."

"What things?" she asked, sounding calmer.

Jake swallowed. "She wanted more than I could give her."

She blinked, looking bewildered. "Like money?"

"No." He shook his head. "Like . . . a more serious relationship than I was into. That's all."

"Why weren't you into it? You didn't feel the same way?"

"Not that exactly." If anyone else asked him such nosy questions, he'd tell them to go to hell. Not Shondra, though. He couldn't help wanting to teach her about life, what to expect, how to survive. It was just hard sometimes knowing how much to say.

"Well, then, *what* exactly?"

"Remember I told you about my wife, who died?"

She nodded.

"Thing is, it just doesn't feel right to have a serious relationship with somebody else. Makes me feel guilty."

She blinked and he sat there waiting for her to think he was a noble guy, but her expression said something else. "I don't mean to get all up in your business, but if you ask me, that's pretty damn stupid."

He flinched, widening his eyes on her. "How do you figure, O wise one?"

She tilted her head, clearly considering her answer, then looked down at the black sandals Stephanie had picked out for her. "Well, if I was your wife, and *I* died"— she lifted her gaze back to him—"I'd want you to hook up with somebody else and be happy. It'd be real selfish to expect you to stay all faithful to me, since I couldn't be with you no more. Know what I mean?"

She was blushing a little, but he pretended not to see it. And her reasoning made sense, yet . . . "Thing is, it's a lot more complicated than I can explain." *I caused her death.*

Shondra didn't need to know *that* sort of horrible truth—that you can love someone and still be responsible for letting them die.

She only shrugged. "I'm just sayin' . . . I don't think your wife would want you to be alone. You've seemed a lot happier than when I first met you, and I figured it was Stephanie makin' you that way. I *liked* you that way."

As the office's inner door opened and the vet came through, Jake and Shondra both stood up. "How is he?" she asked with anxious eyes.

The doctor—a clean-cut guy about Jake's age—smiled warmly, and already Jake knew the mutt was gonna make it. "Scruff's a tough little guy and he's going to be okay," the doc said.

"See, what'd I tell ya?" Jake added with a light smile.

She smiled back and he felt a little like a hero again.

"He's got a concussion and a bump on the head, but both of those will go away and he'll be good as new in no time."

"For real?" Shondra asked, her gaze gone wide.

"Absolutely," the vet said. "You'll want to take it easy getting him home, and he might move a little slow for the next day or so, but after that, he'll be just fine."

Shondra gave a little jump for joy, grabbing onto Jake's arm. "Did you hear that? He's gonna be fine, Jake! Good as new!"

Jake put his arm around her shoulder, happy and relieved on her behalf. Then he caught the eye of the receptionist—the woman was watching them, and looking at him like he was a child molester. Pissed off, he pulled his arm away.

A moment later, when he handed the woman a credit card, she said, "Does that girl's parents know where she is?"

He took a deep breath. "For your information, she's a runaway."

"And you're. . . ?"

He really disliked this woman's nasty, unspoken accusations. He answered through slightly clenched teeth. "Like an uncle to her."

As they drove home, Jake said to Shondra, "You know, it's a shame Scruff doesn't have a nice yard to run around and play in."

She simply rolled her eyes at him. "Bump the psychology, dude. You're bad at it."

He couldn't help laughing. This was the Shondra he'd come to know and love.

"And besides, we already got a dog at home. Mama wouldn't let me bring Scruff home, even if I *went* home, which I'm not."

"Thing is," he said, getting serious again, "if anybody found out you're stayin' with me, I'd be in a lot of trouble, and you'd be goin' to child services—and God knows *what* would happen to Scruff."

This all seemed to catch her attention. "Who's gonna find out, though?"

He eased up the freeway ramp that would take them back to the French Quarter. "That woman at the animal clinic thought somethin' funny was goin' on between us and she didn't like it."

"So? She's nobody."

"She has my name—it was on my credit card. If she wanted to, she could call child services. I'm not that hard to track down."

"You don't think she'd *do* somethin' like that?"

"I don't know, *'tite fille,* but my point is—if it's not her, it might be somebody else, and I don't think you, me, or Scruff want that kind of trouble."

She pulled in her breath and sat up a little straighter. "Then maybe Scruff and me should bounce, head back out on the street."

"Peter, Paul, and Mary," he muttered, "no goddamn way are you goin' back out on the street."

"Well, where else can I go? And don't say home."

"Don't worry—I don't want you goin' home, either. But I'm bettin' there's somebody else in your life who'd be a more . . . *appropriate* person for you to live with."

She stayed quiet, looked pensive.

"I could do some diggin' if I wanted to," he said quietly, eyes on the road.

"Diggin'?"

"I know your last name now, Shondra Walters. And I used to be a cop, so I still have connections."

"Holy shit—*you* used to be a cop?"

"Yeah. And I could probably get a friend to search some databases and find out where you came from. But I don't wanna do that." He sighed. "All I want for you is someplace safe, someplace where you'll have a good shot at a decent life. Isn't there *somebody* who might be able to help us out on that?"

Next to him, Shondra let out a long, acceptant sigh of her own, staring at the dashboard. Finally, she whispered, "My Grandma Maisy, maybe."

"Grandma Maisy—she's somebody you love, somebody who loves *you*?"

She nodded. "My daddy's mother. She don't like my mama's boyfriend none. But . . . I don't think I can tell her what happened with him."

"I could do it if you want."

She turned to look at him. "Straight up? You'd do that for me?"

"Yeah, I'd do that for you. I'd do a lot for you."

"Guess you already have."

"Tell you what," he said. "We'll talk about this more tomorrow, figure out the best way to fill Grandma Maisy in. How's that sound?"

Across from him, she looked sad, and he understood for the first time that maybe his *'tite fille* had a little crush on him. It turned his heart on end—although his heart didn't need any more exercise tonight than it had already had.

The phone woke Jake the next morning, sending him jogging to the kitchen, past Shondra's sleeping form on the couch. "Yeah?" he said, picking it up still half asleep.

"It's me." Tony. "Are you sitting down?"

Whoa, this sounded serious. He plopped into a chair. "I am now."

He listened to Tony take a deep breath. "The guy with Stephanie's sister, Nicholson? He's the kingpin, Jake. Of the whole damn operation. He's the guy who ordered the hit on you."

The hit that killed Becky instead. Jake couldn't breathe, bent over to rest his head in his hand.

"Those girls Raven mentioned? Tracked 'em down and they still deal for him, have been for years, and they IDed him as Typhoeus. Our hunches were right—serious drugs are being moved through Sophia's *and* the CBD, by the escorts. These girls and a couple of higher-ups they turned us on to are all willing to turn, so that and a few well-placed wiretaps and we'll have enough to put him away."

Nicholson was Typhoeus. The man responsible for his wife's death.

To think he'd just talked to the bastard last night.

"You there, man? You hearing this?"

"Yeah, I'm hearin' it—just . . . a little overwhelmed."

"I know," Tony said. "I probably should have come over and told you. I just didn't want to wait. I know it's hard to hear, but it means Becky's killer's going to jail, man. And not just on drug trafficking. Before we're through, he'll face murder charges, too. If nothing else, Jake, we're going to get some justice out of this."

"Jesus" was all he could mutter. Finally getting his head back about him a little, he said, "We found Tina Grant, just last night. She'd been livin' with that asshole until yesterday."

"You're kidding."

"He was at Sophia's and I asked him about her. I was face-to-face with him, Tony." As shock slowly transformed into rage, he spoke through clenched teeth. *"Face-to-face."*

"Listen, man," Tony said, and Jake could already hear the calming tones—they'd learned about those in the academy, how to talk to people who were on edge to settle them down. "You don't want to do anything crazy where this guy's concerned—if for no other reason, you'll mess up our case. And after all this time, I know you don't want to do that. I know you want to see Becky's killer get put away for a good long time. You're hearing me on this, right?"

Jake took a deep breath. "Right." He wanted to rip Nicholson limb from bloody limb—but more than that, he wanted to watch him rot in a prison cell. "You think this is what the feds were *really* lookin' for when they came down on the brothels a few years back?" he wondered aloud.

"Truth is . . ." Tony began, then stopped.

There was some *truth* Tony had never told him? "What?"

"The feds put a buzz in our ear a while back. I didn't get the idea about drugs on the third floor all by myself, and I had more than just a hunch. The FBI thought that's how it was going down—just couldn't nail it and suddenly had bigger fish to fry after nine eleven. They pulled us in on it a couple of years ago—not long after Becky died—but you were in too bad a way to tell you about it."

Jake shook his head. "Why? I know I was bad off, but why not tell me?"

Tony hesitated. "It's like this. Danny didn't offer you the job at Sophia's just out of the goodness of his heart. I asked him to, Jake."

"Why the hell would you do *that*?"

"You were closing down, shutting everything and everybody out. But I wanted you there, at Sophia's—wanted you in on this when it eventually came down. Because you're a cop to the bone, whether or not you're carrying a badge, and I needed your eyes and ears. And because I knew you'd *need* to be in on it when we found out who was behind Becky's death."

Just then, Shondra stretched and eased out from under the sheet on the couch, careful not to step on Scruff, who lay on the floor next to her on an old pillow Jake had pulled from a closet. She gave a sleepy-eyed, messy-haired wave good morning before scurrying off to the bathroom in one of Jake's old T-shirts he'd given her to sleep in.

"Jesus," Jake murmured, still trying to absorb it all, and part of him wanted to chew Tony out for manipulating him—but he couldn't. It all made sense. And Tony had done it because he'd cared.

They talked a little while longer, Tony making sure Jake wasn't going to go looking for Nicholson with a baseball bat, and discussing some more details of the case the NOPD would be building against the son of a bitch. It was so damn much to take in. They knew now. They knew who'd killed his wife.

He was just hanging up as Shondra exited the bathroom in a pair of shorts and a pullover. Scabs adorned each of her knees.

He pointed at them. "What happened?"

She shook her head as if the answer were a nuisance. "That's how Scruff got loose last night."

"What do you mean?"

"Some boy I know was botherin' me." She said it like it was nothing.

But Jake stood up. "Botherin' you? Botherin' you how?"

She looked almost ashamed to tell him and he prayed to God it wasn't anything like what had happened with her mom's boyfriend. "This boy called P.J., homeless kid, like I was. I seen him on the street a couple times lately and he's been givin' me shit ever since I got new clothes."

Jake blinked, not quite understanding. "Why?"

"Figured they meant I had some cash. Last night I went out to get some dog food, and P.J. saw me and hit me up for money. When I said no, he sorta . . . knocked me down, grabbed what change I had, and ducked off when Scruff got hit."

Jake couldn't believe he hadn't seen her skinned knees last night, but now he was noticing scratches on her arm, and a bruise on her right thigh, too. His blood began to boil. "This kid, P.J., what's he look like and where can I find him?"

She drew back slightly. "Why?"

"Just answer the question."

"He's got a nappy Afro, all uneven, and wears a dirty old Saints T-shirt with a number seventeen on it. During the day, he sleeps in an empty building down close to the river." She told him where.

He stormed past her into the bedroom, where he traded in the gym shorts he'd slept in for last night's jeans and T-shirt. "Don't leave this apartment 'til I get back," he commanded, trudging past her out the door.

He traveled to the abandoned building she'd described with tunnel vision. He didn't see morning traffic in the Quarter or people on the streets hosing down sidewalks or opening businesses. He saw nothing but a little girl's skinned knees. What the hell was wrong with people in this world that they thought they could just go around hurting other people? What gave them the right? It was gonna stop now—with him and this little jerk-off, P.J.

He pushed through a tall, half-shut door and found a handful of kids, varying ages, sleeping on old mattresses, car seats, blankets on the floor. The Saints jersey stretched out in a reclined bucket car seat drew his eyes. Damn, the kid was big—and too old to be hanging with the other young teenagers scattered about the place. It made him even angrier.

He yanked the kid up by the shirt, ready to scare the shit out of him. The kid's eyes popped open and as soon as he saw Jake, he drew back his fist and swung. Jake jerked to the right quick enough that it didn't hurt much, despite the coppery taste of blood in his mouth—but it was the last straw with this loser. In instinctive response, he delivered a hard left to P.J.'s jaw.

"Wha . . . ?" the kid muttered, dazed from the blow.

"From now on, try pickin' on somebody your own size!"

"Huh?"

"Last night you stole some money from a friend of mine. Attacked her, knocked her down, got her dog hit by a car. Ring any bells?"

The guy just made a face. "Yeah, but . . ."

Jake slugged him again, this time in the gut. The jolt sent P.J. doubling over with a grunt and the rest of the homeless teens had come awake to simply watch in fear, as if they were afraid to move, lest Jake notice them. As soon as P.J. rose back up, Jake countered with a right to the eye. The kid fell with a *plunk* to the old wooden floor and Jake leaned down over him. "She's just a goddamn little girl! Just tryin' to get by, like you are! You had no right to hurt her, so I'm just makin' things even here."

P.J. didn't answer, simply lay there gaping up at him in the morning shadows.

He doubted he'd actually made the kid understand anything, but at least maybe he'd think twice before mugging somebody again. "I oughta hurt you a lot worse," Jake said through gritted teeth, "but you're not worth it."

With that, he stomped back out the door. His hands hurt as he walked up the street, the right one beginning to swell a little.

He didn't want to go back to the apartment just yet—wanted to cool down first—so he headed to the Café Du Monde to get some beignets for Shondra. He wasn't proud of his actions just now, but seeing those scabs and hearing her tell him what happened as if it had somehow been her fault—it'd been the final straw, the thing that made him blow.

The last couple of days had just been . . . too damn

much to handle. Stephanie, Raven, Tina, Scruff, Shondra—and now they'd found Becky's killer, after all this time. *Merde,* no wonder he'd blown a gasket.

By the time he got the beignets and made the walk home, he felt calmer. Sorry he'd gone off on the kid, probably more than he should have. If he'd still been a cop and heard about someone dealing with a homeless kid the way he just had, even a *criminal* homeless kid, he wouldn't have been happy.

When he walked in, Shondra stood in the same place he'd left her, as if she hadn't moved in all the time he was gone. "Where'd you go?"

"Just had a little talk with P.J." He held up the beignets. "And got breakfast."

"Your hand's red. So's your cheek." Her eyebrows knit. "Did you beat him up?"

He nodded, still not proud. "Pretty much."

To his surprise, she let out a sigh of what looked like . . . relief. "Cool."

"What?"

"He's a jerk. Nobody can stand his ass. Whatever somebody has, even other homeless kids, he thinks it should be his. He thinks he's so bad and . . ." She let out another sigh and took on the innocent look she sometimes forgot to hide. "Well, now I don't got to be scared to go out. After last night, I kinda was. So . . . thanks, Jake. I wish there were more guys in the world just like you."

She took the white bag from his hands and went into the kitchen. He, on the other hand, simply stood there feeling numb. Strange. Good strange. Like maybe . . . he'd saved somebody. Even if just a little. Even if just for right now.

Maybe he hadn't gone about it the best way, but as

Shondra's words replayed in his head, he couldn't help feeling satisfied, and thinking maybe he'd somehow managed to show her there were good men in the world and that maybe she wouldn't live her whole life being afraid of them all.

"OJ?" she asked from the kitchen.

"Yeah," he murmured. "Thanks."

As they sat down at the little table together, Shondra knew she had to tell him what she'd done while he was gone. He'd be glad, but she hated to think this was the last time she'd sit eating beignets with Jake, and she just wanted to enjoy the quiet companionship they shared.

So it wasn't until she picked up their sugar-covered plates and carried them to the sink that she said, "While you were out beatin' up P.J., I called Grandma Maisy."

He blinked. "Really?"

She laid the plates down and turned to face him. "I figured you done enough for me already—and it seemed like a thing I should be able to do. I mean, I've lived on the streets. I oughta be able to call my damn grandma, right?"

He gave her a small smile, one of the things she'd miss—his smiles. "I guess so," he said. "Did you tell her . . . everything? About your mom's boyfriend?"

She nodded. "She said if I come live with her, she won't let him nowhere near me. Said her and me'll go through the court and see what to do so I can live with her permanent, until I'm old enough I wanna move out. And best of all, she's down with me bringin' Scruff. She's got a little fenced backyard and I think he'll like it."

His smile widened on her. "That's real good. I like Grandma Maisy already."

"She likes you, too. From all what I told her, I mean. And she's . . . expectin' me tonight. She's makin' breaded pork chops for supper 'cause they're my favorite—so I guess I better be there."

He nodded quietly, and she liked to think maybe he seemed just a little sad, too. Probably wishful thinking, but she loved that Jake liked her, she loved making him laugh, and she was going to miss him something awful. He was the best thing that had ever happened to her. Well, him and Scruff. They'd both come along right when she'd needed them the most.

That evening around five-thirty, Jake pulled the truck to the curb outside a well-kept little shotgun house on the West Bank. He saw a few kids out playing, and an old man working in a flower bed, and immediately felt good about leaving Shondra here. "Got all your stuff?"

They'd packed her clothes in the shopping bags they'd come in, and her old backpack was hoisted on one shoulder. Scruff sat in the seat next to her, on his leash. She nodded at Jake's question, but seemed nervous, as if she couldn't quite look at him. Clearly, she'd learned early in life to hate awkward good-byes as much as he did.

"If you ever need anything, you got my number, no?"

She nodded again, glancing up at him, then back down.

"Or even if you *don't* need anything, but you just wanna talk—call me. Okay?"

She nodded more vigorously this time.

"Well then, I guess that's it."

Her lip started trembling before she said, "Thanks for everything. I might've died if not for you." With that, she leaned past Scruff to throw her arms around Jake's neck.

It caught him off guard for a second, and he wasn't sure at first if he should hug her back, all things considered. But then he did, for a long minute that wrenched his heart a lot harder than he'd ever expected. She raised her head and kissed his cheek, just like Tina had done, before returning to her side of the truck.

After that, she seemed embarrassed, hurrying to get out with all her stuff, saying, "Come, Scruff. Come on." Only after she slammed the door did she pause, looking back in through the open window.

"Take care of yourself, *'tite fille*. Have a good life."

She looked utterly forlorn as she nodded at him one last time, quietly saying, "Bye."

He lifted a hand in parting. "Bye."

He pulled away, discovering about a block later that something was clouding his vision as he drove. He reached up, wiping at one eye, and his fingertips came away wet. Tears.

You see her sitting naked and beautiful in a dark room. A pale spotlight shines on her, yet her face remains in shadow. Slim knees are drawn up, her arms curved around them, and in one hand she holds a daisy. With the other, she plucks off the slender white petals, one by one. "He loves me," she says.

Her voice is the faintest whisper as she pulls the next.

"He loves me not."

She lifts her gaze just slightly, and you feel her eyes on you.

"He loves me."

You want to go to her, but you can't seem to move.

"He loves me not."

Another petal falls to the floor in front of her as you reach out.

"He loves me."

But you're not there with her, you suddenly realize. It's as if you're watching from behind a glass wall.

"He loves me not."

She cannot see you. Which means you're both alone.

"He loves me."

She glances down at the remains of the flower, one last petal left. She plucks it off and lets it drop as a single tear rolls down her cheek. "He loves me not."

Chapter 26

The first night after Stephanie got Tina back, they'd stayed up all night talking. They'd shed a lot of tears, and done a lot of apologizing, and by morning, Stephanie felt she knew more about her little sister than she ever had before. They'd worked through all the mistakes each of them had made and Stephanie felt real hope for Tina's future, and hope for the future of their relationship, too.

She'd been upset but not surprised when her sister admitted that her reactions to Tina's decisions had ultimately been part of what had driven her away, but she'd just have to deal with that knowledge. She'd told Jake he couldn't hold on to his guilt about Becky forever, and she'd meant it. Right now, she felt *horribly* guilty about Tina, but she knew time would ease it.

The next morning, she'd again found herself sneaking off to Mrs. Lindman's kitchen for muffins to share with her unauthorized guest, and just like when the guest had been Jake, they'd giggled over prim and proper Stephanie engaging in such a deception.

"Not so prim anymore, though, right?" Tina had asked.

"I mean, once you've masqueraded as a hooker . . ." They'd both laughed, but clearly Tina had seen memories of Jake dancing in her eyes. "Or . . . is there something more I should know?"

Stephanie shrugged, not wanting to give her affair with Jake as much power as it truly held over her. "I . . . sort of had wild, crazy sex with Jake a few times, in between looking for you."

Her sister's eyes had gone wide and appreciative. "Jake, the ex-cop bartender who rescued me? My God, Steph, he's a total hottie and a half."

Stephanie had sighed. "Don't I know it."

Tina tilted her head, too perceptive. "Why do you sound sad about this? Wild, crazy sex is usually fun."

Stephanie, who'd gotten very honest with her sister over the previous hours, had said, "I'm in love with him."

Tina gasped.

Yet Stephanie wanted to move to a new topic as quickly as possible. "But he's not in love with me. He has a dead wife he's still mourning, and that's fine, because the sex was great and I shouldn't have let myself get emotionally involved. End of story." She'd said it all in one breath, then continued with, "The upshot is that I have a new appreciation for sex, which I hope to put to good use from this point forward."

She didn't mention that, at the moment, she feared she'd never want to sleep with anyone but Jake again. *Great, he makes me love sex and ruins it for me at once.*

Fortunately, Tina hadn't pressed for more, and soon after eating breakfast, they'd both fallen asleep 'til the afternoon. After waking, Stephanie had called her mom, soon passing the phone to Tina. Neither let anything slip about the escort business, only saying that Tina had been living with a guy she'd met, now they'd broken up, and both sisters would be coming home in a couple of days.

Stephanie e-mailed Curtis to alert him of her return as well. The letting-him-down-gently part would come later. She'd also e-mailed Melody to share her good news and thank her for all her help—hoping as she typed that Tina would somehow end up with the same happy ending Melody had. Meanwhile, Tina placed a call to one of the shelters where Jake had directed Raven, getting lucky on the first try. Raven had come to the phone and informed Tina she was entering a rehab program, and both girls vowed they'd keep in touch. "Even though we probably won't," Tina had said sadly after hanging up. "But she was a friend when I needed one, and I hope she gets better."

Last night, Stephanie had taken Tina out to dinner. Over glasses of Chardonnay, they both resolved not to dwell on the past any longer, but to look forward. "I think I want to try college," Tina said. "And study retail. Is that stupid? To go to college just so I can get a job in the mall?"

Stephanie had shaken her head. "You'll have a leg up on everyone *else* working at the mall, and you can get a job in the meantime and start getting practical experience."

"*And* I'll get a discount!"

They'd both laughed, and Stephanie had actually managed to enjoy the meal—even if she wasn't particularly looking forward to going home, or back to her job. It felt like returning to something meaningless, a world that was about nothing but money and glitz and expensive business suits that in the end boiled down to nothing real—and she also feared it was going to be hard leaving behind the city that held the man she loved, but she didn't have a choice; Jake hadn't given her one.

Now Stephanie had just returned from another trip to Mrs. Lindman's kitchen, explaining yet again to the old woman that she was very busy working in her room and just wanted to take back a muffin—or four. When she came in, balancing muffins and a couple of bananas, Tina announced, "I just got over a big hurdle."

"What's that?" She let all the food collapse gently to the desk, then plopped on the foot of the bed where Tina still lay, wearing a pair of Stephanie's pajamas.

"I almost just did something awful. I almost called Russ. But I stopped myself. Because why would I chase a guy who doesn't want me? There's nothing to be gained, right?"

Stephanie nodded. Precisely the reason she was going home. She might have ended up begging Jake for kisses and for sex, but she wasn't going to beg him for love. "I'm glad you stayed strong," she told her sister.

"I guess I've made a lot of decisions out of fear," Tina said. She shook her head softly. "But you wouldn't know how that feels—always being so in control."

"I'm sorry about my tendency to be controlling," Stephanie replied, although she'd already apologized for it many times over. "I've just always been that way— because *I'm* scared, too."

"Of what?"

Stephanie sighed. "Of . . . everything. Life. Men. Sex. Failure in general. Isn't everybody scared, at least a little? I just hide it better than you, that's all."

Tina looked stunned. "I didn't think you ever got scared, Steph."

"Surprise," she said, trying for a smile, but knowing she'd failed. She got up and walked across the room for a couple of muffins. "Heads-up," she said to Tina, tossing one toward the bed.

Tina laughed. "You really are different. I mean, you've loosened up, big time."

"Because I'm goofy enough to throw a muffin across the room?"

Tina tilted her head. "Well . . . yeah, kind of. You wouldn't have done that before." She leaned slightly forward. "I don't think you should come home with me."

Stephanie flinched. "What?" They'd made their flight reservations last night—they were flying to Chicago late this afternoon.

"I think this place has been good for you." When Stephanie only stared, Tina added, "I think that *man* was good for you. I think you need to get things resolved with him, Steph."

Stephanie steeled herself. "Things are as resolved as they're going to get. We've both stated our feelings. And we've said good-bye," she added softly. "I even gave him the scarf." She'd told Tina about her crocheting project. "And it's like you said. Why do I want to chase a man who doesn't want me?"

Tina didn't hesitate. "Because you and I are different, Steph. I fall for every guy I meet. I even fell for Robert before it was over. You, on the other hand, save up your love and only spend it on special people. You shouldn't let this go so easily."

She could have told Tina about the tears she'd shed since their breakup and how tempted she'd been to do exactly what Tina was suggesting—call him up, show up at Sophia's, try again to make him love her—and how hard it had been to resist. He'd tempted her into places she'd never gone before, but now she had to go back to real life and leave Jake and his bayou behind. It was a private place for a private man who chose to be alone. So she simply said, "I *have* to let it go, Tina. I have to."

To Jake's surprise, the impossible had happened: The apartment was too quiet. There was no clicking of little dog claws, no Shondra blaring the TV or clunking dishes together or calling him a slob when she went around collecting laundry. He missed her, and he even missed the damn mutt, too.

He lay in bed, trying to think of a reason to get up, and he realized that even after parting ways with Stephanie, Shondra had been providing *that,* giving him a reason. She'd been the one thing keeping him from slipping back over that edge into the no-man's-land his life had been for the last two years.

He should be happy this morning, he thought. Shondra was in a good place where she could build a normal life. And he and Tony were going to bring down Typhoeus— Becky's killer had been found. Even in the midst of returning depression, he felt a deep satisfaction over that. Finding out who'd ended Becky's life had been among the hundreds of things he'd chosen not to care about since her death, but now he knew he really *had* cared all along.

So *that* gave him enough of a reason to get up, at least for today. He wanted to go to the cemetery. He'd never gone, not once since the funeral. He'd just been unable to let himself get that close to her again. Life had been hard enough. But today there was a reason—there was justice, closure. Today he would go.

After dragging himself up, getting showered and dressed, and forcing himself to eat a little of the cereal

Shondra had bought, he walked outside to find an unusual chill in the air. Only October, too soon for it to be cold, but he went back and grabbed his old leather jacket from the closet. He started to close the door when he caught sight of something on the shelf above the hangers—the scarf Stephanie had given him.

Slowly, he reached up and pulled it down, let it unfold in his grasp. The loose stitches were uneven and the whole thing had a curve to it he didn't think was supposed to be there. But hell—he tossed it around his neck anyway and walked back out the door.

Half an hour later, he strode up one of the picturesque aisles at Metairie Cemetery, where Becky's parents had insisted on laying her to rest. Jake hadn't argued because his family's dead were buried out in Terrebonne and Metairie's cemetery was the nicest in the city. Now he moved past a row of tombs—miniature cathedrals and temples that lived up to the nickname used for all New Orleans cemeteries: Cities of the Dead. Angels and crosses and Jesus looked down from just above him, each vault topped with a tiny statue that made Jake think of hood ornaments as he walked by.

He found Becky's family tomb—her name had been added to a plaque attached to the front. A particularly pretty stone angel overlooked her resting place, and it gave him a weird sense of peace and made him sorry he hadn't come before. What if people who died really were *here,* at their graves, in spirit somehow? What if she'd been waiting for him?

He looked around, glad to see no one nearby. He'd never talked to a tomb in his life and he generally thought it was silly when people did. But he felt the urge to talk and didn't squelch it. "I'm sorry I haven't been here before," he said, low. "But it hurt too much, and I've . . . been in a bad way, Beck. You'd hate me like this, the way I've been," he said, realizing it just now. Shondra wasn't the only one who liked him better when he was happy.

"Anyway, the man who was responsible for your death—he's gonna go to prison. And he won't get out. Because if he ever comes up for parole, I'll be there to remind people what he did, what he took from me. From you."

The man who was responsible for your death. Damn, but talking out loud made him pay more attention or something. Had he just admitted—to her, to himself— that maybe someone else truly *was* to blame, not just him?

He took a deep breath, glanced up at a strangely blank sky of white, and felt a sharp breeze cut through him, making him pull Stephanie's scarf up around his neck. "There's more," he said. "More I need to tell you."

"Jake? Is that you?"

He cringed, then turned to find Becky's mother walking toward him. Peter, Paul, and Mary—the one time he comes here . . . "Yeah," he said. "Hi."

She wore a severely elegant black coat with a shiny brooch on the collar. Every dyed brown hair lay in place as if unaware it was a windy day, her red lipstick cut a grim line across her face, and she didn't look any happier to see him than he was to see her. She'd never approved of him, only tolerated him, and they hadn't seen each other since Becky's funeral—neither had picked up a phone or driven to see each other over the two years they'd been suffering the same loss. He'd figured Becky's family held him responsible, too, and that thought reminded him . . . "I have some news."

"News?"

"We've found the guy who ordered the hit," he said, going on to give her the rough details, mainly that there would eventually be a trial and the guy would be put away for a long time, at the very least.

When he was done, she drew in her breath and splayed diamond-clad fingers across her chest. "Well, praise God for that much. I hope it will let her rest in peace."

"Me too."

It was then that she bent to place a bouquet of plastic flowers in one of the vases affixed to the vault. Surprised, he spoke before thinking. "Becky loved fresh-cut flowers—she hated plastic ones, even silk ones."

The woman glared at him in shock and he realized how rude he'd been.

"*Mon Dieu,* I'm sorry—I didn't mean to say that."

She looked at him a moment longer before turning her gaze back on the tomb. "The plastic ones are the only ones that hold up to the weather. At least until someone steals them. It's silly to bring anything else."

But Becky would rather have real flowers for a day than fake flowers for a year. "You're right," he lied instead, wishing like hell he'd thought to stop on the way and bring a fresh bouquet.

"I'll go and leave you to yourself," she said then.

"You don't have to," he replied, feeling bad.

"I come all the time. I can come back another day." Translation: *You* don't *come all the time. You might never come again.*

But he would. And he'd bring fresh flowers the next time.

He watched as the woman walked away, her well-coiffed hair still showing no signs of the swirling wind.

When she was gone, he looked back to the tomb, old memories suddenly overflowing. He'd forgotten until just now how insanely Becky loved flowers—flowers of any kind, so long as they were real. Her grandmother had grown an English perennial garden and taught Becky all about flowers, and she'd filled their little house with them—everything from carnations to tulips to roses cut from the bushes she'd planted in the side yard. She'd said flowers were God's most beautiful example of life, living.

Damn.

Flowers.

In the dreams.

It hit him like a tidal wave. Every dream he could remember had flowers in it.

Whether they were real or a pattern in a piece of lingerie or in the words to a song, weren't there always flowers?

"Am I losin' my mind?" he asked out loud, peering at the tomb. Then he shook his head. "But why would a part of you be in my dreams about . . . ?" He couldn't even say it. *Another woman.*

"That's the other thing I need to tell you, Beck. There's . . . a woman. I care for her. Too much." He swallowed, hard. "I wish I didn't, keep tellin' myself I don't. Because I always thought there'd only be you. Forever." He stopped, sighed, stuffed his hands in his pockets because they were getting cold. "But she's still in my head, all the time. And I don't know . . ."

Had he come here to ask Becky for permission?

And were dreams of Stephanie and flowers her way of giving it?

Was she there in the dreams, too, telling him it was okay to need someone new?

"You *are* losin' it," he told himself. "Unless . . ." He looked up at the stone angel, then to the stark empty sky. "*Are* you tryin' to tell me somethin', Beck?"

He lowered his gaze, shook his head, and let out a sigh, feeling like an idiot to be standing here trying to read signs into dreams, trying to converse with a slab of concrete.

When he caught sight of something white in the air around him, he looked about, confused for a few seconds, trying to figure out what it was—it looked like tiny bits of fluffy confetti floating down.

And then he realized. Snow. It was snow.

A chill that had nothing to do with the weather ran up his spine.

He'd never been farther north than the Louisiana border and he'd only seen snow one other time in his life—it had fallen on the December day he and Becky had married almost five years ago.

And it was falling again now, on a brisk October day.

And he might well *be* losing his mind—he might be bending the facts to believe what he wanted to believe, that his dead wife was sending him messages from the grave. But as the snow fell from the New Orleans sky and the wind stopped blowing and the world suddenly felt almost at peace for Jake for the first time in two years . . . he believed.

As Jake drove back to the Quarter, other words he'd spoken came back to him—words he'd said to Tina the other night. *Just let Stephanie help you and things will work out like they should.* Didn't that apply to *his* life as well? And hadn't he known that for a while now?

As he turned up his street and approached his building,

he saw a good parking spot—but he drove past it. He kept heading northeast—toward Esplanade.

What if she was gone already? What if she'd already packed her bags and taken her sister home to Chicago? *Merde.* He pressed down on the gas pedal.

A minute later, he barreled into the parking lot at LaRue House and spotted a familiar-looking car—thank God, she was still here! Killing the ignition, he walked briskly along the winding pathway until he was rapping on her door.

When it opened, Tina stood on the other side. "Jake," she said.

"I need to see Stephanie." His heart pounded against his rib cage.

"She went to find *you.*"

"What?"

Tina nodded, as if to assure him he'd heard correctly. "She left a little while ago, walking to your place." Behind Tina, he noticed packed suitcases lined up at the foot of the bed. Damn it, she was just about to leave.

"Thanks," he said, then headed back toward the truck.

Two minutes later, he parked outside his building and rushed into the courtyard. She'd never been to his apartment before—only knew the location from when they'd taxied here for the truck the other night. The courtyard and interior verandas were empty and quiet but for the hum of a washing machine coming from the laundry room.

He walked over to find Mrs. LaFourche standing guard over the machines. "Taken," she said when he leaned inside.

"Any chance you've seen a pretty woman wanderin' around here lookin' for me?"

She tilted her head, narrowed her eyes. "Jake, right?"

He nodded.

"Yeah, I seen her. Pointed her to your apartment, but she knocked and didn't get no answer, so she left."

Damn. "Thank you," he said quietly, then wandered back out to the street.

Where would she have gone? Not back to the LaRue, or he'd have passed her while he was driving. He thought next of the bayou house, but her rental car had still been at the B and B five minutes earlier.

As he glanced in the other direction, a new thought struck him. Chez Sophia. It was the only other place.

He took off in a sprint, realizing that somewhere along the way the sun had come out, the wind had died, and it was turning into a pretty day. He was starting to sweat, so he shrugged out of the jacket and scarf, gripping them in his fist as he ran.

When he reached Sophia's, all was quiet, but the front door was unlocked.

He heard people working inside—the clink of bottles, the sound of a chair scooting on the floor somewhere, and low music playing—but no one was in sight. He didn't bother seeking them out, just walked on through like he figured Stephanie might have done in the same situation.

Unlike at night, no one stood guard at the door leading to the stairwell that rose toward the secret third floor. He took the stairs two at a time. He was winded when he reached the top, having to stop and catch his breath before pushing through the red curtains.

All was still inside and his heart sank as he tossed his jacket and scarf on the bar. *Stephanie, where are you? I need you.*

But then a blast of memory washed over him, and he

took slow, silent steps toward the place where their passion had first ignited—the red room.

He walked in to find her seated on one of the lush divans, her head in her hands. She wore denim shorts and a summery red top. Her pretty blond locks curled at the tips, falling around her face.

"Hey," he said softly.

She looked up, clearly startled. "Jake."

"Been lookin' for you, *beb*."

"I was looking for you, too." She pushed to her feet, appearing a little confused, like maybe now that she'd found him she wasn't sure why she'd been looking in the first place.

He wanted to remind her without another second's delay, so he took sure steps toward her until he could lift one hand to cup her smooth cheek. "I've ached for you every second we've been apart."

"Me too," she murmured.

He looked into her eyes, tried to let everything he felt for her pour from his gaze, then lowered his mouth onto hers in a slow, deep kiss.

A shudder echoed through them both. *"Mon Dieu,"* he whispered. "I need you, *chère*."

He replaced that kiss with another, and another, until, just like the last time they'd touched, they were both trembling, filling the room with ragged breaths as they clung to each other. Her arms twined around his neck and his molded to her slender waist.

But this wouldn't be like that night outside her room. He needed more than that, and he had so much to give her now.

Pulling back just slightly, he eased her top over her head, then ran his hands down over the delicate white lace of her bra. His thumbs caught on beaded nipples, so he stroked them—again and again.

"More," she whispered up into the silence.

"Much more," he said.

She pushed his T-shirt up and he yanked it off before reaching deftly behind her to unhook her bra. Looping his fingers through the straps at her shoulders, he drew it down, letting his gaze feast on her lovely breasts.

He didn't know yet if this was the last time, if it was too late for him to save things. He didn't know if this was a parting gift from her or a last plea from him. But he'd never thought he'd get to hold her, touch her, again—and he intended to soak up every second, every blessed nuance, of this liaison.

He shivered when she reached for the button on his jeans, glancing down to watch her delicate fingers lower the zipper. He cupped her breasts and her pretty sighs grew labored when he sank his mouth to one turgid pink peak, licking and suckling her.

"I feel that between my legs," she whispered, and it nearly undid him.

"Wanna make you feel so much more, *beb*," he murmured, lifting a kiss to her forehead, then taking her in his arms to ease her down onto the same lush red sofa where he'd first touched her.

Raining kisses onto her pale, perfect breasts, he undid her shorts and tugged gently at the waistband, pulling them off, along with the lacy panties underneath. He wanted her so badly he could barely breathe. He pressed another long kiss to her mouth as she pushed at his jeans and he shrugged free from them—underwear too—so that they lay completely naked together, as naked as the women in the paintings that seemed to float on the red walls above, as naked as Jake knew they were meant to be together.

He rolled her to her back, easing between her parted thighs, pushing his way inside her. They both moaned and peered into each other's eyes, and Jake watched her lovely lips tremble, watched her head fall back in passion, watched a single tear roll down her cheek.

"No, no," he whispered, reaching to blot it from her skin. "Don't cry, *beb*. I love you."

Her eyes shone on him, warm and blue with shock.

But he kissed it away, not wanting to talk anymore right now, just wanting them to move together like they'd been made to do.

He pushed deeper and she met the pressure, lifting her hips, and they held like that for a long, quiet moment, until finally he closed his arms around her and sat up, swinging her up astride him with one swift move. He wanted to take her to heaven.

She bit her lower lip, her eyes falling half shut with heat as she began to ride him. He nibbled at her breasts, roamed her lush body with his hands—he wanted to give her more, more, everything. Her fingernails dug lightly into his shoulders and her breath caught, making him murmur, "*Oui, beb, oui.* Come for me." She thrust faster, moaning, moaning, until finally the ecstasy washed over her face for a few long, glorious seconds.

That was all it took and he was gone, too, erupting inside her, losing himself in the profound, burying pleasure, and finally just holding her tight as the energy drained from him and he tried to recover from the sweetest few moments of life he could ever remember.

Because this was different. This was freedom. Freedom to love her.

When she eased back on him, their eyes met, and she looked wistful, sad. "I decided," she said slowly, "I'd rather have one last time with you to remember . . . than to not have it . . . even though that's scary for me."

He lifted his hand, pushing her hair back from her face. "Aw, *chère*—you've got no idea how much I admire the way you never let fear hold you back."

"Yes I do," she argued softly.

He shook his head. "Not from findin' your sister, no matter what it took. Not from puttin' yourself out there in a dangerous situation with bad men, or even paddlin' out after me in a leaky pirogue." He cast a gentle smile.

She returned it, saying, "I didn't know it was leaky."

"It was still brave as hell."

She relented, her body relaxing against him. He was still inside her. "Well, fear *did* hold me back from one thing. Sex."

"Not for long."

"Yes, for long."

He grinned. "Not for long once you met *me*." He grazed his hands up her arms onto her face and she leaned forward until their foreheads met. "Stay," he whispered.

She drew back slightly. "What?"

"Stay. Don't leave me. I need you. You're the only thing that's made me feel good in a long time. What I feel when I'm with you, I want that every day. I want it for the rest of my life."

She quaked in his arms, and this time he hated it—because he wanted her to believe him, to understand that things had changed.

"I'm in love with you," he explained. "Desperately, wildly in love with you. I was just too afraid to say it. I lost so much with Becky, and felt I *owed* her so much, too.

I was afraid—afraid of somehow sullyin' her memory, and just as afraid, I suppose, that I'd somehow lose you, too. I was afraid I wouldn't be able to take care of you."

She blinked. She'd stopped shaking, mostly. "And now?"

"Now I wanna be like *you*, *beb*. Brave, even though I'm afraid. I wanna love you. Take care of you. Do my very *best* to take care of you."

A slow smile spread across her face, reaching into those blue, blue eyes. Her gaze felt like sun shining into his heart. "I want to take care of you, too, Jake. And I like who I am when I'm with you." She let out a pretty, trilling laugh. "I steal breakfast for two from Mrs. Lindman when I'm with you. I actually *like* having my underwear torn off by you. I walk out into the bayou naked without a care for anything in the world . . . except being with you."

He smiled, filled with pure joy. "*Mon Dieu, chère,* you make me happy."

She finally eased off him and they wordlessly lay back on the red sofa in a loose, easy embrace. "But this is . . . quick, Jake. In some ways, we don't know each other at all."

He only cast his typical sexy grin. "But in other ways, we know each other *intimately*. I'm not afraid. The rest'll come. I feel it in my soul."

He watched her draw in a deep breath, meeting his gaze. "I'm not afraid, either."

"I knew that," he said with a sure nod. "But still . . what about your job?" It had just occurred to him, how much he was asking her to give up. Her whole life.

Yet she only shrugged. "I'll get another one. Or maybe start my own little ad firm."

"Didn't you work awful hard to get where you are?"

"Yeah," she said, "and it's scary to go back to square one, but . . ."

"You'll be brave," he finished for her. And then he swallowed, ready to lay something heavy on her. "I'm thinkin' about rejoinin' the force. Can you handle that? Danger every day?"

To his surprise, the question brought a warm smile to her face. "Jake, you were born to help people. I've known that about you from the beginning."

As he looked into her eyes and felt her belief in him, he knew he'd been wrong: He *could* save people. He'd saved Shondra. Maybe even Tina. Hell, maybe even Raven, in some small way. But mostly, he'd saved himself, by letting himself love the only woman who could breathe life back into him.

And he knew that, finally, he wouldn't be having any more sexy dreams. She'd made them all come true, so he'd be living them from now on.

"Well," she said, "but I'll be sorry to see back to share a lobster."

"We'll be here," he flanked to her. And then he glanced back to the something fuzzy on her...

...

...Then shrugs. The question though I am unable to face. "Are you sure from tomorrow? I whirled the...

...

As he looked back at me and felt me deep in her...

Epilogue

tephanie sat on the dock, listening to the night sounds of
e bayou and eating a slice of the apple pie Jake had
ought home for her the night before. Inside, he nailed up
e crown molding he'd carved for the bedroom, the last
ch in his refurbishment. It had turned into not a place for
m to be alone, but a place for them to be alone *together.*

She thought of the existence they'd built over the last
ar. Life was stressful some days in the Quarter—but her
e-woman ad agency, where she could do the work she
ed without the corporate atmosphere, was slowly get-
g off the ground. And even when Jake came home to
ir pretty little Royal Street apartment tired and wrung
from something that had happened on the job, she
ld see the satisfaction from his work shining in his
s, and she could feel it in the sureness of his touch
en they made love. So life was good in the city, but
n better when they escaped out here for a few days and
hts of peace and great sex.

They'd married in Chicago—a big, no-holds-barred
ir that her mother had loved planning and her sister

had loved helping with. But they'd opted out of the traditional honeymoon and instead headed straight to their bayou house, where they'd made love for a week to the slightly scratchy sounds of *Mamère*'s old records. Jake had joked it was a damn good thing she'd gotten lots of lingerie at her bridal shower because, despite his best intentions, he was destroying panties at an alarming rate.

If there was any dark cloud in their lives, it was enduring the arrest and trial of Robert Nicholson. But that was also a good thing, the last thing he needed, Jake said, to say good-bye to Becky. Nicholson had been sentenced to life in prison just last week.

When the hammering had ceased, she called to him, "Jake, honey, can you come out here for a minute. I need to tell you something."

A moment later, he exited the house with two cans o beer. As he popped the top on his, she only set hers aside unopened and looked out over the dark water. "There ar angels in the bayou tonight," she said.

He grinned, sliding his arm around her shoulde: "That's what you called me out here to tell me?"

"No." She shook her head softly, eased a forkful of pi into his mouth, and then passed him a booklet of Ne Orleans real estate listings. "I called you out here to te you we're going to have to start looking for a house a litt sooner than we thought."

He glanced down at the book. "Why?"

Setting her pie plate aside to place a hand on the wo denim that stretched across his thigh, she whispere "I'm . . . a little bit pregnant." They hadn't planned have a baby right now—they'd only talked of it as som thing for a distant future—and given the child he'd on lost, she wasn't sure how he'd feel.

He leaned forward slightly. *"A little bit?"*

"Well, completely." She smiled and rolled her eyes at her own silly wording. "I was just nervous to tell you."

He set his beer on the dock and lifted his hands to her face. "Never be nervous with me, *chère.*"

"But we haven't talked about . . . and I wasn't sure how you'd . . ."

His smile unfurled slowly. *"Beb,* I love you. And you're havin' my baby. And that's damn scary. But also . . . perfect, and wonderful. You gotta know that."

"Deep down, I guess I did." She bit her lip thoughtfully. "I was thinking, if it's a boy, we could name him James, after you. And if it's a girl, we could call her Meghan." The names, he'd once told her, that he and Becky had discussed that fated evening over dinner.

"Becky would like that."

"I thought it might . . . keep her alive for you a little or something."

"Mon Dieu, you're sweet," he said, bending to kiss her. "But Becky's gone, and as much as that hurt, life is about me and you now, *chère.* Me and you and this little *bébé* inside you."

He pressed his hand against her abdomen and they exchanged soft smiles.

"Now let's look for angels," he said.

About the Author

Toni Blake knew she wanted to be a writer when she was ten years old. She fondly recalls sharing her ambitions with her mother one day over breakfast, then proceeding to write her first novel—nineteen notebook pages long. Since then, Toni has become a multipublished author of contemporary romance novels, as well as having had more than forty short stories and articles published. She has been a recipient of the Kentucky Women Writer's Fellowship, and has also been honored with a nomination for the prestigious Pushcart Prize. When not writing, Toni enjoys traveling with her husband, genealogy, snow skiing, and working on various crafts. You can visit Toni on the web at www.ToniBlake.com.

THE EDITOR'S DIARY

Dear Reader,

Like two magnets, lovers either attract or repel. And when they attract, heaven help whatever is caught between them. Don't believe me? Test out the science of love yourself in our two Warner Forever titles this July.

Romantic Times BOOKclub Magazine praised "you couldn't ask for a more joyous, loving, smile-inducing read" than *Sue-Ellen Welfonder*'s previous book. Well, hold onto your kilts—she's outdone herself with her latest, **ONLY FOR A KNIGHT**. The last thing Robbie MacKenzie desires is to abandon his bachelorhood and wed a complete stranger…but he will. For only the promise of this union has kept the peace between two rival clans and it is time for Robbie to face his destiny and claim heir to his father's lairdship. But on his way home, he sees a beautiful woman on the verge of drowning. He saves her and an attraction ignites within him hot enough to sear his soul. Though he is sworn to another, Robbie cannot bear to leave this bonnie lass who knows nothing of her past. But when the truth of this tantalizing stranger's identity and mission comes to light, can these two star-crossed lovers resist the love that burns in their hearts?

If your sister was missing, is there a limit to what you'd do to save her? Stephanie Grant from **Toni Blake's IN YOUR WILDEST DREAMS** knows there are no bounds to what she'd do. So, as she steps onto the secret third floor of Chez Sophia, her resolve is only strengthened. Amid heady champagne, wealthy men, and stunningly beautiful women, Stephanie begins a dangerous charade to find her beloved sister. But she never expected to find an ally in Jake Broussard, the strong but sexy bartender and ex-cop. Since he reluctantly agreed to help her, she thought she'd feel only gratitude for him. But his gentle touch and soft Cajun accent send her senses reeling. Can she trust him? More importantly, can she trust herself with him? *New York Times* bestselling author Lori Foster raves "with sizzling sensuality and amazing depth, a book by Toni Blake is truly special" and she couldn't be more right. Pick up a copy today and find out why.

To find out more about Warner Forever, these titles, and the author, visit us at www.warnerforever.com.

With warmest wishes,

Karen Kosztolnyik

Karen Kosztolnyik, Senior Editor

P.S. Love doesn't always come before marriage in these two irresistible novels: **Kimberly Raye** delivers the wickedly funny story of a woman marrying to get rid of her mother and finds unexpected romance in **SWEET AS SUGAR, HOT AS SPICE**; and **Paula Quinn** makes her Warner Forever debut with the exciting and unforgettable story of a woman forced by the king to marry who soon vows to win her new husband's heart in **LORD OF DESIRE**.

Want to know more about romances at Warner Books and Warner Forever? Get the scoop online!

WARNER'S ROMANCE HOMEPAGE

Visit us at www.warnerforever.com for all the latest news, reviews, and chapter excerpts!

NEW AND UPCOMING TITLES

Each month we feature our new titles and reader favorites.

CONTESTS AND GIVEAWAYS

We give away galleys, autographed copies, and all kinds of fun stuff.

AUTHOR INFO

You'll find bios, articles, and links to personal websites for all your favorite authors—and so much more!

THE BUZZ

Sign up for our monthly romance newsletter, and be the first to read all about it!